2811
5

The FURY and the POWER

The FURY and the POWER

John Farris

A Tom Doherty Associates Book
New York

THE FURY AND THE POWER

Copyright © 2003 by John Farris

All rights reserved, including the right to reproduce this book,
or portions thereof, in any form.

This book is printed on acid-free paper.

A Forge Book
Published by Tom Doherty Associates, LLC
175 Fifth Avenue
New York, NY 10010

www.tor.com

Forge® is a registered trademark of Tom Doherty Associates, LLC.

Library of Congress Cataloging-in-Publication Data

Farris, John.
    The fury and the power / John Farris—1st ed.
        p.   cm.
    ISBN 0-312-87728-5
    1. Las Vegas (Nev.)—Fiction.   2. Psychics—Fiction.   3. Devil—Fiction.
I. Title.

PS3556.A777 F78   2003
813'.54—dc21

                                                                        2002032534

First Edition: February 2003

Printed in the United States of America

0 9 8 7 6 5 4 3 2 1

For David Schow
Thanks, David

The story of the lion that attacked an elephant and paid for it I've adapted from a similar anecdote in Katy Payne's very good book *Silent Thunder,* recommended not only for its wealth of information about elephant families and social groups, but because it is wonderfully written.

The aphorist Lewis Gruvver is quoting on page 66 is the early Jewish philosopher Philo of Alexandria.

ONE

MONTH OF THE BLOOD MOON

WHEN ITS TIME HAS ARRIVED,
THE PREY COMES TO THE HUNTER.

—PERSIAN PROVERB

Just before his throat was torn out by a husky teenage boy he had never seen before, the Reverend Pledger Lee Skeldon had been distracted from the task of his lifetime—wresting souls from the wiles of the devil and delivering them to the lamb of God—by the face of a quietly ecstatic, weeping girl in the crowd of mostly young people filling a carpeted space in front of the arena's temporary stage. Waiting, like all of the others, for the touch of the evangelist's hand and, perhaps, a personal message at this time of their rebirth in Christ Jesus.

Fifteen thousand souls. Dating couples, pensioners, drifters off the street, busloads from tiny communities as far away as Arkansas or the hollows of Appalachia. Admission free.

The arena lights were purposely low. A follow spot channeled Pledger Lee's own presence. There still were streams of people in the aisles above him, coming down to the arena floor in response to his call. He looked up for a few moments, closed his eyes. He had poured himself out to them and now stood emptied to the naive, fevered emotions they returned to him. His pulses tingled. His heart quaked from their heat.

When again he looked down and directly into the face of the girl, he was certain that he was seeing Pearl Lee, his youngest daughter.

That would have been a miracle to reckon with: Pearl Lee had been lost to the family for more than two years. She had drowned while on a kayaking trip with other Teen-Lifers on North Georgia's Ocoee River. Six hours had passed before her body, wedged upside down by the gushing weight of the water and deep between boulders in a narrow chute of the river, could be recovered.

Pearl Lee was buried in the hilltop cemetery beside the Baptist church in Georgia's Blue Ridge country where Pledger, when he was little more than a child, had received his call to preach. Therefore her weeping appearance before him on this night, flesh and blood though she seemed to be, was an illusion, a trick of his wearied mind.

Pledger Lee was finishing a demanding schedule with this final meeting of his Christian Triumph Revival Crusade at Philips Arena, and he was exhausted. Yes—an illusion, an apparition produced by the sharp-edged grief he'd thought was also buried in the density of time behind him. Yet as he reached out to her, oblivious of the young man moving in close to him on his left side, another thought transfixed the evangelist: perhaps this was the work of the Evil One traditional theology identified as Satan, but whom Pledger Lee knew by another name.

The young man who attacked and killed the evangelist was Jimmy Nixon, sixteen, of Stone Mountain, Georgia. Lived there with his divorced mother, a travel agent, and two younger siblings. Jimmy was, as the subsequent police investigation made clear, known for his cheerful disposition and athletic ability. Didn't drink, didn't do drugs. He had never been much of a churchgoer, so it had been something of a surprise to his mom when Jimmy mentioned after dinner that he was going to drive downtown, alone, to take in a revival meeting.

Jimmy was muscular, carrying 220 pounds on a six-foot frame. Pledger Lee was no lightweight, but he was totally unprepared for a maniacal onslaught. Also unprepared was Smith Ballew, the Christian Triumph Revival's Chief of Security, who, in crowd situations, always positioned himself a couple of feet to the evangelist's right, studying the faces of those within arm's reach. Any public figure attracts head cases, some of whom might be dangerous, but Ballew had seldom encountered problems with the faithful: invariably those who came down to the floor of whatever venue they were in to accept Christ's blood as absolution for their trifling sins were either in a subdued, worshipful mood or tearfully rejoicing, floating free as balloons from sinks of despond.

There was nothing about Jimmy Nixon (Ballew would recall, when his short-term memory was restored) that agitated his curiosity or put him on alert. Jimmy's rusty hair was quite short, like a number-two buzz, growing in after a ritual head shaving at his high school's football camp in mid-August. A deep summer's tan was only beginning to fade from his skin this second week in October, leaving a dark scatter of freckles and pink peel spots across his snub nose and forehead. Dry-looking lips were slightly parted over white teeth girded in metal braces. His eyes were pale, almost an incandescent blue, and (Ballew realized he should have made more of this passing observation) they had no more expression than the eyes of a well-mounted trophy head in spite of the intense atmosphere following the evangelist's message. (Only Pledger Lee Skeldon knew that he believed very little of what he had been preaching for the last ten years, the myths of a two-thousand-year-old religion, albeit a religion that still satisfied most hungers of the spirit. That was the reason why he was still in the Gospel Game. If he preached what he *did* know to be the truth about Good and Evil and the potential fate of humanity, he would have been shut up in an asylum long ago. So he had learned to live with his loss of faith and the assumption of a vital duty.)

Pledger Lee was sixty-five years old, still with an eagle's darkling authority. His long legs were tired, and his knees ached. He wore rimless bifocals. His throat was dry after deliverance of hellfire (in that he certainly could believe, amen). There was a hard pulse in his carotid artery, which lay, as it did in all human beings, less than half an inch below the loose skin and thin flesh of his throat. The pulse may have been visible to the boy who killed him, an irresistible beacon to the metaled teeth.

Before biting, however, Jimmy Nixon seized the evangelist's trachea with the strong fingers of his right hand, rupturing the larynx even as he was forcing Pledger Lee backward against the hip-high, carpeted edge of the stage. Onstage and close by, two of the evangelist's adult daughters, Penny Lee and Piper Lee, were singing the Christian Triumph Revival's signature hymn ("Praise Jesus, I'm Born Again"), in concert with two of Christian Gospel's most popular male personalities.

Piper Lee happened to be looking at her father as she paused before resuming harmony; she let out a scream that cut through the hush of the arena like the clang of a fallen bell. Smith Ballew attempted to get a grip on Jimmy Nixon and pull him away from the preacher. It was like trying to budge a steel pillar bolted to the arena floor. The boy reacted by striking Ballew with an elbow between his eyes. Ballew landed, unconscious, on the back of his neck.

Two more security men lunged through the crowd of seekers, most of whom were stark-still from terror. One of the men leaped on Nixon's broad back as he hunched over his victim. Penny Lee joined her sister in screaming into their open mikes. A prickling current of fear illuminated the body of the congregation. Nearly all of them had a good view of the scuffle below, although it was diffi-cult to comprehend just what was happening.

Pledger Lee, the upper half of his body jammed against the lip of the stage, looked up through skewed glasses at the faces of his daughters. Stunned by the attack, he knew only that he couldn't breathe. If he'd had a coherent thought at this moment it might have been: *I am going to die like the others.*

Whatever his thoughts, recognition flickered in his mind like a will-o'-the-wisp as the boy's face moved to within a couple of inches of his.

If he was aware of the efforts exerted to pry him loose from Pledger Lee Skeldon, whose gristly windpipe was still locked in his right hand, Jimmy Nixon didn't show it.

"You know who I am," he said to the evangelist.

No one else, in the frenzy of the moment, recalled hearing Jimmy speak. Possibly Pledger Lee himself, so close to the eerie deadness of the boy's face, didn't hear him either.

But he already knew.

A member of the security detail was flailing at the attacker's shoulders with a telescoping baton. Another worked on Jimmy's waistline and the backs of his knees. It was as if the boy could feel no pain. Didn't know he was squirting urine from wrecked kidneys. Jimmy jerked his right fist sharply, like opening a stuck gate, uprooting the preacher's trachea and stems of bronchi from the lungs. At the same time Jimmy bit deeply into Pledger Lee's throat, severing the flimsy artery. Piper Lee, on her hands and knees a few feet away, fingernails in the carpet as she implored Jimmy to leave her father alone, was splashed by his lifeblood; it covered her face like a shroud.

Jimmy Nixon was still into Pledger Lee's neck when an arena rent-a-cop imprudently delivered a solid blow to the back of Jimmy's head, driving shards of skull into the hindbrain. Jimmy's body vibrated; he lost his grip on the preacher and was dragged away from him, handcuffed.

With no one to support him, Pledger Lee slumped to the floor, hands patting his body down as if he were trying to put out a fire; but it was the storm from his heart blowing unchecked through the rent throat that quickly did him in.

No one thought to dim the rainbow cross of lights still trained on the evangelist. Or turn off the cameras that were recording his death, the shrieks of those compelled to watch it.

"SHUNGWAYA" · LAKE NAIVASHA, KENYA · OCTOBER 10 · 0310 HOURS ZULU

Eden Waring awoke as darkness began to leave the sky, earth's purification ritual, brief quiet time of renewal before the storming of the birds. Hibiscus flowers outside her windows had not yet unfurled in huge crimson splashes against screens fogged by their golden pollen. The short rains from the south hadn't materialized in this autumn of a third drought year, adding to the woes of a nation whose prosperity and infrastructure had been steadily crumbling for two decades.

There was a morning chill at this altitude in the Great Rift Valley, gusts of wind across the valley floor and the dwindling freshwater lake. On the wind, the primary odors of what remained of primeval East Africa—of herds and their fresh scrape, of sage, resin, jasmine; of wood embers still containing heat from last night's cookfire in the pit outside the kitchen pavilion.

The estate, now a game reserve, had been established by Tom Sherard's grandfather after the First World War and named by him "Shungwaya," after an ancient, possibly mythical southern Somalian kingdom of great power and prestige.

Tom and Joseph Nkambe had left before moonrise to destroy a leopard that had killed the ten-year-old daughter of a Masai ranger in Hell's Gate Park. Although there were, as usual, houseguests to be entertained, Eden had been inclined to invite herself to the blind that the men had constructed at some distance from where the leopard was laying up in daylight, a *kopje* Tom had discovered after days of patient tracking. She was also curious to see the leopard's pug marks although Tom, after looking at one of her careful drawings, had told her the footprint of the leopard was not the mark that had been showing up in her dreams.

In Africa, Tom's mother had written in one of her journals, treasures that he had generously shared with Eden, *there is always too much to see when you are awake. Dreams are the refreshments of the weary eye, as well as the actuality of other layers of existence—fantastic, subtle, strange—here in this valley where human life on earth began.*

His mother, dead at a time when he was barely old enough to remember her. In photographs she had a lanky frame, close-cropped copper-red hair, some cheekbone pitting from acne, a long face, a tentative smile, a gravely inquiring manner. Tom was almost a replica except for complexion and something more aggressive in the hard jawline, his father's long gaze and weathered durability.

"What else have you been dreaming about?" Sherard had asked Eden, with a hint of caution—or fear of trespass—in his gray eyes. They'd had four months to get to know each other; still he was not altogether at ease with Eden, daughter of the woman he had loved. Or, more exactly, he was not comfortable with Eden's wild talent and the destiny it proposed.

You, she might have responded, but she didn't want to attempt an explanation. Her feelings for him were complicated. He was almost her father, although they shared no blood. Under different circumstances—she was willing to acknowledge, but only to herself, this sensual irritant in the heart, like the grain of sand the oyster must make into a pearl—they easily could have been lovers. But it was enough, common sense demanded, that she owed him her life.

Also Tom belonged to Bertie Nkambe, and Bertie to Tom, as surely as if they were already married. And Bertie, another wild talent, had become Eden's best friend and advisor during Eden's period of recovery and reconciliation with herself at the Naivasha game reserve.

She still faithfully recorded every dream in her dream book, now volume number seven. A habit she'd imposed upon herself in childhood, now unbreakable. Hundreds of pages of dreams—mundane, perplexing, and (sometimes) prophetic. Only with Bertie was she willing to share their imagery and symbolism.

Bertie hadn't read much into the recurring dream of pug marks.

"Cheetahs, lions, even leopards—you see them almost every day. No wonder you dream about them. So do I, sometimes."

"Yeah, but—this cat's different."

"What does it look like?"

"I don't know yet. I haven't seen it. I only know that when I do— it'll be different."

"Well—there's tigers. But there are no tigers in Africa, not in the wild. Maybe two thousand years ago, in an Emir's menagerie."

"This cat's not in a zoo or in the wild. It's—"

In my head.

Sitting up in near-darkness in the four-poster bed draped in blowsy mosquito netting, Eden shuddered. She habitually slept in a man's extra-large flannel shirt, but with that and the down-filled comforter on the bed, still she was cold to the bone. The guest bungalow in which she lived was one of the oldest at Shungwaya, and it lacked central heating. There was in her bedroom an eighteenth-century Austrian ceramic stove, delivered long ago by ox wagon from the Indian Ocean port of Mombasa, but sleeping with a *muta-*

mayo fire going (from the wood of the wild olive tree) gave her a stuffy nose.

It wasn't only the chilly dawn that had her shivering. The pug marks that had appeared in her most recent dream had been in an unfamiliar place, not alongside an African streambed or by a salt lick. She had seen these marks very clearly; they glowed in dim light on the marble steps of a staircase. The steps ascended to a gold-toned portal of great age and narrow doors. All of it, the plain gray building, the wide stairs, seemed vaguely to have a religious significance.

Although in previous dreams Eden had been unable to get a true impression of size, it was obvious to her that the pug marks on the marble were very large.

And red.

Eden knew their maker had walked in blood, and for several minutes she could not control her trembling.

Full light, like darkness, comes quickly to Equatorial Africa.

In the ten minutes that it took Eden to wash and dress in shorts and a light sweater, the waters of Lake Naivasha, now receded three hundred yards from the house and farm outbuildings of the wildlife reserve, glowed through drifts of mist. Alberta Nkambe had begun her daily half-mile swim in the infinity pool at the edge of the east lawn, overlooking a landscape of farms, bush, and extinct volcanoes, still a little scary in their gaunt passivity. Her best dog, Fernando, a mix of Labrador and mastiff, barked at her every stroke as he kept pace with Bertie on one side of the heated pool.

Around the farms and coffee-growing estates in the Naivasha region, eighty kilometers up-country from Nairobi and remote from the rest of the world by any reckoning, Eden was known as Eve. Bertie was a superstar model whose face had been appearing on the covers of fashion magazines since she was sixteen. If anyone Eden had been introduced to, at Shungwaya or on rare social occasions at the Naivasha Country Club, recalled her face from satellite TV news, they respected her need for anonymity. She was good-looking, obviously American-bred, and a beauty when she bothered. But at Shungwaya Eden didn't wear makeup and her hairstyle was strictly utilitarian, an expression of psychological isolation from the society she was half afraid to rejoin. She felt no further obligation to its madness.

She never discouraged the attention of guys near her age whom she'd met—in particular a Belgian graduate student in ethnobotany from the University of Ghent, and a Canadian climatologist—but most of the time she made herself unavailable, feeling secure only in Tom Sherard's and Bertie's company. Harrowing times made steadfast companions. Eden badly missed the only mother she'd ever known; but Betts soon would be joining her, coming from California, with a brief stopover in England to visit a younger sister whom she rarely saw.

The climatologist, a Quebecois named Jean-Baptiste, was camped with several older colleagues on the reserve. They were engaged in extracting core samples of sediment from Naivasha's depths to study catastrophic drought cycles. Two or three times a week he appeared for breakfast and the opportunity to chat up Eden. Jean-Baptiste was one of those homely young men with a rump of a nose and a dark squeeze around the eyes, but he had a brisk mind and a sense of humor.

This morning Jean-Baptiste was in conversation with Pegeen, a model chum of Bertie's, and her husband, who had the bronzed look of the well-heeled, gadabout sportsman but who seemed serious about making "docs"—documentary films. They had dropped in a few days ago. There was seldom any such thing as an unwelcome guest in Kenya, where "close neighbors" were defined as being within fifty kilometers of one another.

Eden crossed the lawn to the main house through the drifting vapors of the pool, droplets gleaming like gold dust in the air. There was a flock of emerald-spotted wood doves in one of the old Albizias growing in the middle of the lawn, thick trunks as smooth as ivory. The lawn was about the size of a cricket pitch, which it once had been. There were a couple of reticulated giraffe at one end of the lawn, oxblood in color with a lacy overlay of white lines. Pretty, horned heads and elfin eyes. Just standing around politely, as if they wouldn't mind an invitation to breakfast. Two more of Shungwaya's mixed-breed dog population caught up to Eden and she paused to rub behind their ears before joining the others.

It had been a dry dusty year, but the jacarandas and frangipani, green and healthy from water piped up from the lake, were in full bloom by the recently rebuilt, split-level veranda. The twin roofs that steeply overhung the veranda were thatched in woven papyrus and rested on elegantly twisted, polished cedar posts. The thatch was pink with fallen blossoms, and a young member of the household staff—all Somali males—was sweeping petals from the steps.

"*Jambo, memsaab,*" the boy said, giving Eden a shy glance.

"Good morning, Ahmad."

Pegeen, her husband, and Jean-Baptiste the climatologist were having wake-up coffee and watching the news from London on *Sky*. Jean-Baptiste flashed Eden a smile that had a lot of meaning and a hint of suggestion in it—*Hi, missed you, do you sleep in the nude?* Like a lot of men with middling looks, Jean-Baptiste had developed an intricate understanding of and easy rapport with women.

Eden dropped a friendly hand on his shoulder and sat next to him in a split-bamboo armchair with lion-toned cushions. She was in time to see, on the newscast, a face as familiar in Africa as it was in the U.S.: the evangelist Pledger Lee Skeldon. It appeared to be bad news.

"What happened?"

"He was killed last night," Pegeen said with a slight shudder. She was black Irish, with very full lips and Bambi's eyes. Bambi on Prozac. And, according to Bertie, Pegeen was fey. Eden sensed by the way Pegeen sometimes regarded her that she'd haphazardly picked up on Eden's other life, if not her status in the Psi world. She didn't feel uncomfortable about Pegeen's knowing. Eden was reading auras with more confidence, a talent in which Bertie had instructed her. According to Pegeen's aura, she lacked guile or duplicity. Unfortunately the dead were too much with her, and they could be a nuisance to a latent spiritualist.

Pegeen's husband, an Englishman named Etan Culver, had no clue what was wrong when his bride drifted into one of her melancholy, speechless moods. Bertie had decided that she and Eden needed to work with Pegeen before her new marriage foundered.

"Killed? Accident, or—"

"Murdered," Jean-Baptiste said. His English was lightly accented. "Before a crowd at one of his revival meetings. They have the footage, apparently, but—"

"Much too gruesome," Etan said. He had a three-day growth of beard that didn't become him, and his eyes all but disappeared when he was hungover. Today made three mornings in a row. "A high school boy attacked and bit him in the throat before anyone could interfere. The bite severed his carotid artery. He was dead within a minute."

Pegeen shook her head nervously, then leaned against his shoulder on the loveseat they occupied.

The chief Somali houseman, seven feet in his red fez, brought Eden a cup of the green tea she preferred drinking in the morning, with ginseng added for mental acuity.

"Why did he do it?" Eden wondered, looking at what must have been a high school yearbook photo of Jimmy Nixon.

"We'll probably never know," Jean-Baptiste said. "A security guard became overanxious and bashed his skull with a riot baton. Report had it the boy is in critical care, and he may be a veg."

Eden glanced at him, then concentrated on the televised image, the appealing smile on Jimmy's broad face. Not ashamed to show his braces, which had turned teeth into choppers. But the flavor of him wholesome, untainted. True-blue innocence, this Jimmy, who had been overtaken by a swift madness, had done an incomprehensible, savage thing—the bite a kiss of death, orgiastic—and now lay in a state of twilight forgetfulness.

A shadow appeared on the TV screen, over Jimmy Nixon's face. Eden looked away quickly, into Pegeen's astonished, fearful eyes. She was about to speak.

Eden said quietly, "Not now."

Apparently no one else had witnessed the quick shadow. Etan

Culver opened his eyes slightly, from slits to slashes of chilly blue, giving Eden a puzzled look.

"What's that, luv?"

Eden shrugged. The TV news moved on. To a war zone. One of the bleak places of the earth. Asia, Africa, South America. Didn't matter, Eden thought. Always there were refugees on a long road with black smoke rising behind them. The faces, always the same. The dispossessed. Children with the fixed gazes that only extreme terror can provide. Men who want to cry but can't. Old women in black, their faces carved into rigid masks of rage through decades of abuse, despair. On the move again. Grab and carry or drag what you can. A pot. A goat on a rope. Nothing at the end of this road. They're all the same. The same old nothing. Live another day. Or don't.

Eden closed her eyes. She hated the morning news, never more than when she'd been part of it herself. Up only thirty minutes, already her heart felt sore, the day seemed devoid of promise.

"Didn't this happen before?" Jean-Baptiste said, and Eden nodded. "No, I mean, how the preacher was killed. I remember reading—"

"Yes," Pegeen said, in that just-smoldering, loamy Irish voice. "There was another mairder similar to this one. My roommate in New York"—she named an actress beginning to make a name for herself—"was quite upset when she heard the news. It would've been about a year ago, just before I met you, Etan. Tams and her boyfriend had spent several weeks in India, at the ashram of Tams's guru. I don't know the name, but he is, or was, famous provided one is keen for that sort of spiritual trip. He was supposed to have been a god on earth, with uncanny powers."

"He must have read his tea leaves wrong the day he got offed," Jean-Baptiste said, then interrupted himself with a yawn. "Who killed this guru?"

"No idea. Another sojournor, a disciple, I believe it was. But the method—" Pegeen's eyes went to Eden again, who smiled sympathetically. Pegeen drank coffee, giving memory her full scrutiny, then continued in a hushed voice. "It was the same ghastly method. Neck was bitten through, the artery severed."

"Let's-pretend vampires," Jean-Baptiste said with a grimace. "All the kids these days into cult stuff. Goth." He closed the subject with a palms-up gesture. "Your roommate was Tamora Pass? I saw her in that *Mission Impossible* sequel."

"Bloody film looked as if it were edited in a blender," Etan grumbled.

Breakfast was served; they moved to the table. Jean-Baptiste soon had them laughing about the way some of his colleagues spent their off-hours, obsessively staging and betting on cockroach races. Cockroaches the size of Matchbox automobiles. They kept their huge and pampered pets in lozenge tins that they carried with them in their shirt pockets during the day.

"Bugging out in Africa," Jean-Baptiste said.

"Of course," Etan said, sucking up coffee, "only in our obsessions do we meet the promise of a truly meaningful life."

"Cockroaches are meaningful?" Eden asked.

"As long as they don't finish out of the money."

Pegeen didn't laugh. She continued to look at Eden, seeming adrift and dismayed, wanting confirmation of what they'd both seen on the tube during the bad news from Atlanta.

The opaque orange *shuka* Bertie had put on after her nearly nude swim billowed like flame as she crossed the lawn barefoot, followed by adoring dogs.

"Here comes enough body heat to leave an imprint on stone," Jean-Baptiste said wistfully.

"Behave," Eden chided. "She's spoken for."

"None remain but you and me, Eve. I may not be the First Man, but I'm just as deserving, *mon cher.*"

"And an optimist," Eden said, but with a smile, acknowledging the sacrifice of his pawn. And not unwilling to continue the game. He had a face like a bloodhound with a bad head cold, but his body was lean and fine. Just one of those guys you could feel guilty about for not liking them. Actually she did like Jean-Baptiste, although he could be talkative while never revealing much about himself. In that respect, at least, they were a matched pair.

Tom Sherard and Joseph Nkambe, Bertie's father, returned at twenty past eight with the body of the leopard Tom had settled shortly after daybreak, when the leopard returned from nocturnal prowling to his customary hide, where he laid up during the day. They all went out to the lake side of the house to have a look at the body, tied down on the bonnet of a Land Rover.

On the point of one shoulder there was a punched-out floret from the .375-caliber expanding bullet that had killed the cat, blowing pieces of bone like shrapnel through the chest cavity. The open eyes were a glazed yellow, like the flesh of a cut lemon left all day in a saucer. The six-foot leopard had been tagged, with the particulars of the kill noted on the tag. The remains would be turned over to the Kenyan Wildlife Service.

Sherard looked drawn and tired. Probably he should have left this hunt to another pro, Eden thought, because of a left leg that still pained him and lacked strength after an assassin's bullets had nearly demolished the knee. Hunters of leopard often turned out to be the hunted if a shot only wounded the animal, which was often the case. Nervous exhaustion, not exhilaration, was a common reaction to those who remained unscathed after a leopard hunt. He had waited motionless in the dark for hours, never knowing if the most cunning of big cats might be creeping up behind them, just outside the blind in the leaning tree that he and Joseph had constructed after Tom patiently tracked the leopard to his lair.

The hunters handed over guns and Tom's leopard bag, which was filled with practical items like body armor, disinfectant, and Syrettes of morphine, to Hassan, the Somali head of the Shungwaya household. There was a reflection of a cruising vulture on the Land Rover's windscreen. Pegeen Culver approached the dead leopard, shading her eyes against the sun flare off glass.

Small shapely head, the sprawled body supple even in death. A beautiful creature, claws like razors, retracted now. The leopard had eviscerated and eaten most of a child. Her husband photographed

Pegeen with the leopard. He had a kitful of the latest in digital video equipment. At Etan's urging Pegeen diffidently touched a dangling paw. Retreated, shuddering.

Etan Culver interviewed Sherard, who submitted graciously but had no use for it. He wanted a bath and breakfast.

"Is that what you saw?" Eden said quietly in Pegeen's ear. "On the face of the boy who killed the preacher?"

Several dik-dik sauntered along the driveway, attracted by the tasty buds of bougainvillea. One of the estate dogs loped toward them, chasing them away. Hippos were lounging and splashing in their muddy pools. White pelicans flew along the lakeshore where stubs of drowned trees had reappeared from the blue depths. There was a sizzle of tiny insects nearby, weaving a universe in air, one day and they were done.

"No," Pegeen said. "A catlike body, but huge-r. And the head was not that of a cat. It had a sneering, thuggish face."

Eden nodded glumly. She was familiar with the animal described, although Pegeen hadn't been in Africa long enough to have seen one.

Bertie Nkambe, who had an arm around Tom Sherard's waist as he responded halfheartedly to the filmmaker's questions on camera, glanced at them. Bertie looked serenely happy. Eden felt a pang of envy. It was like the touch of a fly on her skin, to be brushed away. She looked again at Pegeen, whose eyes were dreary. Pegeen, who had asthma, massaged her throat with a pale childlike hand, as if the dry air was choking her.

"Sure and it'll be comin' here," Pegeen confirmed.

"You don't have to be afraid, Pegeen."

"What does it want? Why is it comin'?"

"I don't know yet. But when it does come . . . Tom will kill it."

If it can be killed.

Pegeen looked at her husband, who was absorbed in his craft.

"I hate it here," she said, suddenly in tears. "There's too much of death, everywhere. But Etan won't listen. He won't leave."

His Holiness Pope John the Twenty-fourth, born Sebastiano Leoncaro in a small Piedmont town seventy-two years ago, awoke as was his habit promptly at five A.M. in the papal apartment overlooking the Piazza of St. Peter's.

Espresso with a dash of whipped cream was waiting outside his bedroom door, brought to him by Sister Pasqualina, one of the staff of elderly nuns of the Sisters of the Poor who looked after Leoncaro's daily needs.

Following his prayer for guidance during a long working day and a set of light exercises prescribed for a chronic back condition, Leoncaro treated himself to music—Elgar's *Dream of Gerontius*—which he listened to on headphones while he made his first diary entry for October 10. There had been a thunderstorm during the night, breaking the heat wave that had lingered well into the month. The windows of his study next to the bedroom had been opened for him. The curtains stirred in a predawn breeze that held the sweetness of the summer's air at Lake Albano, only fourteen miles away but fourteen hundred feet higher than smog-plagued Rome.

His source of light at this early hour was a green-shaded student's lamp that had been with him since his early days at the Angelicum and through his globe-trotting years as a Vatican diplomat. The lamp sat directly in front of him on the writing desk. A pool of light illuminated both his diary and proof pages of one section of the papal *Anuncio* he had been working on for three years. The rest of his study was in deep shadow.

After a few minutes it became apparent to Leoncaro that he was no longer alone. He continued his writing for another minute, then closed his diary, removed the headphones, and laid them on the desk. He looked up over the edges of his half glasses at the figure seated on the small divan opposite him. Hadn't been there when Leoncaro entered his study. The door remained closed. So it was a Visitation. And the news was likely to be grim.

Leoncaro's upper lip had been scarred during a brief pro career in boxing after World War II. The scar glowed whitely when his lips compressed in an expression of shock and concern.

"Sorry to disturb you, Sebastiano," his visitor said deferentially, in his familiar North Georgia drawl.

"So it's happened to you," Leoncaro replied, looking at the hideously torn throat, the bled-out, slightly evanescent body.

" 'Fraid so."

"I'm deeply sorry."

"It appears he's on a rampage," the Shade of Pledger Lee Skeldon observed. Vocal cords had been destroyed, so the Shade's lips didn't move. But the form of communication they were using was older than spoken language. And they shaped their thoughts colloquially, not in formally rhymed voice.

"Again."

"Yes, again."

Leoncaro didn't feel uncomfortable conversing with a corpse. He'd seen far worse examples of inhuman butchery. He fingered the plain rosewood crucifix on his breast with two stubby fingers, considering the significance of Mordaunt's message to them. *Rampage.* Well, they'd had it good for too long. And perhaps become complacent in their stewardship of the human race.

Leoncaro had a broad workingman's hand. Knuckles broken and rebroken, now swollen, inflamed by arthritis. He was paying for the long-extinguished need to put another man down, in the ring or brawls wherever he'd chanced to find them. He had become a scholar, a theologian, a world leader, but he was peasant stock and had grown up during a war that devastated his country. He understood the despair and rage of the majority of his vast flock born to low fortune and doomed to hard times. For every audience he held at the Vatican he held six for the suffering in their barrios, the depleted, scavenged places. Consequently Leoncaro was the most popular Pontiff—with the people, if not the leaders of the Curia—since the death of Roncalli, John the Twenty-third, forty years ago.

And Pledger Lee at the moment of his death had been the best-known evangelist of the twentieth century, an inspiration to millions of Protestants, a confidant of U.S. presidents. His passing would be mourned around the world.

While the nature of his death caused great fear.

Both souls were among the heirs of those who preceded human ken, myth, and fable, the original Caretakers of Terra. And obviously they had a problem.

"The question remains," Leoncaro mused, "what does Mordaunt have to gain this time? He can only kill or order to have killed that which is temporal. The immortal is beyond his range. Confusion, deceit, and beguilement are his only weapons. The Trickster has turned human beings against themselves countless times. But we manage to put things right after each convulsion."

"I believe something's made him bolder this go-round," the Shade of Pledger Lee responded. "The latest economic depression is deepening. It's already destroyed all of the social optimism and positive energy generated in the past—well, since the last Great Depression ran its course in '49. Now, *this* depression is shaping up to be a humdinger, Sebastiano. Serious economic depressions result in mindless rage and the madness of crowds. And, inevitably, as if the recent crimes of Islamic terrorists are not enough, we get another world war, raising the consequences to chaos and nuclear holocaust. 'A wind-age, a wolf-age, before the world's ruin,' " he concluded, quoting from the Norse epic of Ragnorok. "Conditions Mordaunt needs for his ascendancy to—it just makes me want to puke to say it—*spiritual leader* of what is left of mankind."

"Not a pretty prospect," remarked another stellar Presence, who had slipped quietly into the Pontiff's study and was leaning against the wall near the windows.

Leoncaro turned in his creaking chair.

"Don Raimundo," he said with a stiff nod to the plasmic representation of the revered Brazilian sorcerer. "Is this going to become a Consistory? I don't remember calling one."

"No, no, Sebastiano. Vibrationally I happened to be in the neighborhood, so—" Raimundo gazed sorrowfully at the evangelist's throat. "It happens, no?"

The Shade of Pledger Lee gave a shrug.

"Was it as unpleasant as being burnt at the stake?" the plasmic image of the Buddhist nun Ling Qi asked quietly. She still retained vivid memories of events in fifteenth-century France.

"Also in the neighborhood?" Leoncaro inquired with a smile. His study was becoming a trifle crowded.

Ling Qi, a living saint to millions in Southeast Asia, bowed politely.

"If it is all right with you, Sebastiano."

"Well, as long as you're here," Leoncaro said graciously. Ling Qi was a favorite of his among the Twelve.

He paused for a few moments to allow the representative from Ocean Parkway to slip in under the wire, his frothy white beard sprinkled with points of light. Then, on a sterner note, raising his eyes, Leoncaro said, "No more, please. We have enough for an informal colloquium; let us keep it that way for now."

The slowly diminishing Shade of Pledger Lee made room on the divan for the petite form of Ling Qi, her shaved head radiant as a crystal ball. The Rebbe from Brooklyn, a venerable eighty-six-year-old, eased into the only chair in the study. Don Raimundo of Brazil continued to lean against the wall, arms folded, a brown hard crust of a man with a pencil-line mustache.

They all looked at Leoncaro, who prepared his thoughts carefully, moving objects around on his desk in an absentminded ritual. A bronze replica of the Eiffel Tower that served as a paperweight; a couple of framed photographs, one of Leoncaro's mother, the other a Polaroid snapshot of a pickup truck with a Texas license plate and a bumper sticker that read CONGRATULATIONS, GOD, IT'S A BOY.

"As for Mordaunt's long-cherished hope for Ascendancy, which we have thwarted every time: Mordaunt lacks the power. It is permanently beyond his reach." Leoncaro paused as if expecting a reaction, but they were all in agreement, for now. "True enough, he will benefit from a social crisis, waxing on the despair and doubt of the multitudes in our conservatorship. His atrocities—the savage destruction of Pledger Lee hours ago and of Sai Rampa last year, and the attempt on the life of our number seven, the Dalai Lama, that fortunately only wounded him—may serve to temporarily weaken the restraint we have on Mordaunt. And, speaking of the atrocity that so recently occurred—" Leoncaro looked at Pledger Lee Skeldon's waning Shade. "You won't have the down time you're accustomed to before establishing another human persona. Not with Mordaunt this aggressive."

"Figures," the Shade replied with an understanding nod.

"I'm afraid another takeover will be necessary to increase our strength."

"Ohhh," Ling Qi said in a faint voice. "Those can be rough."

"Begging your pardon, Sebastiano, but there's no one around in my—I mean—the late Reverend Skeldon's league as a religious leader. You know what television evangelists are like—old whores in new paint. The medium expands avarice exponentially. The pious con games. The cynical false promises. All that purely awful rococo gold furniture. Healing cloths, miracle water, it's a theological bazaar, tacky to the max."

"Religion has always been a strong consumer item," the Rebbe commented. He was taking his pulse. Like Leoncaro, the Rebbe was an elder of the Caretakers, and given to ramblings about his pending retirement. In mortal form, at an advanced age, he'd been suffering the expectable hardenings of this, malfunctions of that.

"I wasn't thinking of another career in Protestant evangelism," Leoncaro said to the tattered Shade of Skeldon.

"That's a relief. I almost lost Pledger Lee when I stepped in ten years ago. A good mind, but shallow perceptions. And I surely did underestimate the strength of his ticker."

"Sometimes the best and strongest horses cannot be ridden," Raimundo observed. "There was a time when I was reading entrails for a Magyar chieftain named Trul—"

Leoncaro looked pained and silenced the sorcerer with a raised finger. Don Raimundo was one of the younger Caretakers, and not always as focused as he needed to be.

Ling Qi looked thoughtfully at the high ceiling of the study, where cunningly sculpted cherubs with stubby wings lolled about.

"If I may make a suggestion, Holiness. With Mordaunt on the offensive again, could it be that we haven't kept him busy enough?"

"Or is it possible that we are simply not all that we used to be?" the Rebbe speculated. "And Mordaunt senses it is so."

"Historically we've had our down times," Leoncaro acknowledged. "Those periods of apocalypse and human suffering Pledger Lee anticipates for the immediate future." He nodded to the Shade of the late evangelist. "You'll pardon me if I continue to refer to you as if you remained in your temporal aspect."

"Go right ahead," the Shade replied amiably. "After a long stretch cooped up in a human persona, I tend to forget who I am myself."

"Tell me about it," Ling Qi said softly and a little sadly. "But the Rebbe has made an excellent point. Mordaunt could have something we've overlooked, to our detriment. A means, perhaps, of reuniting the Trickster's halves of his soul."

"We split his black soul and it will stay split," the Shade of Pledger Lee scoffed, and then, upon reflection, "which is a good thing. Don't think it could be done again, without sacrificing the core energy of all the Caretakers. Three of us gone already, burnt out, nothing left but cinders floating derelict somewhere beyond the Lights."

"I suspect Ling Qi and the Rebbe are right," the sorcerer Don Raimundo interrupted. "But I could only be sure of what Mordaunt is up to by settling in his neighborhood for a while."

"We will take no unnecessary risks," Leoncaro objected. "And what can Mordaunt know that is beyond the scope of *our* knowledge?"

"Not beyond our knowledge," the sorcerer persisted. "A growing power we perhaps have been neglectful in not bringing under our control."

"Please explain."

Don Raimundo spread his hands. "I'm speaking of the Avatar. The, uh, most recent incarnation."

"Oh, come now!" the Rebbe protested. "Of course we all know her, but Eden Waring is a child."

"More woman than child now. Don't be too quick to dismiss her," Leoncaro said. "True, she was chosen in haste by her predecessor, but that choice was partly dictated by dire circumstances. Mmm, yes. Eden Waring. She does have one impressive talent that none of the other Psi-actives possess."

"The left-handed Art," the Brazilian sorcerer said.

"Exactly."

"Meaning?" Ling Qi inquired.

"Like the late Kelane Cheng," Leoncaro said, "Eden Waring can produce her doppelganger."

After a few moments of contemplative silence in the Prelate's study, the Rebbe said, "I don't understand how Mordaunt would find that useful."

But the sorcerer chuckled. Leoncaro looked around at him with a nod of approval. Then he smiled indulgently at the other elder of their company.

"I still don't—"

"Rebbe, where do doppelgangers come from?"

"The parallel universe that most closely resembles this one. Dpg's are, in every vital respect, the mirror images of their homebodies."

"Yes; and are there any limits to the ability of the dpg to travel from one universe to the next, or back and forth in time?"

"Aha! Of course."

But the Shade of Pledger Lee Skeldon observed, "That doesn't help Mordaunt. He's earthbound, and he lacks the left-handed Art. We split his soul, took the feminine half away, and that reduced his power by half."

"The only way we could handle him," Ling Qi said.

"He doesn't know where his other half is. Although he might appreciate the irony if he did. And *she* doesn't know who she is, or where she came from."

Ling Qi shuddered slightly, as if in sympathy, and looked away from Leoncaro's reproving glance.

"What if Mordaunt does know where we stashed his, let us say, his better half?" Don Raimundo wondered.

"He didn't get it from me," the Shade of Pledger Lee Skeldon replied. "And I'm pretty sure old Sai Rampa didn't spill the beans, either."

"Both of your personas were dying, and violently," Leoncaro reminded him. "Can you be sure of what was going through your mind during those terrible moments?"

"Pledger Lee's mind. I never make it a practice to store trade secrets in obvious places. And it wasn't Mordaunt himself, Sebastiano; an emissary the Trickster beguiled. So I'm certain that my— Pledger Lee's—assassin didn't learn a thing. Wouldn't matter anyway. He's brain-dead from the beating he took. He was just there to kill. But—now that you've raised the point—maybe next time it will be Mordaunt himself at the throat of one of you."

"He cannot assume another human shape," the Brazilian sorcerer said. "He may only become . . . the beast. That is more of a danger to him than to us. Each time he shifts, it drains and ages Mordaunt's persona."

"We are accustomed to being on our guard; we will now take precautions to assure the safety of our mortal selves," Leoncaro advised them.

"I would like to send Mordaunt a message," Don Raimundo said, fire in his dark eyes. "A flood, perhaps, raging down from that desert mountain, with accompanying thunderbolts—"

"Unacceptable risk to innocent humans," the Rebbe said. "Does the term *Caretaker* mean anything to you?"

Don Raimundo hunched his shoulders, stroked his neat mustache, and appeared to be sulking.

"Let us assume, because we cannot afford to overlook the possibility, that Mordaunt has taken an interest in Eden Waring," Leoncaro concluded. "He is fascinated with her Art and her nascent power, which he hopes to channel to his benefit. Further assume he may have approached her already." His Holiness tapped a forefinger on the cover of his diary, studying the Shade of Pledger Lee Skeldon as it continued to disappear from the earthly plane. "And now we know how best you may put to use your renewed lease on temporal life."

There was no response except for a long sigh.

"Good day, everyone," Leoncaro said, and returned his attention to the *Anuncio* he'd been working on.

SAN FRANCISCO, CALIFORNIA · OCTOBER 10 · 4:18 P.M. PDT

I've always had this lucky streak," Frank Tubner said, with a modest glance at the well-tended nails of his right hand.

"There are nights when he's uncanny at bingo," Pinky Tubner affirmed, giving Frank's left hand an affectionate squeeze. "And when it comes to drawings at the church—well, that's how we happen to be on our way to Rome this very minute! I mentioned bingo, but that's small potatoes—tell Betts how much you won playing blackjack at the Bellagio, Frank, when we were down there for the convention last week."

"A tidy sum," Frank acknowledged with the unassuming smile of the blessed. "But I'm not *that* good. I mean, I've always had luck; the caveat is, know not to abuse your luck. Now Rex—he's our next-door neighbor in Santa Rosa, Rex Tarlock—Rex was in retail hardware until Home Depot came along and put him out of business—he's always after me to get in on these high-stakes poker games. But I tell him, Rex, this is my philosophy. Apart from the kind of 'luck'—quote-unquote—that you make for yourself through hard effort and the stick-to-it quality that's indispensable in sales, the out-of-the-blue kind of luck is a divine mystery—as Rush Limbaugh likes to say, 'on loan from God.' "

"It's God's reward for how you conduct your life," Pinky said, nodding solemnly and touching the gold cross she wore within the cleavage of her freckled breasts. Freckles and faintly blushing skin and natural strawberry-blond hair, baby-doll-blue eyes—Pinky had looks, although her lower lip was the size of a speed bump, and she was, Betts guessed (knowing she wasn't one to be passing judgment here), a good twenty pounds overweight.

Frank Tubman leaned forward on the sofa in the smoking section of United's first-class lounge, wincing slightly as a bolt of lightning outside illuminated an airport full of motionless planes on tarmac swept by sheets of rain. A series of late-afternoon thunderstorms had been delaying traffic in and out of SFO for the better part of an hour: the Tubners' flight to Rome, Betts Waring's flight to Heathrow.

"I don't believe the Lord begrudges my putting a little extra jingle in my pockets from time to time or a big-screen TV in the den, such as I won at the Kiwanis picnic Fourth of July last, but—you said your field was psychology, Betts, so maybe you can understand better than most what I'm getting at here—"

Betts stubbed the last half inch of her Merit in a standing ashtray beside her armchair and resisted the urge to light another one immediately.

"The lesson, or moral, is: don't be greedy. That's a very healthy attitude."

"Exactly!"

Pinky beamed and opened a new box of the sweet-smelling cigarillos she favored, looking idly around the lounge as she peeled cellophane. Frank was a nonsmoker, but he'd had a couple of bourbon and Cokes during their wait. Thunder caused the sandwich glass in the wall behind Betts to oscillate. Betts wished she could take her shoes off.

"So you and Pinky have an audience with the Pope," she said to Frank. "I'm not Catholic, but I assume it's a matter of some prestige."

"In our case, yes," Frank said. "There are several kinds of audiences with His Holiness. The regular Wednesday audience is held in the Papal Audience Chamber, which seats twelve thousand, and anyone can go who can get his hands on a ticket. So those audiences are not, um, that special. But an audience of key lay people from selected dioceses around the country in the Apostolic Palace is, yes, I have to say it: *very* special."

"Momentous," Pinky added, lighting her small cigar and looking at the two men in dark gray business suits who sat silently nearby, where they had been for some time, not drinking or reading or tapping on laptop computers. They did talk to each other, the sort of leisurely conversation that has its share of dry spells; but for the most part they seemed discreetly to be keeping an eye on—well, it had become obvious to the observant Pinky—Betts Waring.

Pinky looked at Betts again, speculatively, holding the cigarillo near her pendulous lower lip, lighter in her other hand as if she'd forgotten about it.

"Fact of the matter is," Pinky resumed, "we've always been very active in our diocese. Confidentially"— she now took the time to get her cigarillo going—"I don't think anyone has raised more money for the new education building than Frank."

"Now, sweetie, it's just a knack I have, persuading people to participate in worthwhile things."

Pinky Tubner dragged on her cigarillo, expelled smoke, and said in a low voice to Betts, "I don't want to alarm you. But those two men over there, that have this sort of *look* about them, you know, military but in civilian clothes, well—they have been paying you a lot of attention since we sat down."

"It's all right," Betts said, not looking at the two men.

"Oh, you mean you know them?"

"Slightly."

"Ohh." Pinky felt emboldened to study the pair for a few seconds. Frank frowned at her indiscretion, then cringed at another bolt from the thunderstorm that seemed to be parked directly over the airport. He smiled weakly at Betts. Frank wore a hairpiece, but he wasn't a bad-looking guy. Kind of a bumpy face. Wens. There was one below his left eye like a petrified tear. He was short and almost as round as his wife, but a fully packed roundness, as if staying in shape was just another religion for Frank. Tennis racket gold cuff links. Sure.

"They're private detectives," Betts explained, deciding it was time for her next Merit. She was wondering how rough it was going to be, a nonsmoking hop to Heathrow Airport in London. Nine and a half hours? But two martinis before dinner, then a prescription sleeping pill and a snooze in roomy first class with her feet up should see her through a no-nicotine stretch.

"You two were in Vegas recently? Would you believe I've never been? I hear they have some great shows."

"Speaking of luck," Pinky said, revisiting a favorite theme, for the moment distracting herself, "we got tickets to see Lincoln Grayle! I mean, not only that, we *met* him." She glanced again at the professional-looking men in gray suits. Private detectives? Did that mean—bodyguards? Obviously there was more to Betts Waring than met the eye. And then Pinky got it, the last name belatedly making a connection in her memory. Wasn't that also the name of the girl who had been in the news months ago, warning a stadium full of graduates and parents that a DC-10 was about to crash just where they were sitting? Pinky felt the downy hair on her forearms standing up.

"Grayle? That name's familiar," Betts said with polite interest.

"The magician. He's done TV specials. Maybe you saw the one, he escaped from a drone airplane that was blown up in midflight?"

"Most incredible illusion I've ever seen," Frank commented. "He definitely was put aboard that plane, wrapped in chains, and handcuffed. The door was welded shut, mind you, and the camera never cut away as the plane took off, rose to two thousand feet, and—blooey! *Then* the camera panned to a rescue truck racing to the scene, and the first man off the back of the truck, dressed in a fireman's coat and helmet, was Grayle."

"Incredible," Pinky seconded. "But I believe his Vegas show is better than anything he's done on TV. The Lincoln Grayle Theatre is a show itself. Like a glass palace, halfway up the mountain, whatchamacallit, five hundred feet above the desert." Pinky gestured theatrically herself, in the manner of a magician about to produce a palm tree from a top hat, her rings glittering in another burst of lightning just outside the shivering window wall.

"Drawback is," Frank said, "Grayle's theatre isn't in one of those posh hotels on the Strip. It's almost a twenty-buck cab ride west if you miss one of his free buses, which we did."

"But worth every penny," Pinky assured Betts. "When the Grayle Theatre is lit up at night and the fountains are going, they say airline pilots can see it a hundred miles away."

Pinky's gaze shifted and she smiled fitfully at a man in a United captain's uniform helping himself to coffee not far away. He also smiled and nodded as Pinky hitched herself a little closer to Betts. The lights in the lounge dimmed following a crescendo of thunder. Pinky shuddered superstitiously, glancing over one shoulder at the torrent outside, the unnatural daytime darkness between flashes.

"I've heard," Pinky confided to Betts, "that other illusionists—you know, all the big names like Copperfield, Lance Burton, Siegfried and Roy—good as they are, even they can't figure out how Grayle performs some of his illusions."

"If they *are* illusions," Frank said darkly.

Pinky finger-polished her crucifix again, nibbled at her plump underlip.

Frank scoffed at her expression. "Oh, now, that's pure showbiz baloney, angel. I was just getting a rise out of you. It's all part of Grayle's mystique, his image. He doesn't have supernatural powers. You're just supposed to believe he does. Takes a lot of the old snake oil to pack the house night after night."

"Well—"

"On the subject of Grayle, 'fess up, Pinky. You were just a little smitten with the guy." Frank held a thumb and forefinger half an inch apart, prompting his highly colored wife to blush a shade of red that almost erased her freckles. "Don't fret, pet. I'm not jealous."

"Oh, Frank." She looked at Betts. "Did I mention that we had a chance to meet him after the show?"

"Lucky Ticket holders," Frank said, now rubbing that thumb and forefinger together. "Which entitled us to a grand tour backstage after the show, by the man himself."

"He's *nothing* like his stage persona. Very handsome, of course; but so down-to-earth."

"A more affable guy I never hope to meet," Frank agreed. "And you can imagine, the demands of doing a couple of shows a night, probably didn't feel all that much like entertaining a couple of nobodies from Santa Rosa. But you'd never have known it. He showed us his gym where he works out, all the ways he has of rejuvenating himself between shows."

"Colored light therapy," Pinky said.

"How's that?" Betts asked.

"The technical name is spectrochrome therapy," Frank explained. " 'SCT' for short. But it's really very low-tech. How it works, Grayle stretches out on an ordinary massage table and for fifteen minutes he projects full-spectrum light through a set of about a dozen colored filters onto various parts of his body. The pincal gland, for instance. Or the navel or, um, his testicles. What he told me, the lights restore the proper balance in the body's complex electrical field. I tried it myself. I was feeling a little frazzled, fighting off a head cold. See, you have to be completely naked to realize the full benefit of the therapy. But doggone if I didn't feel *great* after my session. Rarin' to go."

"You sure were," Pinky said, giving Frank a sly satisfied look that implied a hot-wired libido had been one of those benefits. Frank sat back with a smug expression.

"Then I got up at five-thirty and played eighteen holes of golf. Fact is, since that little session in Grayle's gym I've had more energy than a pack of foxhounds on the scent." He gave Pinky a nudge. "By the way, you never have told me what you and Grayle talked about while I was getting my batteries recharged."

"Scuba diving, I think. He's an accomplished diver, and he's been everywhere. The Great Barrier Reef, the Caymans, Corsica. That's right. We talked about scuba diving." But Pinky appeared to be a little perplexed. Her gaze made a slow tour of the lounge. Her lips were apart, as if she'd fallen into a mild trance. But faces were vivid to her—the private detectives who apparently were there as protection for Betts (why she needed bodyguards at all was an unanswerable question); the airline captain, graying and with a brushy mustache, standing against one wall while drinking his coffee and idly playing with a gold cigarette lighter in his other hand; a Pakistani businessman and his wife; a Japanese couple, quietly but expensively dressed; and—Pinky felt no surprise, only a strange sense of melancholy and, perhaps, dread—Lincoln Grayle himself, sitting in a corner with a tropical fish tank behind him. He was looking right at her, smiling. It was true, she had developed a bit of a crush during their time alone in his quarters at the crystal palace, reflecting the lights of the universe in its dark mountain setting.

Pinky smiled shyly at what her rational mind quickly told her must be a hallucination. As was the artifact Grayle held, uncovered during one of his diving expeditions in the warm seas of Bimini. A small skull of bloodred crystal. Unique in all the world, as old as the earth itself.

This artifact was the last thing Pinky recalled thinking about, before the sky outside the terminal exploded brilliantly once again. A one-hundred-million-volt discharge that dazzled and made her jump and bite her tongue, just as the window wall behind them collapsed in a sparkling avalanche.

After he learned that Betts Waring was planning a trip to Kenya, presumably to join her elusive adopted daughter there, the Assassin had four days to make his own plans.

Betts would be spending a week in England to visit a half sister long unseen. The reunion would take her to the rural Lake Country. The Assassin briefly thought about following her to England, where probably she would no longer be needing the Blackwelder Organization to keep the still-avid tabloid press and fringe lunatics from hounding her. But unfamiliar territory, he realized, would leave him at a critical disadvantage. No, he had to make sure that Betts didn't board the London plane. If he didn't have control over subsequent events, if every move that Eden Waring made in search of her mother was not orchestrated by *him* up to the very moment he broke her lovely neck while watching life fade from her eyes, his chances of success diminished by every unforeseen occurrence.

And Eden Waring did have, of course, certain abilities that had to be accounted for in his planning. An affinity for miracles, perhaps, including the most miraculous act of all: resurrection. He had killed her once, he was certain of that, because he never missed. Yet she lived. Inviting him to try a second time. An invitation that couldn't be refused.

In spite of the success of his subsequent assignment, staging the death of Rona Harvester to look like an accident (thereby elevating the former First Lady, like MM and Princess Di, to elite status in the common people's pantheon of trash mythology: he watched his Rona tapes nearly every day; *loved* a splashy funeral), his slate, obviously, still was not clean enough for Impact Sector. There had been changes in the high command, but the FBI remained paranoid about psychics. It was Impact Sector's responsibility to deal with them. The Assassin had no illusions about his doubtful standing. He would be welcomed back only if he made up for his galling failure.

The Assassin was, in his covert profession, a genius: he had killed thirty-seven men and one woman without leaving a single clue to his identity. Four months ago he had boldly taken both Betts Waring and her husband Riley hostage in anticipation of Eden's arrival at the lake house in northern California. Now, although he stood barely twenty feet from Betts in the first-class lounge, wearing a United Airlines captain's uniform, she had not shown the slightest awareness of him. This was another and possibly most important aspect of his genius: the art of disguise. His face had been reduced to ruin by a splash of lye from his psychotic stepfather when he was twelve. Thereafter, unable to grow hair or eyebrows through scar tissue, with him looking like a poster child for defective genes, his high IQ was easily transmuted into psychopathology.

Only the Assassin's eyes had been spared. In order to go out, even for a visit to the post office or pharmacy, he routinely devoted an hour and a half to building a new face for himself: nose, ears, eyebrows, hair. For most of his adult years he had been a profitable club act in Vegas, doing female impersonations. A serious disagreement he'd had at the FBI's Sacramento field office, resulting in crippling injuries to two agents, had temporarily made it unwise for him to pursue his art in the limelight.

He was sure that Impact Sector would square that account for him, once Eden Waring had unwittingly helped him clean the last trace of tarnish from his slate.

The Assassin always worked alone. Betts Waring's itinerary had been a cinch to obtain from her travel agent's computer files. Offing Eden's adoptive mom would have been mere exercise for a man with his skills. On most assignments he preferred daytime, and crowds. A busy airport, in spite of the appearance of massive security, was ideal. Airport security was only as strong as the weakest link, and there were plenty of those, all working for just above minimum wage, high school diplomas but no real education, birdseed for brains.

But snatching Betts from under the noses of Blackwelder pros, most of whom were former Treasury Department or FBI agents, required rethinking of his usual routines.

He had spent the better part of three days prowling San Francisco's international airport in various faces of altered dimension and contours to avoid a biometric matchup from a three-dimensional scan of his bedrock face, available from FBI files. He had tickets for various destinations, hand luggage filled with mundane traveler's needs. With the aid of a tiny digital camera in one earpiece of a CD player and a scarce, very expensive black market device called "Open Sesame"—concealable beneath a Band-Aid—that instantly deprogrammed and sprang locks ordinarily accessible only to magnetic-striped key cards, he probed SFO's security. One of the call girls who worked an airport hotel where international crews stayed provided him with a stolen pilot's ID, which he transformed into an authentic badge of his own. At three A.M. he was virtually invisible as a stoop-shouldered Hispanic man vacuuming the carpets in United's first-class lounge.

There was no need to leave bodies at the scene of the abduction. He didn't want it to look as if Betts had been kidnapped; he had enough problems with the Bureau already.

Or was he still keeping score in a game he had lost a long time ago?

It was the occasional flash of rationality that caught him unaware, that made him pause while staring at his raw scarred face repeated in the cruelly revealing makeup mirrors. A cave-in around his heart while confidence vanished from his undertaker's eyes. A time when his mind, like the Badlands he came from, was a sparsely settled place. If he didn't look away quickly from the bright mirror-trap at these times his body became catatonic, death collecting in his throat.

Now he was looking, not into a mirror, but a wall of tempered glass, glazed with faces like the dead from his past, among them himself.

The thunderstorm that had shut down operations at the airport was unforeseen, but it would be useful. A gift from the gods.

Betts Waring had been heavier, with frizzy-tizzy hair, a few months ago but had tamed the mop and made herself over, into a hard old beaut of a woman with hair now a natural wolf-gray, short and stiff as the bristles of a military hairbrush. *She'd done it for him,* the Assassin thought, recalling with affection how Betts had cooked breakfast for him at the lake house, played the piano, eager to please and keep him happy, her fear evident in throbbing pulses.

Betts was about to make him happy all over again.

He wasn't quite ready to make his move when the window wall shattered from concussion, but he adjusted smoothly to this diversion. Everyone was on their feet with jangled nerves as rain poured in. During his tour as a janitor in the wee hours two nights ago, the Assassin had prepared the carpet, seeding it with a chemical that reacted with water to produce a colorless but noxious gas. No need now to use the laser in his gold cigarette lighter to activate the sprinkler system in the lounge; the rain blowing in would do.

The Assassin pressed a mask concealed in the palm of one hand against his false nose and waited, eyes on Betts and the Blackwelder ops. The two dozen people in the lounge were scrambling, grabbing hand luggage, purses, laptops, and heading for the door. Confusion, but no panic. Then the gas rising from the soaked carpet hit them like a fast-moving medieval plague.

Coughing, choking, vomiting. Half blinded by their tears and disabled by retching, the two men from the Blackwelder Organization lost contact with Betts Waring, who was in no better shape, down on one knee, unable to breathe.

The Assassin pulled her to her feet with his free hand and walked her to the emergency exit, Betts stumbling, red-faced, gasping, puking.

The alarm went off when he opened the door, as if it mattered. Down two flights of iron stairs then, using both hands to keep Betts from falling.

"I'm with the airline. We're trained for emergencies. Had to get you out of there."

Betts, desperately sucking cleaner air, didn't argue or resist him. He opened a door at field level. Two tugs and a van with a bar of yellow lights on the roof were parked beneath a metal canopy. Rain lashed them as he pulled Betts to the van and seated her inside. She was rubbing at her eyes, still choking. He went around, got in behind the wheel, took a syringe from his shirt pocket. Betts's distress had lessened, but she didn't see it coming. Jumped and tried to pull away from him at the sting of the needle in the neck muscle. Looked at him, momentary fear in her eyes because of the syringe; and he was holding her very tight. Then she lost focus, went slack in his grip. Thirty seconds, and Betts was out.

Solicitously he cleaned vomit from her chin with a baby wipe and sprayed scent in the cab of the van so he wouldn't smell her until he had the opportunity to clean her more thoroughly. He drove at a leisurely pace beneath the belly of a parked 747, seeing the lights of emergency vehicles heading toward him. He used an exit gate near the freight terminal. Four minutes later he lifted Betts from the airport van and put her into a rental car he'd left behind the Dumpsters of a fast-food place on route 82 in Burlingame.

The rain had let up some. The Assassin smiled at Betts, who snored mildly in the seat beside him. He noticed then that she'd lost a shoe somewhere. No matter. He already was anticipating home-cooked meals in their hideaway. Waiting for Eden Waring to come to Betts's rescue, and at last reveal her secrets to him. For months (with the ardor of a stifled romantic who had conceived his unobtainable woman and kept her in a hollow of the heart, consumed her in a lifetime of longing) the Assassin had yearned for the return of Eden.

But the question remained: how did one lay a ghost for good?

LAKE NAIVASHA, KENYA · OCTOBER 13 · 1145 HOURS ZULU

Six of them made the short trip from Shungwaya to the Naivasha Country Club for Sunday brunch: Tom Sherard, Bertie, Eden, and Jean-Baptiste, her date for the afternoon, in Tom's Discovery, with Etan Culver and his model wife Pegeen following in a Land Cruiser.

Sunday brunch at the club was always an event in their neighborhood. From the terrace, past pink clouds of bougainvillea and pastel jacaranda, there was a view of the lake and water-skiers raising graceful plumes in the afternoon sun. Celebrity-spotting on the terrace was a discreet but popular sport. Movie and rock stars, the occasional crowned head. Today they had a junketing U.S. Senator and his entourage, the old boy half drunk and loud and oblivious of the excellent food and calm beauty of their surroundings. There were also a Swedish ballerina and a magician, with whom Eden made unintentional eye contact. He smiled, seemed to wonder momentarily where he knew her from; then his attention was engaged by a member of his party.

"Illusionist," Bertie said. "Name's Lincoln Grayle." She was alert to something in Eden's expression. Bertie leaned over and whispered in Eden's ear while Jean-Baptiste was looking the other way, talking to Pegeen. "Want to meet him?"

"You know him?"

"I know everybody," the globe-trotting Bertie said. She excused herself and walked toward the table for eight where Lincoln Grayle was the centerpiece. Attracting wide attention with her stature, the toned fluency of movement, happily aware of herself, pride in the wealth of a young flawless body.

Eden knew she had seen Grayle before, although she wasn't much interested in magicians and their art. TV, probably. One of the women at his table was wearing a light windbreaker with the stylized NBC peacock logo.

Grayle stood up at Bertie's insouciant approach. Well, *hello*! Air kisses. Never know who you're going to run into. *Habari gani*, darling. Hey, Linc, if you've got a minute—

His turn to excuse himself. He was Bertie's height, six-one, slender, exceptionally fit. Probably had to be something of a contortionist in his profession, Eden thought. Black hair brushed back, glossy and thick enough to retain its shape in a brisk wind without sprays or pomades. A well-basted desert tan. On the surface, that hip male look Eden didn't much care for. But, judging from the mind's-eye snapshots she collected in a few seconds, possibly he didn't have the self-centered vapidity of the he-model caste. Coming closer; Eden was aware of quick, lively eyes. Curious about the world outside himself. An observer. And closer; he bit his nails. One other thing they had in common. The withheld intensity, or complexity, that reveals itself in unexpected ways.

"Lincoln Grayle, Eve Bell."

Gracious smile, a nod, only a moment to appraise each other before the introductions went around the table, Tom last.

"Gregor here at the club told me you know every inch of Kenya and Tanzania," Grayle said.

Tom shrugged. "That covers a lot of territory. It was probably true of my grandfather, who was a professional hunter and guide. He settled in Kenya a little more than a hundred years ago."

"I understand safaris are banned now."

"Hunting game was banned in '77. About two years after I earned my license. But all types of safaris are still available, from bird-watching to eco-tours. I can recommend a couple of guides, if you're interested and have the time."

"Less than a week, I'm sorry to say. Most of my crew and the network people are already in Zimbabwe."

"What's happening there?" Bertie asked.

A fast grin, quirky, as if responding to a joke on himself.

"I'm going to walk across Victoria Falls. At night." He took in their expressions of amused skepticism. "It's an illusion, of course. I can't say more than that."

"Most of the illusions I've seen you do look dangerous to me," Jean-Baptiste said.

"Most of them are, if they're any good." Grayle glanced at his table, where three Samburu waiters had begun to serve from carts with copper hoods. "Here's lunch. Again, it was a pleasure." This time his eyes lingered on Eden for more than just a moment. She had a sense of being ardently probed, and his undisguised intensity, like a bright flash from a masked lantern, startled her.

"Linc," Bertie said, voicing a spur-of-the-moment inspiration, "if you can drag yourself out of bed, say around four A.M., we'll show you some of the sights while you're here. What d'you think, Tom, the Masai Mara?"

"Elephants?" Grayle asked, as if a scene from an old Weissmuller movie had popped into his head. "I've loved elephants since I was a kid."

"Not in the Masai Mara," Sherard replied. "There are about six hundred in Amboseli, where poachers haven't been able to get at them." Bertie gave him an encouraging look. "Best time to visit Amboseli on a day trip is right at dawn, before Kilimanjaro clouds over for the day. The *tembu* population is used to being studied, so we have a fair chance of getting close to a family."

"How far is Amboseli?"

"Ninety minutes by fast helicopter," Bertie said cheerily. "We happen to have two of them."

"I don't mean to impose," Grayle said to Sherard, who smiled.

"Not at all. Haven't been to Amboseli in quite a while, and I have friends at the Research Center."

"Elephants," the illusionist said enthusiastically. "I made one disappear last year from in front of the fountain at Caesar's Palace."

"Good trick," Eden said, chin on the back of overlapped hands, her elbows on the table. Studying him with a little gleam of fascination. She knew now why he'd seemed familiar, where she had seen him, and recently.

"Maybe it wasn't a trick," Grayle said with that quirky grin. "Nobody's seen him since." He nodded to all and turned to go, saying *ni furaha yangu—asante sana.* My pleasure, thank you.

Good Swahili, Eden thought. How long had he been in East Africa, a day or two? Obviously a quick study when it came to languages.

And women, of course.

Where did you meet him? Eden asked Bertie when they had an opportunity late in the day to chat privately. *Vegas?*

Where else? He lives and works there, or just outside of town, in a dinner theatre I think Mies van der Rohe designed. Steel and glass, halfway up a mountain. Looks like it's suspended in the sky at night, remember the mother ship in Close Encounters, *the Spielberg movie?*

No. Eden yawned. Sunset at Shungwaya, the lake deepening to indigo. The hippos a couple of hundred yards to the south and near the shore were a glossy shade of copper as the sun began to set. There was a good breeze and few *dudu* to contend with. Somewhere in the brush a couple of cheetahs of perhaps two dozen that inhabited the fifty square miles of the reserve were talking in their odd bird-chirp language.

Eden and Alberta Nkambe sat back to back and a few feet apart on one of the verandas of the main house. Someone passing by might have thought they were angry with each other, to judge from the tension in their brows, the rigid jawlines. But it was a practice session in subvocalization, Bertie the tutor and Eden the student. One of the psychic talents that had always been second nature to Bertie. Two months before giving birth, Bertie's mother Guan Ke had been struck by lightning while serenely attending to her daily routine of *tai ji quan* a few yards from their house in the highlands of Thika. Both survived. But the lightning (Bertie had surmised, as an explanation of her gifts), or what the lightning had left behind in her almost fully developed brain, was still there twenty years later.

In a certain state, just this side of sleep, I see it sometimes. A mind within my mind. A separate consciousness.

Bertie's powers were telepathic and telekinetic. Eden, since her "coming out" exercise in a frighteningly high-stress situation that involved the disarming of a nuclear bomb in a parking garage next to a packed stadium in Nashville, Tennessee, had made rapid progress in precisely controlling her psychotronic ability—moving objects with the power of her mind. She possessed other talents that surpassed all of Bertie's potential. Eden dreamed prophetically, had done so all her life. And she had the rare "left-handed Art" that set her well apart from other psychics: she could produce her doppelganger, a mirror image, visible to others only when clothed. Eden was, whether or not she liked the idea, an Avatar, lodestone for all psychics.

Did he hit on you? Eden asked after a few moments. She was peeling a small red banana for her pet colobus monkey. Eden had named her young monkey "Uncle Norm" for a relative of Betts Waring, who had the same druidical face, darkening from pure white as the monkey matured. Keeping her hands busy and her mind semidetached made thought transmission less of a chore.

That's just a showbiz formality, Bertie responded, *ritual intrigue of the high-profile crowd, status as an aphrodisiac: you know—*

Aph—? I didn't get all of that. Can we just talk now?

"Sure."

"I'm getting my usual afternoon headache. Blood sugar's low."

Eden pinched off half of the banana and gave it to Uncle Norm, ate the rest, turned around to face the red sun cut in half by the Mau Escarpment.

"I got the idea at lunch that you wanted Grayle and me to meet," Eden said with an idle sidewise look at Bertie.

"You haven't seemed to be making a lot of progress with Jean-Baptiste."

"Progress toward what? The sack? A roll in the hay?" Eden said, wiping perspiration from beneath her eyes with a fingertip. Her eyes had a vexed burn going, the redness of the setting sun. "*Aphrodisiac?* Do you think I need a quick fix in bed from a disappearing act like Lincoln Grayle?"

Bertie shrugged and said with a certain impishness, the appearance of a white dimple in one cheek, "There was maaagic in the air! He couldn't keep his eyes off you, darling."

"A little too good-looking. Not a tooth out of place. He is *so* not my type."

Eden rubbed prickling forearms: goose bumps. She had a brooding look.

"Bertie, fact is, I think Grayle knows who I am."

"You can't hide here forever."

"I'm not—hiding; I love Shungwaya. Just give me a little more time, all right? After Nashville I needed a straitjacket. But you and Tom have been so great to me."

"You're tougher than you think. You don't have to jump into bed with Linc, but he is an interesting guy. Speaks half a dozen languages. Very well read. *Rich* doesn't begin to describe him, but of course you'll be even richer soon. If he does recall having seen your face on TV or in the tabloids, he'll be discreet. Secrets are his business. Give him half a chance, you'll like him."

Uncle Norm climbed onto Eden's shoulder and when she covered her head with her hands so he couldn't run his fingers through her hair, he scolded her loudly. Eden kept her head down until the monkey jumped to an ebony railing of the veranda. Then she looked up, into Bertie's eyes.

"There's more to it than I've told you," Eden confessed.

Only a rim of sun left, clouds like jet trails but smoke-dark in a sky giving up its blue to a twilight radiance of wafer-thin gold. The monkey chittered at a Shungwaya dog, black and wet from a shoreline romp, that came up on the veranda and slumped down with his muzzle in Bertie's lap.

"I've dreamed about him, a couple of times," Eden said.

"Good or bad?"

"He was *Mwanamke* in my dreams." Eden shuddered. Her headache had worsened. "A woman. And I was afraid of her."

AMBOSELI NATIONAL PARK · KENYA-TANZANIA BORDER · OCTOBER 14 · 0530 HOURS ZULU

Amboseli National Park, mostly in Kenya but with one corner overlapping the border of Tanzania, was 220 miles southeast of Lake Naivasha, an hour and a half by air in Tom Sherard's fast, roomy Agusta III helicopter. They left at a quarter to five in silver-tinted darkness, the nearly full moon resembling one of those crudely minted coins of vanished nation-states recovered from Aegean shipwrecks. They overflew Nairobi in a haze of light and followed the A120 south, altered course, and at three thousand feet crossed the perpetually dry bed of Lake Amboseli, meeting the sun as it flashed on the dark horizon, already as bright as midday, drowning leftover stars and striking Kilimanjaro's smooth ancient glacial skin. Another fifty kilometers southeast and almost twenty thousand feet high, Kilimanjaro stood massive and alone, a cloudless throne its dark gods seemingly had abandoned to the cruelty, greed, tribal animosities, and abysmal judgment of those attempting to run things on an earthly level. The political machinery that ground every good thing, like the human heart, to rubble and dust.

So went Eden's thoughts as they flew lower over a brightening landscape. She had never been a morning person.

She looked at Lincoln Grayle in the seat next to hers. He was wide awake and absorbed in the changing tones of the mountain. Hadn't shaved for a day or two. Black sandpaper of beard that humanized him, in Eden's eyes. So did the vivid nicks and larger scars: back of his neck, underside of chin, forearms. He regularly performed an illusion—*no,* he had corrected her at once, it was an escape routine, with a degree of difficulty Houdini perhaps would have envied—which first required him to be bound in barbed wire before being boiled alive. The wire was chrome-plated, for theatrical effect, but the barbs were sharp and real. So he assured her. She hadn't been impressed, wondering only *why?*

Etan Culver, who was a moody fellow when he didn't have a camera in his hands, remote in his reverence for making film when he did, was alternately peering through a side window and doing lens and eyepiece adjustments. Pegeen napped beside him, face relaxed for once, a look of inward stealthy bliss. One of those people who are easily becalmed, on short or long trips.

Tom and Bertie had the controls of the helicopter. Bertie loved flying. Her enthusiasm for any new adventure was endearing but exhausting to others. Bertie never seemed to run low on pluck or zeal; she seldom had a negative or brooding thought about anything . . . even Tom's caution when it came to marrying, or at least bedding her without sanction, which would have been just fine with Bertie.

"Of course I know what I'm in for," Etan Culver was saying to Lincoln Grayle in defense of his chosen art. "Accomplishment without critical recognition is tantamount to serving a life sentence of neglect."

The land turned green and marshy below drifting mist. Daylight spread in a soft flood, wildlife appearing, motionless, like painted figurines in a shop window. The chopper's shadow coasted over flashy groundwater, seepage from the porous black lava into which Kilimanjaro's snowmelt flowed. Entire groves of yellow-bark fever trees looked boneyard-dead in the dawning, destroyed, Tom told them, by elephants for whom acacia bark was a basic food group, or by toxic salts flushed into the root systems when the water table rose in other, wetter years.

Tom set the helicopter down on the dirt landing strip near Ol Tukai and three of the tourist lodges by Olokenya swamp, one of which had five-star pretensions. They were met by a Land Rover and a VW combi from the Elephant Research Center.

Pegeen vomited as soon as she climbed out of the helicopter. She looked wan and contrite. Etan was annoyed.

"Don't know what that's about," he said. "She's been doing it all week. Change of food, I reckon."

Pegeen made a face. Bitter taste in her mouth, or bitterness in the young marriage. Bertie gave her water, glanced at Eden. They knew, from what Pegeen's aura was telling them, that Pegeen was pregnant. They hadn't said anything: it needed to be Pegeen's surprise, once she found out for herself.

They had breakfast at the luxury lodge; Tom was a partner, owning a third share. Then they were on the move again.

The Acoustic Biologist in charge of the Elephant Research Center was a Scot named Pert Kincaid, middle-aged and reedy in a tan T-shirt and khaki shorts. She'd had two operations for carcinoma. She was subject to eye infections and wore dark wraparound glasses. Her body seemed withered by ordeal in the harsh pastoral of Equatorial Africa. She was hardy and unbreakable only in her desire to glean every bit of information from the subsonic language of her elephants.

Elephant families and bond groups make a lot of dust; a low rusty cloud like a stain in a porcelain sink south of the Enkongo Naroke swamp provided their direction this morning. The elephants normally traveled during the day from the acacia groves and grasslands where they fed to the deep swamp interiors where they rested and bathed, undetectable and undisturbed.

Pegeen, the asthmatic, put on a surgical mask. She and Etan rode in the Land Rover with Pert Kincaid and Eden, who drove. Tom, Bertie, Lincoln Grayle, and a young Research Associate followed in the combi. Every day, even when there were guests, was a workday for the Research Center staff. Pert had recording equipment with her and extra headphones that would enable the others to listen for infrasound communication between the elephants in the windless early-morning air.

"Elephants are so big," Pegeen said, looking dubiously at the boxy headphones, "and you don't have any trouble hearing them at the zoo. What is infrasound?"

"Frequencies well below oor range o' hearin'!" Pert told her, voice raised to be heard over the racket the diesel engine and a defective muffler were making. The track they followed was rocky, with dried, sweetly decaying piles of elephant dung Eden took pains to avoid, wrestling with the stiff steering until her wrists ached. "Sound audible tae oor airs travels in short waves and dissipates as it encounters natural objects: particles in the air, heat risin' fr' the groond. Infrasound is composed o' long waves tha' travel great distances through solid rock, or undersea. We ha' known fer many years tha' whales also communicate infrasonically. Audible elephant roomblings, trumpet calls, bellows, and the like are only part o' thir language patterns. Should one o' the elephants recognize oor vehicles and is feelin' chummy today, tha' one may coom close. Then ye will hear a purrin' will lift the hairs on the back o' yir necks. Aye, we'rrre in luke today!"

Still in the hazy distance, thirty or more elephants were visible.

"Fer animals tha' may stand twelve feet at the shoolder and weigh six ton, they oft are remarkably elusive," Pert said, putting a hand on Eden's shoulder. "We'll slow doon naow, hon."

"How close will they allow us to approach?" Etan asked Pert. He was whisking fine dust from a camera lens with a camel's-hair brush.

"They'll not be a bit shy. We ha' been hir many yirs, and I ha' known most o' the Amboseli elephants since they wir juveniles. Naow hir's a nice bit o' shade we will be grateful fer later. Joost pool off hir, hon. The *lugga* is dry, but thir are boreholes the elephants ha' made recently tae gie at water."

Once they were parked beneath a dust-dimmed canopy of umbrella acacia, with the combi twenty-five feet away, Pert passed water around, then fiddled with the dials of her Nagra recorder. The elephants seemed to be moving their way in leisurely fashion, following, as a casually organized group, a familiar trail. All of them were the reddish brown color of the dust they raised. Still a quarter of a mile off, but Eden anticipated the elephants' arrival in the quickening of her heart.

"Thir is protocol tae be obsairved," Pert cautioned, "which we ha' wirked oot wi' the elephants durin' long pairiods o' habituation." She picked up her walkie-talkie and spoke to the others in the combi. "It's pee break rrright now, er hold it 'til ye float. On no account leave the vehicle once the animals are wi'in a hoondred meters o' oos." She put the walkie-talkie down and took a pair of binoculars from a battered metal case. "Thir are elephants both placid and patient, oothers one might describe as paranoid," Pert explained. "A few may simply be off thir feed any gi'en day, er tarmented by ants up the trunk. We avoid males in musth; in tha' unhoppy condition they may attack at the slightest pairceived offense."

"Good cinema," Etan murmured, looking through a telephoto lens at the movement of elephants in their direction, like a small brown range of hills, restless topography.

Pert glanced at him, a look of misgiving. "Any mature elephant kin stomp this vehicle flat as a tin o' kippers. Mind ye dinna ferget tha'."

"What's musth?" Eden asked Pert.

"Rrragin' hormones. The condition affects all mature males fer up tae four months o' the year. But few o' them ha' the opportunity to mate until they are a' least tharty years o' age. The estrous female wants only the best and strongest bulls tae father her calves. Durin' musth the testosterone level makes a bull dangerous er offensive tae others. He lives as an ootcast er wi' other bulls competin' fer the same prize, all o' them stinkin' miserable, contentious, and losin' weight."

Pert raised her binoculars to study the group of elephants.

"Aye, this will be Czarina's clan. A matriarch, quite elderly naow, but fully as big and powerful as inny bull. No males along today except fer adolescents, but, let oos ha' a look—" She scanned a partly denuded acacia grove in which a few trees had been uprooted, focused on a lone independent male yanking up tufts of coarse grass, trailing the group by forty meters. "Karloff," she said softly. "Ha 'n't seen the auld boy o' late."

"Do you name all of the elephants at Amboseli?" Pegeen asked her.

"Most ha' noombers; others ha' been gi'en names, by whim er soomtimes by appearance."

"Why Karloff?" Etan wondered, putting his camera down to wipe sweat from his eyes.

"He is somethin' monstrous, and not merely in size. Years ago he was part o' a bond group o' elephants, eighty strong, a phalanx moving rrrather rapidly through a confined area by Lake Kioko. It happened tha' a male lion found h'self trapped by thir approach, wi' no room tae get oot o' thir way. The lead elephant, oor gentlemanly Boris K., was quite astonished when the frightened lion leapt tae his shoulder and clung thir by the claws of a forepaw whilst rakin' oot the elephant's right eye wi' his oother claws. Whereupon oor enraged patriarch reached across the lion's boody wi' his trunk, plooked him ri' off, then held him by the tail and beat him 'gainst the rrrocky ground 'til the lion was nae but pulp."

" 'Masterful! Towering! Ineluctable!' " Etan said, raising his camera to eye level again.

"He goes off like that," Pegeen explained, "quoting reviewers' blurbs from adverts for the new Hollywood films in the *Times* that particularly annoyed him."

" 'Colossally talented! Wildly ambitious! Courageously moving!' "

"Etan, darling."

" 'Wonderfully playful, with delectable acting!' "

Toward Kilimanjaro there were a couple of striped hot-air balloons, red, yellow, and orange, like fishermen's bobs dappling the surface of a mirage. A popular type of safari in the national parks, Pert said.

"I hope no one minds awfully," Pegeen said, "but I must take a shit."

"Ye ha' aboot thray minutes," Pert advised her. "Please not tae dally. And carry a stick tae stir up the booshes befair ye drop yer knickers; some o' oor local vipers ha' vile dispositions."

"Oh," Pegeen said. She clenched her teeth and stayed in the Rover. Pert grinned at Eden. She had a dead-white spot near one corner of her mouth, the rest of her face hard varnish, like the wood of a coffin in which a perennial handsomeness was interred. Pert indicated that they should put on their headphones.

Eden could hear the elephants already, raucous in their dealings with one another. Calves stumbled about or fed even as their mothers walked. Cattle egrets like white feathers from an exploded pillow floated in the nimbus of red dust raised by the elephants; much higher, there were eagles.

In the air now a power of movement, a gamey effluence, stench of urine. Elephants, obviously, peed a lot.

"The first time," Pert said, "I laid eyes on an elephant group o' this size, I was properly humbled. I knew wi'out a doobt tha' they belonged hir and we did not. Much o' Efrika simply is not suited tae human habitation, except at the tribal, nomadic level. Rhodesia, now Zimbabwe, was an exception. And Sooth Efrika, o' course, until 'instant democracy' happened in 1991. Democracy in the hands o' those wi' no desire tae employ it has been an abomination, an invitation tae despots and thir tyranny, which arrived bang on schedule. Thir once were tens o' thoosands o' prosperous farmers in those two coontries alone, most o' them white. Sooth Efrika raised food enough tae feed an entire continent. Today tha' gooverment's treatment o' the white farmers is destroyin' the coontry's agricultural base. Sooth Efrika has been forced to import basic foodstuffs, unheard of a decade ago. Thir farmers are the highest-at-risk-o'-murder group in the world. Upward o' six thoosand incidents o' black-on-white violence has decimated the farming community. I'm speakin' a gangs o' young thugs armed wi' Russian Kalashnikovs and usin' military amboosh tactics, rrroamin' the coontryside. Sooth Efrikan gun laws limit its civilian farmers tae ownership o' small arms, which are no defense against automatic weapons. A yoong nephew o' mine, married tae a lass o' Boer-Voortrekker descent and managin' a big farm she inherited, was strangled recently wi' barbwire. His wife and twin ten-year-old datters wir gang-raped. The gooverment seldom prosecutes e'en the bluediest ootrage. A policy o' drivin' off the white commercial farmers whilst the incidence o' HIV-positive cases in the population soars past fifty paircent is suicidal at best. 'Strange things are many in this world, and strangest o' all is man.' I often think whilst starin' at the embers o' my fire and listenin' tae the soft nocturnal calls o' the great beasts in the wood close by, how

Sophocles would ha' enjoyed my elephants. I woonder did he e'er sae one."

The elephants—two families temporarily conjoined, Pert explained, because there were twenty-eight of them, not including Karloff, who belonged to no family—were now close enough to distinguish individual features and imperfections: a ragged ear, broken or cracked tusks, Karloff's scars and wizened eye socket. Pert's attention sharpened to her task. Adolescents were bumptious and play-threatening; they flashed young clean tusks like foot-long baby teeth, broke into ambling runs with their tails straight up and ears flapping. Czarina, oldest of the females and the matriarch the others deferred to, had a remnant of one tusk, the other blunt at the tip. She led the others with eyes downcast, trunk swinging close to the ground, sampling odors on a familiar trail. She was a talker, mostly rumblings. Long aware of the two vehicles parked in the acacia grove, when she was within thirty meters of them Czarina stopped and raised her trunk in an S-shape, nostrils moving delicately.

"We will be verra quiet now," Pert advised everyone. "Tha' roomble ye hear is reassurance tae the group. They may tarry a while, er joost pass oos by."

The elephants stayed. There were calves to be fed. Water to be sucked from boreholes in the dry streambed. To the south a herd of zebra appeared in parched short grass. Wildebeest accompanied the zebra, both favored prey of lion, Pert said. "Also high in desirability a' mealtimes is the two-legged species, tha' canna run verra fast nor protect thir tender arses. Which o' carse ye dinna hear aboot sae aften, as it is bad fer tourism."

The sun rose higher; they all were damp with sweat. Pert apparently had no use for deodorant. Etan filmed and Pegeen fidgeted. Her surgical mask had turned grimy. One of the male elephants, adolescent but still a good eight feet at the shoulder, came close to the Rover, flapping his ears, pissing noisily; he sucked up dust and blew it over them. A mature female called him off. She waved her trunk then, casting what might have been an apologetic eye in their direction.

That's when they heard, and felt, Karloff coming, with a roar that could fibrillate an artificial heart.

The Rover trembled on the hard ground. Pert's head jerked around. In spite of the dark glasses she wore, Eden saw her eyes widen in alarm. They all looked back at the monster elephant as he charged the two vehicles in the grove. His show of rage had instantly upset the other elephants, who responded with fright rumbles, bellowing, and screams.

"What's happening?" Pegeen cried.

Etan said, panning his camera, "We should get out of—"

All of the elephants, led by Czarina, began to run, ears flat against their necks, trumpeting madly, raising an immense cloud of dust. The Rover shook from the impact of the stampede around it; the sun went dark. But not a single elephant made contact with them in their headlong panic.

Moments after the last elephant had cleared out, Karloff arrived. He had gone from a charge to a trot. His ears flapped and cracked like sails in a spanking wind. He loomed behind the Rover, less than three feet away but only partly visible through the dust. And passed it, heading for the combi. Trunk curled high, bellowing his outrage.

Eden could only imagine the petrified faces inside the combi; there was too much dust to see anything from twenty feet away. Pegeen whimpered in terror. Pert's walkie-talkie was on, but they heard nothing but static.

The bull elephant lowered his domed juggernaut's head and placed it against the side of the combi, as if he intended to roll it over a few times. Until he'd dislodged all of the combi's passengers like a few seeds from a gourd.

"Uh-oh, what's got him in this state?" Pert said.

Eden heard Bertie, but not over the walkie-talkie.

Karloff had lifted the combi off its right-side tires, tilting it at an angle of twenty degrees. There he hesitated, as if his rage had subsided. Eden heard Bertie again, and now she was receiving mind-pictures, a great jumble, so rapid she couldn't focus on any of them.

Karloff stepped back, head still lowered. The combi fell to the ground, springy on its shocks. Karloff rumbled, lifted his head, shuffled back a few more steps, trunk swinging imperiously. He tapped a six-foot tusk a couple of times on the bonnet of the combi. The flood of images continued in Eden's mind, a life in no particular sequence. She closed her gritty reddened eyes, feeling an end to the elephant's anger, and sighed.

When she looked again through tears washing out the dust, the cloud had settled from treetop height, revealing the sun again. Karloff was walking away, in the direction the herd had fled.

"I believe I've had enough of elephants for today," Etan said in a dust-strangled voice.

"Aye," Pert said. She ran the tip of her tongue around her lips, leaving them muddy. "Wa'n't the auld boy magnificent, though. Woonder wha' upset him?"

"A lion took out his eye," Eden said. "He doesn't like lions."

Pert looked sharply at her. "Elephants fear no creature. And thir wir no lion hereaboot this marnin'."

"Karloff thought there was. A lion. Something like a lion. I'm not sure."

"I need a change of clothes," Pegeen said, woeful again.

STONE MOUNTAIN, GEORGIA · OCTOBER 14 · 10:45 A.M. EDT

The four-man team from Atlanta PD's homicide division assigned to investigate or mop up after the murder of Pledger Lee Skeldon had taken close to fifty statements before it was finally possible for them to meet with Jimmy Nixon's mother. She had been hospitalized shortly after hearing the grim news: shock and an irregular heartbeat. The family lawyer had kept everyone, particularly the media, away from Rita Nixon and her two younger children.

Lewis Gruvver and Matt Ronyak went out to Stone Mountain

when the lawyer consented to his client being "interviewed"—not questioned—so APD could conclude the paperwork. Jimmy Nixon continued to linger, on massive life support, at Grady Hospital downtown, but he never would speak again. Everyone wanted a motive, of course, which Matt thought was bullshit. He was all too familiar with senseless killings. And they had twenty-three open cases that were a lot more interesting to work on.

They checked out a car and took Memorial Drive east through a billboard blight to the Clearview address, a two-story brick-and-frame house on a high terrace. The park and the granite dome jutting three thousand feet above the Piedmont plain was almost in the Nixons' backyard. Mid-October, but summer still had a grip on the weather. The local cops had closed off the Nixons' block on Clearview; phone calls to the house from religious crackpots vowing revenge on the family.

"I went to school near here," Lee Gruvver said. "Redan High."

"Track star, right? The high hurdles?"

" 'Til I blew out a knee my soph year at Morris Brown. Eight months of rehab. The Olympics came to town, all I could do was watch."

"Tough break," Ronyak said. He was twenty years older than Gruvver, hadn't made detective until he was thirty-six. Gruvver breezed in, college man, second cousin to the Atlanta City Council president. Race-based fast-tracking at APD gave Ronyak the redneck, but Gruvver had proved to be conscientious and astute. A good detective. And anyway, Matt's mother had been half Cherokee.

They were met at the residence by the family lawyer, whose name was Zetella. Rita Nixon was on the patio out back with a neighbor, and her other kids were in psychological counseling.

Before meeting Mrs. Nixon, the two detectives looked over Jimmy's room. His computer had been removed the day after the evangelist was murdered and its hard drive scoured to see where the kid's interests lay when he was surfing the net, but apparently he had no interest in porn or diabolism, or straight religion. Mostly paperbacks on his bookshelf, required reading material for school.

He subscribed to *Sports Illustrated*. The swimsuit issue was well thumbed. Posters on his walls were of local pro sports figures. Chipper Jones, Michael Vick. Photos of his mother and father, who lived with a new wife and an infant son in Phoenix. Jimmy and his siblings spent three weeks each summer and alternate Christmases in Arizona. There were snapshots of the kids with R. Palmer Nixon, burly and balding, prosperous in pawnbroking and the used-car biz. Poolside at the house in Paradise Valley, horseback riding in a desert mountain setting. In the photos everyone seemed to be having a good time. Arms around each other, spontaneous smiles, no sulks or resentful faces as if the kids had been made to pose. The APD detective who had gone to Phoenix to talk to the heartbroken Palmer Nixon had heard nothing to indicate that Jimmy might have had a violent temper kept carefully under control.

Albums of snapshots. Proms, parties. Jimmy with girls his age, but seldom the same girl twice. No one special in his young life. Team pictures dating back to Jimmy's first appearance in a Pee-Wee Football uniform.

Gruvver took a closer look at a glossy photo recently Scotch-taped to the mirror over Jimmy's dresser. Jimmy with his dad and a woman who may have been his stepmother; the fourth person in the photo, between the others, seemed familiar to Gruvver. Showbiz type, looking straight at the camera, big smile. And the photo was autographed to Jimmy.

"Know who that is?" Gruvver asked Matt Ronyak.

"Can't place him. An actor?"

"Magician, I think. Not David Copperfield." He puzzled over the signature, all loops and flourishes. "Gray, something. That's who he is. Lincoln Grayle. They must have done Vegas when Jimmy was out there this past summer, taken in some shows."

"Anything else we need to look at in here?"

Gruvver stared at a portrait of Jimmy, age about ten, all ears and teeth and with that sunny smile, face-to-face in winsome profile with his mother. It was a long stare, with sparse expectations.

"Nice kid. No history of substance abuse. Well adjusted as kids come nowadays. Took the divorce okay . . . everyone says. Did his chores, got the grades, played football. He was hoping for a scholarship to a Division I school, but he was undersized for a college lineman these days, no foot speed his coach says. I guess he would have adjusted to that disappointment too. Four nights ago he has a good supper, kisses Mom good-bye, gets into his car, drives to Philips Arena, waits for his chance, then kills a man like a wild animal kills. Or the remote ancestor still hangin' around like a ghost in the atavistic brain. It's almost as if Jimmy—"

Gruvver made a gesture of dissatisfaction and irritability.

"What?" Ronyak prompted with a sour glance. Gruvver was using unfamiliar words again, a not-so-subtle reminder of his superior education.

"I'm not sure." Gruvver shook his head. "Believe in the devil, Matt?"

"Not since I stopped going to church in a mobile home and speaking in tongues."

"I don't go none too regular, but I love Jesus and I still read my Bible. If the devil was real enough for Jesus, he's real enough for me. The devil *and* his legion."

"Why drag religion into this? The kid just snapped."

"No rhyme or reason. Yeah. I'm down with that."

Ronyak nodded. "Good, Lew. Now let's us finish up here, without gettin' melodramatic."

"Somebody could've been in the car with Jimmy Nixon as he drove downtown. Sat with him in the arena, whisperin' a different sermon in his ear."

"Like who?"

"That remote ancestor. Another Jimmy, one he didn't know a thing about."

"Do I deserve this? The Lew Gruvver Twilight Zone Comedy Hour? How about you yank the wild hair out of your ass, and we try to be professional here. Save your bad hunches for your bookie."

* * *

A few minutes after they sat down with Rita Nixon it was obvious they weren't going to get anything useful. She was flanked by her lawyer, Zetella, a neighbor friend whose name was Marge, and her father, whom she called "Powzie." The family name was Cripliver. Powzie Cripliver was one of those elderly men who wear baseball caps with their suits and florid ties. His eyes brimmed with tears and he clung to his daughter's hand.

Rita was still sedated, slow on the uptake, prone to looking around the shady yard with wide vacant eyes. Clearly she hadn't accepted the fact that anything bad had happened because of, or to, her son Jimmy.

Gruvver was able to get in a few questions when she paused in her ramble of reminiscences, questions Matt Ronyak thought were a further waste of time.

"Mrs. Nixon, did Jimmy say much about his trip to Las Vegas this summer?"

". . . I guess so. Las Vegas. I don't remember."

"He saw a show, I believe it was Lincoln Grayle?"

"Oh. The magician. Yes. He enjoyed the show very much. And meeting Mr. Grayle afterward. You see, Jimmy was a Lucky Ticket holder."

"So Jimmy was interested in magic?"

"Well. Not that I recall. He likes sports." Rita Nixon took a long breath. Her right hand trembled. "Jimmy doesn't like to talk about himself."

"He's not a talker, but he is a doer," her father said. "Whatever you ask of him, Jimmy gets the job done. You never hear a whine out of Jimmy, like so many kids these days. Nothing's ever good enough for 'em."

Gruvver kept his eyes on Rita Nixon. "Do you know if Jimmy was ever hypnotized? At a party, or—"

"What are you getting at, Officer?" Zetella interrupted.

"Detective. Mrs. Nixon?"

". . . Hypnotized? I don't know. I don't think so. Would anyone like more lemonade? Marge made it. I love you, Marge. I love you too, Powzie. Everything's going to be all right, I know it. Because otherwise. Simply can't. Bear it." She began breathing rapidly, too rapidly. Bloodless nostrils pinching in.

"Oh, darling," Marge said.

Matt Ronyak cleared his throat. "Thank you for your time, Mrs. Nixon. I'm sure that'll be all." He looked at Gruvver, who was looking at some tall hollyhocks that grew near the patio.

The detectives had lunch at a Hardee's where Memorial Drive passed under 285, the Interstate highway that circled Atlanta.

For the better part of their meal Lew Gruvver was silent, a finger lightly brushing the underside of his chin when he was in deep-think mode. Ronyak did his usual monologue about his missed opportunities in the business world.

"Six-seven years ago we could've taken out a second on the house and used some of that money Easter Belle's mama left her. Bought us that bankrupt AM station in Douglas County, reformatted it Hispanic. We'd have been the first in the Atlanta broadcast area. Hell, I seen it comin'. The construction trades brought 'em north. Now there's at least a quarter-million Hispanics live up here, a Mex restaurant in every shopping center, and half a dozen Spanish-language stations, all making good money. They even do the Braves games in Spanish now."

"Uh-huh."

Ronyak watched Gruvver and muffled a few belches with the back of his hand. The farts would come next. Lately he ate like a dog; chewing hurt his gums.

"Where did you think you were going with that notion about hypnosis? I believe it's common knowledge you can't hypnotize people to do something that's against their will, murder included."

"Uh-huh."

"So?"

Gruvver returned from his reverie with a heavy sigh, drank from his lukewarm glass of raspberry tea.

"Hypnosis seems innocent enough as a party game, but amateurs without meanin' to can surely mess up a mind that's on the edge of overload anyhow. And Jimmy might have had a high level of suggestibility."

"You think Jimmy Nixon was in a fuckin' trance when he killed Skeldon?"

"It could be more complicated than that. I majored in cultural anthropology, did my senior thesis on pathologies of communication—"

"Oh, no shit?" Ronyak said with a smile.

"—Took parallel courses in population genetics, cybernetics, mass psychology, and chaos theory at Georgia State—"

"Anthropology and mass psychology? Your ideal occupation would be running a strip club."

"It all comes in handy sometimes where I do pull my paycheck. Matt, what I know about Jimmy so far bothers hell out of me."

"We don't need to get too involved here," Ronyak cautioned yet again. "They laid Skeldon to rest this morning up there in Lumpkin County. Five thousand mourners and the Goodyear blimp. Chief, the Mayor, the goddamn *Governor,* they just want this one off the books, forget all the *National Enquirer* crap about cults and Dark Forces at work."

"Nothing that sinister."

"You said the devil."

"Devil's in all of us, dude. Nowadays he's called 'The Stress of Modern Living.' "

"Clears that up."

"Jimmy snapped. Like you said."

"Then what was that stuff you were talking, the ar-tistic brain?"

"Atavistic. Primal. The reptilian complex of the triune brain, which doesn't have the neural circuitry that allows us modern folk to cope with new situations. Reptilian mentality is instinctive, limited to flight or fight. 'Snapping' is another way of sayin' that Jimmy underwent a rapid personality change. Puberty can be chaotic. The hormone frenzy. Sexual, parental, and peer-group pressures. Man said once, 'Be kind, for everyone you meet is fighting a great battle.' My daddy had that on a bronze plaque on his desk. He was a bank loan officer, until stomach ulcers did him in."

"Mine was pretty well eat up by adult-onset diabetes."

"Think Jimmy didn't have a shitload of pressure on him, even if he didn't allow it to show? This's the age of information overload. Wars everywhere; atrocities, genocide, famine, disease. Economy's a loser, layoffs, no jobs. Global warming, disappearing rain forests, the poles are shifting, the ozone fuckin' layer's about to disappear, we'll all get skin cancer if terrorists with suitcase nukes don't get us first. Child pornographers, stalkers, rapists, politicians. Not necessarily in that order. Dirty water, air's worse, cows are crazy, can't eat meat. Bitch, moan, sob. Life's tough, school's tougher, football is a grind. Some of these high school coaches are sadistic morons. Summer camps, temperature on the fields around here can hit 130 degrees. Get tough, suck it up, God damn you, Nixon, *dig*; you wanta play football for me this year? Yes, sir, yes, *sir*.

"Now Jimmy, don't you know he could've been burdened with guilt notions about the divorce? *My fault, shoulda done somethin', kept Mom and Dad together.* So he's sittin' there in that arena for an hour listening to a famous and respected preacher pound it into his head that he's nothing but a guilty little shit, a sinner bound for hell because of his sins. Maybe that wasn't exactly Pledger Lee's style, but it's pretty much the same message with all of them. Come forth and open your heart to Jesus. Christ died for your sins. Come and be saved; you're nothin' without Him, a crispy critter. But Skeldon might've had the exact reverse effect on Jimmy—denial first, then extreme anger with at last something to focus it all on: this man down there who is tormenting him. Then *snap*, baby."

After a few moments Ronyak nodded.

"Okay. You're happy now, right? It all makes sense to you."

"Fact is, makes no sense a'tall."

Ronyak grimaced. "I need to use the bathroom. Fuckin' ice tea goes right through me."

" 'Cause there have been two other cases recently of violent, animallike attacks on prominent religious figures. November seventh of last year in Chandrapur, India. A so-called Spiritual Master named Sai Rampa had his own throat ripped out by a twenty-four-year-old woman from Karlsruhe, Germany, who had previously worked as an au pair in the states, guess where? Vegas.

"In February the Dalai Lama, visiting some of the movie-star gong-beaters in Los Angeles, received a flesh wound on the chin when a nineteen-year-old Vietnamese kid made a try for him outside the Beverly Hilton. Misjudged his distance or maybe he stumbled on the red carpet trying to get to the Dalai Lama, then one of the LAPD Special Squad guys shot him through the head. The Veet kid was employed as a busboy in a hotel restaurant in—ready for this?—Las Vegas. Quit his job and took a bus to L.A. the same day the Dalai Lama arrived for his fund-raiser."

Gruvver sat back in the booth and considered Ronyak's lack of expression.

"I did a global on the M.O. before I came to work, couldn't sleep last night 'cause of the hair up my ass. Okay, the applause sign is flashing and I'm ready to take my bow."

Ronyak stood slowly, as if his lower back was paining him. He glared at Lewis Gruvver.

"You are not going to say another damn word about this to anybody. Not now, not ever."

"You're not curious? Three major religious leaders, icons, you could say, two of them dead with their throats bitten through after vicious attacks by, I'm reasonably sure, complete strangers to the victims?"

Ronyak leaned over and tapped a forefinger on the table, his face congested, cheeks reddening.

"Be a smart cop, Lew. But never a smart-ass. It's not our business. *We don't need this.*"

"Matt. Have I done gone and scared the crap out of you?"

"Man, you just let it go!"

"I can let it go," Gruvver said. "But whatever it is, it ain't gonna go away."

On the first full day of her captivity, unusually warm and clear for coastal California north of Frisco, the Assassin took Betts Waring out behind the cottage of the two-hundred-acre farm he was leasing and showed her how the cervical collar that she wore around her neck would work should she decide to attempt an escape when he wasn't around.

He placed an identical collar on the neck of a dummy. He had painted sunflower eyes and a full smiling mouth on the stuffed head, giving it that little touch of personality. From a distance of twenty-five feet, using a wireless handheld detonator, he blew stuffing into the low branches of some oak trees and scattered the birds for a few minutes.

Betts, hands at her sides, flinched at the muffled explosion but watched the demonstration with narrowed eyes. Staying calm. Elevated blood pressure would strangle her in that tight collar.

"A car driving by with the radio tuned to the wrong AM station could set this one off by accident," she said, carefully fingering the padded collar that held her chin rigidly high. Her mouth was almost too dry to allow for speech, but her voice didn't waver. "Or haven't you thought about that?"

"Of course. My little road is gated and there are pitfalls if one doesn't know the way. The nearest state blacktop is three kilometers from the house, which does limit the possibility of accidental detonation." He paused, frowning. He hadn't put on any makeup this morning, not even a hairpiece. It was a grim business to look at his face for even a few seconds. Look him in the eyes, *never*. "But that was cunning of you, Betts. You've learned something you didn't know before. I wonder what other pertinent observations you've made so far?"

She had planned to say as little as possible to him, but now, having seen him blast the head off Sunflower Man, keeping silent might indicate she had been intimidated.

"Those are gulls over there, coasting above the hills. We had fog earlier. I can still smell the sea, so it's probably within a couple of miles. A lot of dried cow flop in the pasture we walked through, but I haven't heard any cows and the farm looks fallow, untenanted. The apple trees are overgrown and need a good pruning." Betts leaned back in order to look up at the sky. "We may be under a north–south flight path for commercial aviation. The plane that flew over us a couple of minutes ago was beneath FL20 and still climbing. So at a climb rate of about two thousand feet a minute for a heavy, it was only eight or ten minutes, say, from SFO." She caught his look. "A nephew of mine flies for American. The road you mentioned is probably the coast highway that jogs inland for a dozen miles before meeting the coast again at, I think, Bodega Bay. So the nearest town of any size is either Bodega or . . . Coldstream Bridge. I could use a drink of water."

"Certainly." The Assassin handed her the water bottle hooked to his belt. Betts squeezed some onto her dry tongue.

"What did you knock me out with?" she asked him.

"Nothing an oral surgeon wouldn't give you before a couple of difficult extractions. And later, a mild hypnotic to keep you blissfully asleep for twelve hours. By the way, what is that patch you wear under your right arm for?"

"High blood pressure." She hesitated, then added, "I've also had a couple of TIAs—transitory ischemic attacks."

"I see. That reminds me, with all that was going on up there at the lake, I never had the opportunity to express my condolences on the tragic loss of your husband. Was it his heart, Betts?"

"Yes." Betts had another squirt of water, rinsed her mouth, leaned toward the ground, and spat. She'd been without cigarettes for much too long, and was mad for a smoke. But he wasn't a smoker. Disapproved of the habit. He did, however, like to eat. And Betts was hungry.

"What's for breakfast?" she asked.

"I've stocked up on all of the ingredients you'll need to turn out a batch of those wonderful bacon-crumble waffles. Also that commercial brand of coffee you seemed to prefer at the one breakfast we enjoyed together. But I am so hoping to convert you to a Jamaican blend I buy at this little Rastafarian grocer's in North Beach."

"Is that where you're living these days? San Francisco?"

He showed her as merry a grin as anyone with a partly melted face could manage.

"Now, Betts. Never ask. *Deduce.*"

"I've deduced that you don't want to kill me"—her heartbeat sprinted again—"yet. And God knows I'm not material for a sex slave."

"That *is* droll, lovey. Not that I don't think you're a very attractive woman, and the new 'do you've adopted is so gray-panther retro."

"Attractive for my age?" Betts said with a poisoned grin. "So if it isn't sex, and it's not just my cooking, what *are* you after?"

The Assassin gathered the decapitated dummy under one arm. She could have done it then, kicked him in the balls from behind as he bent over. But she was still fighting the effects of Versed or a similar tranquilizer, a disconnect of a second or so between impulse and action. And he hadn't told her everything about the heavy explosives-laden collar that was chafing her neck. Only hinted at the possibilities. She couldn't remove it herself, of course, without the damn thing going off. He'd warned her about that immediately.

"*You* know," he said. "I must have her, Betts."

The beating of her heart seemed to stop as it chilled to ten below zero.

"Go ahead and kill me, then. Because it's not gonna happen."

"Oh, I hate that kind of talk! We are going to be together for a while, so I think we should make every effort to be civil to each other. The time passes so much more quickly."

The cottage to which he had brought her in the night was stone with a shake shingle roof, one-car garage. Sunny and open, one large bedroom and a sleeping loft. *House Beautiful* kitchen, cabinet doors inlaid with stained glass, copper pans hanging from a rack over the island range. A "Great Room" beside the kitchen, stone fireplace wall for those chilly fall and winter nights. Wide peg-and-groove cypress wood floors throughout. His taste in art was minimalist abstract.

Betts had the run of the house as well as a small flagstone veranda with wisteria vines and hanging birdhouses, two rocking chairs.

Stick to the premises and she wouldn't explode. Make a run for it, any direction, sensors would respond to her attempted flight, and *bang!*—No more Betts from the collarbones up.

She wasn't sure she believed him. They were all expert at head games, even those with little formal education. Remorseless in their own logic. More often than not bright as quicksilver, quite personable, until they abruptly chilled: *when in silence came the seep of madness to their gaze.* If they were of a certain bent, like her captor, it was the last thing you ever saw.

Satellite TV, magazines that included a couple of trade journals Betts subscribed to, some good novels (he was an ardent fan of Tolstoy); the Assassin had made an effort to distract her from the discomfort and anguish her situation provoked.

What she desperately wanted to know but hadn't been able to pull out of the conversation over breakfast was how he planned to persuade her to give Eden up to him.

There was a dirty blue pickup truck in the garage. Oregon plates. Part of the garage was partitioned in raw plywood, a cozy well-lighted dressing room where, with the aid of multiple mirrors, he did his makeovers into the characters whom he then inserted into the mirage-filled landscape that constituted his exterior life. While he worked he listened to, on shellac recordings, one of the mellow thrushes or gilded-tongue tenors of the big-band thirties. His wardrobe took up most of the loft in the garage.

Betts did the dishes, then watched TV while the Assassin applied himself to the day's disguise. When she heard him speak, from behind her, she thought someone else had entered the cottage. It gave her quite a jolt. She turned and beheld the cowhand—faded denims, calf-roper boots with dirt in the creases, straw hat, talkin' the talk. His left arm was in a cast and a sling.

"Rance Jool, ma'am, from up a Malheur Lake? Jool's been in the cattle business there since silent pitchers was in style. Aw, arm's not painin' all that much, but thanks for askin'. Got it walked on by a ton a bad medicine in the short go last weekend. Heard the sucker crack like a .30-.30 on a winter mornin'."

"Good God," Betts said, staring at him. Brown contacts and a feckless gaze, blond eyelashes, sun-wrinkles, a friendly jut-toothed smile, little sandy ridge of mustache on his upper lip. The latex work so slick you couldn't spot a seam in broad daylight. And that warm baritone drawl. You trusted him for the lonesome in his voice. This hurt westerner. Men would be buying him a round on short acquaintance. Women, well, they'd go for the whole nickel.

"So what are you up to now?"

The Assassin took off the sweat-stained straw hat and spoke in his usual voice.

"I could be gone until quite late," he said. "If you choose to spare me what is bound to be a tedious excursion, we'll just get on with it now, E-mail sweet Eden the instructions I've provided. But then I don't have the necessary code word to reassure her that all is well with you, do I?"

Betts folded her arms, afraid that she might start shaking.

"So I guess the next step is . . . you get out the cattle prod and pliers."

"Physical torture? I am accomplished, darling, and it has been necessary on occasion. But I don't want our relationship to deteriorate so drastically. I admire the spunk you've shown so far."

"Brainwashing? Or one of the hypnotics you're probably familiar with."

"No, no, I'm not an expert in those areas. I understand that drugs do not always have the desired effect. Experimentation would be time-consuming, and I don't want to damage your mind or mar your perceptions. I need your wholehearted cooperation in this matter."

"We may be together a few years, then. I hope you play chess. What's your name, by the way?"

He smiled thinly. "Sorry. I don't care to be reminded who *he* was."

The Assassin went from dour to homespun twinkly in a heartbeat. Rance Jool was back. "Chess? I play a mean game, mama. Fact is I do expect young Eden to be on a plane wingin' to your side in forty-eight hours. She's not *that* fir away, is she?"

"Don't ask," Betts said. "Deduce."

Betts had the cottage to herself. First thing she thought of was a telephone. There were two jacks, kitchen and bedroom, but no phones.

She tried to remember yesterday. Waiting in the airport lounge with the Tubners, Rome-bound, and her personal escort from the Blackwelder Organization. Had they reported Betts missing? Not to Eden. Only Vaughn Blackwelder himself could make contact with Eden, through Tom Sherard, and Blackwelder was in Pakistan, either just starting up to, or coming down from, the summit of K2.

Hours passed. Several times she went as far as the edge of the patio. The birdhouses were empty this time of the year, leaking a little straw from abandoned nests. Temptation became an ache. Step off. *Do it.* He had to be running a bluff. The microwave oven in the kitchen could set off explosives in her collar. So walk. Keep walking. Down the private road to the state blacktop, flag a ride. *Sensors.* All around the house. So James Bond of him. Break an invisible beam, go blooey.

What were the odds that he was lying? Mind games.

He doesn't want you to die, Betts. You're his link to Eden. That whole business he'd tried to articulate at breakfast, Betts drinking the strong Jamaican coffee until she was wired. He sounded loonier at each bend he careened around. Impact Sector. Psychics a danger to national security. Killed Eden once, she came back to life. How did she do that, Betts?

Her neck itched beneath the collar. And no cigarettes, no cigarettes.

Sooner or later he'll kill you anyway. What are you waiting for, Betts? He'll be back soon.

Indecision made her feel weak. Light-headed. She sat down in one of the rocking chairs, nodded off in spite of the collar holding her head erect.

Hours passed. The light changed. She saw two coyotes in the fallow pasture. Hawks in the sky.

Dark at six-thirty. He wasn't back but she cooked for him again, babyback ribs from the freezer, corn on the cob. She should be poisoning his food, but there wasn't anything around the house to discreetly do the job. Comet cleanser and dishwasher detergent in the kitchen, only aspirin in the bathroom medicine cabinet.

At ten-thirty she turned off the stove and let the food go cold.

He didn't come back that night.

Betts was angry the next day, after a restless night of dreams snaking through the fog at the cottage windows, entering her mind like phantoms. Angry at herself because she'd failed his test of her nerve. Angry at the Assassin because he'd peeled her naked, peeled away her sense of rightness about herself. Controlling her with that detonator the size of half a deck of playing cards that he had left on the range counter in the kitchen, so casually, tiny red light aglow. Daring her to touch it in his absence, open it like a letter from a dreaded source, and remove the button-size battery. Before long she found it necessary to hide the detonator beneath the tented pages of a magazine. Dying might have been preferable to this humiliation. But knowing how easily she could die only made her think of Eden, how desperately she wanted to see her baby again.

Daylight all but gone when at last Betts heard his truck. She trembled, almost as if it were a relief to have him back.

The Assassin pulled the truck into the garage, clomped into the kitchen, threw her a look but wasn't surprised to see her there, dropped his creased rancher's straw on the counter, and sat hunched on a stool. The cast had come off his arm. Hands dangled between his legs. Still in character.

"Howdy."

"Oh, drop it."

"So fir you done jes' fine, Betts. Bet you was tempted to try a getaway, though. Couldn't make up your mind if ol' Rance was funnin' you."

She didn't give him the satisfaction.

"Coffee's not on?" he said, looking around. "You cook anything?"

"You can chow down on microwaved from now on," Betts said. "I'm through."

He sucked at his false teeth with a jaundiced grin.

"Then how's about we send that E-mail now? Know you must a been thinken' on it."

"I won't."

He nodded. Lips compressed. He studied her, remoteness in his eyes. She was afraid of that look, and leaned against a wall, aware of faintness. Still unable to bend his gaze away from her soul.

The Assassin got up and beckoned.

"Somethin to show you in the garage."

He didn't wait for her. When at last she followed with a heaviness in her lungs that felt like drowning he had unlocked and raised the hard top from the pickup bed. He motioned again. Betts came closer and saw the child lying fully clothed on her side on a sheepskin that looked new. Eyes closed, face pale, dried spittle on her chin. She was shoeless and looked to be about ten years old. There was a small diamond stud in one earlobe. She was thoroughly knocked out but breathing, which was more than Betts could manage for a few moments.

"Ohhh. God!"

"Name's Saffron Pike. No need to know where I got her. She can go back there; say the word." His voice fell out of character. "Or never show up again on this earth. That is the choice you get to make, Betts."

"*What did you do to her?*"

"On my honor, she's unharmed. Do you think I'm some sort of twisted pervert? No trauma was involved. Saffie merely went to sleep. She will remain asleep for at least another three hours. But, Betts. Make no mistake. The clock is ticking."

There was a hammer hanging on a pegboard nearby. Betts reached it and went after him, flailing. He took one hard blow on his shoulder before twisting the hammer from her fist. Betts was slung half the width of the garage, banged her head.

When she looked up he was putting the top back on the bed of the pickup truck.

"There are many young girls," he said, hearing Betts groan. "How many do you want on your conscience?"

NAIROBI, KENYA · OCTOBER 14 · 1230 HOURS ZULU

You're Eden Waring, aren't you?"

Eden had known it was coming, having deliberately invited him into her space. A space that had come to seem an enormous empty room in a museum where she was frozen like an exhibit. She was tired of feeling shy about him. At her suggestion, following their return from the near-disastrous excursion to Amboseli, she and Lincoln Grayle had driven down from Shungwaya for lunch at the Thorn Tree Café, symbolic of "Old Nairobi"—although the city, a metropolis amid parkland, was as aggressively modern as Pittsburgh or Frankfurt.

The Thorn Tree was a sidewalk café at the Stanley, a much-renovated Edwardian-style hotel in the city's center, where the long bar had been a hangout for famous white hunters and safari guides before the strict ban on hunting in Kenya instantly dissipated their aura of myth and dangerous glamour. Now they were surrounded at lunch by young grad students pursuing obscure careers in paleontology or ethnobotany, by well-off adventurers, Arab wheeler-dealers, prosperous Kikuyu farmers and tea growers enjoying a day in town, and officials of UNEP, the United Nations Environmental Program that was based in Nairobi.

Across the small table from him she leaned back slightly and let the sunlight into her eyes, which after a moment closed. She lifted her face slightly with eyes still closed and smiled a bit regretfully.

"I have a good memory for faces. Yours was everywhere after that plane crash in California. You seemed just to disappear, afterward. I was curious. Obsessed, for a while."

She lowered her head, opened her eyes.

"But not now?"

"I'm good at illusions, probably the best. Psychologies of concealment, a trickster's lures. I thought, *There can't be any secrets she may not know.* And I thought, *How terrible for her.*"

Eden looked around at other tables. Hearing conversations, laughter. Voices, music in the streets. Taxis, buses, crowded ramshackle *matatus,* a busy, noisy place in heavy gasoline heat, the sun deceptively merciless. Her eyes came back to him.

"There are no secrets to tell. It's not like shuffling a deck of cards and always knowing where the ace of diamonds is. I have no tricks. And no illusions, at least not anymore." She drank some of her Tusker beer that was rapidly warming. Froth on her upper lip; she nonchalantly licked it off and he smiled at that.

Eden said, "An anthropologist friend of Tom's has been studying one of the East African tribes, the Amba, I think, for many years. Wizards are very real to the Amba, although they've never seen one. Have no idea what they look or sound like. A wizard could be someone's brother, or wife. Imagine that degree of paranoia. The Amba are certain only that wizards exist, that they rule every aspect of a man's life; they are the cause of all that's miserable about the human condition."

"How do they appease these wizards?"

"They don't. They can't. Wizards exist only to cast evil spells, to deny, torture, destroy. So the Amba live in fear and torment, one village making war on another suspected of harboring a vicious, though invisible, wizard. The social structure of an entire tribe is in chaos because of their unshakable belief. But in chaos—the anthropologist learned—there's also an eerie kind of togetherness. No Amba escapes the doom of his beliefs."

Her gaze shifted, because his smile seemed forbearing.

"These beliefs aren't peculiar to the Amba, by the way. Other tribes, the pathological religions, all have their versions. That man in the nice-looking suit and blue-striped shirt over there, the one with the cell phone, he could be a professor at Nairobi University. Educated at Harvard or the Sorbonne. But in the dark of his heart, at crunch time for the spirit—he's still bewitched.

"I'm not god, devil, shaman, or wizard. But there are many people willing to believe I'm one. Because it's a superstitious world, that wouldn't be good for my health."

"I was thinking of calling a press conference. But I've been on the cover of *People* magazine. Come to think of it, so have you."

"Is a relationship sneaking up on us?"

"That was yesterday. And here we are. Phase two. I knew who you were right away, of course. So I thought, *Get it out of the way first.* You didn't walk out. Trust may come, or not, still you're talking to me."

"Do you find that interesting?" she said. A faint smile.

"Everything about you interests me. The way your left eye turns in a little. Melancholy. The more you talk, though, the less depressed you seem."

"I'm not up to a relationship. I had one. He was spying on me, for the FBI. I don't know what happened to him. In the end I may have mattered more to him than they did, so I'm pretty sure he's dead."

He let that go by with a sympathetic look, and waited. Their salads arrived, chilled glass plates on pewter. She looked at hers without hunger, looked at his face.

"Sorry," she said.

"Are you wanted by the FBI?"

"Probably. I'm not about to call up and ask them. FBI, CIA, MORG, if they still exist—I, I mean *we,* did them some damage—all government agencies who are in the 'secrets' business"— her mouth twisted wryly—"consider psychics a threat to their existence. It's a tribal thing, as I tried to explain." He nodded. "Although the CIA and the Russians and the Chinese, I was told, have tried for years to cultivate a few of us like a cash crop. But extrasensory perception is and always will be one of the mysteries of time and space." Absorbed now, seeming eager to talk, she began also, mechanically, to eat. "The key word is *perception.* I'm a prophetic dreamer, nothing unique about that. Happens to all sorts of people, millions of times a night, I'm sure. I receive images cast as dreams that, like all dreams, need interpretation. In my walking-around life I don't creep into people's minds." A quick shake of her head, sunlight on the bridge of her nose, lighting ardent depths in her eyes. "Who would want to? I do have flashes of intuition. I'm able to exchange thoughts with other adepts; I'm learning to do that. And sometimes—when I'm under great stress—I can call on an energy I don't have a name for. Then improbable or miraculous things happen. But it's a faculty I can't control."

"Flashes of intuition? Anything about me, so far?"

"You don't have any fear," she declared.

"What makes you think that?"

"This morning at Amboseli, when it looked as if that elephant was going to crush the combi, you—weren't afraid."

"How do you know?"

"You were thinking how you could use it, stage an elephant attack as part of one of your TV specials."

He sat back in his cane chair.

"That might have crossed my mind," he said with a grin. "Seriously. Why didn't he go ahead and finish us off, he seemed that angry. Karloff, was that the elephant's name?"

"Bertie stopped him. Calmed him down."

"Oh, Bertie. So she is—"

"She's good with animals," Eden said quickly. "That's all. Count yourself lucky she was there with you."

There was a kink of muscle in Eden's jaw, as if she were forcing away pain or some other distress. She trembled.

"Are you malarial?" he asked, concerned.

"No, nothing like that. I'm good about taking my prophylactics. In Africa you had better be. Would you excuse me, I need to—"

He was on his feet as she left the table. Walking quickly away, onset of menses, perhaps. A cramp. He took a deep appreciative breath, eyes and heart filled with her shape and style, the fine edge of a lingering emotion cutting him deeper than he was prepared for. As he was sitting down, moving his cane chair at more of an angle to the street, another young woman slipped into his field of vision. She startled him. But already, briefly glimpsed, she was disappearing, obscured by throngs on both sides of the wide avenue, the slow passage of a bus. A white female, the image of Eden Waring, even to the cut of her cedar-red hair and the beaded Masai headband high on her tanned forehead. The green of her sleeveless dress seemed exactly the shade Eden was wearing.

Then she reappeared farther down the sidewalk, hesitated, turning her face toward the hotel as if in response to his astonishment. Where she stood a draft of cold air from the doorway of a shop thinned the vaporous haze from a bus's exhaust; he saw her clearly. Those eyebrows like the red of wasps with their little tapered stingers at each end, rising abruptly above the natural arch of each brow. And that cinched it, although he had seen Eden disappear into the hotel only a few seconds ago. He glanced that way to be sure.

Doubles were a part of his business as a magician. He was amazed that Eden had gone to this trouble to stage her sly, jesting illusion for him. Anyway, he liked it. A very different, intriguing young woman.

When he looked across the street again, the double was gone. Show over. He applauded silently, smiling to himself. More than a little curious about the double's identity.

Who were your parents?" Lincoln Grayle asked Eden, on the way to Jomo Kenyatta Airport. Grayle and other members of his entourage were flying in a chartered Learjet to Victoria Falls, where they would complete the last segment for his upcoming television special.

"I never knew them."

"I thought you might bear a strong resemblance to your mother."

She gave him a look, unreadable behind the dark lenses of her smart Italian sunglasses.

"From photos I've seen of her, I suppose I do."

"And your sister?"

Another look. "One of us was all God made."

"Then you have a double in Nairobi. I had a glimpse of her today, walking past the hotel."

He was waiting for her to laugh, reveal her joke on him. Instead he saw Eden's hands, in fingerless ostrich-leather driving gloves, tighten on the steering wheel. No hint of amusement in her face.

"Oh, her. Yes, I've noticed her too. Actually I'm a lot better-looking." Finally her lip curled, a reluctant half smile. "She has a bad complexion. Her eyes are too close together."

On the ramp for departing passengers she pulled into a space behind a minibus discharging a British Airways crew. It was a busy time of day, jumbo jets arriving from and leaving for cities on three continents, a rage of thunder in the sky. The ramp trembled beneath a load of traffic.

They looked at each other, not sure how to end it. Then Eden slipped off her glasses and leaned toward him with a smile. They kissed.

"I don't think we'll be seeing each other again," Eden said.

"I think we must," he said.

She turned her face aside, politely, at the offer of a second kiss.

"*Kwaheri,*" Eden said. "Good-bye" sounded less final in Swahili. And just a touch romantic.

E-MAIL LETTER FROM PINKY TUBNER TO HER SON AND DAUGHTER-IN-LAW • OCTOBER 14

Hi, Gary and Gloria! Back in Rome after two days on the Amalfi Coast. October is busy but not the high season there, August being the big month when the hotels are jam-packed with people who come back year after year. So we were able to reserve this *gorgeous* room at Le Sireneuse in Positano, which is like a dream at night, the lights twinkling up and down this steep cliff by the sea. Our room was all in white with brown accents, Gloria (I took lots of pictures, never fear), and the bath even had a whirlpool tub! Which I could certainly use after the drive down from Rome. Let me tell you how happy I was that Frank decided not to rent a car but hired a car and driver instead, a driver used to the road down there. I have never been so scared! Roller coasters are tame compared to the Amalfi Coast road. It is one steep blind curve after another. The road is barely wide enough for two cars abreast! And then there are the buses and trucks coming at you with horns blatting, I had rope burns from my rosary. You know Frank—wise-cracking all the way. Grabbing me by the shoulder and going, *Oooops! That was close!* But I could tell his heart was in his mouth at least part of the time.

Making matters worse, you know that volcano they have down there, Vesuvius? It was *smoking*. First time in years, the driver said. Just what we needed, after that send-off at San Francisco Airport, glass pieces in my hair and throwing up big time from the rotten-meat stench in the lounge. I've told you guys enough about that already. But it was a bad omen for the start of our trip and of course I was petrified during most of the flight to Rome, until a couple of martinis knocked me out. So getting back to our excursion to Amalfi, there's a volcano acting as if it's going to explode at any time! *Two* bad omens. I was convinced I was going to die in a crack-up before we ever got to see His Holiness.

But we made it, Pinky here on very wobbly legs, and the next morning at breakfast by the heated pool at the hotel you would never guess in a thousand years who was at the table next to ours. NEIL DIAMOND!!! I was like seventeen all over again, totally tongue-tied, but you know Frank, five minutes and they had a conversation going. Neil could not have been sweeter about it. Then, in Ravello the next day, I swear it was Tom Cruise we saw on a red Vespa with this ravishing dark-haired girl, right there on the square. The Passionist Father we were having coffee with, who is my aunt Claudia's second cousin if I have that straight, said a lot of young Italian men resemble T.C. Anyway I took a couple of pictures on the sly and you can judge for yourself when I get back if I was right.

Even though I hated the idea of going *one inch* closer to that volcano, Frank the *National Geo* freak insisted and so we toured Herculaneum, one of two Roman towns buried in an eruption twenty centuries ago. Herculaneum was a spa for rich Romans. I had no idea how well those people lived! They even went to the bathroom *indoors*.

Well, if the vacationing Romans of yore ate half as well as we did for two days, they all must have been happy campers. I can't begin to describe the taste treats! Oyster-stuffed red potatoes. Steamed lobster in a gelatin of tomato and basil, *cannaroni* with little shrimp in a fennel-and-almond sauce—let me get to the desserts, and trust me my mouth is watering as I type this. Too bad the wild strawberry gelato won't travel, I'd bring home a gallon. And just try to imagine the *torta la Zagara,* the house speciality at this wonderful garden restaurant in Positano: chocolate cake, stuffed with candied tangerine!!!! Yes I'm afraid I pigged out.

But we're back in Rome now, at our cozy hotel at the top of the Spanish Steps. And I'm stuffy and wheezing. The bad news is the Holy Father has had to postpone our meeting for three days, an abscess in his ear, according to Msgr. Ramone at the Office of the Prefecture of the Apostolic Household. I don't want to sound like we're too disappointed by the postponement. After all, we're in Rome. The Eternal City!!! We have a walking tour of Bernini's fountains scheduled for this afternoon with that lovely couple from the archdiocese of St. Louis I think I mentioned before. I only hope my feet hold out.

Frank says hey, and God bless and keep you all, with special blessings for baby Jordana!!

Bad complexion? My *eyes* are too close together? What did you tell him *that* for?"

Eden closed her eyes wearily, trying to relax in a tepid bath in her bungalow adjacent to the main house.

"Because I knew it would annoy you," she said to her doppel-ganger. "Because it wasn't smart to show yourself to Lincoln Grayle this afternoon; what were you trying to prove?"

"I'm not annoyed. My feelings are hurt. If I have to remind you again that I have feelings. I'm your mirror image. We are exactly alike."

"No, we're not. At least I have a sense of humor. For the last four months whenever we . . . get together, all you do is moan and complain."

"I'm bored. I haven't been *out* for more than a week."

"That's another thing. When you are . . . out, you don't have to dress like I do. I told you, dare to be a little different."

"I can be different! Just name me, and release me. I promise, faithfully swear, I will never desert you."

"Nothing doing."

"Then I don't have a choice. I have your taste in clothes, your taste in jewelry, *your* interest in Lincoln Grayle."

"Excuse me?"

"I wasn't trying to 'prove' anything. I did what you asked me to do at the university library." Her research in the library had whetted an old appetite. She wanted to read more. Read for herself, season her mind with the life experiences of others, learning apart from what Eden already knew. But there never was enough time. She came and went too quickly, subservient in a monocracy. "After that, because you weren't in a rush to recall me, I went for a walk." Gwen sighed, reliving the blood-perk of blissful freedom. "After all, it was my first time in Nairobi. And I just *happened* to walk by the Stanley. And there he was. I can see why you're nuts about him."

"Whatttt? I don't intend ever to see him again, which I made perfectly—"

"Oh, bull. I know what you know; I feel what you—by the way, if you're having your period, you probably shouldn't be taking a bath."

"Why, are you bleeding?"

"No, of course not."

"Not exactly alike then, are we?" Eden said, with the merest hint of malice. She was tired, and her glands were subtly out of phase.

"Okay, one important difference. I can't reproduce the species, so what's the point of going through *that* every month. Anyway, you can hide me, but you can't hide anything *from* me. You know you put a little extra something into that good-bye kiss at the airport."

"Temporary girlish weakness."

"Can't you just admit you've been lonely, and you were thinking about how nice it would be to curl up in bed with—"

Eden pitched a soapy bath sponge at her doppelganger, who had already stepped out of the way. She said with an impudent grin, "Why bother? I knew it was coming."

Eden sighed and sank deeper into the old zinc tub.

"Okay, I like him, but it's impossible. Let's get off the subject of Lincoln Grayle. Can I have my sponge back?"

The dpg retrieved Eden's sponge for her. "Can't refuse any request. It's in the doppelganger's job description." She quickly held up a hand. "But you don't want to blow the five o'clock whistle yet."

"I'm not. Stay a while. And tell me if you found out anything today."

"Marble staircases, possibly of religious importance. There are a lot of those, particularly in Rome. Do you want me to download all of my research while you're soaking? Based on your sketch, I did about three hours on the Internet and in the stacks at the library."

"Keep it short; I don't need a lot of travelogue stuff cluttering up my brain."

"I counted twenty-eight steps in your sketch. I assume you were certain about that number, because you took pains to make it exact."

"I tried to draw exactly what I dreamed. Maybe the number is important."

"Helpful. I came up with La Scala Santa, the only staircase in Rome designated as 'holy.' It's located across from the basilica of St. John Lateran in an unimpressive little building filled with Christian relics and a couple of sculptures, one of which is the *Ecce Homo*—'Christ presented to the rabble by Pontius Pilate.' That's significant."

"Why?"

"According to legend, that same staircase led to Pilate's office in the Governor's palace in Jerusalem. Fourth century A.D., it was taken apart and shipped to Rome by order of Helena, Emperor Constantine's mother. She was a convert to Christianity and took a trip to Judea to locate objects Christ might have touched. More than three hundred years had passed, but she found what she thought was the 'True Cross'; it also occurred to her that Christ probably walked up Pilate's staircase for his arraignment, Pilate being in Jesus' time the provincial governor of Judea."

"Then Christ walked back down those steps on his way to Golgotha."

"So . . . through tradition the steps became objects of veneration to the popes of Rome. In the sixteenth century the staircase was moved to where it stands today, a ceremonial approach to the papal chapel on the second floor of the building, the *sanctum sanctorum.* Holy of holies. It's one of the major attractions for pilgrims to Rome, who follow the example of generations of popes by ascending the steps on their knees, stopping to meditate or pray. In the photos I saw the building looks kind of dark inside, so you had that part right. But the steps are covered in wood."

"Easier on the kneecaps of the devout. Doesn't change anything. Underneath the staircase is still marble. And I saw it desecrated. Dripping blood."

"Whose blood?"

"Well—it must be—the Vicar of Christ. Pope John the Twenty-fourth. He's going to be murdered, like that evangelist in Tennessee."

"Unless you're reading way too much into some bloody paw prints."

"I'm not! But that's just what Bertie would say. She may be hard to convince. And Tom."

Eden stood up in the tub. Her doppelganger handed her a towel, glanced at the inside of a tanned thigh where blood mixed with bathwater ran thinly. Eden looked down and grimaced.

"You never have an easy one, do you?" the dpg said sympathetically.

"No, and I'm getting another cramp. I'm gonna lie down for a while."

"When are you going to introduce me to Bertie and Tom?" the dpg asked. "After all, it's been four months. I feel like a poor relation."

Eden paused in toweling off and looked at her.

"Well—I don't think they're quite ready for you yet."

"Ready as they'll ever be," the dpg said with a pout. "But you're still the boss."

COLDSTREAM BRIDGE, CALIFORNIA · OCTOBER 13-14 · 2:45 A.M.–6:15 P.M. PDT

The Assassin left shortly before three A.M. with the ten-year-old girl named Saffron Pike still unconscious but breathing normally in the back of his dusty blue pickup truck, under the locked tonneau bedcover.

Betts had made sure that little Saffron was okay before allowing the Assassin to leave with her. Pulse was a few beats fast, but her pupils were equal and reactive to the beam of light from a pencil flashlight. Unfortunately she had urinated, reverting, perhaps in deep slumber, to an old bed-wetting habit. Betts insisted on remov-

ing the soiled clothing, washing and drying panties and shorts
while the Assassin waited in the cottage, engrossed in an old Judy
Garland movie, only occasionally complaining that he had a couple
of hours' drive ahead. But he commended Betts for her motherly
instincts.

"No surprise Eden turned out so well," he said.

Betts didn't want to talk about Eden. "Your makeup looks a little
saggy," she told him.

While he freshened the face of Rance Jool, Betts hung around the
garage demanding to know exactly where he planned to drop the
girl off.

"Not on her doorstep, if that's what you mean. There's a KOA
campground about ten miles from Hum—from the down-at-the-
heels town I plucked her out of. I'll leave Saffie there, only a few
yards from all the ma-and-pa retirement RVs, just as the birds are
beginning to twitter. By then she should be waking up herself."

"In time to make the seven o'clock news?"

"Well—we must allow a little more time than that. Noon, for
sure."

"When I see that sweet face on TV, when I hear that she's all
right—"

"You will f'fill y'r end a' the bargain," the Assassin said, inserting
fresh pads of silicone into his mouth, enhancing Jool's chipmunky,
half-bright, good-ol'-boy expression. He turned away from his triptych of mirrors in the garage dressing room. "And deliver our
message to Eden. Or else—" He leaned a hip against the truck and
spoke Cowboy. "Reckon the next tasty pullet I bring you'll have its
feathers off and its neck already wrung."

Betts responded with a nod, dumb in the face of his sulky antago-
nism, just one layer (and that close to the surface) of his impenetrable lunacy. She was thinking only of the safety of Saffron Pike. Later
she would work out a method of killing the Assassin before Eden
ever crossed his path again.

No sleep the rest of the night.

At seven she was eagerly scanning the television news on San

Francisco and Sacramento channels, but there was nothing yet. She kept the radio in the kitchen tuned to an AM all-news station in Frisco. Maybe both she and the Assassin had made a mistake, assuming that a ten-year-old girl who turned up fuzzy-minded but physically unharmed after having been missing for less than twenty-four hours would be breaking-news material. But the Assassin had assured Betts, without elaboration, that Saffron Pike would indeed be news.

But by the noon hour she wasn't; and the Assassin hadn't returned.

When he showed up at two-thirty he was driving a Volkswagen Jetta with Nevada license plates, and he wasn't in a good mood. He had exchanged the rancher's straw for an Oakland A's baseball cap and was wearing a red NASCAR windbreaker. Sunglasses hid a third of his face. He sat down immediately in his dressing room and began to remove all traces of Rance Jool, peeling latex. No up-tempo ballroom music accompanied this stripping and discarding process down to the deadpan of his grim past.

"Where's your truck?" Betts asked.

"It wasn't mine in the first place."

"How about this one?" she said with a wave of her hand at the orange Jetta.

"What do you think?"

"Are you hot?"

"I'm never hot. Rance Jool assuredly is. But in ten minutes he will no longer exist."

"Is Saffron with the police?"

"I would assume as much. Or with her devoted parents. *He* happens to be one of the state legislature's prime movers and shakers. They will be making public the note I pinned to Saffron's clothing when I dropped her off 'midst the redwoods. The vid journalists are beginning to swarm. We'll watch the show on one of the Sacramento channels at six. Now don't bother me. I'm dead for sleep. Wake me at five-thirty. At which time a few of those little lamb chops broiled medium-well with some of the delectable porcini mushrooms and of course a chilled, mint-scented bell pep-

per salad would be most welcome. That is, if you're not still sulking and refusing to prepare either of us a memorable meal. No?
Splendid. Use the good china."

Saffron Pike led off the local evening news in Sacramento.
She was seen, briefly, getting into a sedan with her mom,
responding with a bemused smile to the usual frenzied show put on
by the media types hustling to get their tidbits, shouting questions at
her. But Daddy did all the talking for the family. He looked like a
man on his way up: magnetic eyes, and he knew which side of his
regal face the camera liked best.

"Of course we're outraged that this group calling itself 'Geo Puritas' would resort to the kidnapping of a child in an attempt to intim-
idate and coerce not only myself but other members of the
California legislature. I can assure you that in spite of the psychological damage visited upon our daughter in the past twenty-four hours,
my vote will not be changed and the Stony Fork dam will be built to
the ultimate benefit of the citizens of our great state."

" 'Geo Puritas'?" Betts said to the Assassin. The face of Rance
Jool, a decent likeness as drawn by a police artist from Saffie Pike's
description of him, was now on the TV screen.

The Assassin yawned, dancing a carpet slipper at the end of a pale
bony foot. "Best I could come up with on short notice." He looked
at Betts. The TV news scene shifted to a particularly nasty-looking
accident on Interstate 80. With the remote he turned the set off. And
there he was, fixed like a vampire from a bad movie in the depths of
the blank tube, juxtaposed with Betts's desperate, petrified face
above the confining neck brace.

"Shall I get out my laptop now, Betts? Or do you need a few
moments more? Call on God, if you like. What is the old Army saying, 'There are no atheists in foxholes'? You are in a foxhole, honey-
chile. I'm the fox. But you know that. And you know that I am
resolute. God is nowhere to be found, as usual. *My* will be done.
There is no way out."

"Yes, I know," Betts said. "Just shut the fuck up."

After an evening meal of grilled tilapia fillets from the lake, *Makate Mayai,* which were Kenyan crepes stuffed with fried eggs and chopped meat, and fresh mango, Etan Culver said over coffee that he had something interesting to show them.

Pegeen Culver, irritable from prickly heat and bitchy to her husband, excused herself, to everyone's silent relief. They moved from the candlelit veranda to the spacious parlor of the house. The furnishings were largely leftovers from the days of Tom Sherard's grandfather Albert, an early settler in the Naivasha bottomland and safari guide to royalty, as well as a one-eyed U.S. President with more zeal than skill as a marksman. There was a faint but everlasting musk of cigars in the parlor. Tom's mother Deborah had contributed feminine touches during her unfortunately brief marriage: batik drapes and slipcovers, graceful Moroccan vases, two paintings by the French Impressionists Jean Beraud and Jean-Louis Forain. And an eighteenth-century French backgammon table. Deborah had been passionate about the game, and spent many hours during her husband's absences subsidizing her acquisitions of fine art with winnings from houseguests who lacked her touch with the dice.

The most recent addition was a digital projection TV with a sixty-inch screen. There were two large satellite dishes in the vegetable garden; all of it was surrounded by electrified fencing to discourage the herbivore night feeders, particularly hippopotamuses.

While Etan connected his digital camcorder to an i.LINK port in a Sony VAIO Notebook, which would enable them to see footage stored in his camera he had shot in Amboseli that morning, Eden wandered around the parlor with its cabinets full of museum-quality artifacts from prehistoric Kenya, the brute heads and

curlicue horns mounted along walls paneled in termite-resistant
mopane wood, and an arsenal of well-used weapons, some quite
rare and all carefully maintained, from the days of legendary
safaris.

There also were oil paintings: a male lion ready to charge, his tail
standing straight up from his body; portraits of Albert Sherard wearing a squared-off red beard, with the naturalist and hunter Frederick
Selous and two brawny lion dogs. A spacious landscape of an area
Eden was familiar with, the unstable mirage-filled geography of
plains and hills, evanescent in the barely tolerable scorch of noonday
light. Horned animals by the thousands in a cratered place, shimmering miraculously into being from the ground up.

The last painting was a family portrait over the fireplace, Donal
and Deborah Sherard with Tom, buck-naked, age about a year and a
half. Slender Deb held her son serenely on crossed forearms, the
crown of his head beneath her chin. She had a straightforward gaze
and a large bowie knife on her belt.

Eden had come across Tom on more than one occasion, sitting
alone in a favorite leather chair facing the hearth, his walking stick
with the gold lion's head across his knees, gazing profoundly at the
painting. His mother had died in an accident on the Longonot road
when Tom was two. His father's health failed not long after. Bertie's
father, Joseph Nkambe, already forty and with grown children, had
seen to most of Tom's raising. Joseph was a self-educated man who
had elevated his status from gunbearer to a full partnership in
Shungwaya Safaris, Ltd., eventually becoming a landholder in the
Central Highlands. At fifty-eight and a rich man, he took a fourth
wife. Alberta was his last and youngest child, named for the old
safari hand who established Shungwaya.

Joseph had a severe, proud face, bewhiskered to hide the out-of-
kilter jaw he'd received from an elephant-tossing, as he modestly
described one of his many near-death experiences in thornbush and
grassy savanna. A cardiologist had limited his use of tobacco to a
single pipeful after dinner. He packed his old white pipe, carved
from warthog ivory, and settled down on a small sofa next to

Bertie, who was wolfing a dish of huckleberry pie, to watch Etan's picture show.

Eden stood behind Tom, who was also sitting to take the strain off a knee shredded by the gun of the assassin who had killed Tom's wife. And Eden's natural mother, the two of them permanently separated soon after Eden's birth.

What a strange, haunted pair we are, Eden thought, looking down at Tom. Wanting to touch him, but she'd never known how.

They were looking at Czarina's elephant family now. Then Eden saw her own rapt, perspiring face, and Pert Kincaid, wearing headphones, listening with half-closed eyes. A mature female elephant came close enough to the Land Rover to shade it with the flapping canopy of one ear. The picture on the TV set blurred momentarily, as if the Rover was moving to the footsteps of the elephants on baked ground.

"Here it comes," Etan murmured, turning up the sound. His camera panned quickly to pick up the arrival of Karloff as he charged the combi. A cyclone of dust, enraged bellowing. Karloff's immense head swung side to side, tusks slashing the air above the roofless combi. More faces, frightened, as Tom, Bertie, and the Research Associate ducked below the heavy roll bars away from this potentially lethal saber play. Only Lincoln Grayle had the nerve to look at Karloff, but his face was a blur.

"*Now,*" Etan said, and slowed the action. "This is what I noticed earlier, and tell me if I've completely lost it, darlings."

A dark smudge or shadow appeared on the screen and grew in successive images, achieving a recognizable shape. It seemed to come out of the combi, but there was a problem with depth perception and the unsteadiness of the camera. The shadow creature was moving, leaping, perhaps, at Karloff the elephant, reaching a height of ten feet or more above the ground.

Bertie dropped her fork in her lap.

The image broke up in layers of digital chaos.

"That's all I have," Etan said. "But it looked like a lioness to me, except for its size. Of course there could be a distortion effect. The head is difficult to make out, unfortunately. The image is there for only about two seconds of normal running time. Blink and you've missed it."

"Why don't we see it again?" Joseph suggested, as Eden tightened a hand on Tom's shoulder. He looked up at her, puzzled by her intensity. Bertie was watching both of them.

They studied the shadow, or cloud, or whatever it was, three more times.

"The body shape is typical of a tiger's," Joseph concluded. "I saw several of them at the London Zoo, including a male Siberian that weighed nearly seven hundred pounds."

"Phylogenetically lions and tigers are closely related," Tom said.

"But even the Bengal tiger is larger than the largest lion I have ever seen. The image captured by the camera appears to be moving purposefully, not randomly." Tom nodded. "If it is the image of a tiger, or the ghost of one, the head, what we were able to see of it, is not right."

"Tiger's body, the head of a hyena," Eden said. That got their full attention. "I know, it's a physical impossibility. So are two-headed calves, but they exist. And I don't think you've forgotten Moby Bay, have you, Tom? They were real, and this thing is real too, although it wasn't actually *there* this morning. It was like a dark spoor in the air. Karloff got wind of it and charged. If Bertie hadn't been in the combi with the guys, it would be junk now and we'd be burying everybody tomorrow."

"So it wasn't just a figment in Karloff's addled old brain," Bertie said softly. "What d'you know?"

Etan was staring at Eden, which made her uncomfortable. She shrugged before he could start asking questions, turned, and walked out of the parlor.

Tom, Bertie, and Eden had a meeting an hour later in Eden's bungalow.

Eden explained everything her doppelganger had told her about the sacred staircase in Rome, without mention of the dpg.

Tom said, "So there was a guru in India, according to Pegeen; the evangelist in Atlanta last week; and now you think the Pope is a likely target for . . . whatever it is."

"Yes."

Bertie said, "I'm bothered by the whatever-it-is, now that it's shown up here." She was looking at Eden, smiling, but her smile seemed cool to Eden.

"Hold on," Tom said. "We haven't seen much of anything yet. An image, a shadow."

"But Eden has seen it—I mean, enough of it—to believe that it's real."

"Yes," Eden said, and compressed her lips, shoulders tensing. It was Bertie who looked away first.

"You know I love you," Bertie said. "But—"

"You think I'm inventing—*it*? Bringing it to life? Oh, God, *why* would I do such a thing?"

Tom was uneasy. "Let us not jump to conclusions, here."

Looking for ticks, Bertie parted the short hairs behind the ears of Fernando, the hulking mixed-breed dog that lay between her sandaled feet.

"Eden. You went through so bloody much in so short a time. When we first saw you, in Moby Bay among those shape-shifters, you were so deep in shock I thought you were a goner."

"And you don't believe I've fully recovered from that experience, is that what you mean? I'm hallucinating? Well, I didn't hallucinate that fucking dead evangelist, Bertie! And I've always trusted the messages of my dreams. Otherwise that city in Tennessee would be a glass-lined crypt."

"I haven't said you ought not to trust them," Bertie replied. "But your powers have no checks or balances yet; you can blow wild sometimes, like an uncapped oil well."

"But Pegeen saw what I saw the other morning, on the face of Jimmy Nixon there on the tube—and it *was* a tiger with the head of—"

"We both know Pegeen is highly suggestible. Give me five min-

utes and I'll have her convinced she saw Santa Claus on the roof with
the Ghost of Christmas Past."

"This is not very fair of you," Eden said bitterly, turning from
Bertie. There was a catch in her voice; her eyes shimmered by firelight. "Tom, don't you want to listen to me? I know the Holy Father
is in danger. We have to do something."

Silence in the sitting room of the bungalow. The fire on the hearth
popped and crackled. Fernando broke wind vigorously as he got to
his feet. Bertie made a face and fluttered a hand. *Outside.* The dog
padded away.

"Yes. I agree something should be done." Tom was looking at
Bertie.

Bertie got up and put her arms around Eden, who for the moment
was unyielding but offered a bruised smile, taking in Bertie's
warmth.

"I've always liked Rome in the fall," Bertie said.

Eden was in bed at half past midnight but not asleep, although the
genets that lived in one of the fig trees not far from her bedroom
usually lulled her with their nocturnal rap, huffing sounds like fat
men jogging up a steep hill. Voices from the nightly chorus, under-
scored by the ceaseless metallic peeping of tree frogs and the tym-
pany of bull toads. She'd also been hearing the alarm calls of a
baboon troop half a mile or more away; that almost always meant a
leopard in the neighborhood, their most feared adversary.

Tom Sherard knocked on her bedroom door, identifying himself.

Eden got out of bed, stripping off the comfortable flannel shirt
that hung to her knees. Shivering—the temperature outside had
dropped into the high forties—she pulled on a pair of green coveralls: *snap snap* and she opened the thick carved door to him. Raking
a hand through her hair where it had flattened on the pillow.

Tom had a glass in one hand, two ounces of whiskey and a melting ice cube, but she knew it wasn't his first. Probably he'd
camped out on the veranda with only a couple of dogs and Uncle
Norm for company, his boots up, as sleepless as Eden, eyes nar-

rowed but alert in flush moonlight, hunter, caretaker, knowing the night of his birthplace but not the strangeness in his heart. *So it was to be tonight,* she thought, looking solemnly into his gray eyes for confirmation, nipples sensitive against the fabric of her coveralls. She had known how to touch him after all. Reach him. Then a twinge that snaked into a livid cramp reminded her that she was seeping blood. *Not this night.* When he reached into a pocket of his safari jacket and rather awkwardly handed her a couple of folded pages his computer had printed out, Eden realized with a different twinge that she had misread him. She smiled in a self-bemused way.

"What's this, Tom?"

"I know it's late, but I thought you'd want to—E-mail, from Betts. It was received by my office at the Bellaver Foundation in Geneva earlier tonight, and they passed it on to me according to our arrangement."

He turned from the doorway but she motioned for him to stay.

"It's all right. Don't go, please. I'd like some company."

While he poked at the embers of the fire in the sitting room and added logs, Eden pulled up a chair and turned on a lamp with a tasseled shade. She read eagerly, gasped, stopped, looked up.

"Tom!"

"What's wrong?"

"Betts. She's not coming. She *can't* come! Omigod!"

For a quarter of a minute Eden stared at the pages in her hand, breathing through her mouth. Then her eyes closed; tears that were squeezed from the corners of her eyes ran down her face. She sat there heaving from sobs.

Tom came to Eden and gently pried the E-mail pages from her cold hand.

"May I read this?"

"Y-yes."

Eden slumped back in the chair, scrunching against the black-fringed zebra hide. An animal reaction, emphasized by a long wail of despair.

He tilted the lampshade, holding the pages close to the round globe. He had left his reading glasses in his small study next to his bedroom, which had been his parents' bedroom. But with enough light he could make out Betts Waring's words. Eden knotted up in the chair, going, "Oh shit. Oh shit."

> My darling
> this is going to be a rough one I
> know because you have no warning.
> Even after it happened I still wanted
> to come there to Kenya & when the time
> was ripe brag it up (assuming there can
> ever bee ripe time for the noose none
> of us ever want to wear?) but my flying
> to anyplace now is Im sure out of the
> ballpark. Youll understand why.
> My flight from SFO to London was delay
> by a bad storm that bombard the
> airpoor a cup of horse, so I had rumcoke
> in the first class lunge to wait out
> with a very nice people from Santa
> Rose, who were on their way to Rome
> to see the Pope. (Im writing this
> slow but still probably doing some
> whistles wrong but cant tell which ones
> youll understand why)
> You know how my little strokes used
> to happen, because once you were with
> me & I have to pool over ask you to
> drive which you didnt have your license
> yet? I got this warm feeling the side
> of my neck and vision was fuzzy for a,
> copper mints. But weenie they check
> me at the Med that time all the
> dynasty whatzits didnt pick, up
> anything wrong with me.
> That was yours ago but only two little,

episodes after the first one & I
never told Riley told you. Over in
a few mints no harm, done & my
reaction of course was light up
another Pall Mall, self-dialysis &
put it all out of my mind.
But the one that hit me in the San
Fran airpoor wasnt so easy to dismiss.
I know I blacked out but not how long.
And my left urn was numb from elbow
down. Funny feeling, looking & there's
my hand like ded bird in my lap. I
felt weak and had to go to the garden.
Heaved and heaved but didnt feel much
better. Looked in the mirror while
I swallowed my face but already knew
it was deep caca. The pupil of my
right eye bigger than the short one.
Left everything so I guess my kit
is in London now but Im in a big
hurry thinking Im going to die &
took a taxi to Pal Alto. Where
they have the best special lists
at Stanford. They did all the tests
and I guess its pervious by now the
rest of my life is a blank table.
Weenie we look at the skull pix I
know its waste of time to go in
there dig & dig because this squat
little monster has more urns than a
Hondo diety, thats all she rot &
fuckit babe, Four weeks is about
what Im left so pleese I need you to
come here where I am while I can
still make senz and will know who
you arse.

I didnt want to go home to an empty
well. Getting tired now must finish.
Im staying with dear old friend from
college almost married him but those
things happen & anyway he has been so
kind to me. His name is Edmund Ruddy
& will pick you up at San Fro weenie
you rive then its just one oar to the
marbles where Edmund pizza greek. I
miss you so bad pleese mall me right
away you are coming
bye now dear one

"What a terrible thing to happen!" Eden shouted. "Can't the War-
ings get a break anymore? Tom, what am I going to *do*?"

"You have to go to her. The Gulfstream can be gassed and ready
by dawn. It's a sixteen-hour hop, I'd hazard, to San Francisco, so
Reggie will need to round up a full second crew. I'll ring him while
you pack; then I'll fly you to Kenyatta Airport."

"But—we were going to Rome tomorrow! The Holy Father—"

"Bertie and I will go. First I need to get in touch with your grandmother, ask her to set up an appointment through the U.S. Ambassador
to the Vatican. It was going to be a tough sell even with you along, but
we'll make our pitch and trust they won't think we're raving mad."

"I'm sorry—" Tears again.

"Betts is your priority," he said kindly. "We'll somehow convince
Leoncaro to keep a low profile for a few weeks. Then we'll join you
in California."

"You will? Oh, God, Tom, you don't know how grateful—"

"We're a team, Eden. We back each other up. That's how it will
always be."

She flew out of the chair and pressed her wet face against his chest,
aware of his heart, the closeness of his bones, but still miles from the
moment she had opened the bedroom door to him, thinking in her
drowse that he had come to make love to her. A girlish thing, a
lonely infatuation.

"God bless," she whispered.

"Be strong."

She felt the hard point of his chin against the crown of her head.

Bertie was almost always a sound sleeper, but even in those depths she heard the big turbine of the Agusta helicopter winding up for flight. She popped up out of a dream like a glistening fish from deep water. Left her room by way of the interior courtyard that separated the new octagonal wing with its conical copper roof from the original house. Flanked by two silent dogs like dark escorts she walked through the house out onto the moon-blazoned veranda.

She saw Eden, fifty yards from the house, slip beneath the moving blades on the concrete pad and climb into the helicopter while Tom raised the RPMs and turned on the fuselage running lights. Eden had gear with her, a midsize duffel slung across her back.

Almost as soon as the door closed behind her Tom lifted off, turning first toward the lake and then southeast, a heading that would take them to Nairobi. For what purpose Bertie didn't know.

She heard a cabinet clock inside chime twice.

When the roar of the helicopter became too faint to hear against the cold wind blowing down the Rift Valley, Bertie returned to her bedroom and lay down, but with her knees up and her hands behind her head, looking up through the mosquito netting at the moonlight on motionless fan blades. Seeing the two of them in the helicopter with some rendezvous in mind, and her normally contented expression turned glum. After a while she got up again with no more thought of sleep, put on a jogging suit and sandals, and crossed the wide lawn to Eden's bungalow. In the sitting room there was still faint warmth from the redeye fire. Also a glass of watered whiskey that Tom (she thought) might have left there.

She went into the bedroom but couldn't tell anything except that the bed had been slept in and then Eden had packed in a hurry, leaving cabinet doors open and drawers pulled out.

Bertie felt bad for herself, with no real evidence to explain the feeling. It was just something that had been coming on for a month or so.

Tom and Eden, Eden and Tom.

When Bertie went outside again she heard faint but frenzied human cries that seemed to be coming from the campsite of the climatologists and earth scientists down at the lake.

The animal that had snatched Jean-Baptiste Chabot from his cot in the floored tent he shared with another member of the climatology team was described by the frightened survivor as a huge hyena. Which he had only glimpsed by moonlight through large rents in the tent's back wall. A striped hyena, he said. That was a dry-country variety usually seen in northern Kenya and Ethiopia; the smaller spotted hyenas were common within a few kilometers of Shungwaya. But mysteriously silent this night. Jean-Baptiste, his head locked in the jaws of the hyena, had not uttered a sound; his tentmate had been alerted by the jangle of an alarm clock prematurely activated when it fell from an overturned table as the hyena exited with its nearly naked prey.

Joseph Nkambe and the Somali house staff boss named Hassan, also an experienced hunter, looked at the long rips in the tough tent fabric. Hassan devoted half a minute to turning his head in all directions and sniffing deeply.

"Hyena? I do not think so," the tall Somalian said. "*Felid.*"

With the aid of a million-candlepower torch, a beam with a throw of half a mile at night, Joseph found on the dusty floor of the tent faint pug marks that measured more than eight inches across.

"Nor was it a lion," Joseph said. "Scarred in some way that gave the impression of stripes."

They looked at each other, perplexed. They carried double-barreled rifles, a number two Jeffery's Express and Joseph's old Evans Double Express with a bead of non-yellowing warthog ivory for a night sight. Their bush jackets were weighted with five-hundred-grain cartridges the size of small cigars.

Outside there was scant blood spoor, but the body of Jean-Baptiste had left a drag track they easily could have followed by the light of the red-tinged full moon.

October. Known as the "month of madness" in many parts of

Africa, or the Month of the Blood Moon when winds hot or cold raised the red dust from pan to plain in drought years, carried it howling for a thousand miles.

The track crossed a hippo path to open water and continued upland in moderately heavy cover two hundred yards from the campsite. From the stride of the unknown *felid* Joseph judged it to be a dozen feet in length.

That was extraordinary, if not impossible.

They paused before entering the wood, listening. African night is never quiet, and in spite of the wind coursing through the trees Joseph identified sounds from grunts and guttural coughs to cooing and sharp barks. His knees hurt him already. So did an arthritic elbow from carrying a heavy rifle at high port arms.

Hassan, whom Joseph knew to be a brave man, seemed to be trembling in light clothing. Of course it was a chilly hour of the night.

"There is so little blood," Hassan said in a low voice. "And where is This One going? If not to feed, what did it want with the young man who was the friend of the *memsaab* Eve? I am afraid of this *felid*."

"It is sensible to be afraid. But we must see for ourselves what it is."

"An enchanted thing," Hassan declared. "Part *fisi*, part *felid*. The lover of a witch, for whom the young man is intended as an offering. The stripes described to us may well be the markings of the witch that raised it and gave it power."

"That will be enough witch talk," Joseph said, not immune himself to the mention of witches and their enchantments so deep in the night and with a blood moon low across the lake. "I'm surprised at you, Hassan."

"Let us wait now for Bwana Tom. Or the Bwana Game from Hell's Gate. Do you know where Bwana Tom has gone in his helicopter?"

"*Sejui*. He may not return tonight. This stalk will be our business alone, Hassan."

Joseph led Hassan into the wood, the brilliant torch restoring mistily to life daytime colors of the fringelike mimosa, creeper orchid, and tall green acacias. But moonlight was enough and Hassan preferred it; artificial light distorted senses that were finely tuned to the nuances of the night. Farther into the wood the odors were musty and stale from lack of rain. Hassan sniffed nervously left and right with the nostrils of a horse as they walked. For one mile, and the better part of two, as the terrain changed and the trees thinned, becoming mostly scrub oak growing on the banks of ravines choked with tangled brush.

The track they had been following vanished.

Hassan looked around with his finger on a trigger of the Jeffery's. A hyena clan was in an uproar somewhere, their repertoire of wails and chilling moans borne on the wind. They had been hearing them for a while. Joseph felt something windblown, viscous, and stringy, stick to his bare forearm. He turned on the light and saw a clabber of blood. He brushed it off and swept the torch beam through the boughs of the trees around them: high in the tossing canopy a slim body swayed head down, wedged by the waist in the forked wands of a stout limb. The head was soggy and unrecognizable after almost an hour in the jaws of the creature that had carried Jean-Baptiste this far, then climbed nearly straight up the trunk of the tree for twenty feet to secure its prey. A leopard might also cache food in this manner.

Hassan stared up at the body, then smacked his lips loudly, an expression of opprobrium.

"You see? This One did not intend to eat." All Somalis have a keen instinct for impending disaster. "Nay, it lured us here and now it has gone."

Joseph already had grasped that they had been deliberately drawn away from the house, where now, except for the Englishman Culver, there were only servants, women, and dogs. Etan Culver was not familiar with guns.

"Listen," Hassan said. "Do you hear the *farasi*? They have got wind of This One. *Mbeya Sana.*"

They were less than a mile directly overland from the house and grounds of Shungwaya, and the *boma* constructed of dense blackthorn where the horses were safely stabled away from predators.

Only elephants were impervious to thorns like needle-tipped steel spikes that exceeded four inches in length.

Without another word Hassan began to run, striding through brush that was only a minor obstacle for his seven-foot frame, his heavy rifle at arm's length above his head.

Joseph was too old to run. Instead he took a walkie-talkie from a pocket of his bush jacket.

Yes," Alberta Nkambe said, in a voice so low her father barely understood her. "I see it. I see *them*. Hyena. A large clan, at least thirty. They're following it. The horses have gone crazy."

Not to mention the dogs surrounding her on the veranda. Two servant boys came running from their quarters to the house, yipping from fear. Bertie motioned them inside. She was looking west to a *lugga* behind farm buildings and the corral where the hyenas had appeared, rambling along with their strange crippled-looking gaits (although they could outrun horses over short distances) behind the powerful *felid*, its head in the moonlight three times larger than theirs, but with the same black snout, crooked jawline, and bad dental armature. An *uber* hyena, godlike, with the heavy but lissome body of a tiger.

Bertie didn't mention the nude, spectral woman she saw astride the tiger, like a limerick she vaguely remembered, because she felt certain that she was the only one seeing this blank-eyed, evil apparition, long black hair silkily afloat in the argentine light. No need to compound the madness, or the fear Bertie heard in her father's voice. Although by now the goony screams of the approaching hyenas made it hard for her to hear him.

Another Somali servant, wearing only a breechclout, whipped past her into the relative safety of the stone house. The dogs were leaping and snarling, rolling their eyes at Bertie, waiting for a command to attack. Six of them, brawny mixed breeds with emphasis on durability and courage. They all would have been dead in twenty seconds if Bertie let them loose on the hyena clan.

"Go in the house at once," Joseph Nkambe said, unnecessarily. "Arm yourself."

"Yes. But don't you come here. I can take care of it." *Maybe.* She was beginning to swallow her heart. Bertie wondered where Hassan was. Probably returning at a dead run, one rifle, sure death for Hassan as well.

She ordered the dogs into the house. They retreated reluctantly. Bertie followed, glancing at the scared faces inside.

"What in God's name?" Etan Culver said. He was in his pajamas but had a camera with him. Pegeen was holding on to him with both hands, mouth moving soundlessly, appearing to be in a fearful state of near-collapse.

"The thing we saw in your picture show? It's real. And it's here. Brought a pack of hyena along as well."

"I told you, I *hate* this place!" Pegeen said, slamming a fist into her husband's rib cage. "Get me out of here *now*, Etan!"

"Go back to your room and bar the door," Bertie said. "Push an armoire against the windows. And don't come out until I call you." The kitchen pavilion seemed to be the best place for the house staff; she sent them there with similar instructions for sealing off possible points of entry. Although Bertie had no intention of letting any marauder close to the house. She tried to close her mind to the din they were making outside. Hyena had a wide range of vocalizations. For now they were tittering and guffawing like elderly ladies telling each other dirty jokes at their bridge club luncheon. Hyena didn't bother her; she'd been listening to them all of her life. It was unlikely they could break in; they were by nature sneaks. Their strength was in their jaws, which could crush the bones of elephants.

She knew nothing, yet, about the strength of the were-beast and its ghostly accomplice, her pale face resonant in Bertie's subconscious mind.

Bertie went quickly into the parlor and opened the twin gun cabinets, looking over the weapons available to her. Everything from a five-shot, seven-millimeter. Rigby to a double-barreled elephant rifle that had a recoil massive enough to dislocate her shoulder. No point in trying to kill the were-beast and its mistress, she guessed. But she wanted to give their hyena entourage something to remember, if they should be tempted to return en masse to Shungwaya another day.

Her choice from the gun cabinets was a Benelli semiautomatic shotgun, which she loaded with five incendiary shells called "Dragon's Breath." Not the best ammunition to use in a dry season; more than hyenas were likely to be ignited from a single round. But they had fought fires before at Shungwaya. The water tanks were full, pumps in good working order.

And she was one woman, one gun. Three weeks past her twenty-first birthday.

She saw Etan Culver's face in a doorway and heard Pegeen sobbing as she walked back toward the veranda.

"A hyena will pull your face off from the eyebrows down. Or castrate you with one bite. But if you still want to take pictures, I can't stop you."

She didn't look to see if Etan had followed her, but she was careful not to let any of the bloodthirsty dogs out.

The were-beast was in the yard now, striding past a big jacaranda laden with pink foam in its blooming season. Hyena in their rump-sprung prowling around the *boma* serenaded the terrified horses with death threats.

Wouldn't do to fire in that direction, Bertie thought.

Instead she brought the muzzle of the shotgun to bear on the ugly brown head closest to her, observing how the hyena's hard tufted skull did not seem a complete mismatch with the tiger's elegant body. Both animals had powerful necks and shoulders. But it was like admiring the anatomy of a nightmare.

The eyes of the spirit form astride the tiger's body were as empty as holes drilled in wet stone. Her body and teeth both bared, raven hair swirling around lush nakedness. She raised her hands above her head. There was a jingle of shackles, silvery notes in the air as Bertie jacked an incendiary shell into the chamber of the Benelli.

What the hell, she thought. *Let's see what you're really made of.*

The were-beast was fifty feet from the veranda steps when Bertie fired, and was nearly blinded by the flame and smoke that spouted from the muzzle of the shotgun. She had only a blurred glimpse of the tiger's long leap, the hyena's contorted, contemptuous mouth. Then it was gone, and she blinked at a narrow blaze on the lawn, like a bolt of lightning fallen horizontally and blackening the grass. She whirled on the veranda, expecting claws nearby, a fatal slash, but she was alone, the faces of dogs raging and demonic behind the beveled glass panes of the doors. They lunged against each other and the doors until one shattered. Then the dogs tumbled past Bertie in a dark torrent and were gone in spite of her screams, streaking over the burning lawn toward the hyena gang.

The were-beast had leaped twenty feet from the ground to a veranda roof and now she heard or sensed it climbing, claws digging into thick papyrus, woven tightly enough to shed a tropical cloudburst. Both roofs, one above the other, were slanted at a sixty-degree pitch from the ridgepole.

She couldn't tell yet if the thing was trying to dig down through the papyrus to get at her, but the roof seemed to bear up okay beneath tremendous weight. Shaking from her adrenaline rush, she swung the muzzle of the Benelli in a tight arc above her head. But the shotgun would be no defense, unless she wanted to burn the house down.

Bertie was backing into the house, eyes on the underside of the larger of the two roofs, when her attention was diverted by the jarring but welcome noise of the Agusta helicopter flying over at fifty feet, barely treetop level. Tom was back; and the searchlight mounted beneath the chopper was focused on the hyenas.

Charging dogs and blinding light; they disappeared in moments, almost magically, finding the cover of the brush-filled *lugga*. They easily outdistanced the savage dogs if not the helicopter, which continued the chase for half a minute. Then Tom turned toward the concrete pad. The fires on the lawn didn't seem to Bertie to be a big problem. The problem was the were-beast, and for a few very bad moments she had no idea of where it had gone. Her back was to a stone wall next to the shattered veranda door. She was looking, looking, strained to the breaking point, when she heard, above the racket of the landing helicopter, a high-pitched scream. Could've come from one of the houseboys, or Pegeen Culver. *The courtyard,* she thought, freezing in horror, crying and pissing now like a two-year-old child, couldn't help herself.

Then she saw the were-beast on the south lawn where pool mist drifted, heading away from the house with great loping strides. Momentarily bold in the moonlight, a beautiful monster but without the spirit-rider Bertie had seen a minute ago.

The were-beast covered fifty yards in less than three seconds, reaching the bungalow where Eden lived.

Bertie jumped at the crunch of broken glass in the doorway and threw down on Etan Culver. He jumped too, a good three feet away from the muzzle of the Benelli.

"No, no! It's me!" He fumbled with his movie camera, but the were-beast had vanished again, in tree-darkness near the bungalow.

"Get any pictures?" Bertie asked breathlessly.

"Are you insane?" Etan looked at Bertie's shotgun. "You bloody might have shot it!"

"Give me a break. Did you see how fast it moves? Who screamed?"

"Pegeen."

"Well, is she *okay*, damn it?"

"Oh, uh, I think so. She saw, thinks it was, a spectre, she said."

"Forget about the ghost. Anyway, it wasn't." Bertie was still on edge, feeling soggy and ill-tempered. Tom Sherard was coming toward them, a fire extinguisher from the chopper in his hands. He doused clumps of fire as he limped heavily across the rough farm-yard. She wondered fleetingly what he had done with his lion's-head walking stick.

"Bertie!"

She wiped her eyes, which were still leaking. "We're okay! It's down by the bungalow!"

"What is?"

"You didn't *see* it?"

"All I saw were hyena about to massacre our dogs."

Four of the dogs had turned back and were catching up to Tom.

Two missing. Hyena were whooping it up from cover, and no matter how often Bertie had heard them, still their eerie voices raised goose-flesh.

"Oh, man," Bertie said as Tom came up the steps to the veranda. "You have a treat in store. Better get us a couple of rifles, Tom. Fifties. It's the size of a Land Cruiser, I am not kidding."

"What are you talking about?" He looked in irritation at Bertie's shotgun. "What did you load that with?"

"Incendiaries." She shrugged. "It seemed like a good idea at the time. But I missed."

He noticed the wet spot on her trousers, smelled it probably, but didn't embarrass her by commenting. He couldn't remember having seen her scared, by anything.

"It's our phantom tiger-hyena thing," Etan volunteered. "Only in the too, too solid flesh, from what little I saw of it." He looked regretfully at his expensive camera. "I'm afraid I didn't get a good shot myself."

Bertie nodded, teeth fastened to her underlip. Looking a bit windy, as the old safari hands put it. Tom took the shotgun from her and gently guided her inside.

"Sit down. Stay here."

"But—I feel safer with *you*, Tom! You haven't seen it. You don't know how fast it comes at you."

"Faster than a charging lion?"

"I—I don't know!"

"Survived a few of those. So I can cope, you see. Now you've done enough, let me take it from here."

Bertie's best dog, Fernando, came into the house on three legs, left hindquarters laid open to the bone by a hyena's near-miss. Fernando's tongue lolled, he was hurting, but he looked pleased with himself. He spread himself slowly at Bertie's feet and began to lick tattered flesh, eyes half closed.

"I'd better go find Pegeen," Etan muttered. "Left her beneath our bed." To Tom he said, "I don't suppose—"

"Absolutely not. One of us is all I can look after."

Tom went to the parlor and was back in thirty seconds with the .447 Holland and Holland double rifle his father had ordered for him when he was a year old.

Hassan came in from the veranda with his own rifle, not very out of breath after running a five-minute mile through bush.

"Where's Joseph?" Tom asked.

"He will soon be coming."

"Good," Tom said. "Well, shall we take a crack at this mysterious critter, Hassan?"

"If you say we must, Bwana Tom."

Five minutes past four in the morning. The moon was down, the brilliant litter on all the pathways to Eternity flashing forth in the black sky.

It would have been useful, Tom thought, to know what they were stalking. Lion, leopard, Cape buffalo; all dangerous game he had hunted, known their spoor, their cunning, and their power. A tiger combined with a hyena was not only an abomination, unearthly; it could possess a supernatural intelligence beyond his calculation.

Hassan wasn't happy either. They maintained ten paces apart, each covering the other's flank, as they walked slowly toward Eden's bungalow. A clump of fig trees on one side of the stone bungalow; otherwise there was no place for a large animal that had left no sign of its passing in the lush green of the lawn. All of the roof was visible. There was a stub of a stone chimney, thread of gray smoke visible against the Southern Cross.

The only door, oak with iron hinges, had been broken down and scattered like matchsticks. So the were-beast had gone inside. And possibly was still there.

Hassan let out a low moan as the sitting room of the bungalow became visible to them. He stopped, refused to budge with a taut shake of his head.

Tom didn't blame him. He saw it too.

Any sort of animal he'd been more or less prepared for. But not this.

She was near the hearth in near-darkness, the remaining coals in the deep fireplace glowing through the translucent, nude body. By

contrast the sheaf of black hair between her shoulder blades, taper-
ing to her tailbone, was as stark and earthy as a male lion's thick
mane. She turned her head in response to their presence. Faint fire
was reflected in the otherwise empty pits where eyes should have
been.

Hassan moaned low in his throat. Hair crept up the back of
Tom's neck.

When she turned full-front and began a slow drift away from the
hearth, coming toward them, holding her hands bound in silver
shackles away from the coldly beautiful, waxen body, Hassan broke.
He dropped his rifle and departed with a strangled cry.

"Tom," Bertie said softly, and he'd never been so glad to hear anyone's voice. She was out on the lawn behind him. He didn't look
around, but he was grateful that she'd ignored him and followed. He
had had some weird experiences in Bertie's company, but this was
totally beyond his ken.

Bertie spoke again.

"Ask her what they want."

"Can't you ask her?"

"This One and I, we're natural enemies. She won't speak to me."

"All right," he said, not understanding but not doubting Bertie,
who had access to worlds of the afterlife where he could never go.
"What do you want?" he said, his words followed by a tight involun-
tary grimace, the facial muscles a little out of control. Talking to a
wraith.

Where is Eden?

He heard the voice in his head; his ears picked up Bertie's quick
intake of breath.

"Answer her, Tom."

"What the f—"

"Please, Tom."

"I don't even know what this thing *is.*"

"I do. Answer her."

"Eden isn't here," he said to the wraith. "She's gone away." He
swallowed and added, "Nor will she be coming back to Shungwaya."

The wraith hovered three feet above the floor inside the doorway, quaking like hung silk in a faint draft. Tom felt its disapproval, then a scour of fear across his face, a burn of deep cold. God damn it, he was shaking too, and that made him angry.

Where has she gone?

"Piss off, sweetheart," Tom said, with more bravado than he felt.

Die then, the wraith responded.

She broke apart like a large frowzy cobweb as the were-beast bounded toward him from the dark of the bedroom. Tom fired and had a half second to throw up an arm to protect his face. He was wearing an old leather shooting jacket of his father's, the arms layered with strips of linoleum and steel studs. He was thrown over backward with his arm in the jaws of a hyena, a bolt of pain stabbing to his shoulder as if he were being electrocuted. Then he heard another shot and the beast spat out his arm, moaned, and used Tom's body for a springboard, leaping away from him. The force of what amounted to a body blow from a heavyweight champ drove the air from his lungs. He heard the *crack* of another shot.

Half a minute to get his breath back. Bertie and Hassan were bending over him. Bertie's face was pinched from pain, her right arm hanging limp.

"We know two things," she said, breathing hard herself. "It doesn't like getting shot. And it bleeds real blood."

"Where—"

"Long gone. Won't return."

"Help me up, Hassan."

"I ran, Bwana Tom," Hassan said, looking sick from shame.

"But you came back." On his feet, Tom looked at the rips in the tough leather sleeve of his jacket, the mangled strips of linoleum ripped loose from studs. Hassan helped him out of the jacket, and he had a look at his bare forearm. It was contused and swelling, but not bitten through the bones. He made a fist, then probed with two fingers of his left hand. It hurt. Couple of fractures, he thought. Nothing serious.

Tom looked at Bertie. A massive surge of adrenaline had drained away, left him feeling wobbly.

"You fired that first shot?"

"Yes. Hassan's double-Jeff. I think the recoil broke my shoulder. Hassan took the second shot." She grinned through considerable pain, pitched her voice like old Gabby's. "Shoulda seen the ornery critter jump and skedaddle on outta here."

Tom smiled at the dialogue from Roy Rogers movies. Bertie had lived with Tom and Gillian from ages twelve to eighteen, when she graduated cum laude from Columbia University. Already a darling of the editors of high-fashion magazines and working on her second million dollars.

"Reload," Tom said to Hassan, then realized the Somali would have done so even before looking to see if Tom was still alive. Tom picked up his own H and H, seeing blood on the grass. "Let's finish this," he said. He took two steps and felt his bad knee give. Shook his head in frustration and annoyance. His body no longer capable of the effort he demanded of it. Arm broken, chest badly bruised so that breathing sent shock waves to his temples.

"We both need doctoring," Bertie said. "Three of our dogs have to have surgery. You can't kill it, anyway."

"I can make a damned good try."

Etan Culver was crossing the lawn, trying to make pictures in near-darkness. "Did you get it?" he yelled.

"Tom, I think it's changed shape by now. But we'll be seeing it again."

"Why? And what does it want with Eden?"

"You mean *they*. Don't forget our soulless wraith with the empty eye sockets. It's Eden's soul she needs." A shudder; Bertie held her injured shoulder, gritted teeth, and looked past Tom into the bungalow Eden had occupied a few hours ago. "But if she can't have it . . . then Eden's body must do. That's even more terrible. The were-beast has her spoor. I think it exists only to mate with Eden. And it will if it gets another chance."

Ten-thirty in the morning.

Bertie lay in a woven hammock on the veranda beneath a cooling ceiling fan. Her arm was in a tight sling, left hand cupping her separated right shoulder. Surgery, she had been told at the clinic in Naivasha, was the obvious remedy. Healing herself was another, but that was a choice she hadn't mentioned to the attending physician. It was something she had never attempted before, because she'd never been seriously hurt.

Healing was one aspect of the Gift Bertie had possessed even before birth; it had emerged when she was three years old. Joseph Nkambe had been bitten by a black mamba and lay dying on the floor of their home by the Thika River in the Central Highlands, his body vibrating from deadly muscle toxin injected by the mamba's fangs. The mortality rate from mamba toxin, even when antivenin is promptly administered, is higher than ninety percent.

But at the concerned touch of his only daughter, Joseph's trembling ceased. He later spoke of the experience as a calming warmth that rushed the length of his swollen arm toward his fibrillating heart, from there spreading swiftly through the rest of his body.

After a nearly sleepless night Bertie was beginning to feel drowsy, her attention diverted from the CNN news on Kenyan television. She began to feel warmth in her palm, which radiated down into her hurt shoulder. And she was aware of a change in the light around her, which seemed to emanate from her solar plexus. After several minutes of this she gripped the shoulder tightly, action that a few hours before would have had her screaming, squeezed, then relaxed her hand. Swaying gently in the hammock, she breathed deeply for a while, then sat up and removed the fasteners that held the sling and her arm tightly to her body. She placed her right fist in her left hand and raised the elbow higher than the formerly separated shoulder. It still felt a little stiff. She worked the shoulder carefully, without pain.

"Doing okay now?"

Bertie glanced at the slender smiling girl sitting in a cane armchair nearby, wearing a Cal State Shasta Lady Wolves' basketball practice jersey and cotton shorts. For an instant Bertie almost lost her balance and tumbled out of the hammock.

"Oh, hey! Thought you would be starting across the Atlantic by now."

She uncrossed her legs in the armchair and adjusted a favorite Masai beaded headband that held her russet hair off her forehead.

"Eden ought to be. But I'm not Eden. I'm the girl she left behind. Kind of a last-minute inspiration just before she took off at four this morning. She thought, you know, maybe I could be helpful when we all get to Rome."

"Uh-huh," Bertie said, still flustered. "Then you must be—"

"Eden's doppelganger. Pleased to meet you, after all this time." Her smile was wry, appearing to shade after a few moments to bitterness.

"Doppelganger. *Right*. And it *is* a pleasure. What do we, uh . . . I mean . . ."

"I think the best way is to forget I'm a dpg and just treat me like Eden's long-lost, lookalike sis. We don't want to spook the natives. By the way, whatever Eden knows I know too, which will save you a lot of explaining. I can find my way around the old homestead. Shangri-lala."

"Shungwaya."

"Just goofing. As you can see, I borrowed some of Eden's stuff to wear. When I'm not wearing clothes—might as well get this out of the way—I'm invisible to everyone but Eden, although animals get kind of a shadowy impression. That's pretty much my entire bag of tricks. I can't brain-lock like you can, melt glaciers with my X-ray vision, or turn into a feathered serpent. What do you call me? *Guinevere*. That's the name I've picked out for myself if, let's make that *when,* Eden decides to release me. Gwen for short.—What's the matter?"

"You've already talked more than I heard Eden talk the first two months she was here."

"Well, Eden was getting over a crapload of trauma. Also, I may be her mirror image, but I have an independent mind when I'm on assignment, like now. I'm a social animal. Naturally fun-loving and loquacious. Eden's big fault, you didn't hear it from me, is high seriousness."

"What did you mean," Bertie said, still playing catch-up, "if Eden 'releases' you?"

"Oh, that. It's every doppelganger's goal. Eden is my homebody, so of course she has complete control of my destiny. But she can relinquish me to a life of my own. Ancient tradition. Eden is the Eponym, the Name-Giver, which is an aspect of her left-handed Art. The matrix of which is, of course, quantum physics."

"Of course."

Gwen looked across the lawn at the stone bungalow with the smashed door. A couple of workmen were removing shards of oak from the hinges, measuring for a new door.

"Maybe you could fill me in on what went down here last night, Bertie. Some animal peed all over Eden's bedroom. As if he was marking territory or something. What a stink."

"Well—"

Tom Sherard came out of the house, one hand on a cedarwood staff his grandfather had made seventy years ago. His right forearm was in a cast. He looked at the dpg.

"Good morning, Gwen."

"How're you, Tom?" The expression on Bertie's face had her howling with laughter. When she calmed down she said, "We met at the airport last night. Eden introduced us. I came back with Tom in the helicopter, but I guess he forgot to tell you."

"Under the circumstances," Tom said, "completely slipped my mind." He sat down carefully on the edge of the hammock, looking at Bertie's shoulder.

"I fixed it," she said. She shrugged, touched his nose with a forefinger, touched his mouth, sealed his lips, kissed him.

"So when do we leave for Rome?" the dpg asked as the kiss continued for much longer than just a friendly greeting. Bertie seemed in the mood to affirm something to herself. Tom didn't mind. The dpg began to squirm in the cane chair. "Since Eden took the Gulfstream to California, I suppose we're flying commercial."

"Yes, tonight," Tom said when Bertie reluctantly gave him space to speak. "I've just been on the phone with Katharine Bellaver. She'll meet us in Rome tomorrow."

"Eden's granny! Terrific. I've always wanted to meet Katharine. And tell her just what I think of her." Bertie was touching Tom's face again, a distant look in her eyes, mouth relaxed, even dreamy. Gwen said, "Bad enough she cheated Eden out of a mother, bet she's planning to cheat her out of her rightful inheritance. What's Eden worth, anyway? I can't believe she's never asked you."

The doppelganger flinched suddenly, stiffened, let out a cry, and grabbed her head with both hands. Bertie had gone from dreamy insouciance to a fiercer look in an instant.

"Oww! Hey! What are you *doing*?"

"Just something from my bag of tricks," Bertie said. "And if we're going to get along for the next few days—*Gwen*—you need to learn to zip it."

WESTBOUND/NAIROBI–SAN FRANCISCO · GULFSTREAM N657GB · OCTOBER 15 · 0840 HOURS ZULU

When the door to Eden's cabin opened, letting in the white blaze of high-altitude morning light, she smelled coffee from the galley of the Gulfstream V jet and opened her eyes. The flight attendant was a Kenyan girl of mixed blood, with long tilted eyes the reddish brown of oxblood. She was too tall for the doorways and limited ceiling height of the forty-million-dollar executive jet, even though she wore flats. She bumped her noggin on the bulkhead above the doorway, smiled in apology for her presumed clumsiness.

"Miss Bell? I'm sorry, but Captain Lyle asked me to advise you that we will be landing in Lisbon at oh nine twenty to pick up a second crew before we start our transatlantic leg. Would you like breakfast now?"

Bell? Eden thought, then remembered that she was traveling on her Kenyan diplomatic passport. Legitimate, but costly; she'd never asked Tom how much money he had donated to a dozen charities dear to the hearts of government politicians—several of which were probably located in their own deep pockets. She and Tom seldom talked about money. Eden had seen her mother's will, and she knew about the trust funds. She knew that she was well off and with each passing year would become richer, in spite of the deepening global economic crisis that financial soothsayers lacked the nerve to call a depression. A little more than five months ago she had almost cleaned out a modest savings account at the Cal Shasta branch of B of A to pay for her graduation dress. Now she could walk into any of several banks from Zurich to San Francisco and be whisked immediately into one of the baronial private rooms those institutions reserved to transact business with the supremely well heeled. Or she could send an E-mail and a senior trust officer would gladly fly to her.

That kind of money.

Impressed with yourself, E.W.?

Sure. I'm zipping along at forty thousand feet in a jet with gold bathroom fixtures that belonged to a movie star who was so shocked by the initial terrorist attacks on America that he gave up his career and became a Jehovah's Witness. I'm not sure where I'm going or what I'm going to do when I get there. I can't use my own name to travel for fear of attracting the wrong kind of attention. Betts is dying, and I may not be able to handle that one. I didn't even make it to Riley's burial. Riley and Betts were my parents, not some insane kid who spent half his life comatose inside a bubble and my biological mother, who I only met in my dreams. I wish Tom were here. But if he was, sooner or later I'd probably make a fool of myself like I almost did last night. Oh, the hell with this. Things get lousy sometimes. Deal with it.

Eden smiled at the flight attendant. "Thank you, Marthe. Give me a few minutes, please?"

After a quick shower in the gold and onyx bath of the master cabin, Eden approached breakfast without appetite. A glass of fresh pineapple and papaya juice woke up her taste buds; she discovered that the intermittent pain in her stomach was hunger. Before they landed in Lisbon Eden had cleaned up a plate of scrambled eggs, bacon, and soughdough French toast.

By then she also had the stomach to retrieve from between the covers of a signed first edition of *Out of Africa* that she was rereading the folded pages of the E-mail from Betts. A few hours ago she had stumbled through them with tears distorting her vision and a nervous, shocked heart. While they took on another flight crew she read the sometimes incomprehensible message again, with a dwindling fund of hope that Betts's situation could not be as bad as it appeared. She paused to look blankly out a window several times, the last time with a frown.

Who was Edmund Ruddy, and why had Betts never mentioned him?

Once they had taken off again, Eden asked the girl who was alternating with Marthe on the long flight for a pen and paper.

For several minutes she pondered the E-mail, circling several words. Then she composed a brief message and gave it to the flight attendant to fax.

Tom said I could depend on you if I needed help . . .

They were westbound over the Atlantic Ocean with the sun behind them. In San Francisco it was about one-fifteen in the morning. But Tom had said that Danny Cheng, whom he described as "like the CIA, but without the overhead," didn't keep bankers' hours.

The fax went through. Eden did some stretching exercises. The Gulfstream's captain, Reggie Lyle, and his copilot were snoozing with their shoes off in deep leather reclining chairs in the darkened compartment behind the flight deck. Eden paid a visit to the third pilot, recently retired from the French air force, who had taken over the left-hand seat in Lisbon.

"Will we be making a fuel stop?"

"Yes, in Newark."

"I wonder if we could stay there for a few hours?"

"Yes, of course, as long as you wish."

That dog is still hanging around," the Assassin said, coming into the kitchen where Betts, looking weary and with dark smudges under her eyes, was making coffee. "Did you feed it again?"

"No," Betts said, keeping her back to him and leaning on the island counter.

"But you fed him yesterday. That's why he's still here."

"Show a little mercy, why don't you? He's dirty and bloody and can barely drag himself around. He might have been clipped by a car on the road. I think the breed is called 'Pharsyd Tosa.' " She knew exactly what the dog was; one of her friends in Innisfall raised them. Guard dogs imported from Japan. Rare and expensive. Someone would be searching for him. "Don't you like dogs?"

"No." The Assassin, wearing a gold silk bathrobe with a red and green dragon embroidered on the back and his *Phantom of the Opera* face (Lon Chaney's 1925 version), sat down at the counter. He plugged in the laptop computer that, when he wasn't using it, he kept locked up in his bedroom. After he was on-line he entered Betts's password. Waited. "I had a cat once. She had kittens. My stepfather put all six of them in a feed sack, then beat the sack against the well pump in the yard, just a-swingin' that sack around his head, drunk as a barroom mouse, honey, hammering away until their blood was all over his nasty hairy belly and dripping down his face. Did I ever tell you about him?"

"Not much, and I don't want to hear any more."

"I thought primo nutcases were an endless fascination for you, given your line of work." The Assassin scowled at the screen of the laptop. "You've got mail, Betts. But naught from Eden, yet."

Betts didn't want him to see the look of relief on her face. Her blood pressure was so high this morning she was seeing black spots dancing before her eyes. She sugared a bowl of cornflakes, added milk from a carton with a trembling hand.

"Betts, look at me."

"If you don't mind, you're not the most endearing sight first thing in the morning."

"Oh, but you can be cruel."

"I didn't intend it that way. It's just a plain fact."

"Then make it up to me," he said, a pout in his voice.

Betts sighed. "Would you like me to fix you an omelet?"

"There's a sweetie! Fluffy in the middle, crisp at the edges, filled with yummies like melted chocolate and bits of chicken breast? Betts, my mouth is watering. Now why do you suppose Eden hasn't responded?"

Betts opened the refrigerator, took out a cold chicken breast she'd saved from the previous night's meal, four eggs, and a piece of Gruyère.

"I've tried to explain. The E-mails I send her don't go direct. There's a routing procedure. For her safety." Betts nearly choked on the last word, pulses rampant at the thought of her betrayal.

They heard the injured dog whimpering on the patio.

"If the dog is so bad off, perhaps I should put it out of its misery." He took a knife from a pocket of his robe and the blade winked out of the handle with a push of his thumb. A four-inch, partly serrated blade. A fighting man's tool, designed for swift death. Betts had watched the Assassin work for half an hour on the edges until they were sharp enough to split a thread lengthwise. "Don't look so stricken, Betts. You asked me to be merciful. I can assure you that there is very little pain associated with a severed artery. The sharpness of the blade is everything. I'm not asking you to help, although he is a very large animal."

"Just wait," she pleaded. "Have your breakfast first."

He shrugged. "Whatever." He snapped the knife shut and dropped it back into his pocket. "Pour me a cup of coffee, then. I'll drink it while I attend to nature's call."

Betts gave him the coffee. When he was out of the kitchen she separated egg whites and yolks and grated cheese while the iron skillet was heating on the range. She diced the cold chicken breast, cut a rectangle from a two-pound bar of Baker's dark chocolate.

While she made these preparations, she glanced several times at the computer he had left plugged in. A few keystrokes, a cyberspace cry for help; she could route it to a dozen friends in a matter of minutes. Usually he took a lot of time in the bathroom, sometimes calling for a second cup of black coffee while brooding over his sluggish bowel. It was known in Betts's profession that most criminal psychopaths had great problems with constipation. In fact this internal blockage had been the subject of a recent scholarly monograph. But the Assassin's hearing was preternaturally acute; Betts knew he would apprehend the light tapping of the laptop keys through the thin panel in the bathroom door. He just might be anticipating it. Leaving the computer up and running and so temptingly close was a part of the gamesmanship he enjoyed so much, at the expense of her morale.

No point in cooking the omelet yet. Instead Betts took the bowl of cornflakes she'd fixed for herself out to the patio.

The Pharsyd Tosa lay in a corner of the patio, covered with the quilt from her bed. He hadn't moved very much during the course of a chilly night. There was fog again this morning, the apple trees in the orchard indistinct, although the twisty branches had begun to brim with sunlight where the fog thinned ten feet above the ground.

Tosas were warrior dogs trained to silence and not given to complaint. This one had a solid red coat and appeared not to be full grown, although he probably weighed more than a hundred pounds. Two hundred pounds was not uncommon for the breed. He wore a studded leather collar but had no tags. These days a good many dogs had a chip implanted near the shoulder when they were puppies, with tracking information available to a vet.

There were spots of blood on the quilt near his muzzle that looked to be fresh. His jowls were matted with dried blood. Betts suspected internal bleeding. How long could he live without immediate help? In spite of his condition he held his head up and regarded her with the somewhat sad but dignified expression typical of Tosas.

She put the bowl of milk and cornflakes where he could lower his head and lap it all up. He tried a few licks before laying his head down. His eyes were still fixed on her. Then his floppy ears twitched and he raised his head a couple of inches.

Betts heard it too: another dog barking, somewhere over the hills separating the farmland from the sea.

Then the sound of a motorcycle, or an ATV. Above it, an amplified voice, a man calling.

"Pommmm-peyyyy!"

Betts distinguished two engines running at low speeds, saw lights flashing through the fog. They appeared to be driving ATVs in slow intersecting circles, a search pattern. Calling, calling, at least two men and a woman.

The Tosa managed a strangled bark they couldn't have heard. But the dog with them did. His barking became frenzied.

"Pompey?" Betts said to the dog on the patio. "Is that your name?"

"Come back into the house, Betts," the Assassin said behind her.

She didn't look around. "What if I don't?" Immediately she raised her voice and shouted, "*Here!* Pompey's here! The house!" By now the searchers must have been able to see lighted windows, the roofline.

"Whoever they are, do you really want to cost them all their lives?"

"No," Betts said. Satisfied that the searchers had a fix on the house, she opened the screen door. He stepped aside as she entered. His knife in one hand, unopened, concealed, but she had a glimpse of it and was sickened.

"For God's sake. Let them take the poor dog and be on their way."

"I fully intend," he said, not keyed-up or even annoyed. He gave her a soft push toward the kitchen. "You can put the omelet on now. Don't show yourself no matter what you hear."

"Oh, no no no. Oh, Jesus."

"Really, Betts. They're complete strangers. What do you think I am?"

"But your face."

"Face is Face. A blob of deadness no one really wants to look at for too long, as you have so often reminded me during your stay. And I shall remain here, behind the screen, while they gather up their unfortunate mutt. Now, shoo."

Two, no, three ATVs converging behind the house, the dog riding with them perking up Pompey's big ears. He was trembling.

Betts retreated to the kitchen. She looked again at the computer. But from where he was standing the Assassin could keep an eye on it, and Betts too, with only a slight turn of his head. She gave the eggs another few whisks, then poured them into the omelet skillet. She heard the screen door open, and her nerves prickled. He had gone outside after all, as the ATVs approached. But, moments later, he was back, as she gave the laptop another calculating glance.

Voices, the ATVs pulling up outside the patio, engines idling. Excitement, heartbreak. *There he is! Pompey! Pompey! Oh, God, Drake, he's hurt!* And the Assassin: *He must have been struck on the road. Did everything I could for him, but of course I had no way of knowing who he belonged to.*

The omelet was crisp at the edges. Betts folded in chicken and chocolate, turned the gas flame low. Outside, from what she could gather, they were tenderly loading the big Tosa into a flatbed trailer behind one of the ATVs. And soon, with sun melting the fog around the house, they were on the way to the nearest animal hospital.

With their departure Betts felt a sense of ease like sleep coming over her, after a nearly sleepless night. Her trials were far from finished; but after four days she at least had a glimmer of hope.

He put the bowl of soggy cornflakes in the sink, sat down on a stool at the counter. Betts served him the omelet.

"Oh, aren't you having any?"

"No."

"Pompey's full name was Pompey's Bold Runner. His sire, if I remember correctly, is champion Kingstar Law West of Dodge. Interesting the names that the kennel club crowd come up with for their doggies. Well, I'll just dig in, then. Oh, my *dear! Wunderbar.* A touch of Gruyère in the egg, yes? A really bewitching blend of—" He hesitated, swallowed. "But I almost forgot! With you looking so benign all of a sudden; if you were a cartoon cat I would swear those were canary feathers floating from your lips."

"What do you mean? I'm just happy that his owners found Pompey, and—"

"I did not, of course, let them get away with *this,*" the Assassin said. He reached into a pocket of his robe and held up the leather collar he had severed from around Pompey's neck in those moments before the arrival of the ATVs.

"Say *ahhh!* Betts, open your mouth and let Tweetie Bird fly away."

Betts felt the all-too-familiar hammering of her pulses again.

He turned the collar over to the smooth side that had been next to Pompey's thick neck.

"Why, what have we here?"

With a thumbnail he picked at the Scotch tape holding a folded note the size of a chewing gum wrapper to the collar. It fell to the counter. The Assassin looked at it, then had another forkful of omelet, screwing up his devastated face in blissful appreciation.

"I don't suppose there's any point in my reading that," he said after a few moments, then flicked the folded paper in the direction of the wastebasket. He pitched his voice to emulate Betts's contralto. "'Halppp! I am held hostage. Wired to explode. Extreme danger. Contact FBI at once.'" He resumed his own voice. "Or something to that melodramatic effect. Good try, Betts. So resourceful. I am going to miss you when at last we part."

He finished the omelet in silence and pushed his plate across the counter. Betts picked it up and put it in the sink, rinsed. Then she gripped the edge of the sink with both hands. Beginning to choke in the collar around her neck, her face reddening.

The Assassin used a gold toothpick to clean between his teeth.

"Please don't have a spasm, Betts. But the hours are now dwindling down to a precious few. Now that we've had visitors who might come around again to express their gratitude at greater length, I suppose we should think about giving up this place. And I was hoping to brush up on my Dolly Parton today. The *Hindenburg* of bustlines, bless her heart. I'd lip-synch 'Muleskinner

Blues,' cracking my little whip over the ass of some conventioneer I coerced out of the audience. It was an absolute panic. So. Hmm. Let's see if there are additional messages." He pulled the laptop to him, opened Betts's mailbox. "Well, well. About time, I should think."

Betts turned from the sink to stare. His eyes were on the screen.

"Yes, Eden has arrived. All the way from darkest Africa. Hear my heart pound, boss, like Congo drums. There is some mechanical difficulty with her plane, however."

"Where is she?"

"Newark, New Jersey." He read further. "Not certain when she'll reach San Fran. She's requesting that Edmund Ruddy meet her by the mermaid fountain in Ghirardelli Square. Eleven o'clock tomorrow morning. She will be wearing a red turtleneck and—a beaded Masai headband? Cool." He looked up from the screen. "Now why do you suppose she wants to meet Mr. Ruddy there?"

Betts said promptly, "A friend of Eden's from college, they were on the basketball team, is working in San Francisco. I assume Megan lives in North Beach, and Eden plans to stay with her overnight."

"Megan what?"

"Pardo."

"P,A,R,D,O? I'll check that out." He looked again at the laptop screen. "She flew from Nairobi in a Gulfstream jet? That's rather pricey."

"Eden's biological mother was one of the wealthiest women in America."

"Oh, yes. Gillian Bellaver. Another psychic of alarming prowess. I believe they are called 'Avatars.' "

"And Eden can make you a very rich man."

He straightened on his stool, clasping hands behind his hairless head.

"If only I will agree to release you and go quietly on my way, clutching my loot bag. Rejoicing at my good fortune. What kind of money are we talking about? Say, fifty million U.S. cash, numbered bank account in the Channel Islands, that sort of jazzy intrigue?"

"Whatever it takes, whatever will satisfy—"

"But what you won't acknowledge, Betts, it isn't *money*. I have money. Need I remind you that I was a very successful lounge act in Vegas and Reno for more years than God Almighty has wrinkles? While otherwise employed. It is my status in *that* occupation that matters. My rep with Impact Sector. My integrity."

"Killing Eden is a matter of integrity?"

"You just close your mind and refuse to understand," he said in a whining tone.

"I understand you. I want to see Eden again. You'll grant me that wish, won't you?"

"Well, why should I, Betts? I'm not your fairy fuckin' godfather."

"Think about how—entertaining—it could be for you."

The Assassin looked long and thoughtfully at Betts, who didn't flinch.

"There is that," he conceded. "Clever Betts. To know so many of my weaknesses and appetites, on short acquaintance. And to have the gumption to try to manipulate me. Oh, mama. Betts," he said with an attempt at a winsome smile, "I hope I haven't fallen in love. That *will* make our final parting a real heart-tugger."

WESTBOUND/NEWARK–SAN FRANCISCO · GULFSTREAM N657GB · OCTOBER 15 · 6:45 P.M. MDT

Fifteen minutes after they landed at Cheyenne Airport in Wyoming, Eden saw a well-traveled SUV with oversized tires and a dozen extra lights mounted on top of and the sides of the cab. It stopped near the Gulfstream and a petite girl about Eden's age hopped out of the front seat, her short blond hair riffling in a sunset wind. She wore soft fringed knee-length boots with her jeans and a shawl-collar, knitted sweater coat. From the back of the SUV she retrieved a Fender Strat guitar and an orange outdoorsman's pack, waved good-bye to the driver, and walked briskly with her stuff to the steps of the Gulfstream jet, where Reggie Lyle was waiting.

"Hi, I'm Chauncey. I'm expected. Been waiting long?"

Moments later she stood in the doorway to Eden's quarters, smiling but not all that sure of herself.

"Great to see you again. Some airplane. Is it yours?"

"I don't know. I can use it whenever I want." Staring only made Chauncey ill-at-ease, but Eden couldn't help herself. Chauncey had a small nicely shaped face and large eyes the color of brandied plums. There wasn't a trace of the bullet hole in the center of her forehead, probably the last grisly memory she had of Chauncey McLain.

Chauncey knew what was on her mind. She brushed a couple of fingers across her unlined forehead.

"I can explain this," she said casually. "So is that why you wanted to see me, Eden? By the way, who is Danny Cheng?"

"Oh, he's—someone who knows how to find people in a hurry. Kelane Cheng was his sister. Do you know about Kelane?"

"Died in that plane crash that messed up your graduation. She was the Avatar, before you." Chauncey frowned slightly as the Gulfstream's engines revved. "Are we going somewhere?"

"San Francisco, if that's okay."

"Sure, why not? We played Colorado U. last night. Couple of days off before Tucson. We're opening for Zero Body Count on the last leg of their world tour. Rest of the guys left this afternoon on the bus, and I caught a ride to Cheyenne."

"Pussy/Whip, isn't that the name of your band?"

"You remembered! Should I sit down and buckle up or something?"

"I'm sorry. I didn't mean to be rude. Would you like a drink, Chauncey, or maybe it's dinnertime for you? Long trip, my body rhythm's out of whack."

"Know what you mean. We've been on the road three months. I could really go for a beer."

"Sure." Eden placed the order with one of the flight attendants. Chauncey dropped into a leather armchair opposite Eden.

"You have a great tan. Where've you been keeping yourself the last few months, or is that a secret?"

"Africa."

"Oh, right. The tall Brit white hunter type, and that stunning black kid with the Chinese eyes. The ones who snatched you away while we were occupied with the FBI. I just assumed those two were part of the SWAT team that dropped in on our Memorial Day barbecue." There was a long silence as the Gulfstream taxied, Chauncey ill-at-ease again. "I want you to know this, Eden. No one in Moby Bay had or ever will have anything but your best interests at heart. We were trying to protect you, and ourselves, from Outsiders, which is our God-granted right."

"Okay," Eden said, not understanding more than she had ever known about Moby Bay or Chauncey, but in a neutral frame of mind. Chauncey seemed unthreatening, even vulnerable, to Eden. And they had been friends, for a brief time.

Chauncey was admiring Tom Sherard's *mopane* walking stick, with the gold lion's head the size of a child's fist.

"Is that yours?"

"No, but I have the use of it, sometimes. Like this jet."

"I'd swear that lion is keeping a close eye on me," Chauncey said with a knowing grin. "Enchanted, huh? Enchantments can be a heck of a lot of fun. Or is it serious business today?"

"Serious business," Eden said, closing her eyes for a few moments.

"Let's do it," Chauncey said.

When Eden opened her eyes again, the sound of the jet engines was just a whisper. Chauncey was smiling at her a few feet away. Eye to eye, both of them unblinking, and between them rose a mirage: the redwood house of the McLains, saturated in sunlight on a treeless headland overlooking the Pacific Ocean. Memorial Day. A dazzling sea, storm clouds building in the east. The McLains were hosting a barbecue for about forty people. The

entire community, for all Eden knew. She hadn't been in Moby
Bay for very long.

Now she saw the two of them, Eden and Chauncey, walking up
the slant of the lawn from cliff's edge to the patio. A wind was whip-
ping up, paper plates and napkins beginning to blow. Chauncey was
holding Eden's hand, and Eden felt chilled. She shuddered, glancing
at the sky.

What did you hear, Eden?

*I heard Geoff's voice. Geoff McTyer. Trying to warn me. His
father was the head of the FBI. They thought I was dangerous. Geoff
said, "I can't stop them, Eden. Get away!"*

*You know what happened next. But you don't have to be afraid
anymore.*

(There on the patio. Eden's gaze jumping to Chauncey's face as
Chauncey raises her other hand to brush hair out of her eyes, jumping back to the sky. Seeing the first of the helicopters, the sniper's
bullet coming from a third of a mile away. Eden seeing the bullet
whole, as if it has become suspended in air.

(Then the sharp-nosed jacketed bullet ripping through
Chauncey's upraised hand and head. Her falling weight pulling
Eden's arm taut as she slumps to the patio floor. Some fragments
gleaming like fish scale in the welling-out of blood and cere-
brospinal fluid near the middle of the dead girl's forehead. Eden's
head moving downward with the slumping of Chauncey's body, so
that the second shot from the sniper's rifle misses Eden, instead
flattening an elderly guest of the McLains' standing behind her.

(Eden spiraling into shock, leaning over Chauncey and trying
hopelessly to wipe away the gore with the edge of her palm. The
pupils of Chauncey's open eyes fixed and expressionless. Then suddenly coming to life and focusing on Eden. Her small breasts
swelling as she takes a breath. And reaches up to touch the hole in
her forehead.

("Jeez. That'll give you a headache.")

That's as much as I remember. I guess I freaked.

*I promised to explain. In terms of your life span, all of us in Moby
Bay are immortal. And maintenance-free, you might say.*

Oh. Immortal. That's an explanation? But what happened then? To the helicopters, and the men who came for me?

Who tried to kill you, don't forget. To satisfy the obsession of Geoff's father. We destroyed them. All but Geoff and his old man. They escaped in one of the choppers. But it ran out of fuel, or something, twenty minutes south of Moby Bay in a wilderness area. Where we found them, later that night. Near their wrecked helicopter. It must have been a rough landing.

Was Geoff killed?

No. But his father was badly injured.

Then you—and the others—finished them off.

That's not allowed, off our turf. We permitted them to redeem themselves. Listen. And you will understand everything about the fate of your lover. You will know all you need to know about me and my kind.

Small foaming waves were coming farther up the spit of beach, washing across the floor of the helicopter. If there'd been an electrical fire aboard, an automatic suppression system had smothered it. Geoff moved his father to a dry ledge twenty feet wide and a few feet above the high tide line, gathered wood, and built a fire inside a ring of stones. There was no liquor in the survival kit. He made strong tea and scrambled eggs from an MRE pouch. His father drank some of the sweetened tea but wouldn't eat. Geoff choked down a high-energy bar. He was wearing a flight jacket. That and the other blanket should get him comfortably through the night, he thought, if the air temp didn't fall below forty degrees.

(He gathered more wood to feed the fire. By then it was past nine o'clock and a few stars had come out above the darkening sea. Closer to shore the sky was hazy. His father needed to relieve himself but couldn't stand without help. He complained of pain in his kidneys. With the flashlight Geoff looked for blood in the fitful stream of urine. It was darker than it should have been. After making his father somewhat comfortable again, Geoff also examined his head wound. No further external bleeding. There was no way to tell what was going on inside his skull. Some men could absorb hard blows with no significant damage to the brain. For others survival could just be a matter of luck. His father was conscious and restless, hot but not sweating. Unresponsive even when Geoff tried to talk to him.

(Then Geoff lay down exhausted on the mossy ledge, using one of the survival kits for a pillow. He had a flare gun in a pocket of the flight jacket. He resolved not to close his eyes. He hoped the caffeine from the tea would keep him awake.

(An hour and a half later he was awakened from uneasy sleep by his father's scream.

("Dad!"

(Sounds of fearful weeping froze his heart, and the next thing he saw as he looked frantically around almost shattered it.

(The narrow bay, filling with the tide that had nearly submerged the helicopter, was misted over. The forest rising steeply on three sides of the bay was shrouded. The moon was directly overhead, its light giving some definition to the tall straight trees, like Christmas cutouts in black paper, through which the sea mist flowed. Here and there rocky ravines cut back into the mountains away from the creeping water. There were some huge boulders at the mouth of the largest ravine. Atop one of them, as if it were a rounded stage, stood several still figures unrelated to humanity [that much was clear in spite of the mist] and, at their feet, another figure all too human and recognizable, writhing slowly, an arm held above his head to ward off whatever violence or terror the silent watchers threatened.

(Geoff reached for the Glock automatic he had put beneath his flight jacket, but it wasn't there.

(His father sobbing. Pleading.

(He couldn't find the pistol. All he had was the flare gun with a single load, and a flashlight.

("Dad!"

(Geoff splashed down off the ledge into ankle-deep water and started toward the ravine, aiming the beam of the flashlight at the creatures on the rock.

("Get away from him! Leave him alone!"

(Instead they changed positions, coming closer together with their backs to Geoff, blocking Geoff's view of his father. They kneeled slowly around him. Then the sobbing stopped abruptly.

(Geoff slipped and fell on the slick rocks of the beach, losing his grip on the flashlight, which flickered out as it rolled away down a sloping shelf underwater. Screaming in frustration, he lunged to try to retrieve it, getting a faceful of water that stung his sore eyes.

(Groping beneath the surface, he touched a bare foot and an ankle; his hand slid higher, to a slender but supple calf, before he snatched it away and scrambled back, opening his smarting eyes.

(Girl, blond, pretty, early twenties, standing in a slosh of seawater that came nearly to her bare knees. Standing where no one had been moments ago, hands at her sides, looking calmly down at him. She had a very small face that made her eyes seem as large as the plummy eyes of children in a Keene painting.

("Oh, *shit!*"

("Scare you?"

("Where'd you come from? Fall out of the sky?" No idea why he had said that, but it made her laugh.

("Yes. But not like you did," she replied, glancing around at the swamped Conan helicopter. She turned her face back to him. She would have been pretty, but there was something wrong with her mouth; it had an ugly twist to it. And there was a mark of some kind, a round scar on her forehead that gleamed like the moon that was in and out of clouds above their heads.

(As if she knew what he was staring at, she covered her mouth with one hand.

("I know. It's not pretty to look at. Can't seem to get the lips right, but I will. Takes practice. I need a mirror, but I haven't had time to just sit and work at it. Try to imagine what *you'd* look like if you had been shot twice in the face today. Oh-oh. Sorry. That scared you, didn't it?"

(Geoff's lungs felt like sacks of cement in his chest. He made strangled noises trying to breathe.

("Don't worry, bud. I wasn't implying you were going to get hurt.

What happens to you from now on is your choice. I'm Chauncey. What's your name?" Behind the hand held loosely to her mouth it looked as if she were chewing.

("Geoff," he said with a winded sigh. He tried to get up. He was only in about two feet of water, but his knees had washed out. He couldn't stand. This frightened him more than her supernatural appearance.

(Chauncey showed him her small mouth again. "This look any better to you?" She smiled. It was a terrible-looking smile, but he nodded. "Okay. Like I said, I'll work on it. That's the thing about suffering trauma when you're in an alter shape. I don't think I'll be able to do anything about my left foot for a while."

(She lifted her leg slowly out of the water. It was as shapely as the right leg down to her ankle. But she had, instead of a petite foot, the paw of a lion, beads of water dripping from the ebony claws.

("Like walking with a bucket on my foot," she complained. Her grimace of a smile shot halfway up one cheek as if her face had suddenly become highly plastic, unmanageable. A shattered front tooth gleamed wetly in the long gap of her mouth. Chauncey felt the anomaly and with her thumb smoothed her mouth back to approximately where it belonged. But now it was too big, grotesquely wide. She softly patted her lower lip, reducing an ugly lump. "Oh, damn," she fretted, licking and patting. "But I don't want to bother you with my little problems; it's all cosmetic. We should be talking about your future. Your father has already made his decision, as you can see."

(Geoff had forgotten about his father and the shadow-creatures surrounding him. But when he looked he saw that his father was alone on the boulder at the mouth of the ravine, sitting up cross-legged. His face, white by moonlight, was turned toward Geoff. Were his eyes open? Geoff was too far away to tell.

("Dad? Are you okay?" He made another attempt to get to his feet.

("Better than okay," Chauncey said. "He's recovered his honor."

(Geoff tried to wade through the water, but it felt thick and heavy, dragging at his legs, holding him back. He paused, trying to catch his breath, and in those few seconds he saw his father raise the Glock automatic, muzzle first, beneath his chin. Holding it in both hands, he pulled the trigger, and the mist flushed red around him as what remained of his head pitched forward.

("Dad . . . ddddyyy!"

(Chauncey's hand was on his shoulder.

("It's all right. Our honor has been satisfied, and your father has redeemed himself in the most honorable way left to him."

("No! Get away from me! You're a fuckin' freak show, all of you! You *made* him kill himself!"

("Not true. We don't have that kind of power. We can't make anyone act against his will. We may not seek revenge, or kill in cold blood."

("You did a good job of it today!"

("That's where you're wrong. We can defend ourselves on our ground, in our home place, by whatever means we find necessary. That dispensation ends at the boundaries of the home place. You're angry and you're frightened, but I can't hurt you, Geoff. All any of us can do is reason with you. Explain your choices."

("What are you talkin' about! What have you done to Eden?"

("We gave her sanctuary. Which you violated today. I don't know where Eden is. While we were . . . busy, the others of your force took her away."

("What others? You don't make sense. None of this. Why did he have to die?"

("Don't you know who they were?" Chauncey persisted.

("No!"

("Or where they've gone?"

("Oh, God!"

(There was no sound accompanying the appearance of flames. He noticed them first reflected in Chauncey's large dark eyes. He felt the heat; then the mist of the bay was tinted orange. He looked around and saw the body of his father engulfed, still seated on the boulder like a holy immolator at an Asian protest rally. Standing well away, almost into the trees, were small groups of watchers, dark except for the vivid amber of their slanted eyes. The flames leaped and whirled. The heat was intense. The heat and the burning father, corpse though he was, made Geoff dizzy from nausea and despair.

("So you have nothing to tell me."

(Geoff stared at the pyre, swallowing, weeping.

("Just leave me alone."

("You haven't heard your choices."

("There'll be search teams. They'll find us in the morning. I have to get through the night, that's all."

(She nodded. "That's one choice. To be rescued."

("Yes."

("Geoff, you see the Auditors waiting over there, don't you?"

("The what?"

("If you choose rescue, then we'll go away and leave you here. All of us but one, whom the Auditors will choose from their number to be your companion for the rest of your life. Give yourself a few moments now, look the Auditors over, and try to imagine what that life will be like. You'll be constantly watched, by eyes that never blink. Never close. The Auditor won't speak to you. He'll have nothing to say. He will only watch, and wait."

("Wait for what?"

("For you to go balls-up, dungeon-style paddycrackers. Forty-eight hours to fracture time is about average, I'm told. That's when you'll begin to talk to your Auditor. Talk, talk, talk. Plead, moan, and whimper for him to forgive you. But forgiveness is the Pardoner's game. He's only an Auditor. *Your* Auditor, until the end of your days."

(Geoff ran his tongue over his broken front teeth. His lips twitched into a frozen position, a kind of snarl.

("Or—" Chauncey had been working on her smile. She almost got it right this time. "You can go back to Moby Bay, and live there. A few mortals made that choice, and many of them adjusted nicely in time. You will be . . . tolerated, and we're not so hard to take, really, in our everyday appearances. You might even marry one of us. It's a simple, undemanding life in Moby Bay, except for occasional disturbances like today's. There are always problems with the Bad

Souls, the Fallen of Malterra. Those who have no hope of God's forgiveness. I'm telling you, it makes them *mean.*"

("Geoff was trembling. He couldn't look at Chauncey any longer. He looked instead at the flames, at the diminished wisping remains of his father.

("The third choice, of course, is the best one," Chauncey said. "It satisfies—"

("Your honor? What sort of honor do monsters have?"

("There you go, confusing appearance with evil. Not all of the Fallen were evil. The Bad Souls are permanently locked into human form. All except Mordaunt, who is *Deus inversus,* the Darkness of God. All of you mortals can consider yourselves lucky that this is so. Gives you a fighting chance, at least, although evil has had the edge for the last hundred millennia. Maybe because it's never boring. Why *we* are shifters is part of the whole Redemption package. Unlike the Malterrans, eventually we may return to a state of Grace. First we do our lessons. In order to understand the nature of all creatures that swim, fly, walk, or crawl, we assume their identities." Her smile was okay now, somewhat rueful in tone. "But damn it can be tricky! Learning how to shift, I mean. Want to see my paw again? I guess not. I've been working on this damn gryphon for the last year and a half. Mom says I've always been too ambitious. She's probably right. Combining different parts from the avian and animal worlds and getting them to work together, kind of a hoot but it's exhausting. My brother says I should have started with a chicken, the little jerk.

("But anyway, getting back to you. That third choice. If you're buying the total Redemption package. It's really a bargain. Spare yourself in this life, you wrestle a lot of heavy baggage into the next. You go with scabs, murk, and mildew. The soul deserves a clean delivery, Geoff."

("His eyes were smarting. He rubbed his throat, trying to ease the choking tension there. He turned away from Chauncey, seeing the flames on the rock again like radiant branches of a tree nourished by the consumed heart of his father.

("Oh, Geoff?"

(He turned back to her. Chauncey's right hand was out. He saw a compact Glock automatic lying in her palm.

("This is yours, isn't it?"

(He stared at the pistol for a few seconds, then waded three steps toward Chauncey. The surf beyond the misted bay was like the blood rushing through his heart. His fingers closed over the dull black slide of the Glock, fingertips grazing Chauncey's wrist. It was unexpected, that touch, comforting in a way. Imagining himself blind and finding a flower in the dark. A single beat of his heart said *courage.*

(Geoff looked up and into her eyes.

("Thought I'd lost it," he told her. He lifted the Glock from her hand. Held it as he might've held a key poised at the threshold of a lock on a mysterious door. "Thanks."

("What you think is the end is only another place to go to."

("I wanted to see Eden again." There was no strain in his voice, no sorrowing notes. His mind felt clear, open to possibilities, raised remotely above the ruck and misery of self-pity and other merely human perceptions, immaculate as an observatory. The reality was clear as well, like the gleam of new stars; his purpose now etched plainly in firmament but only large enough to accommodate the humble event.

("I know," Chauncey said. "I can promise you this. If she ever needs our help, she'll have it.")

That's enough," Eden said. "Don't show me any more. I don't want to see him die."

Chauncey's small face had a rosy flush; there was a touch of euphoria in her blue eyes from the residual energy of psychic communication.

Eden felt darkened, exhausted. She took a few minutes to regain her composure, staring sightlessly out the window next to her chair as the Gulfstream jet rose through streamers of cloud to the assigned flight level for the Cheyenne to San Francisco flight.

"I do need your help," Eden said finally.

"Ask."

Eden described the dreams and visions she'd been having, of a tiger with the head of a hyena, and the bloody paw prints on the sacred staircase in Rome.

"It couldn't be one of us," Chauncey said.

"My friend Bertie Nkambe, the Kenyan girl you were talking about—"

"Oh, yeah," Chauncey said, with a wry scrunch of her mouth, "the shooter. She plugged me twice when I was in an alter shape, trying to keep them from toting you away. Sorry to interrupt; what about Bertie?"

"She's Gifted, particularly at Peeping and brain-locking. Bertie thinks I may subconsciously be creating this thing. Slowly bringing it to life. But that's horrible. Obscene. I *know* I can't be doing it. I mean, why would I want to?—What are you smiling about?"

"This conversation. What do other girls our age dish about? Hair, clothes, what we saw on TV last night. And guys sex sex guys."

Eden smiled too, painfully. "I love your boots."

"Aren't they awesome? Thirty-seven bucks at this little trading post near the Navaho rez in New Mexico. I like the way you cut your hair. Are you bleaching those streaks in?"

"No, it's just the African sun. Want another brew?"

"Frankly, I wouldn't mind getting blitzed. It's been a tough tour."

"I wouldn't mind, either. But I have business to attend to tomorrow morning, and something about—this gentleman I'm supposed to meet doesn't seem right to me. That's another story, Chauncey."

"Getting back to the were-tiger—I don't believe you're just freaking out. Other than the Fallen of Moby Bay—and we're the good guys—no one else on earth has the power and the ability to shapeshift. Except for Mordaunt."

"*Deus inversus.* But who is he, and where is he?"

"Dunno. In human form he can be anyone he wants to be. He's been on earth for, oh, a couple of hundred thousand years."

"Where did he come from?"

"Where all the Bad Souls are, except those who have slipped

through the Barrier with Mordaunt's help. Malterra. *Terra inversus.* The Dark Earth, what the occultists call the Invisible Planet orbiting between Earth and Mars. It isn't invisible, actually; just one level removed from our vibrational pattern. If you want to get technical, I could—"

"What I want is another beer," Eden said with a smile that came more easily this time. "Was that your stomach I heard? How does a cheeseburger and fries sound?"

They were thirty minutes from SFO when they finished eating.

"The killing of the evangelist and the guru in India sounds like something Mordaunt would be up to," Chauncey said as she wiped a smear of mustard from beside her mouth. "A warm-up for his assault on the Pope. How many Catholics are there, about nine hundred million? And the truly devout believe he is literally God on earth. Mordaunt could be rigging a spiritual crisis for a lot of believers. We'll be seeing *God Is Dead* on the cover of every supermarket tabloid. It'll be prime-time network hysteria. As only the media knows how to feed hysteria. Evil Wins. Tough luck, mankind."

"That's not very hopeful. You're immortal, so why do you care?"

"Hey, I go through my life-death-rebirth cycles like the rest of you. For all practical purposes, I'm one hundred percent humanoid flesh and blood, so don't blow me off like that."

"Yeah, okay. My bad."

"We have to coexist with all of you, so of course we prefer peace and prosperity to *Sturm und Drang.*" Chauncey took a few moments to think something over. "If the Pope is about to get the same treatment Mordaunt handed out to Pledger Lee Skeldon, and obviously you're meant to do something about preventing it—otherwise what's the point of your dreams?—aren't you traveling in the wrong direction?"

"Tom and Bertie ought to be on their way to Rome by now. You don't just barge in on His Holiness with dire news about a psychic's premonition. Diplomacy is required. My grandmother is our ambassador to the U.N. I suppose she knows all of the formal dance steps. *This* is the reason why I'm going to San Francisco."

Eden opened her first edition of Isak Dinesen's great memoir of farm life in Kenya eighty years ago and took out the convoluted E-mail from Betts. She gave it to Chauncey to read, explaining who Betts Waring was, and how much she'd always meant to Eden.

"What does this mean, she's dying of an inoperable brain tumor?" Chauncey said after struggling with the syntax and odd wordings for a couple of minutes.

"It is true, as she said, that she had at least one minor stroke, a few years ago. I was there."

"You've circled a few words."

"Betts smokes a lot. Merits, never Pall Malls. And she's never drunk hard liquor. She wouldn't have had a rum and Coke in that airport lounge."

"But if her mental processes are messed up by whatever it is they diagnosed at Stanford Med—"

"According to Danny Cheng, she was never there."

"She could have gone to another hospital in the Bay Area."

"I know. Confusion. Mr. Cheng is looking into that."

Chauncey studied the last page of the E-mail. "So she's staying with an old boyfriend somewhere close to San Francisco. Where did Betts go to college?"

"Where *didn't* she go? Oregon State, Berkeley, USF, UCLA, are the ones I remember. She has advanced degrees from two of those schools."

"She could have met Edmund Ruddy at any of them. I suppose he'll straighten that out for you when you meet him. He's going to pick you up at the airport?"

"I didn't go for that. I changed our meeting place to Ghirardelli Square tomorrow morning."

"Which will give Danny Cheng time to check him out? Who is Cheng, a skip-tracer?"

"A lot more sophisticated than that."

"Do you have a reason to be suspicious of Ruddy?"

"Huh-uh. It's just that Betts never said anything about him."

"Probably wouldn't have, if she was happily married." Chauncey finished with a questioning look.

"Yeah. They were happy."

"So there's really no reason not to believe Betts is . . . in a bad way."

"No," Eden said, blinking, sniffing a couple of times.

"Are you meeting this guy alone?"

"Yes. I guess so."

"I could go with you."

"*Would* you?"

"Some things you don't want to face alone."

"Really appreciate that. Megan would've offered to go, but she has this job and she can't get away. We'll be spending the night with Megan. My best friend. She's house-sitting for her aunt and uncle in North Beach while they do the round-the-world cruise thing."

"Great. I've been working on some tunes, if you want to hear them. Do you play an instrument?"

"Don't play, can't sing. I spent all of my formative years working on my jump shot and trying to figure out who I was. Not that I've made a lot of progress there."

"I had a thought. Maybe I shouldn't bring it up, probably has nothing to do with this situation." She handed the E-mail back to Eden.

"Go ahead."

"It's a good bet Mordaunt knows all about you. And he would see you as an adversary. Do you know for sure this E-mail is really from your mom?"

"Yes. There's a code word. She used it a couple of times. *Weenie.*"

"I wasn't trying to scare you. About Mordaunt, I mean."

"If *you* don't scare me, nobody else ever will."

Chauncey grinned. "Just be aware that he's around, that's all."

"Uh-huh. Could be I've got better moves than a two-hundred-thousand-year-old man."

Eden hesitated, shook her head in a perplexed way.

"Or woman," she said.

The Assassin had spent most of the day in his garage dressing room preparing for his new impersonation. He had filched the identity of Edmund Ruddy, whom Betts had reluctantly come up with when he requested the name of a boyfriend from her college days.

"Why does it have to be someone I actually knew?" she had asked as the Assassin paged through the details of Ruddy's life, gathered from dozens of sources available to anyone handy with a computer.

"Because I'm assuming our Eden is nobody's fool. And she has powerful protectors. They will want to be certain there was, and still is, an Edmund C.-for-Coombs Ruddy."

"Ed was arrested for soliciting sexual favors from an undercover policewoman? In *Minneapolis*?"

"Eight years ago."

"How do you come up with—my God, a *nude photo*?"

"Except for the bandanna. He did, after all, grow up in the freedom-loving, tie-dyed decade of Aquarius. Like yourself. Shall we amuse ourselves for a little while researching Betts Waring?"

"Not the kind of laughs I'm in the mood for right now."

"The vast majority of people have no conception of how often, usually on a daily basis, their lives are being vacuumed for dirt by one electronic search engine or another."

"Including *your* life?"

"I am the sum of many lives, all stolen for a specific occasion. There is no cyberspace trail that does not quickly fetch up against a stone wall. Not even a government's supercomputers can hack the core of my existence."

The Assassin had taken an hour to study all available photos of Edmund Ruddy, including the one that should have been deleted from police files once charges against Ruddy for solicitation were dropped. And finally concluded: "I suppose he must do."

He had left a dinner menu for Betts to prepare, and he liked his meals served punctually; in this case, seven-thirty. He was five minutes late for dinner. Betts didn't care for cold or warmed-over food either. Because he had been sequestered for nearly eight hours with his latest creation, she decided a discreet knock on the plywood door of his dressing room was in order, although he had severely warned her not to disturb him.

Maybe, Betts thought as she edged around the big Winnebago he had stolen late last night and which took up most of the space in the small garage, he'd had a heart attack, and she'd find him stone-dead inside the dressing room, his head on his makeup table. Maybe God was thinking about her after all.

But when she knocked, he answered her.

"What is it, Betts?"

"Dinner's ready."

"So soon? Oh, it *is* getting late. I'm at the finishing-touches stage, but I suppose I could use a break. Come in, why don't you? See what you think of my work."

Betts pulled open the door, bottom edge scraping on the concrete floor. Bright bulbs surrounding the triptych of narrow mirrors on his makeup table assaulted her eyes.

Then it was Betts who had the heart attack as she witnessed the image of his artistry repeated in the three mirrors.

"Oh, no! My God, you wouldn't! You *can't*! No, no, no—!"

The Assassin turned awkwardly; he wore a back brace during the hours he put in creating a new face. All of the gray-haired simulacrums stared in astonishment as Betts staggered back two steps and collided with the front of the Winnebago, hands clasped tight to her breast.

"*Betts.* What's wrong? I've worked so hard. It was pure inspiration. Don't you *like* us?"

Betts barely heard him. She was on her way to the floor, eyes rolled up in her head.

By the time he got to her she was turning blue. She had swallowed her tongue.

Frank Tubner was having a dream about God.

He lay on his back in the king-size bed in the suite that he and Pinky occupied in the Hassler while they waited for word from the Vatican that their audience with His Holiness John the Twenty-fourth was a go. He was breathing sibilantly and there was a contented smile on his face.

In his dream he and God were at the Oakmoor Lanes, where Frank had bowled regularly until he was thirty-five or so, when tendonitis in his elbow forced him to give up the game. Some of his old teammates also were there at Oakmoor: Jesse and Cal and Owen. He could tell by their covetous glances that they knew he was bowling with God, but they were shy about coming over. No need to introduce themselves to God, of course.

So Frank was well on his way to a crackerjack 220 game, not a single twinge from his formerly bad elbow. Relishing his camaraderie with the Almighty, although they hadn't spoken to each other. God occasionally hooked His ball just to keep things interesting. Needless to say, He could roll a perfect game anytime he wanted.

Frank had worked up a sweat. He wondered if after their game he should invite God to have a cold one with him. Maybe get the answers to some questions that had nagged him from childhood. Like what happened to all the methane gas on the Ark when there was only one small window for ventilation? Frank's father had been a dairy farmer near Mendocino, and Frank had grown up mucking out cow barns. He knew that the eight people aboard the Ark with thousands of different species of fauna would have had to shovel shit practically nonstop for the duration of the Flood, or wade around in it up to their necks. But ask a question like that in school, all you got was a ruler across the knuckles from one of the nuns.

In Frank's dream God was about five-ten, gray hair clipped short, muscular, a little saggy around the middle but with a definite aura about him. You just knew He was God, that's all. He had a way of looking at you.

Nearly all of the thirty-six lanes at Oakmoor were filled. An infinity of graceful gliding bowlers like mirror images in shadowless brilliance, that sharp echoing thunder of tumbled pins. The more Frank sweated, the more he thirsted. He retrieved his solid gold ball for the last frame and was embarrassed to discover that there were no holes for his fingers and thumb. Oh-oh. Under the suddenly disapproving gaze of the Big Guy he perspired as if rooted beneath a cloudburst, cradling the heavy gold ball against his midsection, trying to hide it. His friends had vanished. So had the Oakmoor Lanes. The bowling emporium had become a steep ancient street in the Quirinal, at the end of which lay the magnificent Trevi Fountain. Now it was late beneath a cat's-eye moon, and no one was about. Except for Frank's wife Pinky.

She had shed her clothes and was astride the husky shoulders of Triton, calling to him. When he didn't respond Pinky stuck out her tongue, licking the moonlit air, the droplet moisture around the pagan sea-god and his winged horses, a come-on that gave Frank an immediate erection, which he hoped God wouldn't see beneath the gold bowling ball. His trophy of a lifetime. Not counting Pinky.

The ball had become slippery. He lost his grip and it rumbled away down the street, pursued by a snarling pack of wild black dogs. Frank experienced the sort of gloom that can come over a man who finds himself inexplicably in a strange place among strangers, bereft of his God, devoid of Grace.

He awakened with a hand on his hard penis. The other side of the king-size bed was rumpled but empty. The door to the sitting room was nearly closed; a vertical slash of lamplight glowed in the darkened bedroom. Frank sat up, straightened his twisted pajama top over his convex belly, glanced at the digital clock on an antique commode—it was past two in the morning—and went silently to the sitting-room door. He hesitated there, didn't open it. Instead he looked through the half-inch space at his wife, who was seated in profile to him twenty feet away.

Pinky had ordered room service again. She was eating voraciously. It was what she ate and how she handled her late-night snack that disturbed him so.

On the plate she was hunched over was a large serving of ground beefsteak tartare. And Pinky was eating with her fingers, shoving the raw meat into her mouth as fast as she could gobble and swallow. There was blood on her fingers and blood on her chin; because steak tartare was served raw but not bloody Frank reckoned she must have bit her lip or tongue. A strand of blood mixed with saliva hung almost to the free-swinging crucifix on the chain around her neck, which she took off only to bathe. Twice while he watched in amazement and—yes—disgust, she lifted her head to gulp air. Then she bent to the task of cleaning her plate, a fierce gleam in her eyes.

The Tubners had been married twenty-four years. In all the time Frank had known Pinky she hadn't been much of a meat-eater. Preferred seafood. A broiled lamb chop on occasion, if they were dining out. But steak tartare? *Never.* And of all places to suddenly develop an appetite for it. Three nights in a row.

Pinky had almost finished. She picked up noisettes left on the plate, then licked her fingers. He heard a low groan, or growl, of pleasure. Then she turned her head quickly, as if she had detected him spying on her from behind the door. But she couldn't make him out in the dark of the bedroom, Frank was sure of that. Anyway, her eyes were unfocused, drowsy, now that her hunger was satisfied.

Frank retreated to the bed and pulled up the covers. A little later Pinky came quietly into the room and entered the bath. Frank heard her pissing, then the handles squeaking as she turned on the bidet and "watered her flower." As she liked to say.

Twenty years since their second and last child had been born. But Pinky was only forty-seven, not yet menopausal. It was possible that she was pregnant, and just hadn't wanted to say anything yet. Still getting used to the idea herself.

Yes, pregnancy could account for Pinky's otherwise unexplainable craving, her lack of caution in spite of recent outbreaks of mad cow disease on the Continent.

Frank breathed easier, although the idea of raising another child at their age wasn't entirely welcome. They already were grandparents. Frank recalled dietary mismatches she'd blithely concocted during her first two pregnancies. Peanut butter with sweet potatoes. Ketchup on her pancakes—dear Lord, it gave him heartburn to think about it.

Pinky got into bed like a little mouse so as not to disturb him. When he felt her cold but clean hand momentarily on the back of his neck, he was all nerve ends, flinching beneath the covers.

"Oh, I just wanted to touch you. I'm sorry. Good night, Fuzzi-nuts."

"Good night, baby duck."

"Love you, Frank."

"Love you too."

SAN FRANCISCO · OCTOBER 16 · 11:00 A.M. PDT

Megan Pardo's uncle and aunt lived on Russian Hill, half a block from that famous part of Lombard Street that made its brick-paved, serpentine way downhill between Hyde and Leavenworth. Eden Waring and Chauncey McLain left the house where they had spent the night and caught the Powell-Hyde cable car for the precipitous drop down the bay side of Russian Hill to the end of the line.

It had been gray-blue skies and pale sun atop Russian Hill; halfway down there was fog and the sun disappeared.

When they left the car at the Hyde turntable, visibility was fifty feet. Car and truck fog lights tinted the gloom a hellish saffron shade;

fuming neon faded away along the street. The temperature here on Frisco Bay was ten degrees cooler—in the high fifties—than it had been a few minutes ago.

Eden was wearing the red sweater and Masai headband, articles of identification for Mr. Edmund Ruddy, Betts's former flame, about whom Danny Cheng, the Information Man, had provided Eden the basics of his life. Ruddy had attended USF when Betts was a student there, later worked for a Bay Area corporation. Twenty-three years and out the door, early retirement and his pension. For the past two years he had lived in a duplex condo in an East Bay community but was seldom around, according to the neighbors. A lifelong bachelor, he spent a great deal of time traveling in his Winnebago and indulging a passion for fly-fishing. According to the photo on his driver's license, he looked like ten other men you could expect to run into during any week of the year. On the nerdy side, with gray bangs and a shaggy gray mustache (nerdy men never seemed to realize that the mustaches they grew only emphasized their nerdiness). He wore glasses with heavy black rims. Those, at least, were making a come-back within the literary/intellectual set. He was fifty-six, a year older than Betts. There seemed to be nothing about Edmund Ruddy that would have sustained Betts's (secret) interest in him all these years. But you just never could tell, Eden thought, looking around in the soup. Her teeth chattered; her face felt clammy. She hadn't been able to manage breakfast, and ice seemed to be forming inside the hollow of her stomach.

"I c-could have done without this," she said, tucking Tom Sherard's lion's-head walking stick under her right arm.

"Which way to Ghirardelli Square?" Chauncey asked with a canarylike tilt of her pert blond head.

"Opposite direction from the Cannery, which is over there," Eden said, pointing. "I think Ghirardelli's only a block or two."

Traffic was moderately heavy, mostly delivery trucks and vans. There were not many tourists about on this Wednesday morning. Only half a dozen people had left the cable car with them: a young Chinese couple who had been waiting at their stop on Russian Hill, and a family of four. All of them, including a girl who looked to be about eight years old, had New York accents and that aggressive chumminess of family groups who communicate largely through bickering.

The New Yorkers headed for the Cannery, large old buildings converted in the sixties to a mall and a museum. The Chinese couple looked around as if they were lost. She was wearing a purple break-fast orchid pinned to the lapel of her pinstriped suit jacket. They talked in low voices—their language—sorting out a mild disagreement with the politesse of newlyweds on a new and still precarious level of intimacy. Eden and Chauncey walked ahead of them to Ghirardelli Square.

There was something invigorating about a good fog. Waterside chill, droplets of moisture on Eden's hair, the tips of her eyelashes. Pigeons materializing in glum nearly motionless groups as the Square opened up to them. Seagulls glided at the upper limits of visibility. There were more people now, congregated around the welcoming burnished lights of shops and cafés across Fountain Plaza in the old red-brick buildings of a former chocolate factory. Bronze mermaids sat back-to-back with the modest fountain plume between them. There were, on a fogbound morning, fountain-sitters, most of them solitary and as still as the mermaids, others eating from paper bags as pigeons waddled close to check for handouts.

Eden looked around at bodies half realized in the fuming grayness, faces dim as saintly frescoes in a medieval church. She felt like a wildfire in her red turtleneck sweater. Against her better judgment she was about to trust someone she'd never seen before.

"I smell coffee," Chauncey said.

"Good a place as any to wait," Eden agreed, shuddering.

They were crossing the plaza when one of the fountain-sitters, wearing a hooded cape and holding a shopping bag, raised her head to look at them.

"Eden," she said, in a frail but recognizable voice, "I'm here."

Eden stopped as if she'd come within an inch of walking off a cliff.

"*Betts?*"

"Yes, dear one."

They were about thirty feet apart. Betts made an attempt to rise as Eden sprinted across the bricks toward her, scattering pigeons in a brisk flurry. One of the pigeons flew close to Betts's head and she tottered, the shopping bag falling from her hand. The loose hood fell back from her face. Betts's short gray haircut was unfamiliar, but not her hazel eyes nor the rest of her features, such as the tiny mole high on her upper lip.

Eden lunged to help her, but Betts recovered her balance rather easily and faced Eden with a peculiar slanted smile, right hand coming out from under the short cape.

"Hel*lo,* lovey." This time the voice was not at all recognizable. Eden only knew that it wasn't Betts talking.

Eden! Knife!

Eden reacted to the telepathic warning with the reflexes of a gifted athlete, jerking her head aside a fraction of a second before she saw the blade in the Assassin's hand slicing in a short arc toward her throat. Instead of slitting the carotid artery, the sharp blade glanced off the gold lion's head of the walking stick in Eden's left hand. Before the Assassin, exceptionally quick himself, could reverse his initial thrust with the knife, Eden hit him in the padded breast with her lowered right shoulder, sending him sprawling over the fountain's ledge into the water.

She looked down in a moment of horrified incomprehension at Betts's cunningly duplicated face underwater, at a contact lens that had popped out of one eye and clung to mascara'd lower lashes like a worn penny, at the gray wig now askew from the collision of the Assassin's head with the coin-strewn bottom of the fountain. Then he scrambled up and was coming for her again.

"*Simba!*" Eden said.

The plenipotent walking stick leaped from her hand, the lion's head coming to life. It met the knife thrust in midair as Eden stood her ground and snapped the blade in its jaws. The stout stick flashed like a propeller and struck the Assassin under the chin, snapping his head back. The soggy wig flew off, leaving strips of tape fluttering, a line of glued-down latex visible across his scarred head. He would have been in the fountain again, but the lion's head had grasped him and was holding him erect, feet dangling several inches above the fountain's ledge. Dazed, he stared down at Eden with mismatched eyes.

Six seconds had elapsed since Eden had heard the telepathic warning. They had attracted some attention from the fountain-sitters, but devoutly minding your own business in a city like San Francisco was always the wisest course.

"Wow," Chauncey said behind Eden. "Where can I get one of *those*?"

A sixteen-passenger van crossed the plaza and stopped close to them. Eden turned and looked past Chauncey at the young Chinese couple who had followed them to Ghirardelli Square. He had a gun in his hand. The girl was smiling.

"Hi," she said. "I'm Lu Ping. This is Ted; he's a private detective." She looked up at the suspended Assassin leaking blood from a corner of the mouth he had redrawn to more closely resemble Betts Waring's. "Guess you got my message okay," the Psi-active Lu Ping said to Eden, no longer smiling. She regarded the hung-up Assassin, who was half conscious and had a broken jaw, with martial sternness. "I never expected to run into this sack of pig offal again. Our ride is here. Do you need help getting him into the van?"

"Why should I go anywhere with you?" Eden said.

"I forgot to mention, Danny Cheng is my uncle? He thought there was something, you know, fishy about all this, so that's why—"

"I have to find Betts! Do you know this bastard?" Eden's shakes had returned. "What's going on? Why is he made-up to look like Betts? Why did he try to kill me?"

"We'll find out. Don't worry. Right now we had better get the lead out, Eden."

Unaware as a daydreaming child of time passing, Eden silently watched thoroughbred horses and colts, ten of them in shades of ebony, chestnut, or bay, in a fenced pasture of an astonishing green that brimmed and flowed with glossy light when the sun returned, powerfully, from behind clouds piled like a gilt-edged snowbank above the Marin Peninsula. The horse farm belonged to Danny Cheng and his elderly father Chien-Chi; it was, Danny's niece Lu Ping had confided to Eden, one of his several enterprises, like antiques, that were visible on the surface of Danny's complex business affairs.

Chauncey McLain kept Eden company and observed her need for silence. Chauncey liked the horses, their every liquid, elegant movement evidence of important speed, but none of them would come near her, no matter how she coaxed or attempted bribes with treats she had appropriated from the kitchen of the low white farmhouse with its overhanging roof of bloodred quarry tile. Sugar cubes, carrots, apple sections—nothing lured the horses to the fence. Possibly they all sensed what was alien in her. In both girls, perhaps: the other with her closely held African walking stick of mysterious properties and, when called for, occult force.

Finally Chauncey gave up her efforts and tossed the fruit and carrots into the pasture. She unclipped the pager Danny Cheng had given her from her belt and glanced at the message.

"They want us at the house. Maybe Lu Ping was able to get something out of—*him*."

Eden looked at Chauncey, folded her lower lip tight between her teeth but still said nothing. Worry was like a fever in her eyes. They got into a golf cart and Chauncey drove them the quarter mile up to the house.

Lu Ping sat with her uncle on a small patio outside of Danny's office, which was dominated by a mainframe computer. He wore dark glasses, the third pair Eden had seen today. The lenses of these glasses tightly fitted the sockets of his eyes. Lu Ping looked as if she were getting a few minutes of fresh air following a lengthy illness. Her skin color a cloudy shade of brass.

She looked at Eden and shook her head slowly, wincing as if in apology.

"Is Betts dead?"

"I don't know, Eden. Couldn't find out."

"Let me try, then," Eden said with quiet savagery. The gold head of the charmed walking stick flashed above her clenched fist.

"We could steam his balls in a sauna," Danny Cheng said thoughtfully, "then stab them with a fork. But even that probably wouldn't get a reaction. He's in a state of tonic immobility. He sits where you put him, doesn't move for hours. Raise one of his arms, even into an awkward position, it stays suspended in the air. Mind's in lockdown. Extreme dementia."

"He's faking!" Eden cried.

Lu Ping shook her head again.

"But I would know. You can't deceive a Peeper. There's no mind left. I was in there. It's like an old empty movie house. Projector's running, flickety-flick, but all that's on the screen is a single repetitious memory of—" She paused. Her glossy black hair that she wore tightly pulled back into a single elaborate braid reminded Eden of a playmate she'd once envied, because her own hair as a child had been too lax and flyaway for supple braiding. Lu Ping tugged mnemonically at her braid, which was draped over one shoulder like a Victorian bellpull. "—A terrible thing that happened to him, probably when he was very young."

"An accident? Is that how he got that face?"

"No. The incident he's totally focused on, that he has ritualized as part of his trauma, had an even more drastic effect on his psyche. I saw him taking these . . . *things* out of a bloody feed sack. Slowly. One by one. Kittens, puppies, who knows, they were destroyed to the point they're unrecognizable. Just lumps of flesh and mashed bone. He sits with his scabby little legs crossed and the sack between them, removing, holding each little body, laying them in a neat row in front of him. Tears? No tears, he's too deep in shock. He goes to a great deal of trouble to be sure the row is perfectly straight, the bodies evenly spaced." Lu Ping's own eyes watered; she wiped her lower eyelashes. "Devastating. Once the sack is empty, there's almost a total void in his—adult—mind. He's aware of lights, voices. Doesn't know where he is. External stimuli have no coherence. Then the childhood memory repeats. It's chilling."

"I couldn't care less about his crummy childhood." Eden looked at Danny Cheng. "You said he was a professional assassin."

"Yes."

"Working for the FBI."

"No, not recently. My information is that Impact Sector was purged along with some other rotten elements at the Bureau when Nick Grella was appointed director a few months ago."

"Not all of the rotten elements, apparently. I almost had my throat cut this morning."

With thumb and forefinger Danny massaged a somewhat cruel-looking but sensual mouth. He was a handsome man in spite of weak eyes he hid behind the several changes of dark glasses and an occasional bout of shakes and sweats Danny amiably identified as his "three-minute ague."

"I think the Assassin was acting for someone else."

"Doesn't matter right now. He used Betts to get at me. If he took her place in Ghirardelli Square, means he didn't need Betts anymore—doesn't it?" she added with aggressive anxiety. Her eyes flashed to Lu Ping. "Where is she? Alive? Dead? I have to *know*!"

"I'm sorry, Eden. I tried. It won't come from him."

"Do you mean today? When *will* he get over this 'immobility' bullshit? Next week? Next year? *Never?*"

Danny shrugged slightly. Lu Ping looked at the patio floor. Eden walked away from everyone, shouldering her oppressive burden of fears, getting her face under fragile control.

"Yeah, okay," she said in a quieter voice. "Thanks for trying to help. Coming to my rescue. What are you going to do with that head case you've got in the barn loft?"

"Waste disposal," Danny said after a few moments, "is another business I'm invested in. Meanwhile Teddy is keeping an eye on him, and a finger on the trigger of his Bullpup."

Eden nodded grimly, and turned back to them.

"Does anyone remember what happened to the Assassin's knife?"

Danny looked at Lu Ping, who shook her head. Chauncey said, "Your friendly lion bit the blade in half. The Assassin dropped the rest when his jaw was broken."

Eden said, "It could still be there, by the fountain. Who would want to pick up a knife with a busted blade? Chauncey, I need to find it."

"Why?" Danny asked her.

"If Betts is dead, and he, that sorry shit, killed her with the knife he was going to use on me, I'll know. Just by touching it."

"Telekinesis," Lu Ping explained to her uncle Danny.

"Doesn't always work for me," Eden said. "I need to have a lot of emotional energy invested in order to get feedback." Her lips were chalky. "Like now. But if it happened, I'll be able to see—when. Where."

Danny was already on his feet. "Let's get going," he said.

PLEASANT HILL, CALIFORNIA · OCTOBER 16 · 4:25 P.M. PDT

The weather north of Missoula had turned, with snow squalls accompanying plunging temperatures for the second day, so Edmund Ruddy returned ahead of time from his two-week fishing trip to Montana to find someone else's Winnebago motor home jutting out into the drive from one of his allotted parking spaces beside his snugly covered BMW convertible.

The elaborate covenants of the Heather Ridge garden condos complex in the East Bay community of Pleasant Hill prohibited residents from leaving motor homes, boats, or trailers anywhere but in the fenced, key-entry lot in a far corner of the thirty-six-acre grounds, out of sight behind a tall screen of Italian cypress.

Ed's reaction was irritation and indignation. He checked with those neighbors he could find at home, but they didn't know who the unwelcome Winnebago belonged to. It was late on Sunday. There were a couple of relief handymen in Maintenance, neither of whom spoke good English. No help there.

After unloading his gear and leaving it in the foyer of his two-bedroom unit, he drove to the out-of-the-way parking lot and left his own twenty-one-foot motor home there. Trudged back past the north tennis courts and the indoor pool pavilion with its tall windows opaque from condensation. Brooded about the intrusion on *his* space. They were probably weekend visitors unfamiliar with the rules, but they could be anywhere. There were four hundred condos situated for maximum privacy along the winding, hilly drives.

Or, just possibly, someone was inside. The Winnebago's engine wasn't running, but the sun had been in and out of clouds and the temperature was only in the high fifties.

Before leaving a firmly worded note taped to the door, he knocked and called, "Excuse me? Anyone here?"

No reply. Ed shrugged; it was all he could do, but there was still that tiny kernel of indignation bobbing around in his heart. He was a man of order in a disorderly world. He left the reprimanding note and went into his house, closing the door firmly. Here he was in control. He had no wife and kept no pets. He enjoyed his library, his old shellac recordings of Irish tenors, and his coin collection of early American issues, worth a tidy sum, recession-proof.

He turned on a lamp in the front room where he watched television and had his solitary meals on a tray. Then he crossed the parquet hall floor to the kitchen to make coffee.

The coffee was already on.

Ed stared at the coffeemaker, at a used cup and saucer and crumpled paper napkin on the counter. Beside the coffeemaker there was half a bag of a speciality blend he knew about but never would have bought for his own pleasure because it was both hard to locate and damned expensive.

Then he saw the message that had been left for him on the chalk-board mounted on the wall by the refrigerator, Things To Do Today.

Upstairs, Ed, and make it snappy!!

His heart lurched; the skin on his forearms crept coldly and made livid wormlike ridges, as if he were breaking out in hives. His throat closed when he looked up at the ceiling in response to a muted spectral thumping.

Ed's bedroom was above the kitchen. He grabbed the tool closest to hand, a meat tenderizer with studded metal plates on the mallet head. A glance at the space where the cordless phone was plugged in, but only the recharger remained on the wall. The other phone was, of course, beside his bed.

Parquet steps to the second floor of the duplex condo, the staircase lined with framed photos of his departed parents—as teenagers during the last Great Depression; as newlyweds far from St. Joe, Missouri, in even more turbulent times, his father wearing the uniform of an officer in the Army Air Corps; and posed, finally, white-haired, in a tenderly lit portrait for their twenty-fifth wedding anniversary. Ed had not known until he was well into his thirties that his parents were first cousins. A subject no one in the family, those survivors who knew about it, had ever touched on. No matter; he cherished them still, and sometimes reflected on the passion that had made it unbearable for them to ever be apart, fortunate to have had each other in spite of the inevitable censure and muted scandal back home. Memories—trampled on, despoiled by an intruder in *his home*. Nearing the top of the stairs, Ed got his voice back, more or less.

"Whoever you are! I have studied aikido for five years! I won't hesitate to use what I know to defend myself!"

He paused, eyes on his bedroom door a few feet away. The meat-tenderizer mallet raised in his right hand like a Vandal's mace.

"I want you to come out *now* with your hands on the top of your head!"

Thump. Thump. As if someone was—but he couldn't be sure. The sound seemed, however, unthreatening. A helpless kind of banging. On the concave walnut headboard of his bed? It also had been his parents' bed. He had been conceived there, probably, had first lain in the bed beside his mother when he was two days old. Ed had tears in his eyes, but he was furious. Edmund Ruddy was not someone you could push around and expect to get away with it.

He stood back from the door, reached out for the cut-glass knob with his left hand. Turned it, pushed the door open with a cautious foot. Light from the hall illuminated the inside of his bedroom like a torch in a cave.

The figure on the bed leaped out at him in shadowy relief. It was a woman, bound hand and foot and with a wide, soiled, double layer of adhesive tape across her mouth. She wore a flashy aluminum-gray jogging suit with red piping. She was pushing strenuously against the headboard with the top of her head, nostrils pinched and white as she sucked in air. Her hair was so short she appeared to have a crew cut. The bumping of the headboard against the wall beneath a small Winslow Homer seascape (it had been in the family for eighty years) was what he was hearing. Her eyes were tightly closed, face a mottled red and glistening with perspiration.

Edmund Ruddy switched on the overhead lighting fixture, bringing new definition to familiar things. He was alert for further surprises, someone else lunging at him from the closet or bathroom. Heartbeat at full acceleration. But what caught his eye was a white business envelope that was cheerily pinned to the jacket of the jogging outfit with one of those ready-made Christmas wrap bows, green with twinkly threads of gold.

"Stop that!" Ed said sharply.

Her eyes opened and she looked toward the doorway. Probably she saw more of the meat tenderizer in his hand than she did of his face. She shook her head furiously, now fighting the tight cords holding ankles and wrists together and to the bed frame on either side.

It occurred to Ed that she assumed he was there to silence her with the mallet. But the glimpse he'd had of her eyes and that curt head-shake, accompanied by a clenching of jaw muscles, were images that bolted at him from the mists of thirty-odd years ago. No one else like her, ever; one reason why he had gone unwed until, really, it was too late to think about—

"Oh, dear God! Betts? Betts *Burkhalter*?"

TWO

MAKING FRIENDS WITH DEATH

THE DEVIL IS ANY GOD WHO BEGINS TO EXACT OBEDIENCE.

—JOHN COOPER POWYS

LAS VEGAS, NEVADA · OCTOBER 19 · 2:00 P.M. PDT

They had been in Las Vegas barely long enough to unpack in their room at the Brazilian-themed mega-resort called Bahìa, and already Lewis Gruvver's girlfriend Charmaine was complaining.

"Lew-is, you're on vacation! I thought we were in Las Vegas to have *fun*."

"We are, baby. Cornell and Lourdes are taking us to dinner at the Eiffel Tower Restaurant. It's up the Strip there in the Paris Hotel. Then we have tickets to see 'Legends of Doo-wop' at the Riviera."

"*Le Tour Eiffel*," Charmaine said. She was a senior at Clark Atlanta University, majoring in computer science. But she had taken two years of French and was in the habit of repeating something he'd said in the Gallic language. Working on her accent. Gruvver had been going with her for three and a half months and still found this cute. Other quirks he just put up with. He was willing to put up with a lot from Charmaine. Most of her complaints were concluded with an appealing smile. She was beautiful as well as smart, cool as chocolate mint, and so graceful she could slip between the drops of a spring rain. She put on blue jeans like a snake getting back into its skin.

Wearing only bikini briefs for now, Charmaine was riffling through an entertainment guide she had picked up in the room, which was furnished in blond bamboo, decorated in shades of orange, pink, and pistachio. There were two large paintings of parrots over the bed. The room was about as restful as a pinched nerve.

" 'Elvis Presley in concert'? Thought the man died."

"He did. Now he's a legend. That's an Elvis impersonator you're looking at. It's kind of a new-age art form."

"Are all the entertainers here legends?" Charmaine said, turning more pages.

"Guaranteed." Lewis was changing out of the jeans and sweatshirt he'd worn on the flight from Atlanta, which had arrived late. He checked the time, then chose a light blue shirt with a button-down collar to go with his dark gray summer suit.

"I hate it you're going off and leaving me. Why can't I go too?"

"It's business. Unofficial, but still business."

"*Police* business?"

"Yeah." He leaned toward Charmaine and kissed the bridge of her nose. "While I'm gone you can visit the spa."

"The one where it said in the brochure they have a 'Zen relaxation and meditation chamber'?"

"Uh-huh."

Charmaine tossed the entertainment weekly on the double bed and looked out the window. From the fifteenth floor the view north took in the faux skyscrapers of New York New York, Bellagio, and Caesars Palace on the west side of the Strip. To the west, where the sky was the color of a molten steel ingot at two in the afternoon, there was a desert mountain range that she whimsically saw as a scarred, miles-long, burnt-out dragon. Near the highest peak, where she would have expected the dragon's eye, she saw instead something like a million-carat diamond embedded in a blue fold halfway to the blazing sky.

"Lew, what's that way out there?"

He paused while buttoning his shirt and looked over her bare shoulder.

"Couldn't say for sure, but it might be the Lincoln Grayle Theatre."

"*Le théâtre du Grayle.*" Charmaine turned and brushed a cheek against his. One hand groped playfully behind her to his trouserless lower half.

"Sure you need to go someplace?" She closed her eyes and sighed for emphasis. "What I have here is a part of you that wants to stay in this hotel room with me."

"We got three whole days yet. Promise you, I'm back in an hour. Okay, fifty-nine minutes. *Ohh*, now. Easy."

"Easy? You're the one taught me to play the meat flute. I was pure as granny's boiled milk 'til Lewis Gruvver showed up in my life. Now look how shameless. I just want to practice practice practice all the *time.*"

"My sweet Lord! Fifty-*eight* minutes, and I don't lie."

"Well . . . maybe I'll just go down to the pool for a little while, save that spa for when I'm needin' a real tune-up."

"Now you're talking."

Charmaine mercifully let him go and rummaged through her carry-on for a swim ensemble, holding up a couple of bikinis for his approval. Gruvver could've put her entire bikini collection in his wallet.

"What did you say Cornell was to you again?"

He quickly finished dressing. "My half brother. From Chicago. He works undercover for Gambling Control, and Lourdes, she's a shop steward in the Culinary Workers' local. They've done real well for themselves. Four-bedroom house with a black-bottom pool. We'll be over there Saturday for a western-style barbecue. Lourdes says ordinary hotel maids were earning thirty large a year in Vegas until the economy tanked and some of the hotels here started goin' under."

"Your half bro's married to a Mexican woman?"

"No, she's from Honduras. This knot in my tie look okay?"

"Yes, stop fussin' with it. You calling on royalty? *Les royauté?*"

"Part of the job is always to look professional. Gets them to respect you right up front."

"Big-bucks white folks, you're talking about."

" 'Specially them," Gruvver said.

The Spicer family, Jack and Shelley and their two young children, lived in the priciest section of Lake Las Vegas, a gated community called "Miramonte." Waterfront villas in Miramonte started at a million-five. Gruvver drove in his rental car the seventeen miles from the heart of the Strip and waited a few minutes at the gatehouse while the guard confirmed his appointment with Mrs. Spicer. Then he followed directions to a mustard-yellow house with tiled roofs that was surrounded by feather-duster palms. A sailboat was tied up at the dock below the house. Gruvver parked in the circular stone-paved drive near a garage that housed a red Humvee, a vintage sixties 'Vette, and a golf cart. He remembered to leave the windows on the rental down. It was autumn in Las Vegas, but daytime temperatures still approached ninety. He followed a serpentine walk through a grotto with an arched roof of pierced concrete to double front doors.

A Hispanic girl in a smock took him to an interior courtyard. Large enough for a swimming pool, date palms, purple bougainvillea, a waterfall at one end of the pool. There were parakeets in a large ornate cage. The girl asked Gruvver if he'd like a drink, then served him fresh lemonade from a refrigerator concealed in a rock wall. Cool mist drifted over the courtyard from nozzles in that same wall, holding down the heat.

Shelley Spicer was a tall, thin woman with the gloomy face of someone whose liver needs flushing. About forty, dyed red hair dark at the edges like petals of a frost-nipped rose. She came briskly out of a wing of the sprawling house as if she had another destination in mind, then detoured when she saw him, unexpectedly black and looking right at home beside her pool.

"Mr. Grover?"

"It's Gruvver, Mrs. Spicer," he said, getting to his feet. "Lewis Gruvver." He handed her a business card, the one that identified him as a detective but didn't mention the homicide division.

She motioned for him to take his seat again. "I was in Atlanta once," she said, sitting on the edge of a yellow glider near him, knees together and at an angle. She looked mildly uncomfortable, as if she'd never learned to manage her height well. "For a convention. My husband is a cardiologist. The heat was just awful. You feel it more in the South, they said, because the humidity is so high most of the time."

"Yes, it is."

"And you're here to inquire about Lise Ruppenthal? I thought we had put that dreadful business in India behind us."

"Yes, she's in prison, probably for the rest of her life."

Shelley Spicer stared at Gruvver for a few seconds, as if she were on the brink of dismissing him.

"I was one of the investigators assigned to the murder of Pledger Lee Skeldon three weeks ago."

More seconds ticked by.

"I'm afraid I—"

"There are similarities in the attack on the guru in India and the attack on the evangelist in Atlanta. A Las Vegas hotel worker made an attempt on the life of the Dalai Lama in Los Angeles this past February. His attacker also tried to bite through the carotid artery."

Shelley Spicer drew her thin shoulders together with an expression of distaste.

"I hadn't heard about that." She hesitated. "But I was—I have to admit—struck by the account of Reverend Skeldon's death. Because of what I remembered about—Sai Rampa was his name, wasn't it?"

"That's right. A holy man of great prestige. Did Lise Ruppenthal ever mention Rampa to you?"

"No."

"Was she into Eastern religions?"

"Not as far as I know. I'm sure she would have had books or something in her room."

"How long did Lise work for you, Mrs. Spicer?"

"A little over a year. I hired her to look after Jack Junior and Tracy on the recommendation of an English couple we know well. Lise had been employed by the Claringtons for several months, but because of the miserable winter weather in Liverpool she was developing serious asthma. A change to our dry high-desert climate seemed a likely remedy. She looked so wan and tired when she arrived, but there was a change for the better almost immediately."

"Were you satisfied with her job performance?"

"Oh, yes. Jack Junior and Tracy adored Lise. All I expect of our help is that they be clean, honest, responsible, and patient with the children, who I know can be a handful."

Spoiled rotten, Gruvver thought with an understanding smile for Shelley Spicer.

"I've had the devil of a time finding an au pair half as good as Lise," she continued, as if his smile were an invitation to vent. "Even the ones sent by the best agencies in Europe find Las Vegas too much of a temptation. After they've worked here two or three months— and it's the same story for our friends who also have small children— the girls quit to become cocktail waitresses. Or worse."

"But Lise didn't stick around Las Vegas after giving notice?"

"No. We drove her to the airport, where she caught a flight direct to Frankfurt."

"Did she give a reason why she wanted to leave? Trouble with a boyfriend, family problem in Germany?"

"Frankly I don't know what was in her head. And she gave *no* notice. She said only that she must leave immediately. Well, I thought—we had a better relationship than that. It was so unlike Lise. I offered to pay her twelve hundred a year more, and co-sign a note for a car of her own." Shelley Spicer massaged her throat as if swallowing hurt. "I don't think she even heard me."

"How was she acting? Nervous, distracted?"

"No. She was calm but uncommunicative. Up to the moment she was to board her plane. Then she threw her arms around me. I couldn't be angry with her any longer. She was—such a dear child, really. And I had a sense that—but this can't be of any help to you."

"I'm very interested in whatever impressions you might have, Mrs. Spicer."

"Well—this is hard to put into words. I just felt that although I was holding Lise, she wasn't *there* anymore. As if the Lise I'd come to know had undergone some sort of radical change of personality, literally overnight."

"Like Jimmy Nixon."

"Who? Oh, that was the name of the boy in Atlanta. But wasn't he insane?"

"We'll never know. He died yesterday without having regained consciousness. Did you have any indication that Lise might be doing drugs?"

"Oh, *no*! Never. And believe me, I know the symptoms. Sean McGriskin, Peggy's oldest—but that's another unhappy story."

"After she left Las Vegas, did you hear from Lise again?"

"I was very surprised to receive a card from her, from India. There wasn't much of a message. She had been thinking about us and hoped we were all well. Then—three weeks later, was it? That photo of her in the Sunday edition of the London paper Jack buys at Borders. The Indian police took it, I suppose. The photo really didn't look much like her, but the name, Lise Ruppenthal, jumped out at me. Now she's in what I suppose must be a dank, vermin-ridden—Lise was *always* so clean and tidy." Her lugubrious eyes glinted moistly. "Sometimes, when the children were in bed and Lise was fresh from her bath, I'd drop by her room and do her nails for her. And we'd talk. She always was so grateful for the scents and oils I brought her from Neiman's. I enjoyed those times with Lise so much. I miss—"

Shelley Spicer turned her face from Gruvver, to stanch a seep of tears with her fingertips and sniff deeply.

"There's really nothing more to tell you; Jack and the children will be home from tennis at the club any minute now."

Obvious to Gruvver that she didn't want a black man, even a detective, in the house when they did show up.

"I appreciate you taking the time to talk to me, Mrs. Spicer. I was wondering, how did Lise spend her days off? Did she date anyone on a steady basis?"

"There were young men, I suppose; none of them called for her here. Her best friend was a Danish au pair who worked for the Stockwells. Finnish or Danish. She left last month to be married. I can't recall her name. She rode a motorcycle, and was teaching Lise how to ride. I was concerned about that, but I kept mum. They often went to shows together. Rock concerts at Thomas and Mack."

"Magic shows?"

"No doubt. They're very popular; all of the major illusionists are in Las Vegas. Since you mentioned magic—Jack and I took Lise to see Penn and Teller at Rio shortly after she came here. She was enthralled." Shelley Spicer paused, rubbing her high forehead between the temples. "Lise was in the habit of keeping the ticket stubs from shows she'd seen, sticking them inside the frame around the mirror on the makeup table in her room. I was going to throw them all out after Lise left, but Tracy wanted them for a collage she was making. Tracy has considerable artistic ability for a twelve-year-old."

"Would she still have the collage she wanted the ticket stubs for?"

"Oh, yes. I saw it in her room yesterday."

"All right if I have a look at it?"

"I suppose," Shelley Spicer said, with a frown to indicate her lack of interest in continuing the conversation.

"Thank you, Mrs. Spicer. Then I need to be on my way."

Charmaine was still by the pool or had gone shopping when Lewis Gruvver returned to their hyperchromatic room at Bahìa. He hung up his good suit and blue shirt and sat down on the bed in boxer shorts to review the photos he had taken with his new digital camera of Tracy Spicer's Las Vegas collage, which the precocious Tracy had named "Freekorama." She had worked twelve of Lise Ruppenthal's ticket stubs into the four-foot-long collage along with a spectacle of faces, off-the-wall characters, citizens of the underlife, their fly-blown karma captured fleetingly by disconsolate daylight. Some old desert jasper, his smile poignant in its lackadaisical toothlessness. A one-eyed man in a beret, shoulder-length hair with a despoiled whiteness like the wings of a dead angel. A woman who told fortunes in a mobile home, muumuu and turban, small barefoot children sitting cross-legged at her feet with that eerie nowhere directness in their gazes. A man with a handlebar mustache that hung down to his bare deltoids hawking photos of Elvis in his coffin. Autographed. A nearly naked young woman with tufts of orange and blue hair and a ballsy leer for the camera, playing cards tattooed all over her body. (Gruvver wondered if she had an ace in the hole.) Elderly women whose only known addresses were the nickel slot rows in some of the low-roller casinos.

He used the credit-card-size magnifying lens he always carried in his wallet to closely examine the ticket stubs, and found that three of the shows Lise had attended were at the Lincoln Grayle Theatre. The last time she'd seen the show was three days before she boarded the plane for Germany. Across the face of the stub Lise had written *"Lucky!"*

While he was pondering this information, Charmaine came in carrying a small gift shop bag.

"What is this doo-wop business anyhow?"

"Three-part harmony with bass and a lead singer. Those little records that I collect."

"Oh, yeah. All those old-timers. Martha and the Vanderbilts. Dell and the Vikings. The Planters."

"They don't come any better," Gruvver said with a slight wince, once again reminded in a subtle way that he was thirteen years older than Charmaine. What was that, half a generation?

"I can listen to it," she said, giving him a glance to see if that made him proud of her. She sat beside Gruvver on the bed and kicked her sandals off. "What are you looking for, Lewis?"

"I think I just found another Lucky Ticket holder at the Lincoln Grayle Theatre. Like Jimmy Nixon, and who knows? Maybe others I don't know about yet."

"What's it mean?"

"Means they got to meet the Man Himself after his show. Some sort of promotional thing he does."

Charmaine stood long enough to shuck off her tank top and unbuckle her short skirt. She sat down again, a sleek thigh pressed against his.

"What's that got to do with your police business?"

"I don't know yet. Maybe I'll know more after I talk to Grayle."

"Oh, are we gonna get lucky too?"

"I'll see if Cornell or someone he knows can make an arrangement for me."

Charmaine walked the fingers of her right hand down Gruvver's bulky quadriceps.

"Lewis, did you ever notice how our legs are almost exactly the same length? Maybe you got half an inch on me."

Gruvver put his camera aside.

"Yeah, and right now I've got about seven and a half inches *for* you."

Charmaine undid her bra and lay back on the bed, stretching, arms above her head.

"Practice practice practice," she said. "We've got almost an hour until they do the pirate battle at the Treasure Island again."

ROME · OCTOBER 21 · 7:10 P.M.

Eden Waring's doppelganger was crossing the outrageously *luxe* lobby of the Excelsior Hotel on the Via Veneto when she heard Eden's name called—rather, the name she used while in Kenya, Eve Bell.

She looked around and there was Lincoln Grayle, casual in a yellow cashmere sweater, V neck, nothing worn underneath, and khakis, half a dozen newspapers under one arm. Gwen felt a little stunned momentarily, recovered with a gracious smile.

"Hello! Aren't you supposed to be in Zimbabwe?"

"Aren't you supposed to be in Kenya?"

A few heads turned at this exchange, as if those overhearing expected a couple of rootless characters from a Hemingway story. He gripped her shoulder lightly with his free hand and kissed her as she was laughing. Settled on his heels and looked at her with his own trace of surprise but warmly pleased, as if he'd been handed a valuable, unexpected gift on a day that otherwise hadn't gone well. Like her own day.

"You first," Gwen urged.

He shrugged. "The whole trip was a bust," he said. "Except for meeting you, of course. First the plane we chartered out of Nairobi had engine trouble, and we turned back. Laid over at the Norfolk when we couldn't get another plane; then in the morning we heard that the hotel we were booked into at Victoria Falls burned during the night. Sixty percent of it was destroyed, no casualties, fortunately. Some of our crew were already staying there."

"Oh, the Elephant Hills," Gwen said, researching Eden's memory. "Sure, I've heard of it. The world's largest thatched roof, or something." She paused, still smiling, trying to get a grip on their meeting while thinking about how gorgeous he was up close. The word had its own dynamic when applied to straight guys. There was nothing minutely effeminate about Lincoln Grayle. None of that secretive, cool detachment when chatting up a woman. And the mere brush of his lips against hers had had erotic force. "So—walking across the Falls is out? What brings you to Rome?"

"Another illusion I wanted to stage at the Colosseum this week. At night, with an audience. But the Romans suspended our permits today pending a review of possible structural damage—as if my team designed an illusion that would endanger one of the wonders of the ancient world. What it comes down to, of course, is *corrómpere*. They know I can't afford a delay. My theatre in Vegas has been dark for two weeks. I'm all out of 'vacation' time and I have bills to pay. I said forget it, there are just too many palms to cross in this town, and they'll think of some other way to hang me up tomorrow. NBC is pissed and so far I'm out a hundred fifty thousand of my own money, with nothing to show for it." He took her by the arm. "And that's enough of my troubles, promise. Were you going out just now? Or could we get a drink somewhere?"

"Sure, no problem, I, uh, don't have plans."

He looked at his sports-model wristwatch. "Have you been to Caffe Greco?"

"I've never been to Rome before. This is my first day."

"Tough to get a table this time of the evening, but they know me; my picture's on the wall in the back room between Sly's and Catherine's." He turned and curtly signaled a small dapper man in a black suit standing watchfully near the Excelsior's main entrance. The man turned immediately and went outside. The famed illusionist escorted Gwen, igniting covetous interest in other women around the lobby, to a BMW limousine parked on the interior drive. It was a stretch job but not so elongated as to be incompatible with many of Rome's narrow streets. Chauffeur by the rear door, also two men with the vigilant humorless aspect of high-priced bodyguards. Everyone got in and they were driven through the orange-toned Roman dusk and maddeningly disorganized traffic to Via Condotti.

"Some of the best designers in Rome hang their shingles on Via Condotti," Grayle explained with the air of a man for whom the cosmopolitan cities of the world are one familiar neighborhood. "I wouldn't know; I don't have a wife for those dress-to-kill competitions."

"Or girlfriends?"

He smiled, beginning to relax now, not as charged-up over business frustrations as he had seemed when he gave her that kiss. As for Gwen, her heart was still pumping at twice normal speed. Head in a delicious whirl. Lincoln Grayle!

"Diamond bracelet or a gold Bulgari watch, depending."

"Which you order by the dozens," she said, with Eden's flair for deadpan mockery.

"I leave that up to my secretaries. You didn't tell me what you're doing in Rome, or am I not supposed to know?"

"No big secret."

"You heard I was going to be here, and you couldn't wait until you saw me again."

Gwen gave him a mild shot to the shoulder with her fist before setting him straight; he reacted, however, as if she'd hit him with a sledge.

"Oh, God, what did I do? I'm sorry!"

He covered the shoulder protectively with his other hand and shook his head gamely. But obviously he was in pain. He needed a few seconds to get his breath back while Gwen wished she were invisible; both bodyguards were looking at her as if waiting for instructions to throw her into the street.

"Some ligament damage—I haven't had time to repair surgically. I take a lot of MSM and see my chiropractor twice a week." His grimace eased into a smile. "So now that you've caught up with me—"

"I had no idea that I'd ever see you again. Tom had business in Rome and Bertie had a shoot, and I—I didn't want to be left behind. Etan and his wife went to their house in Mallorca until her asthma clears up, so there wouldn't have been anyone to talk to at Shungwaya. I was bored." And she had been annoyed, almost since their arrival in Rome the night before. Right now Tom and Bertie were at the residence of the U.S. Ambassador to Italy with Katharine Bellaver, calling on the U.S. Ambassador to the Holy See and envoys from Leoncaro. A meeting to which she pointedly had not been invited. More than likely if the Pope did agree to meet with them she'd be excluded again. Tom and Bertie had been pleasant and reasonable in explaining why they didn't feel she could be helpful. More likely, Gwen concluded, they were afraid she'd somehow embarrass them. Not being used to or understanding the nature of doppelgangers, even though every living human had one, from birth. So stupid! She *was* Eden, with only one important distinction that someone who didn't know Eden very well would never notice. If Eden had had the confidence to send her to Rome on this urgent mission, who were *they* to deny her the chance to convince the Pope that he was in serious danger?

The more Gwen thought about it, the angrier and more rebellious she became. Two days had passed; Eden hadn't tried to contact her with advice or instructions. Confidence—which Gwen knew she had earned, plenty of times.

"You're doing that thing you do," Lincoln Grayle said.

"Pardon?"

"You rock from the waist up, with your chin elevated. Endearing. But your eyes are half closed while you're rocking, and it's as if you've gone to the other side of the universe."

"Oh. That thing."

"Makes a man feel insecure. Unworthy of your company."

"It's jat-leg. I mean jet-lag."

"Happened twice while we were having lunch at the Stanley, Eve."

"It did? Never again, on my honor." Paparazzi on motor scooters were suddenly buzzing around the limo, trying to detect who was inside, adding to the racy, high-octane excitement pumping through her veins, the thrill of glamour, of *being there*. "You know, I really don't care for *Eve* all that much." She laughed nervously. "New place, new pers—identity. Could you just call me—let's see, how about *Gwen*."

"Okay," the magician said indulgently. Finding that endearing too, from the way he smiled.

"It's short for Guinevere," she said, feeling just a little foolish and then, with a rush, blissfully liberated.

"I know." He moved his bad shoulder cautiously, fingers pressing here and there. "As long as we're on this kick, why don't you call me—"

"No, no, I *love* Lincoln. Linc. It's perfect. For you. Don't change a thing."

They were getting out of the limousine in front of the Caffe Greco, which had a modest dignified facade and cheery lighting inside, when she noticed a spot of red that had seeped through his sweater just below the shoulder.

"Oh, Linc, you're bleeding! Now I really feel terrible about hitting you."

He looked, unconcerned, at the blood spot. "One of your kamikaze African insects. Camel fly I believe it was. I scratched the bite and it bled. I guess the Band-Aid popped off when I was flexing."

One of the bodyguards handed Grayle a blazer, which he draped around his shoulders Continental-style before they went inside.

The Greco's foyer was jammed with standing Italians, mostly men in sharp dark designer suits killing time with an espresso and gossip before meeting wives or girlfriends for dinner. "Italians eat late," Grayle said, making their presence known to a young woman like a beautiful centaur, long-necked, lithe, and curvy from the waist up and with a marvelous flowing black mane, big in the hips and thick-legged below.

Grayle's chauffeur, Gwen assumed, had called ahead; there was a table waiting in conspicuous isolation in the snug back room. The magician nodded amiably to a couple here and a foursome there when they entered, all of them with the shapely auras of big money or secure fame. He paused to kiss the pallid cheeks of a young Roman pop star dressed in trendy tatterdemalion. Grayle spoke to the girl in Italian. The movements of his hands, the lilt in his eyes were second and third languages. The pop star adored him instantly. It was just something he spread around, Gwen thought, like sparkly dust in the air. Or a pleasant sort of flu.

"How do you know so many people wherever you go?" Gwen said to him when they were finally in their seats.

"The entree to the famous is fame itself. A novelist friend of mine wrote that 'Las Vegas is the crossroads of the civilized universe.' He tends to be a cynic, but the fact is, sooner or later the whole world shows up in Vegas. Or if some of the world is slow in coming, somebody puts up a Vegas version, more fabulous than the original. Venice, Paris, New York. Ancient Egypt. You have to go some to outdazzle the Luxor, but I made a good try with the Lincoln Grayle Theatre."

"I wish I could see it."

Campari was brought to them. Gwen had hers with soda. He looked at her over his raised glass.

"You've spoiled my surprise."

"What surprise?"

He leaned toward her with one of his beguiling gestures. Magic on his mind, at his fingertips. She was gathered in as if by the flourish of an invisible cape, cloaked in intimacy.

"If we're forced to scrub the Colosseum shoot, then I'm flying home day after tomorrow. Plenty of room on my Falcon, and there'll be a fun bunch aboard. I want you to come with me."

"When did you decide this?"

"On the way over." He raised his glass. "Chin-chin."

They sipped their drinks. Grayle said, directing her eyes to images of the renowned on the wall near them, "Keats, Goethe, Wagner, Liszt; they all might have sat where we're sitting now, at one time or another. That rake with the big nose is Casanova. Caffe Greco goes back to the mid–eighteen hundreds."

"Casanova? Your patron saint?"

"I love women. What I don't have is time to pursue them."

"Is that why we're moving so fast, Linc?"

"As long as we're going in the right direction."

"I'm charmed. Really. Can't we just enjoy *now*?"

"Yes. And I'm going to enjoy having dinner with you at Il Fiorentino later. And the drive to Naples in the morning. You're not allowed to leave Italy without seeing Naples, Gwen. That's been known to provoke international incidents."

"Okay, but—"

"Or Florence. My God, we have to spend at least a day in Florence."

"But I—"

"I've been pushing myself hard for two years," he said, staring at her as if he were in a somber confessional mood and she was his only hope for absolution. "The TV special I've been working on, Madison Square Garden this past spring, command perf in London right after that. Ten shows a week at my own theatre. I badly need to take some time just to catch up to yesterday. And I want to spend that time with you." His smile was well placed but sweet and sincere. "Please tell me I'm not being unreasonable."

"No, but—"

A British actor with an alcoholic glaze to his face and wise suffering eyes approached to give Linc a friendly pawing, leaning on the shoulder that wasn't damaged and whispering at length in his ear. The illusionist laughed at the anecdote and sought to introduce Gwen, but the old poof turned away from their table with a suddenly lost look, fumbling for a cigarette.

"Sorry. He's like that."

"Rude to his competition?" Gwen said with a wide-eyed smile. "But they're all fascinating." Looking around the clubby room where majestic creative monsters from dimmed centuries had passed some of their down time. She held up her empty glass, blood tingling in her cheeks. "If I could have another of these? Then I think I ought to change for dinner. Roman women know how to dress. But I can hold my own."

Tom Sherard and Bertie Nkambe had returned from their meeting at the Ambassador's residence when Gwen walked into the seventh-floor suite at the Excelsior. Bertie was napping on one of the large beds in the room she and Gwen shared. She fell asleep easily, like any healthy animal with nothing else to do, but her head lifted alertly from the pillow when she heard Gwen going through some of the eight shopping bags lined up against a silk-covered wall.

"Hi."

"Hi, how did it go?" Gwen said, not looking around. She pulled a beaded Fendi clutch from one of the tissue-filled bags, opened three boxes of dress shoes. This season ankle wraps were back in style.

"His Holiness has agreed to see us." Bertie yawned. "Eleven o'clock tonight, in his apartment at the Gemelli Polyclinic."

"Clinic? Is he sick?"

"Just getting over an ear infection is what we heard. Also Tom and I will attract less attention there than we would at the Apostolic Palace."

"Eleven o'clock. Okay. Should I meet the two of you at the clinic?"

"Where are you going now?"

"To dinner. I have a date."

"Oh." Bertie looked at her with muted curiosity, then commented obliquely, "Looks as if you blitzed every shop on the Via Veneto."

"When in Rome. Besides," Gwen said with a pointed glance at Bertie, who was sitting on the bed now with her legs crossed, reaching high above her head, "I had the afternoon off. I—*we*—have really good taste in clothes, just never had enough money." She unwrapped the shoes she wanted to wear, tried them on again. "It's a kick, isn't it? Being goddamned rich." Bertie was still reaching for the coffered ceiling and didn't reply. She had wonderful breasts, Gwen observed. Mahogany-tipped, a shade darker than a brown hen's egg, with overtones of brass in the yellow lamplight: her Chinese bloodlines. The dpg wondered what Tom Sherard was holding back for, with Bertie so crazy for him. Maybe a buffalo had gored him in a bad place. "You would never guess who I ran into today, I mean this evening, right here at the Excelsior."

Bertie exhaled lengthily through one nostril. "I was wondering how it works. If Eden needs you suddenly, you have to go, don't you? Doesn't matter if you're in the middle of the fish course, *bing*, you're out of here."

"Only when there's a dire emergency," Gwen explained with a burn of resentment at Bertie's lack of tact, carelessly reminding the dpg of her inferior, ephemeral status. "Otherwise she lets me know when I'm being . . . recalled."

"How?"

"Quantum physics. Earn your Ph.D.; then we can talk."

Bertie blinked at her juvenile belligerence, then smiled forgivingly.

Gwen modified her tone. "If you want to know how I get from here to there, or wherever, here's an analogy. Think of a superhighway with millions of lanes, all the traffic moving at about the speed of light. So if Eden wants me, I just slip out of the lane I'm traveling in now into a slightly faster lane, then back again; zip, I'm there."

"Speed of light," Bertie said, nodding, not entirely baffled.

"More to it than that, of course. Why the sudden interest? Did you hear from Eden?"

"No. I suppose everything's going okay in San Francisco. You didn't tell me who you saw in the lobby."

"Didn't give me a chance." The small blight of resentment faded. Gwen opened a dress box. "Lincoln Grayle."

"Linc? I thought—"

"His stunt, or whatever, *illusion,* didn't come off. First they had engine trouble flying to Zimbabwe and turned back. Then the hotel they were going to stay at near the Falls burned. Now he's in Rome for his TV special but having more problems; they may not let him use the Colosseum. If it doesn't work out for Linc, then we're going to Naples tomorrow, or maybe he said Florence. Do you like these shoes on me, Bertie?"

"Perfect. What else are you wearing?"

"Basic black." She held up the filmy dress she'd purchased. "The most dress for the money. I know it looks as if I spent a fortune, but everything I bought came to a little over eighteen hundred on the MasterCard."

"You did well," Bertie assured her prickly roommate. "You know, I've never seen you dressed up before. Well, I mean—"

"I know. By the way, if we're seeing the Pope, how does that go? Do I need something to cover my head in his presence?"

Bertie got off the bed and pulled on a T-shirt with Yves Saint Laurent's face on it.

"Look, I'm sorry, but Tom doesn't think you should go with us this time, either."

Gwen flung the black dress on her own bed, bypassing resentment for fiery anger.

"This is such *bull*shit! Where is he?"

"Tom? He's taking a—"

Tom Sherard was standing beside the marble bathtub but still dripping when Eden Waring's dpg stormed in. All of Tom visible from multiple angles in semi-misted mirrors. And clearly, although he had his share of the African huntsman's scars, no lethal claws had come near his groin. Gwen took in that much of him in a flash: the interesting hard-used body, tight weld of flesh and muscle to the long bones, gaunt rib cage, white swath across abdomen and upper thighs where sun rarely touched him. And he was hung with the stones of a giant-killer in a leathern sling.

"Would you please tell me how you're going to explain what *I* should be explaining to His Holiness? They were *my* dreams!"

"Eden's," Bertie commented behind her.

She turned sideways to confront them both as if she held a dagger in either hand. Tom shrugged awkwardly into a terry-cloth robe, one sleeve of which wouldn't slide over the waterproof soft cast on his right forearm. His face reddened to the tips of his ears.

"Of course *I* never dream, but so what? I know every dream Eden's had since she was a baby! And the Pope has to hear about the beast from me, otherwise he'll think you're a couple of loonies!"

"Allow me a minute, would you?" Tom said with a look that was like cocking the hammer on a pistol.

Gwen retreated promptly, still in high dudgeon. Bertie watched her go with a complex expression that was not unsympathetic, shrugged for Tom's benefit, and gently closed the bathroom door.

She found the dpg in the sitting room, on the edge of a chair, rocking from the waist up, dissipating the rest of her quixotic energies.

"Tom is having a hard time dealing with much of this," Bertie said. "He's still embarrassed, frustrated, that he missed his shot the other night. No use in my trying to convince him that you can't kill a shape-shifter with a mere rifle bullet. Oh, and he's deeply confused about who or what you are, though he'll never admit that. Third point, he's never done well with obsessive personalities; try to ease up a little. I have to keep reminding Eden of that too."

"I know."

"Tonight—let me work it out with Tom. After all, three loonies are better than two. Where would the Stooges have been without Curly or Moe?"

"What?"

"Never mind. We wouldn't be seeing the Pope at all if Tom didn't have a long-standing relationship with Katharine Bellaver. I think they had a brief affair when Tom was about my age. She does know him *very* well. Flights of fancy are not in Tom's emotional kit. He's solid, stable, completely reliable in situations where other men would lose their wits and their nerve. That's what Eden—loves about him."

"You love him too."

"Have, since I was a kid. Always will."

"Is he in love with both of—us?"

Bertie answered that with a soft injured smile. "I'm not sure how clear his feelings are to Tom. Is it sexual, or just devotion? Whatever, call it a dilemma, and until he sorts it all out, the guilt feelings, the generational thing—like I care how old he is—his chivalric code and the mechanism for retaining his sanity will keep him at a distance from . . . us."

She spoke from the sadness of her depths, voice going dry over the last words.

They heard Tom in his bedroom, slamming an armoire door with a muffled curse. The belated anger of a man briefly humiliated in his own bath.

Gwen looked at the floor, chastised, hands clasped between her knees.

Bertie broke the tension with a smile. "Why don't you keep your dinner date?"

"You're sure?" Gwen said gratefully.

"I'll fix Tom a drink," Bertie said, getting up. "He's past due for a blast. Then we'll talk. As for His Holiness . . . just show up. Eleven sharp at the Gemelli clinic. Now you'd better get dressed. Borrow anything you like from my jewelry case. And say hello to the master magician for me."

"Sure. Does he have any moves I should look out for?"

"When Linc holds your hand by the fingertips and slips a little

something on to your wrist and looks deeply into your eyes, probably his next move is straight to bed." Bertie gave this conclusion
some thought. "Although I've heard, from a former member of
Linc's troupe, that he has a reputation for being stuck in neutral sex-
ually. He can levitate any number of stage assistants, but when it
comes to his own—" Bertie threw off the rumor with a shrug.
"Probably one of those stories that was started by an old flame who
couldn't handle being dumped by Grayle. Showbiz can be evil." She
glanced at Gwen, naively curious. "None of my business, but—"

"Yes, I can. No, I haven't. It won't be tonight, either. I may not get
out all that much, but I'm no pushover."

Dinner turned out not to be the intimate rendezvous Gwen had
anticipated. By the time she and Grayle made the scene at Il
Fiorentino on a little street close to the Pantheon, there already were
six guests at the table for ten he had reserved, seated amid magnificent frescoes and imperial columns of the choice dining room.

Three Italian men in late middle age, overdressed by the likes of
Versace and Prada, all with the bearing of graven images. Two had
hair as thick as ram's wool, and ringlet sideburns; the third man was
bald as a pumpkin with a pugilist's nose, impudent green eyes, and
two-carat round diamonds in each wing of his fleshy nose. Their
women—second or third wives or new mistresses—were a sym-
phony of pampered consonance, languor in their smiles. All spoke
fluent-to-passable English and responded to Lincoln Grayle as if
they long had been in the capture of his gravity. They responded
politely to Gwen, but without curiosity.

Fascinating people, Gwen reminded herself. They must be, if they
were friends of Grayle's. But in a way they all made her skin crawl
with an unexplainable animosity.

The other two places at the table were taken a few minutes later by
the English actor Gwen had not been introduced to at Caffe Greco
and his companion, also an actor, a lean handsome youth with the
profile of a scythe, his expression a surfeit of self-love. He wore a
velvet suit the color of an eggplant with a triple-collar shirt, open at
the neck.

The older actor's name was Seth Foxe. He was in Rome, he let them know, working ("for condom money, my dears") two weeks that threatened to stretch into six in a historical drama. He was drunk, but apparently one of those alcoholics who could maintain a high level of comprehension and precision of speech until suddenly passing out on their faces. The glitter of his eyes was scary to Gwen when he looked at her.

After an unrewarding day on the set in the garden of an old Benedictine convent where he was playing a Renaissance pontiff, Foxe's emotional gutters were running full of bile. One of the men at the table, a financier experienced in the film business, egged him on.

"It must be gratifying, Seth, after some of the films you've appeared in lately, to have the opportunity to work with a writer and director of genius."

"Genius? What rubbish. The Chismas mystique is based on cult snobbery, and it is rather a small cult. Paul's script, old darling, is murky psychopathology, with a larding of kinky sex and grue to pump up the lagging box office. From my mouth to God's and Paramount's ears. I refer to those pages I have thus far been permitted to read; they are doled out on a need-to-know basis by our writer and director of genius. What *I* need to know is, when I do my big rape scene with Lucrezia Borgia, will they provide a body double? Not for me; for the dear little dimwit essaying Lu. She's such questionable goods I hate to lay a finger on her, let alone my withered old shanks."

"The script has some good ideas, what I've read," Seth's boyfriend murmured, with the sidelong look of one who senses he has invited trouble by venturing an opinion.

Foxe tapped on his water goblet with a salad fork. "Quiet, everyone! Randy has come to the defense of his film-school cohort. Randy and Paul are quite alike, I must admit, in that their brains occasionally do spawn ideas—like larvae in shit." He leaned toward Randy, sniffing. "Is that the scent I gave you for our one-month anniversary?"

"Yes," Randy said, almost inaudibly.

Foxe beamed at the other dinner guests. "Lagerfeld. I like for him to wear it all the time, so I can more easily tell if it's Randy or my Catahoula hound I'm in bed with." That earned him his biggest laugh; Randy just looked down with feverish cheekbones and a troubled jut of his lower lip.

Somewhere within a kilometer's range of Il Fiorentino there was a muffled explosion; the chandeliers in the rooms trembled and chattered. There was sudden silence throughout the restaurant, wariness or fear in the eyes of the diners. After a few seconds conversations began again, tentatively. Rustlings in the stillness, a man's gruff voice, louder than the others, a dropped glass on tile. Waiters resumed like dancers cued from a theatrical tableau.

"Car bomb," Lincoln Grayle said to Gwen. "Or truck, from the heavy sound of it."

"Third one in six weeks," one of the Italians said with a slight shrug.

"Who are they?" Grayle asked.

"Who knows for sure? They all have their causes, and civilization has a way of angering the uncivilized."

"Rome has always been a great city," the green-eyed man said. "What is another monument? Our true test of greatness is how well we survive our maniacs."

Seth Foxe finished the scotch in his glass. "A well-lived life must endure its little spasms of angst." He caught the question in Gwen's eyes. "*Angst,* darling; it's a delicatessen for neurotics." Now he decided to focus all of his attention on her. "American, are you?"

"Yes."

"In England and in the rest of Europe, we've lived with our bombings for many years. I suppose you Americans are still in shock, terrorism being such a recent import to your formerly unsullied shores. A wake-up slap in the face. I'm reminded of what dear Bogie said to Peter Lorre in *The Maltese Falcon.* 'You'll get slapped and like it.' " His eyes glittered maliciously as he concluded his dead-on impression of Bogart. She wished he would shut up or fall on the floor, but the others apparently found him to be a rare delight.

Foxe surprised her by smiling sympathetically. "You mustn't take me too seriously," he said. "I have my warmer moments. I danced at

all of my weddings. I have a daughter, about your age. Strange, all
day I've been trying to remember her name."

"The world can be quite a wonderful place after all," one of the
wives or mistresses said with a winsome optimism.

"Too bad the human race is still around to fuck it up," Foxe
replied instantly, returning to form for his encore.

Il Fiorentino's master sommelier appeared with the Tuscan vintage that Lincoln Grayle had selected earlier. Grayle looked at the
label, nodded. The wine was uncorked. But when the sommelier
attempted to pour a little of it into his glass, no wine appeared. The
distinguished server looked more shocked than if another bomb had
exploded, this time at his feet.

Grayle smilingly took the bottle from his hands and tilted it above
the glass. Water poured out. Grayle looked perplexed. He held the
bottle upright and studied the label. The sommelier, expressing his
sorrow and indignation in rapid Italian, was rigid and turning red.
Grayle held up an index finger, smiled soothingly, then drew Gwen's
glass to his place and tried again. This time the bottle yielded the
appropriate *Castello Banfi Brunello di Montalcino,* a deep purple
splash in the glass.

"Ahhh," the master sommelier exclaimed, belatedly getting the
joke when the others laughed. "*Magìa,* yes?"

"You'd better bring us another bottle, Pietro," Grayle advised.
"This one"—he stripped the label, revealing his picture on a label
underneath—"is my private stock."

The trick had been a good tension-breaker. But now they were
hearing sirens. Foxe seemed to nod off after his first sip of wine.
Randy took him by the elbow and helped him out of his armchair.

"Couldn't manage to eat a bite anyway," the old actor apologized.
"The odor of Semtex is ruinous for the digestion, and as it happens I
do have an early call."

By ten-forty dinner was completed except for coffee, brandy, and
dessert, none of which Gwen wanted. She graciously took her
leave, and Lincoln Grayle accompanied her outside the restaurant to

his waiting limo. Same chauffeur, same two bodyguards. One of them said to Grayle, gesturing, "Montecitorio."

"This isn't necessary," Gwen said. "I could get a taxi."

"Not by yourself, in Rome. It's no sinkhole of depravity, but unescorted women at this time of the night are fair game for thieves, which includes some legal taxi drivers. You'll get an expensive tour of the palazzos and fountains before you're finally dropped at your hotel."

The hoo-hah of sirens; she glimpsed the blue lights of three police cars speeding through the Piazza della Rotunda. Past the Pantheon but at some distance in the yellow aura of the city, above the referenced piazza, one ringed with government buildings, there was a thick brownish cloud like a brutal djinn hovering over more glories of antiquity, now in flames and rubble. The large vehicular bomb random punctuation in the long, secretive history of zealotry. A disagreeable air of destruction had reached the Rotunda. Grayle produced a silk handkerchief for her, shaking it first as if to free a forgotten dove.

"See you tomorrow," he said. "Where are you going now?"

"The Gemelli clinic." In response to the question in his eyes she improvised. "Bertie has a . . . a fever we're concerned about, and they're keeping her overnight."

"Gemelli clinic," Grayle said to the driver. And to Gwen, "It's only a few minutes from here, if the cops aren't barricading bridges on the Tiber. See you tomorrow."

"Are we really going to Naples?"

"You bet." He leaned into the backseat and kissed her. Gwen had a glow on when the limo pulled away from Il Fiorentino. Grayle watched until they were out of sight with a slight bemused smile, then returned to his remaining guests.

They were now in a private room on the top floor of the three-story building. The tall balcony doors were closed. Venetian busts brooded in niches around the walls. There was a fourteen-foot ceiling. The men—now including the owner of Il Fiorentino and the small palazzo in which the restaurant was housed, a man of impeccable fashion that failed to detract from several afflictions, among them gout and palsy—and two of the women were enjoying cigars with their cappuccino and Napoleon served in crystal glasses that were three centuries old.

Lincoln Grayle stepped out of the cabinet-sized elevator and took his seat in a thronelike fifteenth-century doge's chair, a little distant from the others. He was offered a selection of cigars from a humidor by their host, who made recommendations in a hushed voice. The cigar that the illusionist chose, a Davidoff Millennium, was clipped and lighted for him.

One modern feature of the splendidly furnished if somewhat gloomy room was ashtrays that drew off the considerable smoke. Another was a handmade, organic-form light sculpture of some opaque material, nearly eight feet in sinuous height and a couple of feet in diameter. The fluidly changing tones of the sculpture provided the only light within the room.

Grayle's legs were stretched out in front of him, feet on a sculpted bronze footstool that, on examination, was the figure of a man in chains, crouched on all fours, jagged gouges where his eyes would have been.

"What do you think of her?" he asked, after several contented puffs on his cigar.

Their heads turned to the light sculpture, where a holographic image of Eden/Gwen had appeared, hands clasped at her waist, head slightly bowed.

"Delightful," one of the elegant women said. She wore a double strand of gray pearls that cost more than a thousand dollars a pearl.

"Extraordinary," another said. She was the wife of the man with diamonds in his battered nose. Her red coif complemented the brilliant, hectic green of his eyes. "Is she a perfect likeness?"

"Oh, yes."

"But how do you know," asked the third woman, who was heiress to a media lord's fortune, "that she is a doppelganger?"

"I couldn't have known," Grayle said, "if I hadn't met Eden herself in Kenya." He rubbed his wounded shoulder lightly; another

day before it would completely heal, leaving no scar. In the meantime it served as a memento of his last night in Africa, his frustrated
hunt at Shungwaya. The pain a promise. Someday soon he would
have a second opportunity to kill the man who had shot him. But he
had more urgent business, in Rome and elsewhere. "You see,
Stephane, doppelgangers are mirror images of their homebodies. Our
friend Gwen, as you may have observed at dinner, is right-handed."

"Producing one's doppelganger is a left-handed Art," said one of
the men, chairman of Italy's major financial conglomerate.

"If our dinner guest was a dpg," the green-eyed man asked
Grayle, "then where is Eden Waring?"

"I don't know," Grayle said, comfortable with the admission.

"The doppelganger, unfortunately, cannot be of value to you,
Great One."

"I wouldn't say that." Grayle almost shrugged, but remembered
not to. It hurt to move his shoulder, even though only a small fragment of bullet remained unabsorbed. Peevishly he kicked the footstool with the heel of a shoe. The footstool cried out and writhed in
torment, to the amusement of Grayle's Roman coterie.

"Biologically," the financier said, massaging his forehead as if
trying to recall the answer to a difficult exam question, "aren't all
doppelgangers sterile?"

"As long as they remain doppelgangers," Grayle confirmed, thinking of Gwen's pathetic eagerness to claim an identity of her own.

"Then only Eden herself can provide you with—" said the
woman whose lightly flushed, columnar neck rose from a pedestal
of pearls. They took on a glow and began to tighten like a hang-
man's noose, lifting her dimpled chin as she made strangling noises.
Her eyes bulged and sought forgiveness for the indiscreet reference
to the magician's torn and scattered soul. Forbidden, even among his
intimates.

The sulky chill left Grayle's eyes and she sagged in her chair,
coughing up part of her dinner. No one looked at her.

Grayle nodded, and moved on.

"For now I need them both. Eden and Gwen."

"What can Eden Waring's—replica—possibly accomplish for

you?" the pragmatic financier asked. "Isn't she completely in control of her homebody?"

Grayle studied the night sounds of a writhing, assaulted city as if he were a composer alert to nuances in the prelude to a favorite and oft-repeated work. Anticipating the long agony yet to come, that would wither and ultimately crush the sacred heart of the Eternal City.

"Not any longer," he said.

The Eden/Gwen image persisted in the light sculpture, downcast like a penitent ghost.

A replica, yes. But should Eden, growing powerful in ways unknown to him and perhaps now intuitively aware of the hunter and its desires, become too dangerous to approach, the dpg had access to worlds beyond his reach. The illusionist fully understood how to use Gwen, but not how to persuade her to willingly help him.

That would come. Grayle drew on his cigar, eyes narrowing. He was content, for now.

Gwen was drowsy, perhaps from the rich food or the glass and a half of Tuscan wine she'd drunk at Il Fiorentino. Or her spell of drowsiness might have been due to the scents permeating the white silk handkerchief Grayle had given her to annul the effect of smoke flowing south and west from bombed buildings, making the streets near the river hazy. Moments into her ride in the black leather compartment of the BMW limo she was nodding off.

Screech of brakes, a shouted oath from the driver. She was snapped out of her pleasant daze but barely got her chin up before the stunning impact. A van had appeared at great speed from a side street. The crash nearly tore the front end out of the Beamer, lifted and rammed the rest into the steel shutters of a shop across a narrow sidewalk.

Gwen was thrown across the seat. She hit her head on the smoke-toned armored window on the opposite side. Other windows had been cracked but not shattered. She didn't feel anything for a few seconds; then a sharp pain like a meat skewer through the back of her neck made her scream.

The van backed up, green fluid spurting from the ruptured radiator. The van's running lights were barely perceptible through the armored windows. Gwen was aware of men outside, quick shadows, doors wrenched open, gunfire. One of the bodyguards in the car was hit; there was a vivid gush of blood as his head rocked backward.

Then gloved hands seized her by the ankles and she was dragged out of the backseat, lifted off the pavement. An ultraviolet light switched on inches from her eyes.

Strength was squeezed from her body as if she were an apple in a press; she felt literally flattened, mush inside her skin, straining to breathe, the black light saturating her brain like anesthetic. The continuing pressure caused muscles to spasm in her arms and legs. She couldn't speak, beg for the oppressive light to be turned off.

"My daughter's name was Edwina," said the man with the ultraviolet light. "She was married at fourteen to a bastard son of Charles the Second, and died of food poisoning not many years after. Now isn't it odd how you can forget a simple thing like that?"

This while she was being carried to a car behind the van that had destroyed the BMW. She was flung into the backseat and Seth Foxe climbed in after her. Doors slammed shut. Her eyes were tightly closed, but Gwen knew her dress had snagged on wreckage, was torn and riding up over her waist. He pulled the torn dress down to cover her thighs and patted her on the fanny.

"Do we need any more of the light?" he asked solicitously.

Gwen shook her head slightly. The light clicked off. The driver gunned a powerful engine, backed up a full block at high speed, and made a sliding turn onto a broader, busier street.

"What was the light for?" Randy of the velvet suiting said. He was in the front seat with another man, looking back at them.

"Didn't you know, darling? Ultraviolet saps their strength completely. She's quite helpless now. Only requires a few minutes of the light every hour or so to keep her docile and mum. No need for bonds or an uncomfortable gag."

"How do you know so much about doppelgangers?" Randy asked.

Gwen felt one of Seth's gloved hands massaging a still-trembling quadriceps. *Helpless* didn't adequately describe her physical weakness, the dim sense of alarm that told her she was in big trouble. again.

The venerable actor sighed.

"I have been around for a very long time," he said.

CITTÀ DEL VATICANO · OCTOBER 21 · 11:00 P.M.

The papal secretary, a brisk young Frenchman from Aix, met Tom Sherard and Bertie Nkambe at a covered entrance to the Gemelli Polyclinic.

"I'm Laurent Colbert." The monsignor had a quick smile and confident eyes behind Clark Kent glasses. "I was told to expect three visitors."

"She ought to be here any minute," Tom said, mildly vexed as he looked around. The small lobby they were escorted to was empty except for Vatican cops in plainclothes, the lighting subdued. "Her name is Eve Bell."

The secretary nodded. "Well, perhaps we should go up. I'll watch for her." He had the peppy stride of a long-distance runner, leading them to a private elevator.

The papal apartment was on the eleventh floor of the clinic. There was a river view from the windows of the small living room, and to-night a smoke-shrouded sky across the Tiber, turbulent yellow where the car—or truck—bomb had exploded. "Terrible business," Laurent Colbert said, closing opaque curtains but not the drapes. "The Holy Father is in his chapel; I'll let him know you have arrived. May I bring you something from the kitchen? We have soft drinks. His Holiness is particularly fond of Orangina."

"Without ice, please," Leoncaro said, coming almost surrepti-tiously into the small room and smiling slightly, having caught his secretary off-guard. It seemed to be a long-running game of *gotcha* that amused him. Laurent recovered with a quick bow and made introductions Tom and the Pontiff shook hands. Leoncaro was dressed casually for their visit, dark gray slacks, a white shirt open at the throat, black leather sandals. Bertie wasn't Catholic but she kneeled and kissed his ring, which pleased him.

Leoncaro gestured to a small stuffed sofa, then turned and took a couple of steps to a high-backed wooden chair with traces of gold remaining in the deep curlicues of carved wood. The broad seat was heaped with pillows and cushions. There was a Pluto pillow and a Mickey Mouse pillow in the pile, Mickey wearing a baseball cap. Leoncaro arranged the lot to his satisfaction and settled down.

"My most recent niece and nephew sent these to me," the Pope explained, holding up the cartoon pillows. "I've never been to the Wonderful World of Disney. Wouldn't mind a visit to the one outside Paris. But the way things are going in the real world, I'm advised not to appear as if I'm having fun." His English was excellent, his voice low and with a slight rasp to it. His smile when he looked at Bertie appeared gently mischievous. "Signorina Nkambe. I understand that you are more famous than I am."

"Just lucky so far, Your Em—I mean, Your Holiness."

"And very photogenic, I've no doubt, which must have a great deal to do with your secular success." Bertie's impression was that, in spite of his hard line on abortion and disdain of feminist groups, he did like women and didn't consider them bystanders in the human race. "Why don't you call me Sebastiano? In fifteen minutes, twenty at the most, I will fall asleep, whether I am in my bed or still sitting upright in this chair. During this little remnant of my day I am more or less off-duty."

"Thank you," Bertie said. She glanced at Tom, whose attention was unhappily fixed on his wristwatch.

Leoncaro spread his hands, smiling indulgently. "Where can she be? This amazing child I have heard so much about. Who knows everyone's fate, including my own."

"I hope she'll be here soon," Tom said edgily.

"So do I. I meant what I said about falling asleep." He sipped from a goblet of orange soda. "If this is only about the bloody paw prints on La Scala Santa, I know. I have seen them in a vision of my own, glowing like the coals of hell." He paused, touching the gold of his pectoral cross. "Given that visions are not logical and portents require interpretation, still I would like to hear about this daemon, or were-beast, apparently formidable enough to have injured your arm"—he nodded, acknowledging the blue cast beneath the shirt cuff Tom couldn't button—"then survived two shots from rifles made to bring down a rampaging elephant."

"They can't be killed," Bertie murmured.

Leoncaro tapped the rim of his glass against his front teeth. "Elephants?"

Bertie's voice dropped lower, and she squirmed uncomfortably on the sofa beside Tom, who put a hand over hers.

"Shape-shifters."

Leoncaro leaned forward. "Removal of the abscess has only marginally improved my hearing," he said, cupping a hand to his right ear.

Bertie spoke up. "What we saw, and an impression that we have on tape for you to see, was a *shape-shifter*."

"Oh. One of those."

"It was a full-grown tiger with the head of a hyena."

"The combination," Leoncaro said calmly, "of the terror and the power, must have been greatly unsettling. Even though you seem to be knowledgeable about matters beyond the visible world."

"But who knows what form it might take, when it shows up again—"

"To destroy me? Prince of light, God on this earth? True or not, nonetheless it is one of the strongest covenants our faith provides. If this is the will of the creature that made itself known to you, why should it appear in Africa four nights ago?"

"It came to Shungwaya looking for Eden. But she . . . wasn't there just then."

"Could the shape-shifter have been stalking her? Because of her prescience, her status in the Psi world?"

"No, Your—Sebastiano. See, I've been thinking about this until my brain feels raw. But I'm convinced that the were-beast has to—it *must* mate with Eden. It may exist only for that purpose."

Leoncaro's head moved up and back slightly, as if he'd taken a light jab to the chin, reminiscent of his younger days in the ring. He stared at them and past them, eyes narrowing, a hooded appearance. His eyes were hard, but his lips trembled before he spoke.

"Morto un papa, se ne fa un altro."

Then his mouth clamped shut; he returned to them with a stiffened jaw and momentary rage in his expression.

"That obscenity, that *abomination,* must not occur. The girl must be protected with all of the powers available to us under heaven. Why hasn't she come? Do you know where she is?"

"She went out to dinner," Tom said with another look at his watch. It was eleven-eighteen. "More than three hours ago. Please let me try to apologize for . . . Eden's unforgivable rudeness."

"No, no. There was a car bomb in Montecitorio, which of course you're aware of. It is possible, depending on the location of the restaurant and subsequent traffic conditions, that the bombing has delayed her. Was she with someone you know?"

"Lincoln Grayle," Bertie said. "Eden met him in Kenya. Actually I introduced them."

Leoncaro nodded, distance in his eyes again.

"Oh, yes. I have heard of him. Isn't he a magician? What an interesting profession."

The papal secretary returned and stood with clasped hands near the door. Leoncaro nodded again and rose slowly as Tom and Bertie sprang to their feet.

"Thank you for coming to see me," the Pontiff said, taking a hand of each and holding them tightly. "Please have no fear for my life. I'm well protected within the Holy See by the Swiss Guard— not the showy ones with the halberds; I'm speaking of those who are trained by America's Secret Service—and by state security forces in those nations I travel to. But I urge you, when Eden returns, never let her out of your sight again. Eden's life is more important than my own at this critical time. The words I spoke in Italian? It's a saying the pragmatic Romans have. 'When a pope dies, they make another one.' "

He smiled ironically, let go of their hands, made the sign of the cross over Sherard and Bertie. Turned to go to his bedroom as the papal secretary stepped forward to escort them out.

"If it would not be a difficulty," Leoncaro said, pausing, "please bring the girl to me. Tomorrow at three-thirty in the papal library. I'm most anxious to see and talk to her. Laurent will make those arrangements. I'm scheduled for an audience with some distinguished members of the American laity, whom I have had cooling their heels for the better part of a week due to my ear problem. Is it who, or *whom*, in English, Laurent?"

"I'm not at all certain, Holiness. I'll look it up right away."

"Don't you ever sleep, Laurent? Do it tomorrow. Has Pasquale remembered that I needed a new toothbrush?"

Tom and Bertie were in the car taking them back to the Excelsior Hotel when Bertie broke a long brooding silence.

"His Holiness knows something we don't know," she said. "Tom, do I scare easily?"

"You're braver than I am."

"Not now I'm not," she said, clinging to his unbroken arm and huddling close to him. "Tom, please don't make a big scene when we see Gwen."

"I'm just going to quietly strangle her."

Leoncaro, on his Swedish orthopedic bed, a practical luxury to preserve the structural integrity of his aging lower back, had not been able to fall asleep as promptly as usual. There was an odor in the air of the spartan bedroom (in spite of sealed windows and the additional air purification system installed in the papal suite to screen out the tiniest pathogens that were always kicking around inside hospitals) that had something to do with the cloud of disaster lingering over a wide area of Rome toward the midnight hour, more to do with an unspeakable entity already prospering infernally on earth when Rome was a collection of hovels and sheepcotes.

His nose wrinkled at this first disagreeable sign of intrusion, which he had the option to forcibly reject if he chose. Still, Leoncaro reflected, perhaps it *was* time that they meet again.

He abandoned the effort to sleep, reached for a robe, and sat on the side of the low bed. Yawning from time to time, he read his Bible until church bells announced a new day and, at one minute past midnight, the advent of his longtime adversary.

"As usual your foulness precedes you," Leoncaro said gruffly, setting his Bible and reading glasses aside. He looked around the small room, which was mirrorless, undecorated except for the large carved ebony crucifix above the bed.

A coarse smoky image was raveling kinematically while keeping cautious distance from him. An eyespot became visible, expanded from embryonic blandness into a steadfast iris afire with contempt.

"And—as usual—I find *you* in reduced circumstances. Millennia of riches and spoils surround you, but you might as well be in that squalid goat-hide tent on the lower steppes—or do I have the place and circumstances of our last meeting wrong?"

"You know that you do," Leoncaro said, snuffling into a handkerchief, disgust in his eyes.

"Oh, yes, it's clear to me now," Mordaunt said, even as a second, rudimentary eye and a dark mystical rubbing of a face, satirically like that of the Shroud of Turin, appeared to annoy Leoncaro. "On my last visit you were beset by creditors and largely dismissed by your peers. A routinely ignored voice in the House of Lords. Considered somewhat dangerous for your views. '*Fiel pero desdichado.*' Wasn't that the motto on the family coat of arms? *Faithful but unfortunate.* How appropriate even now, in your present coopted persona."

"You seem to be in a gloating mood."

"Why not? You're losing ground while doing my work for me. *Caretaker?* Not much."

"I don't recall losing the Second World War. I do recall the penalty you earned for starting it. Now, how is it I do *your* work, Trickster?"

"Insisting on the doctrines of a mythological, obsolete religion. You don't protect souls with that claptrap; you subjugate them.

What is a pope but a man with a book, a mitre, and the head of an ass?"

"An *enduring* religion. Mythological? No more than the true Eternal Soul is a myth."

"Religious faith is spiritual ignorance. *Credo quia absurdum.* Ignorance spawns delusion. The more fiercely the ignorant believe in the unknowable, the more fanatical they become, and, in groups, horrifically mad. My kind of folks, Caretaker."

"Once it reaches us, the fertilization and evolution of a new soul is slow and arduous. In the beginning of its earthly cycles, each soul requires the sanctuary of a sane system of values so that it may begin to mature. I don't feel that I'm wasting my time in theological pedantry, no matter how many setbacks the Caretakers must endure to graduate a cosmic soul from the earthly plane. Belief in God, through whatever religion inspires it and however 'god' is idealized by the creative unconscious, is essential to the development of metaphysical perception. A liberating force, Mordaunt, achieved only through the steady progress of a soul making its rounds. As for your methods—the more outrageously you behave, the more the souls need *us.* Oh, you have your Malterran misfits to bend to your whims and promises, but you can't construct anything with them that will last. You will never be strong enough."

The large crucifix fell from the wall across the bed, missing Leoncaro by inches. He looked at it, then at the still-unresolved, unreliable shape of Mordaunt hovering futilely in front of him.

"It didn't destroy Him then; it won't bother Him now. Time for you to go."

"I'll be back," Mordaunt said, "in strength none of you can overcome. You left me with a means to heal myself. And now I will use her."

"I wouldn't roll those dice if I were you. If she doesn't know about you yet, she soon will. On the earthly plane you're all flash and not enough powder; no match for the gifts of Eden Waring."

"The beauty of it is, Caretaker, she will use her greatest power against *herself*. And I walk away the winner. Now when shall we two meet again?" he asked mockingly. "In thunder, lightning, or in reign of blood?"

"Get lost," Leoncaro said, but he didn't feel as tough as he sounded.

SAN FRANCISCO · OCTOBER 21 · 2:50 P.M. PDT

On an afternoon when the prevailing winds had gentled and a high-pressure system centered just offshore provided such a mild but radiant atmosphere it was as if all of the Bay Area, with its waters of lapping indigo, its strings of bridges and wharves and towers, had been captured inside a crystal bell . . .

On an afternoon when every breath was a tonic, the heart racing and tingling from the pure enchantment of being outdoors . . .

On an afternoon of pleasantries and nostalgia at lunch with her best friend Megan, and shopping after . . .

On an otherwise agreeable and diverting afternoon, Eden Waring got the pain in her neck.

She had just taken two steps inside the revolving door of the Mark Hopkins's entrance, shopping bags in both hands and a dress box under one arm, when it hit her, penetrating deep like a red-hot knitting needle. The pain similar to what she had experienced the time she thought she'd broken her neck diving for a loose ball her junior year at Cal Shasta.

Eden stopped immediately, afraid to take another step. She dropped one of the bags and grasped her neck with her left hand, a fearful bracing.

The concierge was passing by; he stopped immediately with a concerned smile.

"Are you all right?"

"I, uh, must have twisted my neck coming in the door. I was trying not to drop anything." The pain, an isotope beneath her palm, was at its worst for only a few seconds before tempering to a deep ache. Eden found it bearable then to massage with her fingers, turn her head cautiously left-right on its bony pivot.

The concierge, a silky-looking man with an almost fluorescent pallor, picked up the dropped shopping bag, tucking something filmy back between layers of purple tissue-wrap.

"I can have your purchases sent to your suite for you. It's Miss Bell, isn't it?"

"Yes. I'm, uh, my neck is really beginning to feel okay now."

"You might want to consult Heinrich in the spa," he suggested. "If you're having a muscle spasm. I get them all the time myself, but Heinrich does wonders in only a few minutes. I'll call for you, to be sure he can see you right away."

"I don't know what happened. Maybe I didn't stretch enough this morning. I've played basketball most of my life; my body's used to a certain warm-up routine or I cramp easily. Maybe I'll see Heinrich later, but it's very kind of you."

"Please don't feel shy about calling if there's anything I can do," he said with that tone of unctuous appreciation five-star hotel employees have for the celebrated and the deeply monied.

Eden took the public elevator to the nineteenth floor. There was no one else with her. She used the small interval to press the index finger of her left hand against the site of the occult third eye on her forehead.

Okay, what's going on? What's happened to you?

Nothing specific came to mind. Then she tensed. Black-gloved hands reaching for her. A sensation of being dragged. Bump *bump* and pavement scraping skin, the fiery bloom of a contusion on her hip.

Trouble. Wasn't that just like her?

Eden opened her eyes and felt momentarily displaced, a breath of coldness on her face, as if yesterday had returned. Fog wisping away from the surface of black water. Bubbles where the chain-wrapped body of the assassin had gone down. Open eyes, open mouth, no change of expression at the shocking immersion nor as he swallowed brackish death. Bubbles. Ah, God. She had not blinked or looked

away; she was there at her own insistence, standing in the cluttered
bow of the trawler with men she didn't know and never wanted to
know. Diesel stench and clammy fish rot giving her a sick stomach.
Feeling the chill of three A.M., cheekbones near to freezing. No forgiveness in her heart although he had spared Betts. To Eden he was
only a sharp blade narrowly missing her own throat. Thus his
penalty for failure. The deep salt sleep. It had always been that kind
of world and now she had willingly contributed to its avid mon-
strousness. And gone shopping.

Refocused, Eden realized that the elevator door probably had
been standing open for several seconds. A blond young room service
waiter bent over a wheeled table was looking oddly at her, waiting to
board.

"Sorry," Eden told him, with a lame lipless smile. She gathered her
things and got out of his way, walked slowly to the key-operated
penthouse elevator. The ache in her neck still bearable but not
improving. A dud vacancy in the middle of her brain. *Where are you,
what's happening?* She stumbled on the carpet for no reason; it was
as flat as the baize on a pool table. Disoriented again, feeling zero g in
the pit of her stomach, being lifted, conveyed somewhere—what was
that odor, engine oil? And smoke, and, Jesus! *Blood*—at the speed of
a razzle-dazzle carnival thrill ride.

Come back to me. Now!

Beside the vestibule doors of the secluded penthouse suite Eden
rested her forehead against the wall for half a minute, missing that
buzz around her navel that always told her the manifestation of her
doppelganger was imminent.

Here we go again, she thought dispiritedly. What could have happened to her, with Tom and Bertie around?

She rang the bell. The door was opened by a Blackwelder detective
named Vicky Janssen, diminutive but with a collection of advanced
degrees in deadly martial art forms, and, undoubtedly, although
Eden hadn't asked, she was highly proficient with the .32-caliber
Heckler and Koch automatic she carried.

"Hi, welcome back; how was lunch? Was I right about Kuleto's?"

"Megan and I had a great time. Thanks, Vicky. Where's Betts?"

"Getting some rays on the terrace. She has company."

"Oh. Police again?" Eden frowned. They were required, by the attorneys Vaughn Blackwelder had provided, to make an appointment if they had further questions for Betts about her kidnapping.

"No, it's Mr. Ruddy. He brought her flowers again today."

"Oh," Eden said again. "Bless his heart." His presence, instead of the official interrogators they'd endured, was a relief. Or was it?

Vicky had one of those smiles that served as silent commentary: wry, jaundiced, perplexed. Her response to Eden's expression was cheerful admonition.

"You know, a different hairstyle; and he certainly could use a little help picking out his clothes, but that's the way these old bachelors are. Here, let me carry your things for you. Looks like you cleaned out most of the boutiques on Union Street."

She followed Eden through the living room of the suite, furnished with Chinese antiques and neo-classic pieces, deeply lacquered surfaces reflecting sunlight from the greenery-sheltered, twenty-five-foot terrace. Eden greeted the Filipino nurse on duty, who was on her way to the kitchen. She heard Betts's roguish laughter before she stepped outside, sounds to gladden her heart.

"*There* you are," Betts called out. She was on a chaise with a plaid throw tucked in across her lap. Edmund Ruddy faithfully at her side, sipping a Coke; he stood quickly when Eden approached. She favored Ruddy with a polite smile, gesturing for him to take his seat again, then bent to kiss Betts's cheek. Sunlight flashed and receded on the terrace according to the wind-driven flourishes of arborvitae chockablock in planters along the outer wall. Betts still had very little color, Eden noted, except for the healing abrasions on her throat and neck.

"How's Megan?" Betts asked.

"Dying to see you. I told her another day or two, Mom, we'll all have dinner someplace nice. Mr. Ruddy, how are *you* today?"

He was a man to give considered answers to the most casual questions. "The transmission in the Z3 I seduced myself into buying is acting balky again. I had it to the dealer's only last week. I'm not entirely satisfied with the service I've been getting. When I owned my S-type Jag I must say it never gave me a moment's—"

Betts silenced him by playfully flicking fingers at his sheepdog bangs; he flinched, then smiled ruefully as if the gesture was an old but familiar signal.

"Betts always used to complain that I have a tendency to explain too much," he said to Eden. Explaining further, "I guess you'd call it a nervous habit."

"Relax, relax, please," Eden urged him with a bigger smile, but then she had to ask, "Are the feds still giving you a hard time, Mr. Ruddy?"

"Ed, please. Not at all. I suppose everything about Betts's . . . captivity by that psychotic bird was just so *bizarre* that they've had to conclude we are both telling the truth, and I had nothing whatsoever to do with it."

"You did have something to do with it," Betts said, her voice lowering to a hoarse growl, "after he dumped me on your doorstep. You acted fast and saved my life, Ed."

"Well, I've always been good in an emergency, I like to think." He rolled his shoulders uncomfortably. "But why did he—"

"The feds have found a great deal to interest them," Betts said to Eden, "at the farmhouse near Coldstream Bridge. His theatrical makeup kits and costumes, catalogues of electronic devices, actual explosives—stuff the average citizen can't get his hands on. That should be all they will need, although of course they'd like to know his true identity. A motive, too, which I don't feel obligated to help them with."

It had been Danny Cheng's idea to check all Bay Area hospitals after Eden's futile search for the remains of the Assassin's knife by the fountain in Ghirardelli Square. Minutes later they were speeding across the Bay bridge to the hospital in Concord where Betts had been received following Edmund Ruddy's call for an ambulance.

"But he was a complete stranger to you," Ruddy said, anxiety rising in his eyes.

"That's right," Betts said with a level look at him, reaching up again to fondly muss his hair in another direction. "Complete. Stranger."

"Well, I'm certain I've never been acquainted with anyone who had such a perverted, diseased mind. That's the part I simply can't understand. How could he have possibly known about me and our relationship while we were at USF?"

"I've been thinking about that too," Betts said, very serious. "It might well have been someone we were in school with, and just never noticed. Maybe nobody noticed him. A studious loner type. Silently watching us together. Envious. Obsessed. I've had cases like that."

"Obsessed," Ed repeated dismally. "And he's still at large."

"They'll catch up to him," Betts promised, with the merest glance at Eden's stony face. "He will have left clues. I doubt that we need to worry. After all, it was his intention to bring us together again after all these years. That was in his note to you, wasn't it, Ed?"

"More or less. It's just so damned *creepy*."

"But in spite of his psychosis, there was a streak of humanity in him, somewhere." Betts looked at the shopping bags Vicky had left on a glass-topped table nearby. "Are those for me?" she asked Eden with a gleam of pleasure in her eyes.

"Mostly," Eden said, and confessed, "I think I went a little haywire." She flinched at a fresh twinge and put a hand to her neck. Time to get off an E-mail to Bertie. "Megan took me to some fabulous shops."

"Show me!"

Ed Ruddy, possibly beginning to feel excluded by the prospect of ecstatic clothes talk, got to his feet again.

"I think it's about time that I—you see, I've a four o'clock squash date. Long-running rivalry with my insurance agent."

"Ed," Betts said, sunlight playing over her face so that she batted her eyelashes in a way that seemed coquettish, "I can't thank you enough for the gorgeous flowers. You're being too good to me."

"Oh, no, *no*—my pleasure."

"Did you get a look at that beautiful jade and onyx backgammon table in the library?"

"No, I missed that."

"Have a gander on your way out," Betts said, her voice still stuck in a raw lower register. "And tomorrow if you're not too busy we'll find out if your skills have improved during the past twenty-eight years."

He stood a little straighter, delighted by her challenge. "I wouldn't want to brag, but."

"Give you every chance to prove yourself, Ed. How about three tomorrow afternoon? We'll have supper after I take you to the cleaners. Room service is excellent here."

"Or we could call Tommy Toy's," he suggested, his color high; Edmund Ruddy clearly was ravished by her interest in adding impetus to their resurrected friendship.

"*Now* you're talking."

When she and Betts were alone Eden said, hands on hips, "*Well,* Betts."

"Don't get smart. And nobody said you have to like him right away."

"I don't *dis*like him. Were the two of you really, I mean, back then?"

"Hot and heavy, sugar. That's the second time you've grabbed your neck. What's wrong?"

"Muscle spasm. I think. The mattress on my bed is too hard, or something."

"Did you sleep at all? It must have been after four when I heard you come in."

"No," Eden said, avoiding Betts's eyes. "I didn't sleep."

"Too much on your mind?"

"I suppose."

"You're not going to tell me why you stayed out most of the night, are you?"

"Better that you don't know."

"Oh, God," Betts said, with an invalid's tremulous mouth. "This dodging around and using a phony name like a fugitive, what sort of life do you have now?"

"Shh, I'm fine."

"I should have done a better job of protecting you. This mess I got into—"

"Was never any fault of yours. We won't talk about what happened. What almost happened."

"I was terrified, every minute of the day and night. Now I can't turn it off, even with the tranqs; get *him* out of my mind. And when I'm awake, every face I see could be his face."

"Mom, that evil bastard is gone for good." It was a cold surprise to still feel so shockingly vengeful. "For your sake and mine, I had to make completely sure." Betts stirred uneasily. "No, I didn't touch him. There were others who—do that sort of thing. I really can't tell you any more."

"Those strange friends you've told me about? And that sweet-faced girl with the English butler's name, she couldn't be—"

"I've trusted all of them with my life. Strange? No more than I am."

Eden sat on the side of the chaise, her melancholy face giving way to raw anguish, and put her arms around Betts. She took long shuddering breaths.

"You're safe, Mom. You're *safe*. Nothing matters to me more."

Betts stiffened slightly. Her lips touched Eden's wet cheek.

"You're not leaving again! Oh, but it's too soon."

"Have to," Eden said, feeling like a skunk in the face of Betts's unhappiness and renewed anxiety.

Betts took a fresh purchase on Eden, fingers tightening fiercely. "When you first came into the ER—I was half out of it, but I could see right away. You've aged ten years in just a few months."

"Is that all?" Eden said with a weak smile. Edmund Ruddy's selection of pricey flowers—air-freighted, exotic blooms from Brazilian hothouses—were causing her nose to run. As she had done in childhood, she unthinkingly wiped her nose on the sleeve of the cardigan sweater Betts wore.

"We'll be able to talk again someday," Betts said, "like we used to talk. Won't we?"

"Yes, darling." And now she was mothering Betts, which made her feel desperately sad. "I'll be in touch every day," Eden promised, getting up slowly, swallowing until she forced down her sorrow. She reached for a tissue in the box on the low table beside the chaise. Blotted her wet lashes.

"Betts? Do something for me?"

"Well, of course."

"Talk Ed Ruddy out of those tweedy jackets with lapel tabs and leather at the elbows."

"That's definitely a priority," Betts agreed with a good laugh that her heart didn't feel. The Filipino nurse appeared on the terrace carrying a little tray and several pills in a glass dish, orange juice in a goblet. Betts pounced on her with sudden ferocity. "At least let me have a glass of red wine with those!"

"Cheerio, dear one," Eden said.

LAS VEGAS, NEVADA · OCTOBER 21 · 9:20 P.M. PDT

Lourdes, Lewis Gruvver's sister-in-law, put their rambunctious kids to bed (too many kids, Lewis thought, wondering if he had it in him ever to be a daddy) with Charmaine's easygoing assistance. Lewis gave his half brother Cornell a hand clearing the soak-proof foam plates, empty one-liter plastic soda bottles, and other trash from the patio where they'd feasted on West Texas barbecue and some Honduran specialities from Lourdes's kitchen. Los Lobos on the speakers concealed in low shrubbery around the stake-fenced backyard and pool. Big black western sky with a gaunt moon and field of stars thick as crusty sugar on a doughnut.

While the women wrangled the youngsters with good-natured threats about their prospects for longevity if they didn't cooperate, Lewis and Cornell lit up two of the El Sublimados from the box of cigars Gruvver had brought along with a gift bottle of golden tequila, and they settled down on redwood gliders padded with fiesta cushions. A radiant heater on a pole nearby cut the gathering chill of high desert night.

Sports talk, then technical, aficionado car talk that aroused in both men the lust of pornography without the dirty words.

Cornell was ten years older than Lewis, just into his forties and with the gut of a settled-in family man, half a head of red-toned hair. He had a serious way of cocking his head to listen or observe. A slow-talking man with a deep voice, he only stuttered occasionally, having worked hard to overcome that blight in his life.

"So what's your interest in luh-Lincoln Grayle?" he asked, after their passion for hot wheels neither of them could afford had been talked to death.

"I heard he puts on a damn fine show. You seen it?"

"No. I'll go to hear Gladys Knight or Lou Rawls anytime. Lourdes can get me to Gloria Estefan without too much fuss. But magic shows're not my thing. There's a glut of 'em here anyhow. The Grayle Theatre's an expensive ticket, I know that, but they still sell out even though plenty of the hotel shows got rigor mortis from the fuckin' economy." He looked in admiration at the cigar between his fingers. "Man, this here is a *smoke*. That cuh-cognac flavor comes right through, don't it?"

"Best smoke for the money I know of. By the way, Mama said to deliver you a message. E-mails are fine, and she knows you're a busy man, but she'd like for you to put the kids on the phone once in a while so she can hear their voices again before she's gone stone deaf."

"Her hearing's got that bad?"

"She hears what she wants to. Don't have any trouble singin' in the choir, Rascalla tells me."

"I invited her out to visit twice this year already," Cornell said with a defensive shrug. "Said I'd gladly put up the fare."

"You bring up the subject of manned flight, Mama says ain't no way, I'm not ready to be wait-listed for Eternity."

Cornell laughed. "Heard Peabo's latest fiancée bailed on him short of the altar. Too bad he couldn't hang on to this one. What I saw of her, she had auspicious ways."

"Yeah, Peabo. If love was golf, he'd be a do-over."

Cornell cocked his head. "You hear that?"

"What, coyote?"

"It's quiet in the house. Mercy! We got through another day without a trip to the ER." He exhaled a perfect smoke ring in the direction of the moon. "And Lourdes is already talkin' up number five, if you can believe that."

"Well, Cornell, reckon you own the faucet, you can ration the water."

"It's a superstitious thing with Lourdes; or, you know, the Catholic influence that is in her blood, even though she don't practice. Those half-crazed priests they get in the deep buh-back country down there in Central America? Tell a woman that if she deliberately blocks a child from bein' conceived, then the Lord will surely smite her for it, take away one she's already got."

"The female mind. Need a road map nobody's invented yet."

"Speaking of women—that is one terrific package keepin' you company now. What she wants with a empty-pockets 'Lanta police like yourself?"

"I'm cute," Gruvver said, feeling relaxed, blissful, and a little smug. "Say, Charmaine's dying to see Lincoln Grayle. Think you could get us comped for his show?"

"Not me. Lourdes probably can, but I believe they're duh-dark right now. He's on vacation or shooting a TV special, Africa, I think it said in the paper."

"What do you know about Grayle, Cornell?"

"What I told you. That theatre's earned him a walk-in freezer full of cold cash. He's a big Vegas booster, like wuh-Wayne Newton. Sponsors a big tennis tournament for charity. I don't think I've heard a word said against him, which is not true of plenty other celebrities earn their bread here. Bad drunks, whore stompers, casino welshers. And you know somethin'? Most of those male actors look so imposing on the movie screen, they're runts. Need a stepladder to see over a dime." Cornell looked at the flicker of a bat just above the pool, a spreading ring in the water where an insect had been. "So where's your question comin' from?"

"Oh, I don't know. Just some coincidences got me to thinking."

"You on a case, Lewis?"

"Was." Gruvver explained about the murder of the evangelist Pledger Lee Skeldon, and identical incidents involving other religious leaders. Then that business about the "Lucky Tickets" to the Lincoln Grayle show.

"I don't know yet about the 'Nam kid who took a bus ride down to L.A. to greet the Dalai Lama with a piranha kiss, but I'll be looking into that tomorrow while Charmaine has a back rub and a facial. Also I wouldn't mind getting a look at the list they have of Lucky Ticket holders over at the Grayle Theatre. Those folks who rate a special audience with him after the show. They probably have photographs too, lucky folks arm in arm with Mr. Magic." Gruvver picked a fleck of wrapper leaf off his lower lip with an index fingernail. "Audience. Isn't that what they call it when the Pope visits with dignitaries at his home place in Rome?"

"Believe so. Lewis, you care to hear a piece of good advice?"

"Why not?" Gruvver said, already sure of what Cornell's advice would be.

"You don't want to go near Lincoln Grayle or none of his people with off-the-wall speculations, especially since a vuh-visit by you is in no way connected to official business. Which you have no jurisdiction here anyhow."

"That's true." Gruvver placidly drew on his cigar, admiring his view of the starry night.

"It's all just a weird coincidence, what I'm saying."

"I've always found magicians to be a little scary, haven't you, Cornell?"

"Showmanship, man. Good scare is all part of the fun."

"Some of them are expert hypnotists too, aren't they?"

"Here it comes," Cornell said, puffing out his cheeks in exasperation. "What're you thinking, that Grayle is some kind of evil cult figure, follower of Satan, a spawn of the devil who can get people to do awful things against their will?"

"Spawn of the devil? Probably not. I wouldn't rule out that he *is* the devil." Gruvver put his cigar down on a smokeless ashtray and had a good stretch. "No matter he's not around this week, his business office will be open. I'll take a run over there tomorrow, see if they'll let me have a look at that list I'm curious about."

"Won't happen. You won't get to see nothing without a warrant, which a lawyer is going to read first under a microscope."

"Fuck warrants," Gruvver said, disagreeing with a smile. "Sometimes all you need to do is hit the right note of humble and nice to get their cooperation. One thing I do know about celebrities, there's no such thing as enough good PR."

The women had come out of the house and were walking toward them, ice cubes clinking in their glasses. Charmaine moved with the grace of a deer crossing a dawn meadow, head bent as she listened to squat, solid, cheerful Lourdes.

"And it's hard to say no to a pretty woman," Gruvver mused, studying on Charmaine, who lifted her head and called to him.

"Lewis! Lourdes is saying we don't want to miss the roller-coaster ride at the top of the Stratosphere. And that other deal they got, the Big Shot, lifts you right to the tip-top of the needle and drops you, practically a free fall."

"Not tonight, girl. I'm digesting beans and barbecue and good tequila I don't want to be hurlin' all over Glitter Gulch. How about the late show at the Tropicana?"

"He means the Folies Bergere," Lourdes said with a laugh.

"Uh-*uh*. All those bare boobs? You don't need the stimulation."

"I take that as a compliment," Gruvver said, gathering Charmaine in with one arm. She perched in his lap with a twist and a wiggle and pressed her frosted margarita glass against his cheek as if branding him. He yelped, then had a sip of her drink. Lourdes laughing and laughing. Cornell still with his serious expression, head cocked to one side, watching Gruvver.

"You know there's twenty-four-hour wedding chapels all over Vegas," Lourdes said, giving Gruvver the needle, "and Cornell and me don't have anything to do for the next couple of hours."

"Gettin' hitched might spoil all our fun," Gruvver said, gazing up at Charmaine's face, waiting on that little lift of an eyebrow he knew was coming.

Charmaine bounced on him. "For sure it would spoil your *life* when my daddy got hold of you. You'd be better off dragged five miles behind a slow mule with a bad case of the farts. I'm still his baby and you better not forget it, Gruvver-man."

ROME · OCTOBER 22 · 5:20 A.M.

Have the police come up with anything?" Lincoln Grayle asked.

"If they have, we've not been notified," Tom Sherard said. "It's been a busy night for them anyway. There were eyewitnesses, but the closest was a block away."

"My chauffeur and one bodyguard are still unconscious in the hospital," Grayle said. "I called again before I came down to see you. As you may have heard, the other bodyguard is in the morgue. I'm sick about that."

"Were they reliable people?" Tom asked.

"I've used the same firm for years, every time I come to Rome. Sure, they're the best."

"Would you like coffee, Linc?" Bertie asked him.

"No, thanks. I'm coffee'd out." The magician flexed his talented large hands, strong-looking fingers a pickpocket or concert pianist would've envied, before clenching them helplessly. "I just wanted to express to you both how badly I feel about what's happened." He looked around the sitting room of the suite to which Eden Waring's doppelganger had not returned as if it were an uncomfortable stage without the props he was accustomed to, for bringing off miraculous reappearances. There was a suggestion of guilt in the set of his mouth. Bertie smiled sympathetically, poured tea for herself from the room-service cart, had another sidelong look at his aura, which was flashy as might be expected according to his personality and vibrant health, shimmering two feet out from his body, but also muddled by tension and sleeplessness at this melancholy hour. She settled herself by Tom again, crimson *shuka* floating around her bare ankles. There was a trace of light at the windows. A street sweeper passed on the Via Veneto, bringing dogs in their wrath to barred gates and windows along the wide avenue.

"The best I can come up with," Grayle reflected, "is that they were after me. But, if that were the case—"

"They shouldn't have taken Eden," Tom said. "There is a possibility they might have decided on her as a consolation prize, once they discovered you were not in the limousine as expected."

"Even if they didn't recognize Eden Waring?" Bertie said skeptically.

"An attractive young woman riding in a limo would indicate that eventually she could be worth money to them." To Grayle Tom said, "Did you let on to any of your chums who your date for the evening really was?"

"Of course not. I respected Eden's need for privacy."

"So what do we do now?" Bertie asked.

"Nothing to do but wait and hope we're contacted," Tom said, looking again at Grayle. "Do you plan to be in Rome for long?"

"I'll probably leave later today. After this most recent bombing, there's very little chance I'll be allowed to use the Colosseum for the illusion I planned. And I have plenty to do before I reopen my theatre in Vegas this weekend." He rose to his feet with a defeated little flourish of one hand. "We'll stay in touch," he said. "I do feel as if I let Eden down somehow."

Bertie spoke soothingly to him in a soft voice, accompanying him to the door in the trompe l'oeil vestibule of the suite. There, out of Tom's line of vision (he didn't happen to be watching anyway), she drew fingertips down Grayle's jaw that was blackening with stubble and gave him a mild kiss, sent him back to his own accommodations. She drifted again into the sitting room with a dense glazed face that wasn't entirely due to lack of sleep; Tom knew the look. She tasted and decided her tea had cooled too much and poured a fresh cup from the silver pot. Added sugar and milk, forgot that she had added sugar, and reached for more. Sherard's patience had ebbed.

"Bertie? What gives?"

"Oh," she said, shivering slightly as if he'd startled her. "Well, he's lying about something."

"About what happened to Gwen?"

"Relative to that." She walked around the pink marble floor with its oblongs of Turkish carpets, sipping from her teacup.

"Bertie," he said again.

She looked a little cross. "But I can't be specific. I'm able to brain-lock anyone. I can only Peep minds that are susceptible or unaware. His is neither."

"You have reason not to trust him, though. Or was it just one of your hunches?"

"Trust him? I'm afraid I haven't for a while. Linc is very sophisticated in defense of his arts, which may include the black arts. Always in control of himself, even while we were in danger at Amboseli." She whirled toward Tom before he could say anything, forgetting the teacup in her hand. The tea sloshed and burned her wrist. "Damn!" She put the cup down and licked. "By the way—something showed up in his aura that *wasn't* with him at Amboseli. A bullet fragment in his right shoulder. Big one. Maybe from a .447 or .50-caliber Steyr. Recent wound. Happened only three or four days ago, I'd guess."

"And what does that tell us? One of his magic stunts went awry?"

"I'm not sure. I'll think about it. Meanwhile, shouldn't we get back to the real Eden Waring?"

"Yes. I'm afraid I've had a pretty bad thought. What if the kidnappers of her doppelganger have a change of heart and—"

"Try to do away with her? She can't be killed, Tom." Bertie drank her remaining tea. "You can't off a shape-shifter, either, as we've had a couple of chances to prove. At least not by conventional means." She crossed the sitting room, pulled Tom to his feet, put her arms around his neck, and rested her face in the hollow of his shoulder. She felt deeply flushed. He touched the back of her head, sensing the lightning inside her skull like a dim flare of firelight in a prehistoric cave.

"What unconventional means could be employed? Or is that too theoretical?"

"You could try pulling one of them apart atom by atom, and scattering those atoms from hell to breakfast. That would take a lot of energy. Probably enough to kill a couple of talented psychics in the bargain, even an Avatar."

"The only ammunition I've ever used is Steyr," Sherard reminded her.

"I know."

He took a long breath and exhaled slowly, bathing an ear in his warmth; she shuddered slightly, holding him tighter.

"There's none better. But if 480 grains of powder can't get the job done—just what the hell are we in for, Alberta?"

"Not now. I need to talk to Eden. Then let's turn in and try to get some rest. Can I sleep with you, Tom?"

"No," he said, but in the timbre of his voice she detected reluctance to refuse her.

"Can I sleep next to you and be a perfect angel?"

"That you may."

"Good."

CITTÀ DEL VATICANO · OCTOBER 22 · 3:25 P.M.

The ever-vigilant Laurent Colbert had detected a minute spot of relish from lunch—Leoncaro had invited as his guest the Black Pope (general of the Jesuits), whose guilty pleasure was American cheeseburgers—so there in his study on the third floor of the Apostolic Palace the Pope was obliged to hastily change into a fresh white satin cassock brought to him by his valet. While he was being buttoned up Leoncaro took advantage of this lull in his usual tightly scheduled day to study the photographs and quickly memorize the names of the eight American men whom, with their wives, he was about to meet. All were prominent lay Catholics singled out by their bishops for exemplary service and fund-raising prowess in their dioceses. Not incidentally, all of the men were members of *Opus Dei,* sometimes referred to by cynics or detractors as the "Holy Mafia." The uncompromising allegiance of *Opus Dei* to papal dogma was a source of comfort in these contentious days of cultural imperialism and secularism, and adversarial polemics from within the Church itself. (Speaking of certain members of the Curia he found it difficult to deal with, Leoncaro had grumbled to Colbert, "Whenever things are not going well with the home team, they invoke the spectre of Satan.")

Santa Rosa, California. San Antonio, Texas. Minneapolis, Minnesota—"I thought all of Minnesota had fallen into the hands of the Lutherans," Leoncaro said, setting up his joke as he and Colbert left the antechamber of the papal study and, for the fourth time that day, headed for the elevator that would take them to the *appartamento nobile* on the second floor, then down a corridor to the library. "Please fax Bishop Van Cuse my gratitude for sending me half of his flock today." The secretary chuckled dutifully. "Now tell me again, what is the business of Adamson from St. Louis?"

"His company distributes a line of processed meat products, Holiness."

"And is it *Tub*ner or Taubner from California?"

"Tubner. Liquor wholesaler."

"Mad cow disease and double malt scotches," Leoncaro muttered, assuring himself of a couple of topics for conversation.

Pinky Tubner still had a headache and a case of nerves from bombs in the night as she waited with her husband for the Pontiff to make his entrance into the elegant library. Also she was starved. Frank had fasted for the last twenty-four hours, a weekly regimen that he said kept him mentally sharp and increased his store of energy, but Pinky hadn't been able to hold down breakfast and so had passed on lunch when invited by two of the other women present in the library, Liz Adamson from St. Loo and Pem Carpenter from Cleveland.

She kept a gloved hand in Frank's while they circulated, admiring with the others ancient and modern objets d'art from every part of the world, the oriental carpets that lay on a marble floor as reflective as a glacial lake, dark solid Renaissance library tables and upholstered chairs. The air was sharp with the acidic odor given off by the crumbly leather of valuable old books.

Lined up on one of the long tables were sixteen red velvet boxes containing twenty-four-karat gold medallions, with St. Peter on the reverse and Pope John the Twenty-fourth on the obverse, his sharply struck profile surrounded by an inscription (from St. Irenaeus): *Gloria dei homo vivens*—"living man is the glory of God." All of Leoncaro's honored guests coveted these medallions, each of which had been blessed and would be given into their hands by His Holiness at the conclusion of today's reception.

Frank had smoothly insinuated himself into a discussion of the inroads—or depredations, according to the majority view being expressed—that Islam was making in third-world countries, with Catholic ministries lagging in their influence. "It seems to me," he was saying, "that a religion without the 'radiant mystery' of salvation as its greatest concern is more interested in exploiting poverty and oppression for political reward."

Pinky found herself standing too close to a stylishly barbered man whose aftershave was making her headache worse. She allowed herself to be separated from her husband by another of the wives, Irene Hudlow from the archdiocese of Denver. Irene was tall, ungainly, nearsighted; her glasses gave her blue eyes that watery aquarium look. In the way of homely women on important social occasions, Irene had overprimped. Pinky had found her, during their get-acquainted stage earlier in the week, to be somewhat ditzy. With no encouragement on Pinky's part Irene had proudly showed off her surgical steel tongue stud, which she had acquired at the age of fifty-plus as a means (outrageously misguided, it seemed to Pinky) of bonding with her sixteen-year-old daughter.

"They say his eyes are just so gorgeous," Irene gushed.

"Who?"

"The Holy Father. On TV you don't really notice because of the totality of expression, his ineffable power. But his eyes are a remarkable sea-green shade, according to the monsignor from Vatican PR I was just talking to. An unusual color, even for a northern Italian. I get jittery when I meet celebrities, although it should be old-hat by now. Howard's an exhibitor, you know—multiplexes in three states—and there are scads of movie stars and directors at ShoWest every year."

"ShoWest?"

"In Las Vegas; it's a big convention, basically a promotional deal for the studios trying to sell us their new product. We get advance looks at all the big flicks they have in the works. I'm thirsty; it's warm in here, isn't it? But I don't dare drink any more punch. Even though my tongue sort of swells in my mouth like a toad if I'm trying to talk to, say, Harrison Ford. Or, *forget* it, Tom Hanks. Now, the Holy Father! My knees are already knocking. A league of his own. You wouldn't happen to know where the girls' sandbox is? But probably it's too late to duck out, His Holiness should be here any second."

Pinky glanced at a Vatican photographer, who had smilingly motioned for her to stand a little closer to the towering Irene Hudlow. Pinky obliged, but was afraid afterward that her eyes had blinked shut just as his flash went off. There was another photographer on hand, this one with a video camera. And three men in black suits who didn't appear to have any particular responsibilities. Probably security for His Holiness, Pinky concluded with a feeling of sadness. Necessary even here, within the hushed frescoed magnificence of the Apostolic Palace.

There was an expectant stir and turning of heads to the library's entrance, but still it wasn't the now-tardy Leoncaro: instead Pinky saw a stunning young woman of mixed oriental and African bloodlines, as tall as Irene Hudlow, on the arm of a man with a tanned somber face and a pronounced limp in spite of his reliance on a dark cane with a thick twist in the wood and eyespots where thorns had been cut away. He looked as if he might be recovering from a bad car accident; he wore his English-tailored pinstriped suit coat cloak-style because of a cast on his right forearm. The regal young woman was wearing a vividly patterned *shuka* with a silk headscarf knotted behind her head and a breastplate of glowing pink-tinged cowrie shells on gold chains.

Obviously they were invited guests, but not honorees; a security man glanced at the cane, but from his expression the couple were expected, Pinky assumed, and had been cleared elsewhere in the palace.

"Wow," Irene Hudlow said under her breath.

"Celebrities?" Pinky asked; Irene had established herself as the expert on the breed.

"Hmm. I don't think she's in pictures, but the face is *awfully* familiar. What *presence*. Cripes, I'd love to be able to walk into a room like that. Would you look at the fellas? You can practically hear their eyeballs clicking."

"I wonder what he does?" Pinky said, her attention now on Tom Sherard.

"Hard to tell, but I smell money. May be one of those sportsmen who take big gambles; y'know, racing yachts in the horse latitudes and going for round-the-world hot-air balloon records. That's no health-club tan. This guy *lives*." Irene got a squinched look around her mouth. "Jeez, I think I'll have to chance it and look up the bathroom. How about you?"

"No, what I need is to pop an Excedrin and wash it down with some punch." Pinky grinned. "I'll let you know if you miss anything."

"Don't say *that*," Irene admonished, and sought the ear of a security man for directions to the women's lounge. Pinky fished in her clutch purse for the tin of Excedrin and was served punch in a cutglass cup by a young Irish nun who wore one of those modified habits—simple blue shirtwaist, dark gray pleated skirt, and an unobtrusive black-bordered wimple—that made her look more like a practical nurse than a bride of Christ.

"They do keep it warm in here," the nun said with a smile, blotting the hollows of her eyes with a paper napkin, noting the tablet that went onto Pinky's tongue before she began to drink her punch.

The monsignor in charge of the afternoon's reception and one of the security men were rounding everyone up to form a line near the library's entrance. Howard Hudlow was looking around in annoy-

ance. As Pinky went to join her husband she whispered in his ear,
"Ladies' room."

"Nervous bladder," he said, shaking his head. "Forgot to pack her
Datrol."

"I think we're all a little nervous," Pinky said on Irene's behalf,
then slipped into the reception line beside Frank, who was on his
toes, doing his unobtrusive isometrics, all smiles. *This was it.* A lifetime of adoration and anticipation was culminating this side of
heaven.

Pinky briefly observed the recently arrived couple off to themselves in a corner of the library looking over a piece of modern
sculpture she'd seen earlier, by a Zambian artist. Gray stone and
ebony, a cloaked African mother (she'd had to look twice before she
realized the folds of the "cloak" were really praying hands around
the stylized oval face), two babes at her breasts. Then the Pope
walked in followed by two men, one of whom was a monsignor and
had a flat black case under his arm; the other was probably another
security man who had met Leoncaro in his second-floor apartment
for the brief walk to the library.

The honorees weren't wearing name tags, but the Holy Father
apparently knew everyone by sight. No prompting required by his
secretary, who trailed him down the reception line. Leoncaro clasping hands, smiling, taking his time, a personal reference in each
greeting, as if they were all best friends who hadn't been together for
a while. And, yes, his eyes were an incredible shade of green. Pinky
felt a warm blood-tingle as he moved closer to where they stood
toward the end of the line. She saw that Frank's hands were joined at
the belt line almost as if he were preparing to receive communion;
but Pinky knew he had been trembling moments ago.

"Faith is only as powerful as human nature allows it to be," His
Holiness said in response to a question from one of the wives.

Irene Hudlow appeared at the entrance to the library, looking
flustered and somewhat askew. A security man approached her with
a palms-up gesture. Too late to join the others. She'd have to wait
there. Her husband giving her a deadly look. Pinky had him pegged
as somewhat of an emotional bully.

Irene looked distractedly at the security man as he whispered in her ear. Pinky returned her attention to the Pope, but she caught the movement of Irene's head in the background as she simultaneously seized the security man by his longish hair and yanked his chin up, exposing his throat. And that's where Irene bit and tore before throwing the man, now jetting blood, out of her way.

Afterward Pinky had a lot of difficulty piecing together the sequence of events because much of what happened, in the nature of a small complex riot occurring within the framework of mere seconds, she simply needed to forget for the sake of her sanity.

There was the man with the torn throat staggering and raining blood at the marbled threshold of the library; another security guard drawing a pistol from beneath his jacket and stepping into Irene's path as she rushed toward the Holy Father, one thick lens of her eyeglasses spotted with blood; the reception line breaking up with screams and shouts of warning; Leoncaro turning toward the outlandish, harpylike Irene as she smashed the second security man to the floor with casual but immense strength. Was a shot fired into Irene's midsection? *Time-skip.* Pinky had no memory of it.

Ensorcelled Irene (what other explanation could there be?) nearly had the Pope in her grasp when Laurent Colbert seized him and whirled him out of harm's way. Both men stumbled toward Frank and Pinky, Laurent embracing Leoncaro with both arms. The two of them resembling an awkward ballroom dance team.

Then Frank—

—her own husband—

(The one memory, please God, she could have done without, but no such luck; it was to be forever in her mind like a funerary curse etched at the entrance to an ancient tomb)

—Frank grabbed the off-balance papal secretary and wrenched him away from His Holiness. As Leoncaro fell, Frank and Colbert came head to head.

And Frank, his jaws appearing to unhinge like those of a rattlesnake, bit off half of the monsignor's face, then heaved him in a flying body block toward the remaining two security men.

Irene swooped in, shrieking approval. Pinky's scream froze in her throat.

Time-skip.

When time resumed in its now helter-skelter fashion both Irene Hudlow and Frank Tubner were clawing at the slippery cassock of the Pope, who was facedown on a carpet and covering his head with both hands. Blood was everywhere on the cassock and papal robes in dabs and finger smears, blood made more vivid by repeated flashes as the Vatican's official photographer, as deep in shock as anyone there, metronomically continued to record the chaotic scene. Irene Hudlow's husband, not such a tough cookie after all, had fainted. The Irish nun was screaming, having nearly attained a note that would shatter the glass fronts in the bookcases.

These horrors were more than sufficient to keep Pinky in nightmares for the rest of her destroyed life, but, unmercifully, there was worse to come.

As quick as Frank Tubner had been to pounce on the unprotected Pontiff, he was raised from his and Irene Hudlow's intended prey, jerked almost six feet off the floor by an otherworldly force that Pinky felt in her own wavering bones. She saw a jolt of astonishment in Frank's eyes just as the force bent him double like a giant cramp in the gut and sent him headlong into the wall above a row of bookcases, near the twenty-five-foot ceiling with its fine painting of a gathering of someday-saints in another age of miracles.

A worm of blood crawled down Pinky's upper lip. Pem Carpenter's nose literally gushed into her white gloves as she backed toward the doorway; another woman's backside was staining from an untimely and abnormal menstrual flow. Pinky's eyes flicked from her airily suspended husband to the outstretched hand of the young woman in the Hermes-style *shuka*. Not begging for surcease; commanding it. Her lovely face was distorted, as if reflected from a curved dark surface. Irene Hudlow's elongated face also was undergoing change: a dark shadow like hair on her widening jaw, nostrils flattening and enlarging. Wildness in both their faces: but even

Pinky, in terrified straits, could distinguish the difference. Good was eye to eye with evil and Irene's splayed, knuckly, haired-up hands, inches from the prostrate Pope, were as still as if they had been locked to the wrists in a block of granite.

At the same time Frank, still doubled and hissing like a viper from the Book of Revelation, bobbed against the ceiling above their heads, a grotesque party balloon. Most of the oxygen in the library seemed to have been consumed by the demands of their terror; the heat now was almost scorching.

Leoncaro's secretary, nearly blinded, his face wrecked down to fragments of gleaming bone, threw himself across the Pope's body. The library was emptying; more nosebleeds to fuel pandemonium.

"*You know who I am,*" Irene said with a curt aside of her head; she was cutting new teeth that jutted from her upper gums like ivory stakes. She spat in fury at the tall African girl while simultaneously urinating on the floor.

"And you know who *I* am," Bertie Nkambe returned. Then with an agonized glance at her companion she said, "Tom! They're trying to shift on me! I don't know how long I can hold them off!"

"Give me the chunky fellow," Tom Sherard said calmly.

His Holiness stirred, trying to rise with Colbert's body on his back. The secretary had passed out.

"*Totus tuus,*" Leoncaro said with a lift of his eyes to Bertie. *I give myself totally to you.* He was bewildered from shock or perhaps serene in the light of a vision of the Holy Virgin.

Three men rushed to get Leoncaro on his feet. They half dragged him to the door while Irene struggled, shrieking impotently. Then with a sound as painful as an arrow to the ear Irene split the carapace of force holding her immobile. She bounded on all fours after the Pontiff, now splitting out of her dress as well, revealing the colorful ass of a baboon.

Frank Tubner fell at the feet of Tom Sherard, who smashed his head sidelong with the cane; there was a double *crack* of split skull-bone, first from the impact with the cane, then as Frank's head hit the marble floor, but Pinky didn't hear that hollow-sounding report.

Time had just skipped on her once more. Skipped for the rest of the afternoon.

Eden Waring, accompanied by two tall, bearded Swiss Guardsmen in their amusing orange-and-blue striped Renaissance regalia, was hurrying along the corridor that led to the library when the screaming erupted and echoed throughout the Apostolic Palace, followed by invited guests bailing out of the library with bloody noses, followed by the Pope, more blood on white satin, his zucchetto dangling over one ear, gold pectoral cross swinging as he was more or less carried by three men in black suits, and followed by—

The two guards, unable to believe their eyes, tried to hold Eden back as the Pope was pushed inside a room and a stout oak door slammed behind them. The late Irene Hudlow, now transformed into something else entirely, hit the door hard enough after a leap of more than fifteen feet to cause chandeliers up and down the corridor to tremble and blink. Real ugly, but obviously powerful. What remained of Irene was a nice rope of pearls around its hairy neck. Claws gouged splinters a foot long and an inch thick from the elaborately carved door.

Eden recovered her faculties while the Swiss Guards and others, attracted by the fearful screaming that could be heard, probably, in the basilica, were backing up. Eden crept closer with a grimace white as a scar, moving at an angle in the wide corridor, so far unnoticed by the howling-mad creature. She held Tom Sherard's walking stick level and at shoulder height, gripping it a few inches below the gold lion's head. She calmed herself with an athlete's practiced focus.

The four-hundred-pound, ten-foot-high door began to come off its ornate hinges.

Bertie appeared in the library doorway as the creature acknowledged Eden's approach with a baleful over-the-shoulder look. For a few moments the claws were still while it pissed lavishly on the floor, expressing both contempt and a territorial imperative.

What kept you? Bertie wanted to know. Subvocally she still sounded weakened by ordeal.

Storm over the Atlantic. That's a gorgeous shuka.

Thanks. My guy at Hermes. Eden?

Yeah?

Don't fool around with this beastie. There are people dying in here.

I wasn't thinking of adopting it, Eden told her, curtly shutting Bertie out of her mind; she needed to retain focus and not allow surging adrenaline to pump her heart through the roof of her mouth.

The creature resumed its frenzy of destruction. The massive door came free with a tortured screech of old nails pulling out of wood and wrenched bronze hinges, and was flung end over end down the wide corridor at Eden.

"Simba!"

The lion's-head walking stick streaked end-first from Eden's hand as she dodged away from the tumbling door. The stick was a momentary blur, catching light as it arched toward the open doorway. It pierced the creature in midleap like a heavy arrow from a medieval longbow. Flesh, sinew, bone, and heart skewered in a fraction of a second. The creature fell headlong and skidded in a heap almost to the feet of those who had sought refuge inside the large domed chamber. A leathery eyelid closed in shadowless diffused sunlight.

When Eden got there a stink was rising from the hairy body that was curled limply on one side. Some pearls from the broken strand were rolling slowly across the marble floor.

Eden looked into the eyes of John the Twenty-fourth. His Holiness looked appalled and seriously pissed at the same time. He held his gold cross in one hand, away from the blood-soiled front of his cassock.

Well done, she heard in her mind. Then Leoncaro raised his eyes to something he sensed was lurking above them, on the outside of the small dome with its cupola of stained glass.

Eden had a glimpse of it too—catlike, shadowy, climbing surreptitiously to the highest point of the cupola, looking down into the chamber some thirty feet below. Small brimstone eyes in a blunt monstrous head. She'd last seen it in the video shot by Etan Culver in

Amboseli National Park during the fearful display of rage and power by the elephant known as Karloff. Bright splinters of light from the sky above the cupola hurt her eyes. And the part-feline phantom was already losing definition, as if it had been accidental, a burst of dirty smoke from a chimney, vanishing even before she could be certain it was really there.

"I don't suppose I'm going to get my walking stick back," Tom Sherard grumbled. He was gazing at the gold lion's head and the inch of dark wood socketed between the simian shoulder blades of the motionless creature.

"Remember what we talked about? That thing isn't dead," Bertie reminded him. "Only inert. But it will stay that way as long as the stick is there. How long do you think *mopane* wood is good for?"

"I reckon a thousand years, in a dry place."

"I know of just such a place," Leoncaro murmured, kneeling beside the shape-shifter and making the sign of the cross above its head. An eyelid flickered, prompting a shocked reaction from caped ecclesiasticals drawn to the scene. The Pope wasn't bothered but he did seem annoyed that there was no door to close on the chamber as he rose stiffly, waving aside helping hands. "A tomb," he concluded, "where others much like this one are interred." He looked again at Eden with an unexpectedly warm—considering the tumult echoing through the Apostolic Palace—smile of welcome.

"So good to meet you, at last. We'll talk soon. Right now I believe we both have more pressing concerns, Eden Waring. Do you have knowledge of the whereabouts of your alter ego?"

Eden said, with an expression of surprise—how could he know about doppelgangers?—"Not yet, Holiness. I don't think that's good news. She—she must respond if she's able."

He glanced up at the dome again before giving himself over to a phalanx of Swiss Guards in mufti. The blood of outrage in his face caused the old scar impinging on his upper lip to stand out in ivory relief.

"You must do everything in your power to retrieve her," he said to Eden, "before we meet again."

Lewis," Charmaine complained, "I know you explained it all to me a couple times already, but I'm standing here twenty minutes at this table and I still don't know when you win or lose, or why."

"Mostly I'm winning," Gruvver said, absorbed in the action at the Caesars Palace craps table. He indicated the four-inch stack of red chips, with a growing stack of green beside it. Now that the dice were in the hands of a shooter who had numbers working, Gruvver was making come-bets on every roll, with odds. Working up a sweat, rolling his shoulders, putting his own momentum behind the bouncing dice. "This is when the game gets good."

"What are those green chips worth again?"

"Twenty-five each."

"Oh. And what is the high-roller trying to do?"

"He's not necessarily a high-roller; he's just the shooter. But it's happening for him. What he doesn't want to do now is seven-out." The point was nine. "Yeah!" Gruvver exulted.

"You win again?" Charmaine said, liking this part.

"Four hundred big ones on that roll."

Charmaine helped him stack the chips he pulled in. Behind them the lilt and bingle of slot machine city, a rhythmic patter of payoffs that was part of the megasell come-on, the hallelujah energy of a rural come-to-Jesus beneath spyglass ceilings that hid most of the casino watchdogs and their hard-core eavesdropping technology.

"Come, don't come, stickman, hard-on, everybody gettin' lathered up," Charmaine said teasingly in Gruvver's ear. "This game's just about havin' sex in public. No wonder most of the women watch while the men play with themselves, rubbin' up and blowin' on those dice."

A woman next to Charmaine, overhearing some of this, said in a middle-European accent, "For a man, everything is about sex. Money? It just buys better sex."

Charmaine offered a polite expression of interest but no encouraging comment. Not liking the way the woman was staring past her at Gruvver. Vegas seemed to be full of people who looked as if they harbored secret manias and were there to be exorcised, not entertained.

"It's hard*way*, Charmaine," Gruvver corrected her as she pressed closer to him. He was avidly following the tumble of dice off the padded end wall. "But that's a sucker's bet. Yeah! Man made his point again."

Charmaine nipped his earlobe with her teeth. "Are we ever gonna eat supper tonight?"

"Reservation's at ten."

"Think I'll go play roulette then." It seemed safe to leave him alone; the woman had drifted off to another table.

"That game is easy to understand. It's red, or it's black. Put your money on a number, little white ball lands on that number, bingo, thirty-five to one. Could I have some money, Lewis?"

"There's a fifty in my wallet."

"I'll play your birthday, like I did yesterday at Mandalay Bay."

Charmaine reached inside his suit coat and extracted his wallet. "Why don't I keep this? That way I know you'll come looking for me when you're flat busted."

That wasn't happening yet. The shooter had made another point and Gruvver was in ecstasy. Charmaine dropped his wallet into her purse and sauntered off. What she really wanted was a kir royale, but if she sat down at the bar by herself two things were inevitable. She'd get carded. Because she was still a few weeks shy of twenty-one, she wasn't supposed to be in the casino. Or before she could even order her kir royale, someone from casino security would stop by to chat and then ask to see a room key. Charmaine had one, although they weren't staying at Caesars; but it was annoying to think she could be mistaken for a hooker.

Might as well settle for a Coke at the soda fountain with all the kids.

At a table in one corner of the ice cream parlor she took Gruvver's old wearing-out wallet from her purse and idly looked through it. Receipts stuck just about everywhere; she needed to establish a better filing system for him. And there were a couple of articles he had clipped out of the local newspaper today. One was just a squib under World News Briefs that he'd circled. The supreme Patriarch of Thai Buddhists had been flown to Los Angeles for treatment at the UCLA Medical Center. The nature of his illness was undisclosed. Charmaine had no idea why Gruvver would be interested in a Buddhist; he was benignly negligent about attending his own church, even though his mama called him promptly at seven A.M. every Sunday to remind him. Charmaine had come close on a couple of mornings while half asleep next to him to picking up the phone herself, which probably would have jeopardized the marginally good opinion Lewis's mother had of her.

The other article had a one-column head:

VATICAN DISTURBANCE
BLAMED ON CHILDREN

Apparently, Charmaine learned, hundreds of visitors to the Holy See the day before, at about three forty-five in the afternoon Rome time, had been shocked to hear terrified screams emanating from the Apostolic Palace while the Pope was in audience with a group of "prominent American lay people." A dozen security men had rushed to the second floor of the palace, followed shortly by a medical team. Everyone inside the basilica at the time was quickly ushered out and security personnel closed off all access to the palace.

The official explanation from the Pope's spokesman was that one of the visiting Americans had suffered a fatal seizure, and the sight of the unfortunate victim writhing on the floor had greatly upset a group of mentally challenged children who happened to be passing by the papal library at the time. Thus the screams that were heard.

The alleged seizure victim was not identified, pending notification of next of kin.

Charmaine, although her curiosity wasn't exactly at fever pitch, brought up the newspaper clippings after they'd completed their dinner selections at Spago. Gruvver was still relishing every fortunate roll of the dice that had enabled him to leave the craps table with twenty-six hundred in folding cash.

"You don't happen to know anybody who was visiting the Pope in Rome yesterday, do you, Lewis?"

"Huh-uh. Why?"

"Oh, when I was borrowin' that fifty from your wallet, couldn't help noticin' your little newspaper articles about the head Buddhist from Thailand who is in Los Angeles, and the poor man who died during his audience with the Pope."

"Oh, yeah," Gruvver said, somewhat guardedly.

"So I just wondered why you were interested in them, that's all. More detective work? *Le travail du agent?*"

"Well, the Buddhist Patriarch and the Pope his ownself fit in with what I've been thinking since we closed out the Jimmy Nixon case, particularly that so-called *disturbance* reported at the Vatican yesterday."

Charmaine waited attentively, hands folded under her chin, wondering if she was supposed to guess where his mental processes and nosing around had taken him the past couple of days. Charmaine had occupied her afternoon changing her hairstyle to something smarter, vampish, a big blade of hair downswept over part of her face, the incognito look. Gruvver avoided the tough-love expression in the single brown eye that was revealed to him.

"Sooner-later you're gonna tell me," she said. It wasn't an ultimatum but he knew she was serious. "I'm first-rate, Gruvver-man; don't you go treatin' me like second place in your life, or I won't be there for long." That was the ultimatum; Charmaine let him absorb it. "Now then. Yesterday you had me go out there to the Grayle Theatre with you where I did a number on that nice PR lady they have there, pretend I was writin' an article on the Magic Man for the Atlanta J-C. It upsets me to tell a lie, Lewis, but I was helping you. You said."

"You're a bona fide journalist; that's no lie."

"What I am is campus correspondent for the paper, and once in a blue moon I get a couple paragraphs into the *Constitution*."

"Better things are just ahead," Gruvver said with an attempt at a flattering smile.

A young black man with small eyes, a shorn skull, and powerful sloping shoulders was making his way through the dining room, escorted by ex-pug bodyguards, flashy consorts, and some elegant quail. Complete strangers looked up, smiled, called him Champ. Diamonds glittered in his cruel mouth.

A waiter poured red wine for Gruvver and, without hesitation, a glass for Charmaine.

"Anyway," she said to Gruvver, "thanks to me you got that list you wanted, Lucky Ticket holders to his shows for the past three years. It's a long list, and you were up to three this morning studyin' it."

"Was it that late?" Gruvver said, suppressing a yawn.

"Now suppose you tell me what's important about that list."

"It's a weird fucking story, and I probably don't know half of it yet."

"Lewis, your mouth," Charmaine said, glancing at the diners nearest them in the packed restaurant, hoping none of them had overheard. In the time they had been going together, Charmaine felt she had made good progress in two vital areas: toning down his vocabulary and improving his taste in neckwear.

"Sorry. But too many things add up already, and it's gettin' scarier."

"*You're* scared?" she said with a nervous shrug of her bare shoulders, flicker of lamplight in her widening eyes. Still, she was fascinated. "Of what? The magician?"

"Didn't say *I* was scared. The situation—the case—has a lot of weird elements. What I know beyond a doubt is, at least three young people, Jimmy bein' the youngest, attended Grayle's show and afterward got to spend time with him backstage. Weeks or months later they were responsible for two killings of prominent religious figures and an assault on another, the Dalai Lama, that didn't take his life. Method each time was the same—they bit like wolves or some other kind of large predator. Now, yesterday"—Gruvver joined his hands and leaned toward Charmaine, keeping his voice low—"there was that reported disturbance at the Vatican, and a man died. Today the

Pope went about his business like any other day, held his regular Wednesday audience. So he must be okay. I don't know the name of the man who the Vatican Press Office says had that seizure, but I do know"—he leaned back and fished a folded sheet of paper from an inside coat pocket—"*four* of the sixteen people at yesterday's private audience with the Pope are on the Lucky Ticket holder list as well. Now that just can't be a coincidence." He unfolded the paper. "Their names were published yesterday in *L'Osservatore Romano,* if I'm sayin' that right; anyhow, it's the Vatican newspaper and I took this off their Internet site. The four are Max and Irene Hudlow of Denver, and Frank and Roberta Tubner from Santa Rosa, California."

Charmaine raised her wineglass, staring blankly at him. "Well, so?"

"I'm on the come line that the Pope was attacked yesterday by one of these sixteen people at their audience, and the Vatican has hushed it all up. Which of course they can easily do. If there were any 'mentally challenged' kids in the Apostolic Palace at the time, then that's what they saw, something would really give them cause to have screaming fits."

Charmaine ran a finger around the outer rim of her wineglass. "Lewis, when we get back to the hotel, I think I need to take your temperature."

"I'm runnin' hot, but it's not the flu, baby." He placed the folded papal audience list beside his plate, tapped it with a forefinger. "If it did happen, then all of these people saw it. But curial counselors at the Vatican, their own Catholic psychiatrists, maybe the Pope himself, will have briefed them to keep shut about what went down. Why? Because something diabolical, I'm thinking, was loose in a sacred place, and they don't ever want that kind of publicity."

"*Diabolique?* The *devil?*" Suddenly Charmaine was looking at Gruvver with the rounded eyes of an impressionable ten-year-old. There were Pentecostal preachers in her extended family, and from an early age she'd been subjected to visions of torment and hellfire the way other preschoolers absorbed the gentle morality tales of Dr. Seuss. Charmaine's present level of sophistication, Gruvver reminded himself, was largely physical. He waved away the spectre he'd called up.

"No need to go that far. But we both know spells can be worked on susceptible minds." Charmaine nodded. He tapped the audience list again. "When these people get back home, won't take me but two or three phone calls to confirm what really happened. I can smell a cover-up long distance like it was fresh dog poop on my shoe."

As he concluded that remark the antipasto arrived. Charmaine only picked at hers, looking, in a childlike manner, very worried. She glanced at him a couple of times before saying, "Magicians are kind of freaky, but that's got to be an act. Casting spells on innocent people—what reason would Lincoln Grayle have to do that?"

"Charmaine, I've dealt with criminal psychopaths most of my working life. They're all around us, matter of fact—" Charmaine was instantly uneasy again; he had to smile. "I don't mean here at Spago; but my point is you couldn't easily pick one out of a crowd. They put up a good front, all smiles, easy talkin', but they're all the time wonderin' what they can get out of you. Or how best to get rid of you, if it comes to that. Those people are devious, clever, and emotionally cold. What motivates the worst of them is strictly what they want, got to have, at a given moment. Then their compulsion lights them up like a pinball machine."

"So—if Grayle is one of *those*, and he's got it in for religion or religious figures like Pledger Lee Skeldon or the Pope, then he'll just keep on keepin' on? Is that why you cut out that little article about the Buddhist big shot checking in to the UCLA hospital?"

"Right. Because I'm wonderin', assume I had time enough to check out every name on the Lucky Ticket list, would I learn that one of them is a medical professional on staff or an employee of the hospital? Already programmed by Mr. Magic to do damage to a prominent religious, should the occasion arise? I researched a whole other list of potential victims around the world: Jews, Muslims, Sikhs, the Eastern Orthodox Church."

"But what can you *do*, Lewis? Those lists don't prove anything."

Gruvver's broad shoulders fell slightly, and he looked so frustrated Charmaine felt sorry for him.

"That's the tough part. The man is a solid Vegas citizen. Homegrown. Employs three hundred people in his various enterprises. If he's also programmin' zombies and sendin' them out to commit murder, he's two-for-four to this point, which must be a disappointment, but only one of his zombies is left to wail her tale. If she's coherent at all. I'd have to take a trip to India to find out. Probably Lise Ruppenthal is sittin' in a cell with fungus all over the walls and a leaky ceiling, wonderin' how the hell she came to be there in the first place."

"Do you want any more of this salad?" Charmaine asked him after a few moments, determined not to see him brood about his presumed inadequacies.

Gruvver sighed. "No, thanks, Charmaine."

"Were you plannin' to go back to the tables after we eat?"

"My philosophy is, once you walk away a winner, you're a sure loser if you go back the same night." And he added, whimsically, "Get behind me, Satan."

"Well, we still got two whole days left in Vegas town, so I guess my philosophy is, let's put away those lists and make the most of our time together. I bless you for bein' the man you are. But you can't solve all the troubles and miseries of the world, Lewis."

Gruvver finished the wine in his glass, then drank hers, which perked him up marginally. "If the Forum shops are still open," he said, "we might see after supper if we can get shed of some of this cash in my pocket, buy you something to match that sparkle in your eye."

He put the papers back into his coat pocket as two waiters arrived to serve their dinner. Meat loaf with port wine sauce for Gruvver; a lean veal chop with sage hollandaise for Charmaine.

It didn't seem to be a time to mention—if ever there was going to be a time—that one of the names on the Lucky Ticket list was that of Gruvver's half brother Cornell Crigler. The same Cornell who had said to Gruvver two nights ago that magic shows were not his thing. And that he had never seen Lincoln Grayle perform.

They returned to their room at Bahìa at a quarter past one, Charmaine wearing a Mexican silver necklace with her birthstone, an amethyst, as the centerpiece. They had taken in a late lounge act at Rio Suites before finally calling it a night.

A white clasp envelope, sealed, had been pushed under their door. Charmaine opened it while Gruvver, substantially lit and with a full bladder, occupied the bathroom.

When he came out in his boxer shorts Charmaine was sitting on the king-size bed reading the note that had come with two invitations to the reopening of the Lincoln Grayle Theatre on the upcoming Saturday night.

"It's from Lucy Perkins," Charmaine said. "The PR director for Grayle I sort of conned? This is so sweet of her, Lewis! But actually says here Mr. Grayle *himself* is invitin' us."

"You need to be back for classes on Friday."

"But, Lewis! We can afford to stay over one more day; you still have more than half the money you won at Caesars! What difference if I miss a couple classes, I'll still graduate summa."

Gruvver opened the opaque curtains over the windows and looked west through the dust-laden penumbra of Las Vegas to where the Lincoln Grayle Theatre glowed like a supernova on its dark mountain.

"You *are* dyin' to meet him, and you know it."

"In a professional capacity. Maybe I didn't exactly get across to you at dinner that the Magic Man is not good people. Ask yourself, why is he takin' a personal interest in us?"

"Well, because I can charm killer bees out of their hive, you always say." He looked around at her. She shrugged prettily, pleased with herself. "And I guess Lucy Perkins took a likin'."

"Uh-huh," Gruvver said doubtfully, facing the windows again. The night had chilled down; his breath ghosted the glass in front of him. He was divided between a desire to clear out of Vegas on schedule and his natural impulses as a detective to pursue the mystery that obsessed him to its source, although he knew that source probably was out of his depth as an investigator. He felt a little apprehensive, regretful now because he had involved the faithful and eager-to-please Charmaine in his quest.

As if aware that she was uppermost in his thoughts just then, Charmaine sprang off the bed, long arms going around his bare hunky torso, squeezing blood and adrenaline to his throbbing temples.

"*Please,* Lewis." Charmaine began to play teasingly with his nipples. So deft. She sent a good supply of blood surging the other way, to his groin. "Everybody I've talked to says it's just an amazing show he puts on, as good as Siegfried and Roy. Lincoln Grayle uses animals too. The world's largest tiger."

One hand slid down to just below his navel. Still deft, she opened his shorts and polished his uppity apple with the ball of her thumb, while feeling his heartbeat through the muscle web of his hard back. Gruvver melting inside like Hershey's Kisses on a hot sidewalk.

"It's how he may be using some of his pets that bothers me," Gruvver said forebodingly.

Charmaine purred for him. "I saw this draped silk chiffon dress at one of the Grand Canal Shoppes. It is *so* fly. Wouldn't be like I don't have anything to wear."

CITTÀ DEL VATICANO · OCTOBER 24 · 4:50 P.M.

They were escorted up the back stairs to the third-floor papal apartment. The Pope was waiting for them in his study. He asked Eden and Bertie to sit in the high-backed chairs on either side of his large desk. Tom took the remaining seat, a small sofa where the Shade of Pledger Lee Skeldon had appeared to His Holiness early on the morning of October 10. It was a sunny cool day in Rome, nearly dark inside the study with the heavy drapes over the window facing St. Peter's Square drawn tightly closed.

The only light in the study came from the student's lamp on one side of the Pontiff's desk. Coffee and tea were available on a Medici-era sideboard. The door was closed. Two Vatican security men had posted themselves in the antechamber.

"Again, my profound gratitude," Leoncaro said, nodding to Sherard and the women.

"How is Monsignor Colbert?" Eden asked him.

"After seven hours of surgery on Tuesday, as well as could be expected. He may eventually regain the power of speech. But no matter how many operations are required, how gifted the surgeons are, I have been told that he will never again recognize himself in a mirror." He looked at Tom. "During my visits to several African nations, I saw numerous examples of the hyena's predilection for seizing victims by the head. But one never becomes accustomed to the sight of those who survive such powerful jaws."

"I know. And I've spent most of my life in Kenya."

Leoncaro folded his hands on his desk blotter, leaning into the pool of light on his desk, green eyes and satin zucchetto glistening. "I may tell you, without satisfaction, that the remains of the creature that killed one of our Swiss Guards and maimed poor Laurent have been interred. It lies in the crypt of a fourteenth-century monastery on Monte Capanne overlooking the sea at Isola D'Elba. A very secret, consecrated site. It will stay there along with a few other interesting—*specimens*—that have appeared down through the centuries to terrorize and destroy the faithful."

"All of them shape-shifters?" Bertie asked.

"I'm not at all certain. It might take a modern forensic pathologist to determine the origins of the mummies interred there. This won't happen, of course. And the knowledge of their existence in any form must stay with us."

The Pope kept his study warm, and the near-absence of light and sky made the warmth almost stifling. Their purpose in being there added to a general feeling of discomfort and oppression.

"What happened to the California man who was in on the plot to kill you?" Tom said. "Obviously that one wasn't a shape-shifter."

"Sent home yesterday for burial. His wife, Roberta, I believe, although she rather plaintively insisted upon being called 'Pinky,' was in no condition to accompany her husband's body. She is being treated for emotional and mental collapse and probably will be for the rest of her days. The same is more or less true of all of my other guests at the audience." He clasped his hands tightly. "What a mess," he said, still dismayed and very angry.

"Until a week ago," Bertie said, "I didn't know shape-shifters existed outside of a few places like Moby Bay—" She was about to explain her reference, but Leonaro indicated with a slight smile that he knew about that refuge for the Fallen who were dedicated to restoring themselves to a state of Grace. "So," she continued, "there must have been a breakthrough recently, I mean for the Bad Souls."

Leoncaro nodded. "When terror on earth is raised to a certain pitch, spirituality suffers. Rage is the outlet for unthinking men, and the ethical standards of erstwhile good men become corrupted. They find themselves at each other's throats because of conflicting ideologies, territorial disputes, or other irrational preoccupations. This is the final enigma of history, as Niebuhr proposed. 'Not how the righteous will gain victory over the unrighteous, but how the evil in every good and the unrighteousness of the righteous is to be overcome.' I believe I've quoted him accurately." Leoncaro paused to take a drink from the glass of water on his desk. Sherard asked if he would like tea. "Please." He opened a drawer of his desk and took out the digital tape Tom had left with the unfortunate Laurent Colbert on their previous visit with Leoncaro, at the Gemelli clinic. "I've had the opportunity to review this, which you told me was shot among the elephants at the Amboseli game reserve. Now, if you wouldn't mind describing to me in detail what you saw the next night at your home . . ."

Tom supplied most of the description of the were-beast, with color commentary by Bertie, as he served cups of tea and poured coffee for himself. Eden listened with a hand on her forehead, eyes half closed.

"We forgot about that mopey spectre riding on the back of the tiger," Bertie concluded. "Very symbolic, but of what I don't know."

"How could I forget about her?" Tom said with an uneasy smile in the Pope's direction. "She was eyeless, and manacled. Silver chains, which by moonlight looked every bit as substantial as the beast itself."

"And they were in *my* bungalow," Eden said, raising her head from her supporting hand. "Bertie believes—" She didn't want to go on with it. Leoncaro regarded her patiently, with an expression of such sympathy and concern that she couldn't help feeling he knew what she was reluctant to say. Blood was rising in her cheeks. "It was there, in my bedroom too, sniffing around. Attracted. Because I was having my period, maybe."

"I think it came around, that it probably exists, just to mate with Eden," Bertie concluded for her, Eden grimacing and avoiding everyone's eyes, as if she felt shame, or guilt. "Awful as that sounds," Bertie then added, with an apologetic glance at Eden.

"Why should it have a crush on me?" Eden said with a fretful smile. "You're better-looking." The nails of her right hand dug into the upholstered arm of the chair.

"The evil entity embodied in the were-beast," Leoncaro said to Eden, "is missing half of its soul, also its soul mate. Thus half of its normal strength. This entity is known to me, and to a few others, by the name of Mordaunt, and it has been on this earth since men first walked upright and chose sides against each other. Making it easy for the entity to become the chief tormentor of all men. It has chosen you, Eden, and your doppelganger as well, because of your demonstrated and latent powers as the Avatar. Better to have you on its side now than as a foe later."

"This Mordaunt has Gw—I mean, my doppelganger?"

"You've been unable to recall her to your side?"

"Can't even communicate with her," Eden admitted. "That's a first. Something's blocking me."

"Something as simple, and effective, as bathing the captive dpg in ultraviolet light; this prevents thought transference while greatly weakening the organism."

Bertie grinned incredulously. "Your Holiness—Sebastiano—how do you know so much about—"

"The less attractive aspects of the supernatural? It is my duty to know as much about the unholy as it is to promote the health and spirituality of each precious, developing soul. There is quite an extensive library downstairs, as you may have had time to explore on Tuesday, and another library elsewhere, under lock and key. That library is filled with lore of the occult, the dark fantastic. It is available to each successor to the throne of St. Peter according to his need to know, and prepare for days like these. The church is a beacon of light, the source of which is knowledge—no matter how twisted and forbidding some of this knowledge may be."

"You've lived before," Eden said. "Have I?"

"Oh, yes. You're a very old soul. But your past lives are not relevant to present circumstances, so if we may put inquiry into those lives aside for the time being—"

"I don't know what I'm going to do," Eden said bitterly. "The thing that's stalking me is probably still in Rome—Holiness, we both saw its shadow on the outside of the dome above that chamber."

"No, the entity has left Rome. I no longer feel its presence here. The power of light and love concentrated in this hallowed square mile discourage it from hanging around. Puts it off its feed, you might say. A little down in the mouth." He smiled. "It has withdrawn into its human persona once more, to contemplate its inadequacies."

"Now we have to destroy it," Bertie said with another glance at Eden. "Destroy *him*, while he's vulnerable and unsuspecting."

Eden sat up straight in protest. "But I still don't believe you're talking about Lincoln Grayle!"

"I think about it carefully," Sherard advised. "He shows up in Naivasha, supposedly en route to Victoria Falls, but we're more than a little out of his way. He recognizes you immediately on the terrace of the club, or so he claimed. Is that a coincidence? Try another. Two days ago he turns up in Rome, right on our heels, and a few hours after that Gwen is missing, forcibly abducted. Grayle was one of the last persons to see her."

Bertie said, "The shadow of the were-beast seemed to come from right out of the combi where he was sitting. And he was back in Nairobi the night you left for San Francisco. Plane trouble. No problem for him to get up to Shungwaya, and I'll bet if we could x-ray Linc's shoulder right now, there'd be a piece of a bullet buried in it."

"Okay, okay. But if he's as bad—evil—as as you're trying to make him out to be, why didn't I pick up on it? I'm no dummy when it comes to reading people. Neither are you."

"The supreme Trickster," Leoncaro observed, "has had millennia to perfect his tricks, and his subterfuge. You and Bertie have extraordinary talent, but only by working closely together can you hope to penetrate his defenses, reveal his true nature."

"If he kidnapped Gw—I can't say the name she gave herself; just like that she wouldn't be a dpg anymore—kidnapped my shadow, what good is that to him? She doesn't have powers—oh, naked she's invisible, big deal, and she can scoot around faster than I blink my eye. Quantum physics, she says. Whatever. She may be able to duplicate my physical moves but I have to bail her out of scrapes, and like you said, Holiness, black light or any kind of dog can reduce her to a quivering—"

Leoncaro held up a hand to slow Eden down.

"Let me tell you a little more about Mordaunt, in order for you to understand his motives. In spite of his ability to shape-shift into paradoxical creatures and his considerable talent for creating chaos in likely locations when human affairs go sour, he is a wounded soul. His powers, mighty as they appear to us, were diminished by half when—how to put this? He was separated from his soul mate and feminine half through a group effort by some associates of mine. That soul mate was then dispatched to a place where it remains forever in bondage, with no memory of who it truly is, or what it was on this plane of existence. Mordaunt's other half now goes by the name of 'Smith.' "

"Smith?"

"But it has a masculine form where it now labors in chains with numerous other poor wretches on a day in July in the year 1926. In the state of Georgia, USA, to be more precise. A day which Smith is doomed to repeat endlessly, for all of Eternity." His mouth firmed and he seemed to regret a gloating tone in his last words.

"Chains?" Bertie looked at Tom. "The spectre we saw at Shungwaya was female, but it was also wearing chains."

Leoncaro nodded. "I have suspected that one of Mordaunt's surrogates, during their current murder spree, squeezed from the subconscious mind of one of us—like seeds from a peeled grape—the approximate whereabouts of Mordaunt's other half. He would have programmed them to extract that information. Not that he can ever hope to get to 'Smith' and free him. Mordaunt doesn't have the power to bend time to his uses."

"A Georgia chain gang. Seventy-six years ago," Tom said with an expression of cynical wonder. "My late wife Gillian explained to me when we 'Visited' a few months ago"—he smiled nostalgically at Bertie; the Visit had been all too brief after months of longing—"explained that time isn't linear. Then, Now, and There all exist simultaneously." He settled himself by taking a long breath. His mood became pensive. "Needless to say it's been a troubling concept for me to deal with."

"I'm beginning to get this," Bertie said, looking around at all of their faces, lastly Eden's, where her eyes stayed. "Lincoln Grayle met you in Kenya. Then you had a lunch date, he got to know you pretty well—"

"Let's not go too far with that," Eden warned.

"Won't. But it's Linc's business to be hyperobservant, so of course he saw that you're left-handed."

"I'm sure he noticed. What of it?"

"Then he ran into your doppelganger in the lobby of the Excelsior, took her to dinner—"

"Where he would have found Gwen to be right-handed," Sherard said. "And that little weakness when your left eye turns in when you're stressed? Gwen's eye was turning in before she left on her date. The right eye, naturally. Eden and Gwen, mirror images."

"Thanks for reminding me. So he had her pegged for a dpg, then arranged to have her kidnapped off the streets of Rome? Suppose I buy that. What can he do with her? Incorporate her into his act?"

"Or," Leoncaro said, "he may have in mind sending her to Georgia in July of '26 in order to spirit his soul mate away from the chain gang in spite of the guards and the dogs."

"Doppelgangers can travel anywhere," Bertie said to Eden, "in parallel universes. You told me that yourself."

"Only if that's what I want her to do. But I don't. And it's me, not Grayle, who is in control of Gw—damn, I almost said it. Excuse me, Your Holiness."

"I prefer that my friends address me as Sebastiano. If you wouldn't mind, Eden."

"Thank you."

Sherard said after a short silence, "I don't want to see the two of you at risk again." He was looking at Leoncaro.

"Yes, it is a very great risk to approach Mordaunt," the Pontiff admitted. "Or Lincoln Grayle, as he now represents himself." He took time to think about this, drinking some of the tea Tom had brought him. "But wouldn't it be more of a risk for him to seek you out again? He will, you know."

More silence. Eden shifted restlessly in her chair, then abruptly got up and walked away from Leoncaro's desk, from all of them, seeking isolation in the confined study.

"I know I don't want to be hunted anymore," she said. "But I can't destroy another human being, no matter what. From everything Bertie's said, the two of us together can't handle Grayle's werebeast. His stand-in for stud purposes." In spite of the heat in the study she was shuddering. *"Ugh."* She turned to face Leoncaro, longing for words to release her from her dilemma and her misery.

All he could say was, "It is a very grave predicament, I know."

The teacup and saucer on his desk moved inches away from his hand. Leoncaro studied it, amused, looked up into Eden's resentful, rebellious smile.

"That's about how powerful I am, Sebastiano. *Avatar?* Please. I've learned to move a teacup with my mind. Is that any better than an armless man who can shuffle a deck of cards with his toes? Okay, Bertie can brain-lock just about anything that has a brain, I guess."

"I wouldn't want to throw my *chi* at Grayle. I have a hunch I'd get it right back, like a live wire across my face. He'd laugh."

Eden spread her hands. "And that's where we are."

"I believe you both underestimate yourselves," Leoncaro said. "There was, I believe, an incident involving a nuclear device surrounded by a highly charged electrical field?"

Eden was surprised, again, that he knew so much about her.

"Okay, that. No idea how I managed it. I don't think I could do it again if I lived a thousand—"

"It's simply that you don't *want* to do these things, because they frighten you. As for your powers, Eden: they exist. Dormant most of the time, behind barriers you've erected. But both you and Bertie are, at unpredictable and highly stressed times, capable of tapping into the Dark Energy and focusing it."

"Dark Energy? What's that?"

"The Energy that expands the universe and keeps it humming. That builds galaxies, and tears them apart. A force that even Mordaunt is helpless to deal with."

Leoncaro beckoned the three of them to step around behind his desk with him. From a drawer he withdrew a small but heavy bronze casket that looked as if it might be three thousand years old. Placed it on his desk blotter and invited Eden to raise the lid.

Lying on faded velvet inside were two small chunks of a dark dense metallic substance.

"Each little piece you see here may have traveled for a billion light-years through the firmament before reaching Earth. And each retains a portion of the Dark Energy that formed it—let us say, one-millionth of the power necessary for a firefly to light up its behind."

They all smiled, even Leoncaro. Then he turned serious again.

"Nevertheless, even an infinitesimal residue of Dark Energy can be useful to you, as a means of controlled contact with the entire celestial reservoir through which these bits of metal once traveled for eons. There is one for each of you. Mount them in some manner so that you may always wear them in contact with your bodies." His green-eyed gaze was almost unnerving. "They will work for you, when you most need their help. And, Tom?"

"Yes, Sebastiano?"

"I have not forgotten about you."

Leoncaro rose from his chair and opened a nearby armoire, reached down from a shelf a long bubble-wrapped and taped package that he handed over to Sherard.

"Your lion's-head walking stick, for your continued protection. I know how responsible you feel for the lives of these young women. I couldn't ask you to go in harm's way with nothing more substantial than a side arm."

"But I thought—"

"It was decided to remove your stick from the body of the shape-shifter once a similar length of *mopane* wood, suitably sharpened and consecrated, was also driven through the remains. And of course those remains are now entombed in stone, never to be disturbed."

"By the way," Bertie asked, "what happened to her—its—husband, the one who fainted?"

"He was easily persuaded, once he recovered part of his faculties, to undertake a lifetime of prayer and silent contemplation in an old cloister that overlooks what I am told is one of the loveliest fjords in all Norway."

"What we don't understand," Sherard said, "is how Mordaunt, or Grayle, is turning out shape-shifters to do his killing for him."

"Wouldn't we all like to know?" Leoncaro said thoughtfully. He looked at Eden. "Possibly you could find out for us. Remember that there is not so much to fear while he is in human form. That is when Mordaunt is most vulnerable; when he believes he is in control of you."

The old rotary-style white telephone on the Pope's desk rang twice: a discreet reminder.

"I'm afraid that I have backlogged my appointments until well past the dinner hour." He smiled in apology. "Tomorrow's dinner, very likely."

Eden, holding the bronze casket under one arm, looked at Bertie with a fateful smile.

"Let's go to Las Vegas."

"I will be praying for you," Leoncaro said. "Go with God and in full confidence of your great strength."

Leoncaro arose from his prie-dieu in what had been, moments before, the solitude of his spartan bedroom. Now that his prayers were done, the room began to fill up.

"Let's make it brief," he grumbled. "I still have a lot of work left today."

The Caretaker who until recently had been known as Pledger Lee Skeldon said, "What's this about 'Dark Energy,' Sebastiano?"

"I remembered the term from an article on stellar dynamics I read in *Scientific American*."

"And pieces of meteorite?" said the white-bearded Rebbe from Brooklyn.

"Who knows? They might well have been from the engine block of a Jeep the Germans eighty-eighted, or a tank tread. Leoncaro picked them up in a rubbled lot when he was a boy. They looked interesting, so I have kept them all of these years."

"Telling whoppers to innocent young things," the Buddhist nun Ling Qi chided him.

"I'm surprised at all of you," Leoncaro said. "Have none of you seen one of my favorite Disney movies? The one about the baby circus elephant with extremely large ears? So large he couldn't walk without tripping over them. That, and the laughter of the other elephants, was very hard on the youngster's confidence."

"Dumbo, the flying elephant," said the Metropolitan of the Russian Orthodox Church.

"*That* movie. Well, poor Dumbo was shunned and frustrated because he didn't look like the other baby elephants. But he did have this wise-guy little mouse friend—"

"I loved that part," Ling Qi confided to the group of Caretakers.

"—Mouse friend," Leoncaro continued, frowning at her, "who convinced Dumbo that as long as he had a certain 'magic feather' with him he could fly, flapping his large ears and soaring through the sky with a gaggle of reprobate crows."

"Isn't it 'gaggle of geese'?" said the prominent Islamic Imam and scholar who had just popped in.

"Don't know. Anyway, there was nothing magical about the feather, of course. Dumbo could fly perfectly well without it. The feather was just a—"

"Confidence-builder," the currently unemployed Caretaker concluded for him. "Smart, Sebastiano."

"Can't hurt. Those girls will need all the confidence they can muster." He looked hard at the Caretaker, who was loafing around now that Pledger Lee had been laid to rest. "Don't you think you ought to be on your way to Las Vegas yourself? No need to fully assimilate another persona. Just move in temporarily and as unobtrusively as possible on someone in a position to keep an eye on the situation."

"Been there," the Caretaker replied agreeably. "About to do that. I've already located just the guy. You know, it was a heck of a long time for me between visits out there. Pledger Lee was a child evangelist doing revival meetings in that shabby tent of his in those days. Brother, you don't know how hot it can get until you've done Vegas in the summertime. Hell hath no fury. Anyway, little Pledger Lee was just across the street from where Mickey Cohen was putting up the Flamingo—the Mick was Jewish, but one night he—"

"*Go,*" Leoncaro said, in his most commanding voice.

"It's a good story, Sebastiano."

"Some other time. May we know who you've chosen to coopt while you're out there again?"

"He's a vacationing cop from Atlanta. Small coincidence. He worked my—I mean—Pledger Lee's case. What I could tell *him.*"

"No, you won't."

"And he has a gorgeous girlfriend."

"I'm sure that had nothing to do with your choosing him."

"Yes, it did."

MOUNT CHARLESTON, NEVADA · OCTOBER 24 · 1:15 P.M. PDT

How do you feel?" Lincoln Grayle said to Eden Waring's doppelganger.

"Not any better than I did last night. Like I tried taking a shortcut through a demolition derby. My bones feel soft and my joints ache. Could you *please* turn that horrible light off for a little while?"

"I'm afraid I can't do that. Not until we've reached a level of mutual trust that I'm hoping is not too far in the future—"

"Trust?! You had me kidnapped and a man was shot, probably killed!"

He adjusted the bullet-shaped head of the slender black standing lamp that had been aimed at the middle of his bed where Gwen was sprawled, wearing a pair of the magician's pj's, her weakened body covering the gold script *G* on the black silk coverlet. The bed was about the size of a badminton court. Everything else in the bedroom, including the walls and the smoke-toned mirrored ceiling, was either gold or black. As was the magician himself this afternoon. He wore black loafers without socks, black jeans, a harlequin-style black-and-gold cashmere turtleneck sweater, glasses with elliptical black metal frames and gold-tinted lenses. He straddled a lacquered black Chinese Chippendale chair and smiled ruefully at her.

"I regret the violence. But I had no time to waste. If you returned to your homebody, then I might never have had this opportunity."

"I had you *so* wrong! What a bastard you are. Smuggling me aboard your plane in a theatrical trunk—I could've smothered."

"But doppelgangers, I am told by an expert, can't die: only cease to exist. Something of a paradox, but we'll pass over it for now. The trunk seemed to be the best way to get you out of Italy, with all of the added security at the airport prompted by Al Qaeda and their Italian friends."

A few tears leaked from Gwen's reddened eyes. She barely had the strength to blink. "What do you want? I'm not Eden! Why don't you just let me go!"

"I've always known that you weren't Eden, since I was allowed that glimpse of you on the street in Nairobi. I suppose you were just feeling playful that day, but I was inspired to speculate about the possibilities you presented. Doppelgangers have long been an interest of mine. Now I have one."

"I won't talk to you anymore if you're going to continue t-torturing me!"

Sunlight slanting through the solar-gain windows of Grayle's Mount Charleston hacienda made the light from the hundred-watt ultraviolet bulb in the bullet lamp all but invisible; its power to render a doppelganger nearly helpless was not diminished.

When he continued to study her intently but without speaking Gwen cried out bitterly, "Just turn the lamp off for a little while. I promise I'll—"

"Stay? But you can't make promises to *me*, Gwen. Can you?" Her lips clamped whitely together. "It's Eden who makes all of the decisions for her dpg," Grayle said.

"Sure. You have it all figured out. Without Eden, I'm a big nothing."

"And you hate the restrictions of your situation. You even hate your homebody, at times."

Gwen had no reply. Today she hated everybody.

"What if we can get you free of Eden, so that you can be *Gwen* in more than name only? That's a promise I can make."

"Like hell you can," the hard metal of her spirit beginning to show through her self-pity. It felt good. "You don't understand doppelgangers at all. Neither does your so-called expert, whoever *that* is."

"Someone you know well, I believe. Maybe it's time for him to come in. I have a crowded schedule this afternoon."

Lincoln Grayle activated the cell phone he wore on one wrist like a slightly oversized diver's watch. He relayed a summons, then reached out and, to Gwen's relief, turned off the ultraviolet light.

"I know the effects will continue for several minutes, so you'll be good for now. Can you sit up? Wonderful, sweetheart."

"What's going on?" Gwen said suspiciously, working at keeping her woozy head up.

Double doors to the bedroom suite were opened. Dr. Marcus Woolwine walked in. Legs as bowed and muscular as ever, sunlight forming a nimbus around his deeply tanned bald head, flaring from the surfaces of his mirrored sunglasses.

Gwen blinked a couple of times, bringing him into sharp focus.

"Oh! God!"

"Hello, Gwen. Such a great pleasure to see you again. I would like to apologize for some of the things I once said to you. *A soulless facade, a fake, a nonbeing.* But, after all. It wasn't easy being forced to consume humble pie—a man of my stature in the remodeling business."

Dr. Woolwine was followed into the bedroom by a Chinese male anesthesiologist wearing OR scrubs, pushing a stainless-steel cart of meds and bags of IV saline solution dangling from a short pole.

Gwen's mouth was locked open at a grisly angle as he approached her, his bullet head thrust forward with a smile prepared to be ingratiating. She watched herself withdraw, tiny and insubstantial, in the twin convex mirrors concealing his eyes.

"From the day we both, ah, found it sensible to flee from Plenty Coups," Woolwine said, "my interest in you has grown with each passing hour. I have the good fortune now to be in the employ of a man who shares my fascination with doppelgangers." He turned to Grayle with a courteous expression, unusual for a man with an ego to match his arrogance. As Gwen remembered him. "And now we are ready for her, at your pleasure."

"What are you going to do to me?" Gwen screamed at the magician. She was still too weak from the black light to get much lung power into her scream.

He sat down on the bed and gently ran a hand over her head, stroked a cheek with his fingertips.

"You'll soon have the life you've always wanted," Grayle said reassuringly. "Disengaged at last, freed from the tyranny of a homebody. For your freedom, all I ask in return is a favor."

"Do *you* a favor? I'd rather vomit in my own eyes."

"But we'll talk more about that when I see you tomorrow."

5:20 P.M.

Lincoln Grayle had finished an arduous session on the parallel bars in his gym and was relaxing beneath the hands of his masseuse when Cornell Crigler was brought in to see him.

Grayle dismissed the masseuse and sat up naked on the side of the table, looking at the uneasy Cornell.

"Tell me about your brother-in-law."

"Lewis is my half brother, Great One." Cornell, the childhood stutterer, needed when under duress to think about each word before he spoke. "I'm tuh-ten years older. We never really known each other all that well, although these days with E-mail it's easier keepin' in touch. I grew up in Chicago, and—"

"Let's keep to the point, Cornell. He's a detective with the Atlanta Police Department, you told Gaby. Why is he in Las Vegas asking questions about me?"

"Usin' some of his vacation time. He was a part of the Pledger Lee Skeldon murder investigation team. Case is closed, fuh-far as Atlanta PD is concerned. But Lewis, he made a connection between that case, the death of Sai Rampa in India, and the attempt on the Dalai Lama's life. Said to me last night, 'Cornell, I'm convinced the Pope also was attacked in Rome this week, but you won't hear a word; Vatican's too good at coverin' up when it threatens the stability of the church.' Right now Lewis is attempting to contact a few people on the Pope's invite list Tuesday. So I thought you ought to know—"

Grayle shrugged. "The connection Lewis has made leads straight to me. Which does explain his interest in the Lucky Ticket list that we gave out to his lovely companion."

Cornell said, looking everywhere except at the splendid body on display a few feet from him, "I did tell Lewis right off that he shouldn't mess with important people like yourself, since he don't have a thing to go on but suspicions."

"Cop smarts. Give Lewis credit, Cornell. No need to defend yourself. It's an awkward situation for you."

"Wuh-what do you want me to do, Great One?"

"Don't be nervous. I don't see that we have a problem. Other than to somehow make up for our bad luck in Rome. And it was all planned so carefully." Cornell's brow furrowed in commiseration. "But let's think about Lewis. He's clever and tenacious. Know what I think of clever people, Cornell?" He didn't wait for Cornell to finish shaking his head. "Never can get enough of them. So I look forward to meeting Lewis. And what's-her-name."

"Charmaine."

"Where are they staying?"

"Bahìa."

"On the cheap, of course. Maybe, since one or the other of them is going to do me a favor soon, they should have choicer accommodations for the remainder of their stay. Their own pool, hot tub."

Cornell tried not to look puzzled or apprehensive. The blond masseuse had returned, wearing chrome-plated chains and manacles around her shoulders like an iron maiden's boa; forty pounds if they were an ounce, Cornell reckoned, but she didn't appear to even notice the weight. The masseuse was shapely and missed being beautiful because the iron in her Germanic soul blocked expression from her flawless face like a course of Botox.

She spent two and a half minutes locking Grayle into various contorted positions while Cornell, not yet dismissed, fretted silently, wondering if the chaining of Grayle was a prelude to some variation on kinky sex play that he might be forced to watch. Cornell was a Bad Soul, but he did have his druthers.

The magician and the masseuse, however, appeared to be all business as he supervised his heavy bondage, making suggestions as to how and where the chains could be tighter.

With the last padlock in place she helped Grayle down from the massage table. He was bent nearly double. He could move, only shuffling a few inches at a time and with great effort. The masseuse left again. Grayle made his way to the edge of a ten-foot-square pool. It looked deep.

"Do you have a watch, Cornell?"

"Yes, Great One."

"I'm going to sit on the bottom of the pool for a while, practice getting out of these chains. Let me know when eight minutes is up."

"*Eight* minutes? How do I do that?"

Grayle managed to look back over one shoulder, the shoulder that still contained bits of a .447 brass Steyr cartridge and which hurt like hell. But he loved the pain. Pain was pride. Pain was money.

"Just jump in and hold up your fingers where I can see them, Cornell," the magician said as he began to concentrate, preparing his remarkable body for the ordeals ahead.

After his workout in the pool, from which he emerged thirty seconds ahead of schedule and just as Cornell was taking off his shoes, Lincoln Grayle napped, then shared a light supper with two members of his design team. They were working on an illusion that the magician called "The Gilded Cage." It also involved a perilous escape, with Grayle wrapped this time in barbed wire, adding to the degree of difficulty. He was to be dropped from the highest bridge in North America, which was in West Virginia, into a river chasm some five hundred feet below. He had conceived the Gilded Cage stunt two years ago. The design challenges were enormous. The Gilded Cage would replace the illusion for which he'd been denied access to the Colosseum in Rome. That production, now on the back burner, featured some comely female gladiators, a chariot drawn by six black horses, a pair of lions, and Grayle himself locked inside a body bag with ten pounds of raw liver.

Big, better, best. His perpetual quest as an illusionist. Always searching for an edge over his competitors. Dedication to his art kept his theatre filled every night while other Vegas magicians were closing up shop for lack of business.

When their working meal was over, Grayle rolled up two sets of plans for further study, had a second glass of sauvignon blanc from his Napa Valley winery poured for him. He leaned back in a leather lounge chair on one of the glass-walled terraces with retractable roofs to watch the high-desert sunset flare metallic green along a saw-toothed black horizon. He listened, as he did most nights when he was home, to Christmas music and parodies. He loved Eartha Kitt's seductive "Santa Baby," Burl Ives's jovial "Jingle Bell Rock," and never tired of the tragicomic bonhomie of "Granma Got Run Over by a Reindeer."

Marcus Woolwine found him there. Woolwine had allowed himself only the slightest smile of satisfaction, as if he were fearful that his eighty-year-old face might cramp if the smile got any wider. But obviously he was pleased with himself.

"Would you care to see her now?"

"She's awake?"

"No, no. She needs to sleep for another twelve hours. The minor surgery is done, and we're mentally prepping her to accept her new status, giving no further thought to Eden Waring."

"Her new status, and my proposal?"

"Only Lincoln Grayle, and his desires, will matter to Gwen when she awakens."

"No more of this 'I'd rather vomit in my own eyes'? Fab. No wonder you came so highly recommended by Bronc Skarbeck."

"How did you happen to meet the General?" Woolwine asked.

"After the Multiphasic Operations and Research Group imploded, Bronc was casting around for someone else to sell his soul to, and I offer unmatchable terms."

"I'm also indebted for the opportunity you've given me, to study a doppelganger in such detail. She *will* be mine, once she has fulfilled her obligations to you?"

"Certainly, Dr. Woolwine."

The sky had darkened, stars appearing like flecks of silver in a miner's pan. Grayle finished his sauvignon blanc and followed Woolwine, who in spite of his age bounded like a pneumatic mountain goat up a double flight of outside steps to the wing of the house that Grayle had turned over to the biogeneticist.

In a large room decorated with exotic cacti growing like crude homunculi Gwen lay faceup and completely nude except for a surgical patch on one side of her neck in a mild yellow-green soup of mineral salts more buoyant than ordinary seawater. She was wired to murmurous machines and taking on clear fluids through the IV needle in the back of one hand. There were sunlamps ten feet above the shallow tank in which she serenely floated, breathing almost undetectably, but no ultraviolet light. Her overall deep tan had a beautiful luster, like the painstakingly applied paint jobs to hobby cars. Her dulse-red hair also floated, fanlike, on soothing currents that rippled through the gelatinous solution.

"Why can I see her?" Grayle said. "Doppelgangers in the nude are invisible unless you catch them in black light."

"Her skin and hair are sheathed in an organic compound that maintains the integrity of her image within the spectrum visible to the human eye. I obtained the formula from a Yaqui sorcerer accustomed to dealing with dpg's in his own work. The compound binds to the skin in a layer a few microns thick, hardened by a gentle electrical stimulus, the source of which is the billions of microorganisms in her salty bath. The compound, however, begins to break down after a couple of weeks."

"So she can't disappear on me when she wakes up."

"Had she the desire to do so, where could she go? Back to Eden Waring? The device I've implanted in her neck alters her magnetic field just enough to cancel contact between Gwen and her home-body. Gwen is no longer 'on call,' shall we say."

He paused to mop his steamy bald dome with a paisley handkerchief. It was both hot and humid inside. There were half-moons of moisture on the inner surfaces of Woolwine's mirror lenses. "Isn't she lovely, though? I'm nearly persuaded to jumpstart my libido again, in spite of the potential consequences at my age." Grayle gave him a look. "That is, unless you had a sexual relationship with Gwen in mind. Female dpg's are barren, of course."

"I don't fuck," Grayle said. "Anyway, Gwen's not for breeding purposes. Eden will give me the child I want. A child of power and magicial strength. Charming and ruthless. My equal, once I'm at full strength again. I hope all of this tinkering you've done with Gwen hasn't diminished her ability to do a little time-traveling."

"I shouldn't think. Just point her in the right direction."

"If only it were that easy," Grayle said, brooding over the face and nude form of the girl in the sunlit tank. "Do you know how many chain gangs there were in the state of Georgia in 1926? Almost every county had one. Thousands of prisoners. I don't have a face. All I have is a name. *Smith*. Not very helpful, is it? There are no records anymore of who the prisoners were. The Caretakers did a number on me. I made them pay, but not enough. If Gwen fails me, they've won." He turned to stare at Marcus Woolwine. Who, just for a moment, was treated to a glimpse of what lay behind the handsome facade of the magician. His face felt numb; his Adam's apple bulged in his wrinkly throat. When Grayle spoke again, it was as if his voice were brawling from a chasm like an avalanche in reverse. "I *hate* to lose!"

Woolwine was able to swallow. He smiled diplomatically.

"Oh, I don't blame you! But I have made it a point during my career never to involve myself in the, ah, *politics* of those who acquire my services. Nevertheless—may I wish you luck? It all sounds so fascinating."

WESTBOUND/ROME–LAS VEGAS · GULFSTREAM N657GB · OCTOBER 25 · 0015 HOURS ZULU

Over the Bay of Biscay Bertie fell asleep. Even heading into danger she had the happy faculty of the young and supremely healthy of sleeping almost anywhere and at any time, dismissing the world and its load of cares. She was never a worrier. Eden had a more precarious outlook, dictated by events of her recent past. Hadn't closed her eyes, or so it seemed, in days. She had had a shower but still felt annoyingly out of focus, airborne, not of earth anymore but not in tune with the spheres. Part of her sense of dislocation was inspired by futile attempts to contact her doppelganger. It was like listening to the celestial drone for a different pulse, a beacon of intelligent life half the cosmos away. When she was too long at this mental labor her brain needed an ice bath.

Tom Sherard came aft from the flight deck with a drink in his hand, ice cubes and a generous slug of Glenlivet. He paused to cover Bertie, stretched out nearly prone in a reclining armchair, with a blanket, then parked himself with the slowness of a man expecting pain opposite Eden. She held out a hand mock imperiously and he passed her his glass. Eden had a swallow, then another, a taste she had

begun to relish, twenty-year-old smoke and heather. Developing a
needful thirst. Drinking made her feel less afraid of herself. Even
Avatars, she'd decided, had to have their flaws. She would be watchful, and accommodate this one. A third sip, and she gave back the
glass, looking into Tom's eyes.

"Feeling okay?" he asked.

"Better than dismal, but not as good as lousy."

"Thatta girl," he said with his faintly sardonic smile. "Can't find
your dpg?"

"No. She's trapped, somehow. Black light would be my guess. The
son of a bitch. I almost fell for him, you know."

"Not surprising." Tom picked up his walking stick from the seat
next to him and idly stroked the gold lion's head. The lion's eyes
opened partway and it yawned. Eden touched the Pope's talisman,
which she now wore on a gold chain around her neck, one of the two
mountings that a Rome jeweler had fashioned for Bertie and herself.

"We need to start talking about how we'll deal with Grayle," Sherard said. "If it wasn't against the law I wouldn't mind having a crack
at him with one of the rifles I brought along. Although filling either
Grayle or his alter shape full of lead doesn't seem to be the answer."

"Where are we staying in Vegas?"

"Bahìa."

Eden shrugged. She had never been to Las Vegas.

"It's a Bellaver property. Quite lavish. And losing money. Our
hotel business is faring poorly these days."

She smiled wryly. "What's another half billion or so? I buy my
sneakers at Wal-Mart anyway." She held out her hand again. "Let me
help you with that drink." She helped him by draining his glass
while he watched, still sardonic. Sometimes he only needed to look
at her a certain way, like now, to give her goose bumps. She covered
up her sexual uneasiness by dropping the ice cubes from the glass
he'd given her into a Coke can on the table next to her, began rolling
the heavy fluted whiskey glass back and forth between her palms.
"Tom?"

"Yes?"

"I'm scared that I'll freeze up when I see Grayle, or Mordaunt, or whoever he is. I'm out of touch with G-G—you-know-who, and seriously disconnected from reality. I'm sitting here talking to you and all I see is that ugly saber-toothed baboon-thing bounding down a fifty-foot-wide marble corridor and tearing a huge door off its hinges. And the look in its eyes! The evil. The contempt for all that's sacred."

"You didn't freeze up then, sweetheart."

"I had old reliable Simba to protect me. I knew he'd do his stuff." The lion's head turned inquiringly in her direction. She set the whiskey glass on the table next to the Coke can. Tom looked at it. The glass was lopsided, as if it had been aimlessly reshaped by the rolling action between Eden's palms. "But is Simba up to handling a seven-hundred-pound tiger with the head of a hyena? It immobilized a shape-shifter, but the thing wasn't dead. It's in a place with other undead curiosities the Church doesn't know what to do with. Evil is eternal, but I know I'm not."

The Gulfstream jet had run into turbulence at thirty-nine thousand feet. A flight attendant looked in on them and advised fastening seat belts. Tom requested another scotch from the attendant, then got up to secure Bertie in her seat. But she looked up at his touch, smiled drowsily, and put her arms around his neck, pulled his face toward her. Eden examined a broken nail on her left hand.

"There already?" Bertie said.

"Not by a long shot."

"Need to use the potty." Eden looked up as Bertie kissed Tom, stretched, got up, smiled vaguely at Eden in passing. "Anybody hungry yet?" She went into the bathroom. Sherard sat down again, rubbing his jaw as if bewitched.

After a couple of minutes he said, "That may be an answer."

"What are you talking about?" Eden asked, aroused from a brown study.

"Grayle the illusionist is fond of disappearances. A staple of the magician's art. Let us suppose he vanishes one night, but neglects to reappear."

"Bravo. Where's he going?"

"To a tomb of his own, perhaps."

Bertie came out of the bathroom, still yawning hugely, and popped joints in one shoulder and her left wrist. She dropped into the chair next to Eden and removed her earplugs.

"Have I missed anything?"

"Doom and gloom," Eden said.

"Are you cold?" Bertie asked, looking at Eden's forearms. "Do you want a sweater?" Eden shook her head brusquely. Bertie leaned back and steepled her fingers on her breastbone. "Poor attitudes could make us careless," she warned.

"So you're optimistic that we're gonna handle this okay?"

"Why not?"

"Sure, why not. Well, it isn't your ass the were-beast is after."

"Are we going to fight?" Bertie said mildly. She picked up the misshaped whiskey glass from the table. "Neat. How did you do it?"

"I don't know. I was playing with it and it got hot. I thought the glass was going to melt in my hand, so I put it down."

Sherard said, with a narrowing of his hunter's eyes, "Why don't you see if you can soften the glass more."

"I could, I guess. What for?"

"Without touching it," Bertie suggested.

"Oh, now; that would be like hitting a half-court J with the gym lights out."

"Nevertheless, I'd like for you to try, just as Bertie said," Tom persisted.

"Burns a ton of energy, and I'm half brain-dead already."

"We'll channel the Dark Energy," Bertie said. "I need to use up a bunch of calories. I'm three pounds heavier than when I left Shung-waya. All that lovely Roman pasta, *mamma mia*, just shoot me."

The flight attendant came in with Sherard's fresh scotch. Bertie noted the red in his eyes and gave him a significant look. Tom ignored her. Bertie said to the attendant, "Yvonne, would you bring some empty glasses? Half a dozen should be enough." She gave Eden a gleeful look.

Eden groaned and slumped in her chair, pretending she had fainted. Bertie prodded her in the ribs until she opened her eyes again.

"Come on; it'll be fun! We'll have a competition. And then I can afford to have dessert with dinner."

"Is my nose going to bleed?" Sherard asked.

"Do what I told you to do in the papal library. Just pinch the bridge of your nose with your thumb and forefinger. You'll be okay."

"There's another problem," Eden said.

"What?"

"We could screw up the plane's avionics if we're not careful and take a quick trip to the bottom of the Atlantic. I mean, what do we know about Dark Energy?"

"Good point," Bertie said, fingering her papal-issue talisman. "We need a way to monitor our output."

"Magnetic anomaly detector," Sherard said, getting up and balancing on his good leg while reaching for the walking stick. "There should be one in the flight deck kit. Don't start without me."

Bertie took the first turn in the competition she'd proposed. The quarter-inch-thick glass left the palm of her outstretched hand and hovered a few feet away in her line of sight. Bertie had once levitated a MORG psychic named Mae Purkey in her wheelchair and flown her halfway across the Vanderbilt University campus, but she'd been very angry then; and her *chi* worked best outdoors. Glass, she found, was hard to work with, but in short order she had reshaped hers into a Vasa Murrhina pitcher tinted in shades of lavender and lime green. She turned it around for the others to inspect.

"Very pretty," Eden commented.

Bertie took deep breaths to balance her *chi*.

"I'll give it a six," Sherard judged. He was enjoying his third scotch of the flight and keeping an eye on the MAD readout, which had registered a higher number only briefly during Bertie's efforts, and nowhere near a dangerous level.

"Six?" Bertie cried. "On a scale of ten?"

"That's fair," Eden said with a trace of smugness, her own drinking glass floating free of her hand like a discarded module from a spacecraft.

"Really?" Bertie said, still miffed. "Can't wait to see what you have in mind."

Eden toyed with the talisman on her breast. She didn't feel tired or dispirited anymore. Whatever Dark Energy was, every cell of her body now seemed to brim with it. She melted the glass easily, feeling its sensuous plasticity in her exquisitely sensitive temple bones. Then she willed the glass to draw itself out into a twenty-inch rod. She was gliding quickly on her long wave of foaming, revitalizing energy, through supple twists, turns, and knottings of the glass until her cunning figurine had been sculpted.

Bertie whistled softly.

"What is it?" Tom said.

Eden sent her figurine past his nose, into a dive, then a climb and a final flyby at near-stall speed. Tom plucked it out of the air as deftly as if he were capturing a butterfly.

"Now don't you see?" Eden said with a happy laugh. "It's Dumbo the flying elephant."

They were all smiling now. "This one's an eight," Tom decided. Bertie made a face. "Challenge round," he announced. "Eden, in my judgment, which is unassailable and absolute, you won the right to challenge first."

Eden, flush with the rhythms of her psychokymes, said to Bertie, "How about a stained-glass window?"

"With or without angels?" Bertie shot back.

"Show off all you want, babe."

Tom Sherard found himself sleepless after several hours in the air, uninfluenced by the slumberous sounds both young women were making in their blanket cocoons. Deep, untroubled sleep. The nearly dark compartment was littered with the successes and failures left over from the competition he'd proposed. Bertie's stained-glass window containing the bearded figure of Moses, Eden's marvelously filigreed, rose-tinted Camelot sculpture. Bertie had modeled his own face in glass, but couldn't get the nose right; the bust had the aspect of a disagreeable camel. Eden had bombed out trying to get the strings right on her glass cello. But by then whatever charge was feeding the astonishing neural energy of their minds had waned. They were pooped and quarrelsome, ate silently with prodigious appetites, and curled up soon afterward.

Tom used his alone time to access Lincoln Grayle's Web site on his laptop computer.

Grayle had been born in Ladue, Missouri, a suburb of St. Louis. He was an only child. His father performed routine magic tricks for children's parties; he recognized that his son was a prodigy and generously encouraged him to study the techniques of great illusionists. Linc's twin passion was gymnastics; he excelled in prep school competitions while lopping off fake heads with a guillotine at assemblies.

His parents died within weeks of each other when he was eighteen, leaving Grayle with enough insurance money to support himself while ascending the learning curve of his career in magic. (Sherard wondered at just what point the entity Mordaunt, looking for a new human persona, had settled on the bright and athletic teenager from the Show-Me state and moved himself in. The suspiciously convenient deaths of the elder Grayles might have been the starting point for an entirely new version of Lincoln Grayle.) At twenty-one the young man was a well-publicized escape artist. Headliner in a Vegas showroom a couple of years later.

It took the now-established illusionist six years to design and raise the money needed to begin construction on the Lincoln Grayle Theatre. From the day he announced he was building it he had a lot of detractors. The site he had chosen was fifteen miles west of downtown Las Vegas, and nearly inaccessible. It would have cost him half as much to build the same grandiose theatre on or near the Strip; who, the local showmen and casino owners wondered, would spend top dollar for dinner and a magic show they had to be bused into the mountains to see? He hadn't even applied for a casino license as an added attraction. Complete folly, according to an op-ed that ran in the *Sun*. Rockslides and other mishaps during the early stages of construction only confirmed the majority opinion.

But Grayle knew how to put on a show. From opening night his theatre was a splashy success, the show a must see. Six nights a week beginning at six-forty a dozen red and gray luxury buses began making the run from the shopping plaza he owned on Convention Center Drive. Dinner was at eight-thirty, showtime ten sharp. During the day the buses transported tourists who had been unable to secure show tickets but wanted to tour the theatre and Grayle's Museum of Magic and have lunch with a great view while being entertained by apprentice magicians. Now and then Grayle himself made a surprise appearance, signing autographs and dazzling his guests with sleight-of-hand street magic.

The Web site offered a great deal of information on the construction of the theatre, which in its exposed location on the side of a mountain was subject to a lot of weather, from heavy snowfalls to baking heat to mica-laden desert winds that could exceed seventy-miles-an-hour velocities. The tons of solar-gain glass had a metallic coating to withstand these violent sand blastings. Titanium steel framework allowed for flexing of the diamond-shaped panes. Rocks tumbling from higher elevations were caught or deflected by chainmail-like webbing tented above the spectacularly high, all-glass rotunda of the theatre.

Sherard looked over several photos of the completed theatre. Fragile in appearance from just a short distance away, impregnable as a medieval fortress within in spite of the adroit use of space, an artful illusion of openness. Lair of a monster. No way to tell from the Web-site description how many secret means of entering or leaving there might be into the heart of the mountain itself, perhaps, that Grayle had designed and constructed for his exclusive use.

Sherard turned off the laptop and put it aside.

He was a professional hunter who knew the nature of his quarry, but not its cunning. And nothing much about its habitat. That greatly lessened the permutations of what old-time white hunters referred to as chance control. Even if he were at full strength, stalking Mordaunt would require almost superhuman effort. He had a game leg and his years had begun to weigh against him. He was afraid. But, as a famous client of his father's had observed during his last African safari, being scared is better than being dead of carelessness.

The client whom Donal Sherard had called "Hemindinger," an offhand tribute to the bulky author's shooting ability.

On certain occasions of sinking morale Sherard could recall vividly the odor of tobacco smoke in his father's wiry beard. He smoked a corncob pipe. Recalling textures, hearing in the distances of a drowsy mind dark voices singing the lion song. And a remembrance of firelight shadows, the capering, foot-stomping Wakamba dance in honor of his first lion. His old man hadn't been there to see it. What would he have thought about the hunt his son was now pledged to, what advice might he have offered?

You will ha' two shots, Tommy. One to knock 'im down, one to plow 'im under.

Sure. He had wounded the were-beast already; next time he would plow it under.

Unfortunately the damned thing would not, could not die.

When he looked at the sleeping heads of the women he loved and had to protect, though one of them would be his bait, Sherard felt nearly sick from anxiety. Both Bertie and Eden had incredible powers and prowess; but to go against Mordaunt they literally had to achieve thermonuclear capabilities. There was no magic bullet, walking stick, talisman, or spell that would work on the magician. Undoubtedly he had seen them all.

Sherard reached for the glass Dumbo that Eden had manufactured, tossed it hand to hand. The glass warming from his touch. The little elephant seemed to be smiling at him.

THREE

LAS VEGAS
OCTOBER 24-26

THE SKY IS DARKENING LIKE A STAIN;
SOMETHING IS GOING TO FALL LIKE RAIN,
AND IT WON'T BE FLOWERS.

—W. H. AUDEN, "THE WITNESS"

as Vegas by night—and when else did it matter?—made plutonium look tame, its neural mainline a monster canyon of light like a borrowed galaxy, apocalyptic surge confined, reshaped for entertainment purposes but commanding awe.

Vegas was a city of resurrections and apostasies, of quick love and last flings and second acts that weren't happening; of lifestyle as creed.

Yeah.

Vegas was a deadly sort of flatterer; it beguiled the gullible and put a serious hurt on many of the unwary. Vegas was dreamtime in overdrive, showtime anytime, where even the strays and drifters had production values. Vegas outhustled the hustlers with the dispassionate ease of a jaded old carny.

Yeah.

Vegas—when he first saw it—had the look of something immense but still temporary, the greatest show in the Milky Way but with the wagons parked somewhere just out of sight, ready to roll again when the desert scene was maximally juiced, the last exhausted funseeker on a smoky bus to someplace else.

A young man wise to his own needs, totally aware of how well he fitted in, Lincoln Grayle had fallen for Las Vegas the moment he set foot in town, feeling the energy on his skin like the energy of a populace under a state of siege.

Yeah.

OCTOBER 24 · 7:45–8:10 P.M.

What did we do to deserve this?" Lewis Gruvver said, looking around the grand salon of the high-roller's villa. To which they had been escorted by Bahìa's Vice President of Operations. Charmaine couldn't say anything. She was staring at the heated pool, bathed in pale blue light, just outside the forty-foot square room in a flowery walled garden illuminated by colored floodlights. "I don't think," Gruvver continued, "that I can begin to pay for—"

"But the suite is compliments of Bahìa, Mr. Gruvver! We want you to know how badly we feel about the damage done to your clothing and personal effects."

"Oh," Gruvver said, noting the blissful hypnotized expression on Charmaine's face. "Any idea what caused the flood in our room? I mean, we didn't leave anything running in the—"

"No, no, obviously it was a broken pipe in the wall. Some other rooms were damaged as well, but they were unoccupied. Of course you'll be reimbursed for clothing that can't be cleaned. We put in a rush order; everything that was, ah, salvageable should be back from the laundry and dry cleaners in a couple of hours."

"Well, that's—"

"Please continue to enjoy your stay with us." The Operations VP handed Gruvver his business card. "Let me know if I can be of further assistance. Oh, and dinner is on us tonight."

"Appreciate that, Mr."—Gruvver glanced at the gold and green card—"Havens."

"My pleasure."

The Operations VP wasn't far out the door when Charmaine took a flying leap onto a silk brocade sofa, buried her face in a pillow, and let out a muffled, joyful scream before rolling over on her back and kicking her legs in the air.

"Lewis, I am not *believing* this! A high-roller villa! It's like the Taj Mahal."

"Hope not," Gruvver said superstitiously, looking at a basket of fruit and other goodies the size of a small canoe. There were bottles of French wine on the ebony table with the fruit boat. "Taj Mahal's pretty, but it's a tomb."

"Oh, well, you know what I mean." Charmaine kicked off her sandals in another paroxysm of delight. "So this is how the big shots get treated when they're stayin' here. Wonder who's in the other villas? Think we might be rubbing up against some movie stars?"

"I still don't quite get why they didn't just move us to another room like the one we had?"

"Who knows, maybe half our stuff got ruined. I want to go for a swim and I don't have a bikini." She jumped up and went to the glass doors that opened onto a secluded terrace the kidney-shaped pool embraced. "Or does it matter if I wear a suit; these villas are designed for total privacy, aren't they? Come on, Gruvver, let's take a dip in the altogether, then we'll hot tub it for a while."

"Not now, Charmaine. I had a good workout in the lap pool this afternoon. My shoulders are still sore. And the back of my neck has this tender spot."

"From bumping headfirst into the swimming pool wall?" Charmaine came dancing barefoot back to him, emulating the carioca women depicted in a *Carnivale* frieze that decorated the grand salon. "That's not like you, bein' clumsy, Gruvver." She put an arm around him and rubbed the tender spot just above his occipital bulge. "Hot tub, then. What you need to get rid of those aches and pains."

"Hot tub would put me to sleep, and I need to eat something first." Gruvver closed his eyes, giving himself over to her solicitude. "Don't know how that happened to me. Misjudged my distance, I suppose." He flexed his shoulders. "Funny thing. I was lookin' in a mirror gettin' dressed after my shower and it felt like I was lookin' through somebody else's eyes at a face I had trouble recognizing." He flexed again, stretched, bent to touch his toes while Charmaine watched with a small frown of concern. "Can't seem to get comfortable," Gruvver said. "It's like I'm wearin' a suit that's too tight on me."

"Lewis, you are close to weirding me out here. Why don't we open a bottle of that Bordeaux wine, relax, and decide what to do about dinner? I'm gonna see if I can find a powder room. *Les Dames.* Wonder how you say tinkle in French?"

"*Le peepee,*" Gruvver suggested.

He was prying the cork out of the bottle of red Bordeaux when he heard Charmaine call, "Gruvver, there's a big rec room back here with a pool table and a poker table and a home theatre with one of those flat plasma screens on the wall that cost a fortune even at Sam's Club."

"Do you want a glass of wine?" he called back. "It's just a couple years younger than you are."

"Is that good or bad?"

"I don't think either one of you is past your peak yet," Gruvver judged, sampling.

A little later she called, "Gruvver, you will not believe this! One wall of the master suite is like a waterfall, but quiet as a whisper. And there's tropical fish in a pool."

"Don't fall in; some of 'em might bite."

"And there's a hammock for a bed, feels like pure silk."

"Find the potty yet?"

"Oh, I almost forgot. Be right there."

Gruvver ran his hands over the smooth cocobolo-wood rumps of sculpted Brazilian women lazing on a pedestal beneath a series of angled spotlights. He felt, superstitious again and a little wary, that there had to be more to all of this luxury they'd been introduced to than a mere apology on the part of the Bahìa's management.

Palm fronds in the theatrically lighted garden swayed in a cool evening breeze. The pool and octagonal hot tub steamed invitingly. All of it was a poor boy's dream of paradise. He felt both intimidated and resentful. Mostly it was just pretentious. *Four* chandeliers in one room? Waiting on Charmaine, he sipped his wine too fast, wondering where he could lay his hands on a room service menu.

But that wasn't how it worked on High-Rollers' Street. No sooner had his hunger pangs sharpened than he heard muted door chimes. Gruvver opened the door in the skylighted foyer to find a full-dress butler outside. Swallowtail coat, white gloves. Name of Sven. Nordic blond but not aloof. Whatever they desired for the rest of the evening, Sven was there to provide it. He looked a little dismayed that Gruvver had already opened one of the bottles of wine, and asked anxious questions about the quality. Room service for dinner? Not at all. The villa contained a well-equipped kitchen, and Sven was a master chef.

They had their dinner on the garden's cozy terrace, in a gazebo over-looking the hot tub. Cold yellow tomato soup, sautéed scampi, and broiled lobster tail for Charmaine; an avocado salad and a New York strip medium rare for Gruvver.

He knew he was drinking too much wine, and didn't care. Charmaine's face kept going in and out of focus, and their conversation didn't make a lot of sense to him. He smiled and smiled. While Sven and a maid were cleaning up in the kitchen Gruvver and Charmaine played pool in the rec room, listening to Aretha Franklin. Gruvver was all thumbs and missed easy shots. They were waiting for Sven to leave for the night so they could skinny-dip outside, although the sunken bath in the master suite was big enough to paddle around in.

Charmaine had to guide him across what seemed like an acre of glass floor in the master suite, beneath which tropical fish lurked around an artificial reef. He lay down on the spacious hammock—just for a minute, to get the feel of it, he said. Don't want to go to sleep, night's young, I'll get plenty of sleep when I'm dead. Charmaine kissed him twice but he never felt the second kiss. The water-fall murmured in his brain, and he was riding a long sunset wave to dreamland.

Charmaine, who had drunk only half a glass of white Bordeaux at dinner while Gruvver lit into the red with a vengeance, wasn't sleepy yet. She removed Gruvver's shoes and all of her clothes, gave him a parting kiss, and after dialing down the lights throughout the villa she went outside to slip into the deliciously warm pool. There was music in the air, programmed by Sven before he left. All guys, the great saloon singers from the desert-deco Vegas era, when the mob guys were a saturnine presence around their watering holes. Frank, Vic, Tony, Dino. And the other Tony.

Not a lot of room for swimming in the pool. Charmaine settled into a genteel sidestroke to keep her hair from getting too wet. After about fifteen minutes of this moderate exercise she lifted herself out of the water and, wrapped up in a terry towel, lay down on one of the colorful mats lining the apron of the pool. She used a smaller towel on the edges of her hair, then brushed. Some water had gotten into an ear, which was the main thing she disliked about swimming. She tilted her head toward her left shoulder and gave it a couple of shakes.

That's when she noticed she wasn't alone.

The black dog watching her from one of the gazebo steps was of the cuddly type that Charmaine's aunt Livonia had always owned, six of them running around Livonia's house at last count. A mixed bag of Cockerpoo, shih tzu, and Lhasa apso, a breed which Charmaine's little sister called a "lapsed abscess." Anyway, they were darling.

Charmaine whistled softly. "Hey, there. Where did you come from, stranger?"

The little dog trembled all over from the excitement of being spoken to, but he didn't budge from the step he was on. Charmaine looked around the garden to see if there was a gate he could have crawled under. No way he could have leaped over the seven-foot surrounding wall. Possibly he'd come in under the wall; some of these little dogs were ferocious diggers.

She whistled again; more agitation from the dog, but no real movement. He was, she noticed now, wearing a fancy collar that flashed like gold when he wiggled.

So, if he didn't want to come to her—

Charmaine got up and walked around one end of the kidney-shaped pool to the gazebo on the terrace. The fluffy dog's eyes sparked at her approach; he whined ecstatically but backed off a few feet when she sat on the top step.

"You're okay; I like pooches," Charmaine assured this one, looking him—or her—over. The links of the chain around its neck, from what she could see of it, looked like eighteen-karat gold. Obviously a pampered little darling that belonged to one of the resort's guests, but Charmaine didn't see ID tags on the chain. "So what do I call you?" she said.

The little dog was momentarily still, head tilted to one side, moist dark eyes inquisitive. Charmaine held out a hand, palm down, fingers wiggling invitingly.

"Come on; I won't hurt you, little foo-foo dog."

That seemed to be all the dog had been waiting for—an invitation to jump into her lap and frolic. Which he did, with a lot of energy that nearly bowled her over. With his paws against her towel-wrapped breasts, he—Charmaine had confirmed he was all boy, had that stiff little dipper and tiny furry testicles—lapped eagerly at her nose and cheeks. Charmaine snuggling him tighter, happy that he had no doggy odor; someone obviously took good care of this little charmer.

Slippery licks on her closed eyelids from a petite pink tongue. Kisses, kisses. Charmaine had the giggles; she had also come unwrapped and lay back loosey-goosey on the floor of the gazebo. Frank Sinatra crooned in her ear from hidden garden speakers: "Come Fly with Me." She was willing, the doggie all over her face and breasts, *lick lick*. She felt as light as fog, subtly adrift, lost but loving it in a limbo of lassitude and squirmy animal affections. The animal roaming her body with heated breath and insinuating tongue that now rasped, it was nearly enough to give her an orgasm.

Then, abruptly, there were no more touches; she felt alone again, bereft, flat on her back but a foot above the gazebo floor, moored there by another's will. She heard him breathing.

Charmaine's eyelashes felt sticky; with an effort she batted them free of her cheeks and looked at the man squatting Indian fashion nearby, watching her intently. He was dressed all in black, but there was a gold chain snug at the base of his throat.

"You know who I am," he said with a smile.

Charmaine tried to raise her head to see him better. But she knew. She felt awkward and shy but not alarmed. Lifting her eyelids was one thing. The rest of her body was not under her control. It floated as if on a current of air. A not-unpleasant sensation.

"Yes," she said. "I know. But how do you change from a dog to a man?"

"Oh, I can do many fascinating things, Charmaine."

"Is this an illusion?"

"No."

"Are you going to finish making love to me?"

He shook his head regretfully. She felt sad for him.

"That I'm unable to do. Although I've often wondered what it must be like."

"Why did you come to me as a dog?"

"Two reasons. A barrier was put into place tonight, before I got here. I suspect one of the Caretakers has moved in on Lewis, and is taking precautions. So in order for us to have this conversation, you had to invite me to appear. I thought the best approach would be to show up as one of the little dogs you're familiar with, so you wouldn't be frightened. You're not scared of me now, are you?"

"No. I don't think you want to hurt me."

"That's right. I don't. I love women, Charmaine. I just can't make love to them. Not in the form I'm assuming now. If you'd like, I can come back to you as—something altogether different. But there's no point to our mating. I'm saving myself for someone else."

"Then—what are you going to do with me?"

He looked up at the stars above the walled garden, and smiled.

"Like Frank says, it's a good night to go flying."

"Can we do that?" she wondered, wide-eyed, nerves jumping.

"Of course, Charmaine. Together you and I can accomplish almost anything."

OCTOBER 25 · 6:22 A.M.

When Lewis Gruvver woke up with a start after almost eight hours of uninterrupted slumber, the jerking of his body set the unfamiliar hammock in which he lay in a tangle of bedclothes to swaying, which caused his stomach to roll over and expel a jet of soured wine toward his throat. His mouth, as he became more conscious of his body and dizzied heart, was hangover-parched; his eyes felt as if there were grains of gunpowder beneath the lids.

He lay very still for half a minute while the motion of the hammock and his heartbeat settled down. Whose demented idea had that been anyway, to put a hammock instead of a bed in the master suite? Gruvver doubted that many Brazilians slept in hammocks, because, for one thing, the birthrate in that country would be way down. Never mind finessing your stroke, just trying to maintain a workable erection while swaying side to side would be a difficult feat. He tried to imagine himself on his back, as he now was, but with Charmaine astride him, elaborating on a theme from her sonata for meat flute and trying to maintain her balance in spite of the swing and sway of the hammock. The absurdity of the scene he was imagining had him laughing until he choked up a little more of the soured wine. He flung out a hand, discovered that Charmaine wasn't there, asleep with her knees drawn up to her belly, the way he usually found her in the morning.

But she was habitually an early riser; liked her swim or a mile run to get the day started right.

"Charmaine?"

Gruvver relaxed for a couple of minutes, giving her time to stroll in wearing her faded gold Georgia Tech sweats and her ratty softball cap from Woodward Academy, where she'd gone to high school on a partial scholarship. Carrying a cup of coffee that she'd brewed for her Lewie in the villa's kitchen. Perky as hell and already getting in a sly dig at him for passing out on her so early.

He called again; no answer. And suddenly it was time for him to pee, or way past time; so he scooted woozily across the glass floor with fish scattering colorfully beneath his feet (another dumb idea, Gruvver thought, although you could actually watch the fish, reflected in a mirrored ceiling, while scrunched in the tricky hammock, a pastime possibly of interest only to ichthyologists).

Gruvver relieved himself copiously, then undressed and lurched into a cold shower, multiple showerheads massaging him top to bottom with what felt like cactus needles. Stepped out feeling so *fine,* almost a whole man again instead of a conglomerate of rusty old parts. He put on one of the courtesy robes hanging in the bathroom and a pair of flip-flops and went in search of Charmaine.

Who wasn't hard to find. She was lying full-naked on the pool apron out there in a cold sunless dawning, knees drawn up as was her habit, with everything he cherished and could never get enough of innocently but lewdly exposed. Sound asleep—he assumed, after his initial shock of seeing her like that faded—because a portion of her slender right thumb was caught between her lips and strong white teeth. That sad little reversal to blissful infancy he'd never seen before, in the months they'd been sleeping together.

When Gruvver picked her up in his arms he was shocked anew. The desert air had him shuddering, it must have been around forty degrees this early, but Charmaine wasn't cold. Her skin felt as warm as if she'd been sunbathing. When he rocked her, gently at first, then more urgently in his arms, she was slow to wake up; not a muscle moved in her smooth slack face. Gruvver carefully pulled her thumb from between her teeth. She apparently had bitten down hard in her sleep and there was blood around the quick of the polished nail. A little smear of blood lay across her front teeth, still with the slightly serrated edges from childhood.

Charmaine's throat muscles bulged as she swallowed. Then she opened her eyes, looked blankly at him for a moment. Recognition came like the light of the sun. She snuggled, touched her lips with the tip of her tongue, smiled.

"Oh, man," she said. "Did I ever have me a dream."

6:48 A.M.

A limo was waiting for Gulfstream N657GB when it taxied to the corner of McCarran International where private jets were parked during their owners' layovers in Vegas. They had gone through Customs while the jet was refueled in Boston, so there were no formalities to be observed. The drive to Bahìa resort took eight minutes in traffic that was beginning to get heavy. It was that hour of the morning that sidles around like a whipped dog after the revels have ended.

They sat close together in the back of the limo with the tingling nerves and taut unsmiling faces of people who had of late spent a lot of time continent-hopping. The sun was rising, revealing more fully to Eden, who had never seen the Las Vegas Strip, the collection of hotels lined up like baubles on the dusty shelf of a curio shop, a slapstick mismatch of entertainment architecture still dripping with light in the blue dawn. Everything else in town looked like an untidy playground. Sand and a dearth of trees.

"Fifty years ago you could have had most of this for eight bucks an acre," the limo driver said.

"Overpriced," Bertie murmured. She had been spoiled since birth by vistas of a grander sort.

"But I understand why my granpap never took the plunge. Granpap was a leery sort of guy."

"That so?" Tom said, and pushed a button to close the blackout divider. They had other, private matters to talk about.

Past the ominous obsidian pyramid of the Luxor at the low end of the Strip, a monument to a culture that didn't know it was doomed—but no culture had ever interpreted the odds correctly— the Lincoln Grayle Theatre, approximately fifteen miles west, was dazzling by first light, a star that refused to dim in spite of the advance of morning.

"There he is," Eden said forebodingly as they approached an outsized billboard near the Strip. Lincoln Grayle, looking down on the lines of traffic waiting for a light to change, was the size of King Kong but slim and sexy in a black turtleneck. In a segment from his show playing on a Jumbotron screen, Grayle gestured with both hands as he guided not one but two levitated female assistants through the Twin Pendulums of Death. A digitized newsticker running along the bottom edge of the billboard announced the reopening of his dinner theatre on Saturday night. The show was sold out, of course. Welcome back, Linc.

"We're about to commit murder, you know—" Eden began, as if they weren't all gloomy enough at this hour.

"Is ridding the earth of an ancient scourge against the law?" Bertie interrupted, her tone uncharacteristically irritable. "He may look like a man, but he's a god who went bad."

"—Or be murdered, which is probably an inadequate way of saying what he'll do to us if we're not very lucky."

"We are lucky," Bertie said. "There's not a slot machine in town that won't cough up its jackpot to us after a couple of spins."

"Like we need the money. Crashing slots isn't luck; it's—"

"What I'm trying to say is, we make our own luck, and we're dealing this game."

"But not as long as Grayle is holding . . . you-know-who. What are we going to do about it? I don't even know where she is."

"He'll be devoting a lot of his time and attention to Gwen," Tom Sherard said. "So probably she's under house arrest. His house, of course."

"Where does he live?" Eden asked.

Tom had researched Grayle's living standard. "House in Hawaii, penthouse in New York. His main residence is on the southeast slope of Mount Charleston at an elevation of six thousand feet. Access strictly limited. There's a gated private road, which is patrolled. The house was featured on a segment of the Travel Channel a few months ago. It has the design and opulence one would expect of someone with Grayle's celebrity and resources. Needless to say he'll be well protected up there."

"Think he'll have us over for brunch?"

"I shouldn't have to go inside to find out if Gwen is there." He checked his watch. "I'll be leaving in about an hour, as soon as I've had breakfast and changed into something more suitable for climbing around on a mountain."

"You mean we," Bertie attempted to correct him.

"You and Eden have your deal; rescuing Gwen is mine."

"Tom, you're simply not up to clambering around on rocky slopes in unfamiliar country."

"Couldn't agree more. I'd be a fool to try. But I've been provided with some expert help. Someone who knows Mount Charleston well, all eleven thousand feet of it."

"Who have you been talking to?" Bertie asked.

"Our old friend Senator Buck Hannafin. His son-in-law is an Army general, in charge of the United States Special Operations Command. Rangers, SEALS, Delta Force, tough guys all. I'm getting the loan of one of the Army's Special Forces officers, a light Colonel who grew up in southern Nevada."

"Suppose my dpg is at Grayle's place? Then what?"

"The Colonel and I will go in and retrieve her."

"While *he's* there?" Eden said. "Tom, I don't think so."

"That's where you come in, Eden. If we need to effect entry, it will be up to you to lure him away from home base. That won't be until late today. Meantime the two of you can get some rest. Don't leave the hotel grounds until you hear from me."

9:35 A.M.

Tom Sherard met the loan-out from Special Operations, who was currently on leave, in one of the parking lots at the ski and snowboard center high on Mount Charleston. The temperature at seven thousand feet on this late October day was barely into the fifties, the sun almost too bright for the naked eye to bear.

She was leaning against the side of a dusty maroon Toyota Tundra off-roader, watching Sherard climb slowly out of his rented SUV and limp toward her, right hand on the gold lion's-head walking stick. Her expression betrayed misgivings, although he couldn't read her eyes behind the amber lenses of her mountaineer's glasses. She wore her thick dark hair cut appropriately short for her profession, a dark blue headband, a camo vest over a black sweater.

"Tom Sherard?"

"Yes."

"I'm Courtney Shyla. Nobody told me you had a bad leg."

"Knee. I'll manage."

"How did it happen?"

"I was shot."

She didn't say anything to that, but took off her glasses for a few moments to blow some dust off the lenses. Making up her mind about him. Her eyes matched the color of her headband. True-blue eyes, a firm, possibly stubborn jaw. Mid-thirties, he guessed. He wondered about some of the places she'd been to lately. Afghanistan. Iraq. The terrorist training camps in Yemen or the North African desert.

She made up her mind, gave him a slight nod. "Looks like a stout-enough stick you've got there."

"It has—unusual properties."

"You're looking at about a three-mile hike down to the magician's place. Trails most of the way. Once we get there, we'll have cover some three hundred feet above the house, with our backs to the sun."

"You've been there already?"

"Seven o'clock this morning." She picked up the backpack at her feet, unzipped a compartment, showed him footage that she had shot with her camcorder. "The subject was described to me as being about five-nine or -ten, early twenties, red hair—"

"More of a strawberry blond, with red streaks."

Courtney shook her head. "I didn't see her, but it's one hell of a house. Three levels cantilevered over a gorge. As I said, I got there early. Some Hispanic servants were up and around. And the magician was out jogging. Running, I should say, and on steep terrain. He's got powerful legs and a lot of stamina. I got a good look at him. He came within eight feet of me."

"And didn't see you?"

Courtney smiled confidently. "If I don't want to be seen—" She turned and lifted another backpack out of the bed of her truck. "Yours. I was told no one goes tango uniform, and the Secretary will disavow any knowledge of my actions, et cetera, if I stub my toes. Objective is to exfiltrate the subject and leave no tracks. What kind of physical condition is she in?"

"Good, the last time I saw her."

Courtney unzipped another bulkier compartment and let him have a look inside.

"Taser gun. You have one in your pack. They handle like an oversized .45. Close range. Aim and pull the trigger. Done any shooting?"

"Now and then," he said, semi-amused by her assumption of vast superiority in tactical matters.

"By the way, you don't have to answer this, but is the subject related to you?"

"Rather poor relation, I'd call her."

"Anything else I should know about?" Courtney said, shrugging into her backpack. Sherard did the same. "Is Grayle the badass I've heard he can be?"

"Worse than anything you may have heard. We want to avoid a run-in with Mr. Lincoln Grayle, no matter what."

"Like I said, he was less than eight feet from me. He never had a clue."

"Let's hope he didn't, Courtney. And let me caution you: you may see things before the day is done that are well beyond the realm of your experiences. You could find yourself questioning your sanity."

She laughed heartily. "Are you a magician too? You've got the patter, but you don't look the type, Tom." She glanced at his bad knee. "Let me guess. Grayle was responsible for that wound?"

"No. Actually he owes me one. I'm sure it's still fresh in his mind."

"You shot Lincoln Grayle? This *is* getting interesting. He didn't look shot when I saw him. Picture of health, and so good-looking."

"You can wound him, Courtney, but you can't kill him."

She looked hard at him for a few moments.

"O-kay. Guess I'd head back home right now, if you hadn't been vouched for by some terrific people I really trust."

"I appreciate that vote of confidence," Sherard said sardonically.

"So just what do you mean, he can't be killed? Like, he's a living legend sort of thing? Because we all die. Have to. Otherwise in a few years there'd be gridlock in the supermarkets. Who the hell is Lincoln Grayle to beat the odds?"

They had left the parking lot and were on a wooded trail through moss-covered boulders, birds flicking through streaks of sunlight.

"Grayle is *Deus inversus*. The Dark Side of God. In other words—"

"Tom, I'll bet you're a lot of fun at parties, but could you just cut the shit? Sounds like you're saying Grayle is the devil."

"Most of us are either god or devil, Courtney. But watch out for those who are a combination of both."

Sherard held up his walking stick, gripping it below the lion's head. Might as well find out now, he thought, if Courtney Shyla had the real stuff. Imperishable grit in her soul.

"Courtney? Have a look at this."

She glanced at the lion's head. The jaws opened wide in an unheard snarl. Tom relaxed his grip. *"Simba,"* he said softly. "Fetch." The stick flew from his hand, streaking up into trees beside the trail they were on. There was a flurry within the filigreed, reddened aspens, birds shrieking. Courtney's mouth was ajar; he could almost look down her throat. When the lion's-head stick came back to him like an arrow there was a feathery jewel of a cedar waxwing in its severe metal mouth. Tom took the stout stick in hand.

"Release," he said.

The fright-paralyzed bird dropped from the lion's jaws onto packed-down pine needles. After several seconds its wings began beating feebly. Then the waxwing recovered its wits and ability to fly and swooped off into shadows.

Courtney turned and walked away from the trail to a rock outcropping, sat there with knees apart, her head down. The westerner's alert toughness, that touch of renegade moll, had vanished. She made a fist and pounded rhythmically on one thigh, hard enough so that Sherard was afraid she'd injure herself.

"Oh! Jesus!" she said, shaking her head vehemently.

"You can go home now, if you want," Sherard said coolly.

She stopped beating up on herself. Raised her head, posture hardening.

"Damn you!"

"I know."

"I haven't freaked so bad since I was ten years old."

"I believe that."

"Who *are* you?"

"I like to think I'm one of the good guys, Courtney. Right now some other good guys who are dear to me need all the help we can give them. If you're strong enough."

Courtney filled her lungs. Her lower lip was turning white between her teeth. Finally she eased the bite, pushed herself away from the rock, nodded tautly.

"That's what I'm here for. Just don't pull any more of your magic or witchcraft or whatever the hell it was on me. I like it here in the real world. Wherever you come from, I don't think I could live there."

9:52 A.M.

Lewis Gruvver went into the bath of the master suite where Charmaine, wearing a shower cap, was luxuriating among the bath gel bubbles in the sunken tub. He sat on the rounded marble rim, looking down at her.

"You look like you didn't digest your breakfast too well," Charmaine said, squinting an eye that had a little soap in it. "Tummy still not feelin' so great?"

"What? Oh, my stomach's okay. I wasn't that hungry, but these butlers they keep shuffling in and out of here can't just bake some biscuits; they got to whup up a feast every time."

"That sounds like we are lookin' a gift horse in the mouth, if you know what I'm talking about. *Un cheval cadeau.*"

"Means if somebody gives you a horse, you don't go countin' to see if it has all its teeth."

"*Vraiment*, Lew-eeess." She extended a long leg from the pink cloud of bubbles covering most of her body, pointed her toes at the vault ceiling with its fresco of naked brown-toned Brazilians discreetly having sex behind large palm fronds. She squinted again, at flaked polish on a big toenail. "You're not out of sorts because you didn't like the lovin' you got this morning?"

"What? Oh, *no*. You were perfect, baby. I'm the one jumped the gun and spoiled it for you."

"No complaints here," Charmaine said. "But it's like since we got up you're not even *here* half the time while I'm tryin' to talk to you."

"We didn't sleep together last night, Charmaine," Gruvver reminded her.

"Told you already I don't know how it happened I fell asleep out there after my swim. So are we finally okay with that?"

"What?"

"There you go again! Gruvver, you need to hit the gym this morning, get on the rowing machine; you've got cobwebs on your brain. And will you please look at me, I am *talking* to you."

But that was part of Gruvver's problem; he didn't want to look at her for long because overnight her eyes had changed. They were very old eyes in a youthful face, with something sly and fiery lurking in their depths. Like the eyes his mad old great-uncle Etaw had by the end of his ninth decade, toothless old man but still a hell-raiser. It wasn't just that Gruvver's perceptions were a little off. Charmaine had been a frenzied clawing bitch during foreplay instead of her cuddly, slow-breathing pleasure-giving self. He'd lost his load when she raked the underside of his glans with her fingernails as he tried to mount her. It still hurt. There had been nothing loving in the action of her nails; she'd rejected him, as if she had suddenly found him undesirable and wanted no more couplings.

Heavy in the heart, Gruvver said, "The gym? Yeah. Good idea. First, though, I—"

As he drifted away again Charmaine splashed him. "Don't *do* that. What's going on in your head, Gruvver-man?"

"Oh—I'm not sure. For some reason I need to go next door."

"Go where? That big villa with its own tennis court? What for?"

"Somebody there I need to see. I think," Gruvver said, sorely perplexed and holding his head.

"Like who?"

"Don't know who they are. They just came in this morning."

"You are not making a lot of sense. You don't know who they are, then what business you got botherin' them?"

"There's a van parked near their gate. Watchbirds, I think. But private, not government. It's not a surveillance gig."

"How do you know?"

"I had a look outside few minutes ago. When it first came to me that . . . I should go introduce myself."

"Well, sure. Just walk on over there, tell 'em Lewis Gruvver is here, on important business to discuss if only you can remember what it is."

"Look, Charmaine, I don't even pretend to understand what's got into me since yesterday."

"Makes two of us," she said sulkily.

"But it is driving me half crazy. Maybe when I get there, I'll know what it's about."

Charmaine, deep in the tub, studied him pityingly. "Lewis, I think I know what has you out of kilter."

"Yeah?" He saw the redness in her eyes, and looked quickly away. It was only soap. He wasn't himself this morning.

"What you're telling me is some kind of powerful dream you had and can't shake off."

"Dream? Maybe that's what it was," he said, wanting to believe her. But his scalp tightened as soon as he spoke.

"Sure! I have this dream, I'm late for a test which if I don't pass means I don't graduate. But I can't remember the building I'm supposed to take the test in. I'm walkin' and walkin' and I wake up cryin'. Even after I wake up that dream hangs on for a while. Why don't you get yourself another cup of coffee while I finish up with my bath? Then we'll do something fun. Want to drive over to Boulder Dam? I heard there's dead men in there, fell in while the concrete was bein' poured, which they had to do night and day. Couldn't stop pourin' to fetch out the bodies or else the dam wouldn't hold together when it was finished."

"That's some story," Gruvver said, although the moment Charmaine stopped speaking he couldn't remember what she'd been telling him. One thought was crowding everything else out of his mind. *Have to get out of here and go next door. They know what's going on. Why Charmaine isn't Charmaine anymore.*

As Gruvver got up to leave Charmaine flicked soapsuds at him with a churlish smile. The suds burned hot as lava on his skin. He pawed them away in sudden fright. Redness. Boiling red in the center of her pupils, spreading threadlike through the whites of her eyes. His scalp tightened again, as if he had been gripped by otherworldly fingers that were trying to drag him away from Charmaine, out of the bathroom, through the villa, and on to safety . . .

But what was there to be afraid of?

Charmaine rose from the tub, a dripping hand outstretched.

Never you mind, Lewis. He can't make you do a thing. Listen to me. Do what I tell you to do.

With her voice like fingernails ripping him again, this time tearing through his frontal lobes, Gruvver fled, stumbled across the glass floor of the bedroom, fish glimmer below, stumbled like a clumsy imitation man with too many hinges in his legs. Dragged this way, pulled another.

Let him go!

In addition to conflicting voices he heard sharp clickings in his assaulted mind: pool balls striking together. He glanced through the double doorway of the recreation room and saw his half brother Cornell inside, angled against the pool table, cue stick in his hands, smoothly running a rack of balls. He looked up inquiringly at Gruvver, then laid his stick down and followed him, in no hurry. Music in the rooms. Lionel Hampton, from the big-band era.

Gruvver labored to reach the front door of the villa, the safe outdoors, sunlight. Sanity restored. Each step now as if concrete were flooding over his feet, piling against his ankles. Millions of cubic yards of concrete in a continuous pour. Day and night. Apocryphal dead men in the forms down there, couldn't stop to pull them out. Concrete a thick river and nearly up to his knees while he discovered the doors wouldn't budge. Secure as a slab on his tomb. *It's like the Taj Mahal,* Charmaine had exclaimed on first entering the gift villa. Uh-huh.

Just let me get out of here, God and Jesus, anybody! *Don't let a man die who doesn't know what he's dying* for.

Charmaine, glistening from her bath, stood beside Cornell watching Gruvver as he doggedly recrossed the grand salon, foundering in what he knew to be fresh concrete. Loaded with the stuff. He shoved open the sliding door to the garden and fell awkwardly outside.

The pool apron had been freshly hosed. Birds were hopping around beneath feather-duster palms and pepper trees. The sounds of tennis came to him from the court next door; voices of two young women.

Over the wall! Get there! They will help you.

Some force beyond his comprehension yanked Gruvver to his feet and sent him staggering headlong around the pool. A young Hispanic gardener was at work, trimming vines in one corner of the garden. He turned when he heard Gruvver gasping, laid down his clippers, lit a cigarillo, and watched in amusement Gruvver's stilted, hectic progress toward the seven-foot wall between villas. Charmaine had come outside with Cornell, Charmaine still in the lush altogether, not even a towel for modesty's sake, snapping her fingers, hip-rolling to the big-band jump of "Hamp's Boogie-Woogie."

Gruvver stormed the yellow wall in his madness, pulling his feet out of the grasping flow of concrete. In his clumsiness, feet triple-size from accretions, he misjudged distance, smashed his face against the stuccoed wall, and fell back bleeding.

The concrete slopped over his chest as he lay stunned in a narrow bed of ivy. His hands were covered with the gray, sludgy stuff; when he raised them weakly into his line of sight they looked like the hands of a mummy.

This isn't real. It's all an illusion. You're not helpless. Fight it!

But who the hell are you, Gruvver thought, *to be giving advice, when I'm the one who's about to be sealed up in a dam for the next five hundred years!*

I hope," Lincoln Grayle said when Gwen walked out onto the terrace where he was studying plans for upcoming illusions, "that you're going to tell me you feel like a new woman. If you haven't seen yourself already, let me be the first to say how gorgeous you look this morning."

Gwen stopped a few feet from the glass-topped table and said, eyes narrow in hard sunlight, "What did that creep Woolwine do to me?" She was wearing a soft yellow bathrobe; her feet were bare. Newly aware of the music from unseen speakers on the terrace, she grimaced. Grayle was listening to Brenda Lee's tongue-in-cheek "I Saw Mommy Kissing Santa Claus." "*Christmas* music? How long was I out, a month?"

"Fourteen hours, give or take. This is the first day of your new life. How about brunch? It's time for me to eat. Dress rehearsal's at four-thirty. I usually have only two meals a day, six hours before a show, then after, when I really need to put away the calories."

"*What* new life, damn you?"

"Woolwine said you'd be a little agitated at first, uncertain about your status."

"My status? I'm a dpg until Eden says I'm not, period."

"Not entirely true. Dr. Woolwine, the eminent whatever-he-is, has wrought some beneficial changes. Worked a little, quote, magic to alter your biomagnetic makeup. That's the reason for the little patch you'll find behind your right ear." He waited while Gwen, dismayed, groped with her fingertips. "A small incision. Should heal in four or five days. You still have the best features of a doppelganger, but your dependency relationship with Eden is effectively over. Here's an analogy: if Eden were a disease, you'd have complete immunity."

"Not possible."

"You'll soon realize it's true. There is no contact between the two of you in an otherworldly sense. I suppose you could give her a call on her cell phone, but I'm sure you won't, once you become used to your new independence."

"Thanks for what you obviously assume is hospitality," Gwen said in a deep glower, "but I'll just be on my way."

Gwen unbelted the robe, shrugged it off, and kicked it aside. She turned and walked away from the table, looking back at him, anticipating confusion and consternation. Instead she was a little shocked to see Grayle looking straight at her, smiling, as if she hadn't vanished at the instant of discarding her robe.

"That's another difference," Grayle said. "The new Gwen can't disappear on a whim. You've lost your invisibility. See for yourself." He pointed to the glass doors of the terrace, in which they were both clearly reflected.

Gwen looked slowly around. For a few seconds she couldn't believe she was seeing her nude self in the solar-gain glass. Then, her face reddening, she made a grab for the robe she'd discarded and put it back on.

"The total visibility effect lasts for about four weeks; then you'll need another treatment. Nothing harmful. It's like spending a relaxing day at a good spa."

"Omigod—what else have you geniuses done to me?"

"That's about it," Grayle said pleasantly. "You can, we hope, still do all of your other doppelganger things. Which we now need to talk about. Would you care to sit down? We both have a busy weekend ahead of us. You're going to save my soul and I'm going to become a daddy."

11:06 A.M.

Bertie chased down a long sideline smash from Eden, but her backhand return was weak and she netted the ball. Again. They had agreed not to keep score, play the game on the level of noncompetitive fun, because Eden showed no mercy when it came to games of any kind. For all of the power she could put behind a serve, Bertie lacked Eden's lateral quickness and bewildering variety of shots. But at least playing her was instructive.

"Time out," Bertie said, gasping a little. She put her racket down and pulled off the cableknit sweater she no longer needed as the temperature rose into the sixties.

Eden nodded and twirled her racket in the air, caught it deftly behind her back. "Do we have any Gatorade?"

"How about a couple of wine coolers?" Charmaine suggested. She was perched on the wall where, for the last half hour, she helpfully had been serving as line judge and impartial rooter, applauding every good shot.

"I could go for that," Eden admitted. Bertie gave her a mild questioning look tempered with a smile. In the past few weeks Eden had become something of a drinker, but in present circumstances Bertie didn't begrudge her. Eden never got shit-faced, although on a couple of occasions, trying to match Tom drink for drink during long evenings of talk at Shungwaya, she had come close. It wasn't just nerves. Bertie knew precisely what was going on with Eden where Tom was concerned, and although she felt bleak about the potential for a nasty situation, she tried never to let her misgivings—and jealousy, of course—affect the valuable chemistry of their triad; the vital bond they all needed and depended upon.

"Give you a hand," Bertie called to Charmaine.

"Oh, thanks."

"I'm gonna take a bathroom break, see if we have any calls," Eden said to Bertie.

Bertie used clinging vines for handholds and scaled the seven-foot wall, dropped onto grass on the other side.

"Where did you say you were from?" Bertie asked Charmaine, who was wearing a cream suede tunic with embroidered blue jeans and cork-soled sandals that brought her to within a couple of inches of Bertie's imposing height.

"Atlanta."

"Go to school there?" Bertie said, making a guess about Charmaine's age.

"I'm a senior at Clark Atlanta. You look familiar to me, Bertie, sort of like Whitney before she got wrecked on drugs."

"People tell me that. I do some modeling."

"That may be where I saw you! Swimsuits?"

"Yeah, *Sports Illustrated*. I got the cover this year."

"Oh, you're famous! *Célèbre*. I remember now. My old boyfriend, before Lewis, he never missed an issue of *Sports Illustrated*."

They walked into the villa. "Is this a honeymoon trip for you, Charmaine?" Bertie asked, looking casually around.

"Oh, no, we're not that far along. Can you believe this place? Lewis isn't exactly a high-roller, but he doesn't think *anything* about dropping fifty thousand in a high-stakes poker game." Charmaine shrugged and sighed and led Bertie to the kitchen. "Which is mostly what he's been doing since we got here. I don't mean *losing*. Just playing poker, all night, every night." Sigh. "Does make a girl feel, you know, second-best? And I don't know a soul here in Las Vegas." She opened one of the restaurant-type refrigerators and began handing bottles of wine coolers to Bertie. "We'll find us somethin' to carry those in. Six enough?"

"I should think."

"I feel like I know your friend Eve from somewhere too," Charmaine said, but Bertie just smiled inscrutably. "It's nice of you guys to let me hang out. I get lonesome for somebody to talk to, you know?"

"Glad to have you, Charmaine."

Charmaine looked in some kitchen cabinets and came up with a picnic hamper. They loaded it with the chilled bottles and went back outside.

"Is Eve a model too?"

"No, just a good friend."

"Are you all spending much time in Vegas?"

"Depends."

Bertie went to the top of the wall first. Charmaine handed up the basket and seemed not to notice Bertie's helping hand as she climbed over herself. The two young women settled down in the semishade of a beautifully furnished orangerie. Nearby the surface of the pool flashed in the sun whenever a breeze passed over it. Charmaine tried to remove a stubborn twist-off cap from a bottle of wine cooler and grimaced at Bertie.

"You'll ruin a nail," Bertie advised her. "I'll get an opener. Right back."

Inside the duplex villa she met Eden coming down a free-standing spiral staircase. She'd had a fast shower and changed clothes. Crisp white resort wear with a sleeveless cashmere sweater.

"Tom should have called by now," Eden fretted. She rubbed the mastoid bone behind her left ear.

"Too soon. He's only been gone a couple of hours. What's the matter?"

"I don't know; it hurts here. Like I'm raising a boil." She tilted her head to one side. "See anything?"

"No."

Eden stopped rubbing the spot where Gwen had had a small magnetic device implanted, behind her right ear.

"Well, I wish Tom would keep us up-to-date, at least. What if he doesn't find you-know-who."

"You'll have to think of something. She's your dpg."

Eden shrugged. "It is my fault for thinking she could be helpful. But she's like a jinx. Maybe I just ought to say, you know, the 'G' word; then she won't be my responsibility anymore."

"She would still be your mirror image. How desirable is that? Give Tom some time and try not to worry."

Eden offered a deliberately goofy smile. "Me, worry?"

"If we're not playing any more tennis, I'll take a shower too. If you don't mind entertaining Charmaine."

"She seems easy to amuse. What do you make of her?"

"For one thing, she has less of an aura than a pilot light gas flame. Sometimes none at all."

"What do you think that means?"

"Either she's walking dead, or she's suppressing her aura."

"I didn't know anyone could do that."

"Lincoln Grayle for one. Also the guy from Santa Rosa, California, who bit off the monsignor's face in the papal library."

Eden looked out at the orangerie, where Charmaine patiently waited with an unopened bottle of wine cooler in her hand.

"Do you think—"

"I'm not sure yet, but it's suspicious. Also she hasn't wanted me to touch her. As if she knows I could get a reading. And there are crosscurrents of extremely bad vibes in that villa where she's staying. I felt like I was wading through a tide of stinging jellyfish. Of course vibes hang on in places like this, where there could've been a couple of hundred people in and out during the past month, very few of them perfect in their love for Jesus."

"Then we don't want her hanging around with us."

Bertie thought about it.

"I'd rather know where she is than not know where she is."

"So we'll do lunch?"

"Let's find out what we can. About Charmaine, and those vibes I mentioned."

"You're not planning to—"

"Bad vibes or not, before I clean up I'd like to do a walk-through next door. Just keep Charmaine occupied while I'm snooping. Oh, you'll need a church key for those wine bottles. There's one on the bar over there. And Eden?" Bertie waited for Eden's full attention. "On this of all days we need to keep our wits about us."

"Remember that yourself. And I'll just have a Coke."

<h1 style="text-align:center">11:24 A.M.</h1>

Brunch had been served to Lincoln Grayle and Eden Waring's doppelganger on the terrace of the second of three traylike levels of the magician's mountain home, designed, apparently, by a disciple of Frank Lloyd Wright and constructed of native sandstone with a plentiful use of bronze-toned glass. While Tom Sherard and Courtney Shyla watched from the high-country hide that Courtney had selected on her first foray, Gwen previously had gone inside to put on clothes. And returned of her own volition. Tom noted this with interest and apprehension. After returning she had listened, saying little or nothing, to a pitch from Lincoln Grayle that went on for nearly a quarter of an hour, Grayle pacing around the terrace while Gwen remained seated, motionless, her head bowed, hands knotted in her lap. She looked tensely servile, Tom thought, sharing with Courtney binoculars that would not reflect sunlight. They were about three hundred yards from the house, in a jumble of sheared boulders below a southwest face of the mountain, scrub spruce that clung to deep cracks between the rocks providing good cover for their surveillance.

"What do you think he wants from her?" Courtney commented when Gwen and the magician devoted themselves to their meal. Gwen ate tentatively at first, but after a few bites of beef Wellington her appetite perked up. Food seemed also to loosen her tongue. Her end of the conversation was accompanied by mostly negative gestures. Sherard was glad to see that; he had thought she might have been mesmerized by the Trickster. The only other way to account for Gwen's continued presence on the terrace would have been black light; but obviously she wasn't a prisoner of high-quantum energies. So Grayle had come up with another means of keeping Gwen close to him. And he wanted her cooperation. Leoncaro, Tom thought, might have been right when he theorized Grayle needed the dpg to retrieve the missing half of his black soul.

"Maybe I can answer that," he said to Courtney. "But first you should know that Gwen is not exactly what she appears to be."

"Here we go again," Courtney said, rolling her eyes in mock resignation.

While Bertie supposedly was dawdling in an upstairs shower, Eden toured Charmaine around the first floor of the six-thousand-square-foot villa, this one with all of the Technicolor panache of a 1940s Carmen Miranda musical. Bertie slipped over the garden wall again and reentered the villa next door, not without a heavy baggage of misgivings.

Just inside the glass doors she stood very still for half a minute, eyes closing, hands levitating from her sides, fingertips beginning to tingle. She sensed, as if her outstretched fingers were divining rods, black arts, a household of evil, murder.

Also, thankfully, a benign presence.

"I'll watch your back," the entity said in her mind. "Have a look around."

"Thanks. What am I supposed to see here?"

"You know I can't answer that."

Bertie heard colorful, infectious music: hectic drummings, guitars, tambourines. *Samba.* Her hips began to move involuntarily. *Gotta dance.* When she opened her eyes one of the cariocas on the mural in the grand salon was moving also. Bare to below his slim brown waist, glistening with perspiration. He wore tight-fitting awning-striped bell-bottom pants and an old-fashioned straw boater. As Bertie looked at him with a twitch of a smile and the music became louder, throbbing with good feeling and diminishing some of the nastier vibrations inside the villa, the carioca doffed his boater, rolled it on its stiff brim the length of an outstretched arm, winked, and returned the hat to his head at a cocky angle. His feet were moving all the time to the frenzied beat of Brazilian conga drums.

"Do I know you?" Bertie said subvocally.

"Let us say we have a mutual acquaintance in Rome."

"Okay, let us say. What do I call you?"

"How about 'Bing'? I have always taken a shine to that name."

"Bing it is. What tripped your trigger, Bing? Do I really need to know what went down here?"

"Yes. But be cautious."

"The magician?"

"And his many surrogates. Thousands of them infest Las Vegas. This place is long overdue for a good dose of plague and fire."

"You sound like the late Pledger Lee Skeldon."

"I had the duty and pleasure of assisting him in his long career."

"So what are you doing in Vegas, Bing?"

"Unfortunately I was unable to prevent another terrible murder. The magician was a stronger presence. And I have no license to interfere in human events. Otherwise what need do souls have for human beings?"

"I thought it was the other way around."

"Of course not."

"Could you tone the music down a little, Bing? I can handle whatever is left here to deal with."

"A great deal, I'm afraid. And there's so little time. But you're a resourceful girl."

"Where do I start?"

"May I suggest the master suite? And I wouldn't leave Eden Waring alone for too long with your new friend."

"Way ahead of you there, Bing."

11:58 A.M.

Gwen dabbed her lips with a linen napkin and asked one of the Hispanic girls who had waited on them at breakfast to adjust the tilt of the sunshade above her head. The other girl poured more fresh orange juice into her glass from a pitcher, looked inquiringly at Lincoln Grayle. He waved both of them away and off the terrace.

"The point is," Gwen said, "I've never time-traveled. I know how it's done, but—"

"What do you need," the magician said genially, "a time machine?" He had begun to enjoy her company, now that she was thawing out and accepting the fact that her hostility was misplaced. He really did want to help her achieve her full potential as an ex-doppelganger.

"Time *is* a machine."

"Oh."

"With an infinite number of entrances and exits. How complex do I let this get before I lose you completely?"

"That's enough of an explanation. My question was—"

Gwen had been staring into blue space, running her tongue thoughtfully over the edges of her front teeth, trying to ignore a relentlessly uptempo version of "Ding Dong Merrily on High" pouring out of multiple speakers on the terrace.

"What do I need? To start with, photographs of the period. Summer of 1926."

"Original photos? That would take time."

"No. I think good copies from an Internet archive might do. I'm not all that sure. But all images, even those, let's say, in a faded old Raphael tapestry from the early sixteenth century, can be used to gauge the exact position and velocity of the particles that resulted in the creation of the image, and once I'm logged into that flow of the machine, I know at just what point I 'get off.' It's like riding on a subway the thickness of a human hair, where all the tunnels are wormholes and I'm the only passenger."

"What if you want to travel to the future?"

"The past, obviously, is predictable; the future is not, according to chaos theory, so that's another story. But I'm not going to the future. Yet."

"Could I tag along with you? To Georgia in 1926?"

"No. Nothing personal, it's just that your string section doesn't play the same tune as my string section. Subatomically you'd wind up scattered in an infinity of universes, crying for your mommy."

"Like yourself, I never had a mommy. So explain to me how

you'll know, out of several thousand prisoners on a hundred or more chain gangs, which one is—"

Gwen pushed her chair back, got up, and walked around the table to where Grayle sat, relaxed, smiling quizzically at her. She bent down swiftly to kiss him, one hand going to his face. Her nails raked skin and he flinched. Gwen stepped back, holding out her hand for him to inspect.

"I didn't draw blood or mess up your handsome profile. A little of your skin under my nails is all I need to take with me."

"How will that help you? Maybe you didn't understand. 'Smith' is not flesh of my flesh."

"I'm not hard of hearing," she said with a touch of Eden's asperity. "Remember what I said about your subatomic structure and travel to the future?"

"Yes."

"Once I locate 'Smith' the complexities are just beginning." There was perspiration on Gwen's faintly downy upper lip. "That little matter of chaos theory. The interesting thing about theoretical physics is, almost all conclusions lead to paradoxes. I guess that's why I'm a nut on the subject. Why I'm going to try to do this. When can you have those photos for me?"

Grayle tapped out a number on his wrist pager.

"Give me half an hour. One of my secretaries will deliver them to you. I need to go to the theatre; I have a show to put on. Will you be here when I get back?"

"No," Gwen said. "But I'll leave you something to remember me by. One more thing: please hang a DO NOT DISTURB sign on the door to my room. If I make it back, it could be a thousand years from now, or thirty seconds ago. If a return is possible at all; I may not have a way of fine-tuning it."

"Now you tell me." There was no censure in his voice. Until a few days ago, until Eden's doppelganger came to his attention, he had thought that he was the loneliest entity in the universe.

Bertie joined Eden and Charmaine in the orangerie of the Carmen Miranda villa after her return from next door, a hasty shower, and a change of clothes: bolero jacket, black leather pants with painted peacocks on each leg, and python-skin boots; an outfit Charmaine practically swooned over. Fashions gave them all something to chat about on a level of vapidity that allowed Bertie and Eden to converse about more serious matters subvocally.

"You're still damp behind the ears. Everything okay?"

"Worse than we figured. The magician got to our friend here, however he works his spells, and the results ain't pretty."

"Evil enchantment, you mean."

"As good a description as any. Her lover was an Atlanta detective named Lewis Gruvver. I doubt if he played any poker last night. He's floating faceup in a room-size aquarium beneath a glass floor in the master suite over there."

"Sleeping with the fishes?"

"Don't make me laugh in Charmaine's face. He's very dead. Shot once in the temple."

"Charmaine's not exactly grief-stricken, is she?"

"She hears a different drummer now. Eden, you have to go to Los Angeles, right away."

"I missed some of that, I think. Los Angeles? Tom told us not to get separated."

"This qualifies as an emergency, babe. Gruvver was an investigator on the Pledger Lee case. He got suspicious of Lincoln Grayle somehow, and he'd spent most of his time in Vegas documenting his suspicions. I read all of his notes. We already know what Grayle, or Mordaunt as he's famously known around the Vatican, has been trying to do: kill the world's most prominent religious leaders. Many of whom are also Caretakers in some kind of holding pattern."

"Care what?"

(To Charmaine Bertie says, "Michael Kors, Jean-Paul Gaultier,

Christian La Croix—and Dior, of course—depending on the season and the occasion. I never let anyone except Wendell Wyatt touch my hair, and most of the time I ask for Merope Miglietta or Roque Velacqua to do my makeup.")

"Caretakers. We'll cover that later. Right now there's a a Buddhist Patriarch from Thailand at the UCLA Medical Center, kidney cancer or something. Gruvver compiled a comprehensive list of people who were entertained by Grayle after his shows, going back more than a year. Two of the people on that list showed up at the papal audience intending to murder Leoncaro. A boy named Jimmy Nixon did Pledger Lee Skeldon, remember Jimmy's sweet face? He was also on that list of Grayle's select people. And so are three others who are currently on staff at UCLA Med. A male nurse, a physical therapist, and a resident oncologist. Gruvver concluded that the Buddhist is a likely target of Mordaunt's. Makes sense to me."

(Eden, holding back a yawn with the back of her hand, says to Charmaine, "Couture? Me? Shucks no. I'm more of a connoisseur of lowbrow.")

"What could I hope to do about it?"

"Make certain that none of those three get anywhere near the Patriarch."

"How?"

"Come *on*. You're *Eden Waring*. You're famous for your premonitions."

"Notorious."

"Even better. You had four magazine covers that week. In this country alone. *Der Spiegel* went nuts over you. That Germanic theme of déjà vu. So fly down to L.A., demand to see the hospital administrator, do a number, get the old boy ironclad security."

"You know what will happen. They'll throw my butt out on the street."

"The Fox Network won't throw your butt on the street."

"Oh, God. The Fox Network."

"You must do this, Eden."

(Charmaine says to Bertie, "What are designers like? I mean, other than gay?")

"Bertie, I'm not leaving you alone with this airhead werewolf."

"Yawn again, excuse yourself to take a nap, walk out the front door, get into the van, and tell the Blackwelder guys to run you over to the airport. Don't worry about me and Charmaine. We'll do lunch, have a fun afternoon, and then I'm going to seriously fuck with her mind."

(And to Charmaine Bertie says, "Designers? They're all like monks. The sort who illuminated manuscripts, obsessing by candlelight in monkish cells. In thrall to line and form. Fresh air never touched their eyeballs. Or else they're crazy as bedbugs. Sometimes both at the same time.")

12:22 P.M.

One of Lincoln Grayle's hirelings delivered an envelope to Gwen on the terrace where she'd spent the past hour and a half. Photographs. She looked briefly at several of them, slipped the photos back into the envelope, and said something to Lincoln Grayle, who was talking on his cell phone. He nodded. Gwen got up with the envelope and walked into the house, having a last glance at the magician before she disappeared.

"Looks worried," Courtney Shyla commented, lowering her rubberized binoculars.

"Did you catch a glimpse of any of those photographs?" Tom Sherard asked her.

"Couldn't tell much because of the sight lines from here," she said. "They appeared to be mostly period stuff. Men wearing high collars and bowler hats like my grandfather Wallace when he was sheriff of Rio Blanco County, Colorado. Streetcars, old cars, and trucks, what looked like a line of convicts swinging pickaxes—"

"A chain gang."

"Yeah, old stuff like that." She looked at Sherard. "Mean anything to you?"

"I'm afraid so." Sherard also looked worried. "We need to get her out of there as quickly as possible."

Lincoln Grayle had finished his conversation, closed his cell phone, and was putting it away as he rose from the table. Sunlight flashed from gold chains at his throat and on one wrist. He stretched himself, limber as a big cat; momentarily motionless and bent nearly double with his locked hands high above his shoulder blades, a tortured position maintained with ease, he seemed to look right at them.

"Did you move?" Courtney whispered to Tom.

"No." He wanted to; his bad knee was killing him.

"Okay."

They were eye to eye, faces two feet apart. Her breath had a flavor of spearmint gum. She narrowed her eyes slightly.

"What is it?"

"The sun," she said. She looked down at the walking stick in his right hand. The gold lion's head was alight from a thin shaft of sun slanting through a break in the high greenery above them. "Damn. He might have noticed that."

Sherard moved the stick slightly toward him and the lion's head lost its luminosity.

On the terrace Lincoln Grayle had turned away and was contemplating a small chest on the table.

"We're nearly three hundred yards from him," Sherard said. "His eyesight can't be that keen."

"Mine is," Courtney said a little boastfully. "On a clear mountain night I can see the two largest moons of Jupiter without a scope. Let's ease on out of here. Do we try to retrieve the subject while Grayle is still domiciled?"

"I said as quickly as possible."

"Right." Courtney started to move backward in a crouch, a hand on his sleeve. She stopped. "What is he doing now?" She steadied herself on one knee, raised her binoculars for a closer look.

Lincoln Grayle had opened the chest and was taking out several balls, each the size of a tennis ball but transparent. Plastic or glass. When he had four balls in his large hands he began to juggle them.

Courtney handed Sherard the binoculars. "He's working on hand and eye coordination. Very smooth. And it must be hard to see those balls in full daylight."

"He just added a fifth one," Sherard said.

"What talent."

"You haven't seen anything yet. Take another look."

After several seconds of studying the distant terrace through her binoculars, Courtney said softly, "Be damned." She slowly lowered the glasses, turned her face to Sherard, perplexed.

"He is a magician," Tom said with a slight smile.

"But nobody can *do* that. Leave five balls suspended in air and just walk away."

"You've missed something important."

Courtney had another look. "What? Oh, now I get it. Five balls, five points in the shape of a star."

"Or a pentagram, as the ancients called it. An occult symbol."

"Meaning what?"

"A couple of things. Grayle knows we're here, and why. The pentagram is his warning: stay away from this house."

"Which we are going to ignore."

"You got me this far, Courtney. But the stalk is getting real now. You're under no obligation to continue."

She had a crooked grin that revealed a feral glint of tooth.

"Just like a man. Now that I'm falling in love, you want to get rid of me."

They were more than halfway from their former place of concealment on the mountain, within sight of the ribbon of blacktop that served Lincoln Grayle's secluded house, when they heard a car. They faded back into a shadowy draw where clear water trickled in a dozen streams down the mossy rock facings.

Tom had a quick look at the magician, alone in an antique silver sports car, gearing down to negotiate a sharp curve as he sped away from the house. From the sound of the engine Sherard guessed that Grayle could be driving one of the Cobra Daytona coupes from Carroll Shelby's glory days. Maybe Grayle was just out for a spin, or he was on his way to the theatre. But his absence removed a big obstacle in getting Gwen quickly out of the house.

They followed the road the rest of the way, to a stone-paved garage area beneath the first cantilevered level. Grayle also owned an Escalade, a Dodge Ram 1500 pickup with huge knobbed tires and a snowplow mount on the front bumper, and a sixteen-passenger van. There was an elevator in the garage. No one seemed to be around. They heard novelty Christmas music from an unseen speaker: Jan and Dean's "Surfin' Santa." Courtney checked out the Cadillac SUV, grinned at Sherard, and made a turning motion with thumb and fore-finger together: key in the ignition. Tom nodded. She unzipped a pocket on her backpack and withdrew her taser gun.

On the first level of the stacked house a Hispanic girl with a single long braid down her back was running a polisher on the travertine floor. She had her back to the elevator and was listening to *ranchera* on headphones. She didn't hear the elevator door open. Courtney handed Sherard her taser and pounced on the girl, grasping the con-venient braid in her fist, clamped a gloved hand over the girl's mouth.

Sherard stepped in and wrenched off the girl's headphones; Court-ney sharply pulled her head back by the braid.

"*Calma, muchacha.* Where is the red-haired guest of *El Magico*?"

"*Segundo piso,*" the girl said behind Courtney's muffling hand, rolling her eyes like a horse in a burning stable. "Doan hurt me."

"Don't make us hurt you. Who else is in the house now?"

"*No se, no se.*"

Courtney let go of the braid and flicked fingers in front of the girl's face. One, two, three—the girl nodded quickly at *four,* her best estimate, probably. She was still rolling her eyes when Sherard taped her mouth shut. Courtney grabbed the braid close to the roots and pulled her backward into the small elevator. The floor polisher was still running, maintaining an illusion that the girl's chores were prop-erly being attended to. Sherard stepped into the elevator behind them. They went slowly up to the second level, Courtney continuing to hold the girl erect by her braid, speaking softly in her ear. Sherard didn't understand Spanish, but the girl calmed down; from her expression her brain had vapor-locked.

The door opened again, revealing a preoccupied young man with the high forehead and scoop nose of an Easter Island artifact; he had folders in his hands. As if he were recoiling from a snakepit his upper body jerked back almost a foot at the sight of the girl with duct tape over her mouth. Before he could get his own mouth open to question their intentions or shout bloody murder Tom shot him with Courtney's taser and he collapsed on the floor, a thousand volts blitzing his nervous system, loose papers all around him.

The sight of his helpless thumping and writhing got the girl going again in the direction of hysteria; Courtney shoved her, stumbling, past the young man and down another travertine-floored corridor with ochre walls and closed white doors. Sherard disconnected the young man from the taser and followed, hearing Dwight Yoakum in bluesy Sensurround: "Santa Claus Is Back in Town."

Halfway down the corridor the girl gestured to one of the doors. But she fought Courtney in a flareup of frenzy when Courtney put a hand on the doorknob. Courtney had had enough of her antics; she popped the girl over one ear with the lead-lined heel of the glove on her right hand. The girl wobbled and her eyes lost focus. She sank down with her back against the wall and slowly fell over.

Tom had his own taser gun out; Courtney glanced at him, nodded, then bulled her way shoulder-first into the room.

Which turned out to be the sitting room of a nice suite with a terrace facing pale western skies and a bleak mountain range that marked the northwest boundary of the great Mohave Desert.

Eden Waring's doppelganger was seated at a small table with her hands folded on several of the photographs she had glanced at while in Lincoln Grayle's company. She seemed unnaturally still; her head was slightly bowed in the direction of a small crystalline red skull placed in the exact center of the table.

Only it wasn't Gwen at all. They were seeing a three-dimensional shell, a holographic image of great sharpness, but still a reproduction of what was, in the first instance, a copy itself.

"Lord a' mercy," Courtney Shyla said in a hushed voice. "What have we here?"

"We're too late," Tom said, a twinge of anxiety in his heart. "Gwen's gone."

"Gone where?"

"She's taking a little trip through time," Marcus Woolwine said behind them.

Sherard turned, leveling his taser at the bowlegged, nut-brown man with the silvery mirror glasses. Woolwine, in the doorway, raised both hands in a wry, exaggerated protective gesture. "Please don't," he said. "I have a pacemaker." He didn't otherwise seem very perturbed.

"Who are you?" Sherard said.

Woolwine introduced himself. "And you would be Tom Sherard. I know of you, of course." He looked curiously at the lion's-head stick in Tom's other hand. "Gwen and I are old acquaintances, from Plenty Coups, where I recently was employed. You may have heard."

"What do you have to do with this?" Sherard said with still another look at holographic Gwen. Courtney had edged closer to the image of the dpg, causing a mild fluctuation like a breeze disturbing the surface of a pond, but she seemed more fascinated by the bloody vacancy of the crystal skull. Tom was aware of a resonance in the room; he felt it in his temples.

"Nothing much, really," Woolwine replied. "This is Gwen's doing, in her desire to be helpful to our host. I'm just keeping an eye on things for Gwen, monitoring fluctuations while she's . . . away." He seemed to be about to smile at some irony in this description, but instead said sharply to Courtney Shyla, "Get away from there; you must touch nothing in this room! The image she left with us is a crucial point of reference for Gwen, should she hope to return when her . . . explorations are concluded. Just by your unwanted presence you've already disturbed the several electromagnetic fields she will rely on in plotting an accurate return within the continuum."

"Where did she go?" Sherard demanded. "Where is she?"

"With any luck   " Woolwine adopted a colder tone. "But that is no business of yours."

"Guess again."

"Tom," Courtney said, giving the crystal skull a fishy eye, "I'd swear this evil little thing is talking to me. Sounds like one of those raghead dialects you hear in—"

"It finds you susceptible," Woolwine advised her. "And the language would not be one anyone on earth is familiar with."

"Susceptible to what?" Courtney said, rubbing the back of her head as if to tame a virulent itch.

"You may hope never to find out." Woolwine looked at Tom. "Obviously you will not be taking Gwen with you when you leave here. Which should be immediately. Poor Mr. Dilly by the elevator seemed to be dazed more than injured, so we'll dismiss the possibility of criminal charges being brought against you both. Just go."

They were on their way down the mountain and out of sight of the magician's house when Courtney Shyla flexed her shoulders and said without looking around, "We're being followed."

"Man or beast?"

"Don't know. Haven't seen anything." She looked up at a solitary circling eagle. "I just feel it coming on. It's an instinct you'd better learn to develop in Special Forces."

"Or hunting big game," Sherard amended, although he didn't share her conviction someone or something else was trailing them. The road was empty. The day clear. They were walking along the side of the road, steep sunless cedar woods a few feet away on their left. Across the road there was a steel guardrail and several hundred feet of sheer emptiness beyond that.

"That's what you used to do?" Courtney took a nine-millimeter compact Glock automatic from a holster at the small of her back and flicked the safety off.

"I was raised to hunt." Tom stopped and lifted his walking stick above his head, intently regarding the lion's head.

"What are you doing?"

"I usually can sense when an animal is behind me, even if it's lurking in tall grass. But to detect the supernatural, I need supernatural help."

Courtney said with a sinkhole of a grin, "Do you suppose that crystal skull has a set of crystal bones to go with it?"

"There are worse things around. I've seen a couple of them in my travels."

"Thanks, I don't want to—" Courtney stopped as if her throat had frozen shut. The gold lion's head was turning on the knuckly shaft, eyes and mouth open. Gold eyeballs and gold fangs, of course. "How do you do that?" she croaked.

"It's not of my volition. *Mopane* wood from time out of mind has had special spiritual qualities. As for the head of Simba, it was empowered by someone very dear to me, for my protection. That was, by the way, her doppelganger you saw in the suite at Grayle's house."

Courtney was, basically, nonplussed.

"The, the time-traveler."

"Courtney, keep your wits about you."

"I'm fine! The rest of the world has gone nuts, apparently. What is your—what is *Simba* trying to tell us?"

"It apprehends what we're unable to. Yet."

Courtney, doubting, took a fast look around. They were, she could clearly see, still alone. There was no change in the glistening atmosphere.

Except for a couple of rainbow-hued spheres, each about two inches in diameter, drifting toward them, a dozen feet or so above the road.

"Soap bubbles? Where did they come from?"

"I don't think they're soap bubbles," Tom said. "Remember the spheres Grayle was juggling?"

"Yeah, five of them."

"Here come the other three," Tom said, aiming his walking stick up the road.

"So what?"

"I don't know. But I think we should remain still until we find out what this means."

"I'll show you what it means," Courtney said in a fit of exasperation. She drew a bead on the nearest sphere with her Glock and fired a shot.

The sphere trembled when struck but didn't dissipate or fly to pieces. When it resumed its perfect shape, it seemed a little larger. And the hollow-nosed bullet from Courtney's pistol was perfectly centered inside the sphere, floating along with it.

Sherard saw the slackness in Courtney's face, that near-death look of stupefying shock. He put out a hand to steady her but she dodged away, teeth flashing white in a bizarre grin.

"Courtney, wait—"

She made a snorting sound as she plunged off the road and into the trees, seeking familiar wilderness, deep woods, concealment, the only refuge she respected.

"No, you're safer with me!"

The other sphere that had been closest to them took a new direction, leisurely trailing Courtney in her headlong flight. This sphere too seemed to be increasing in size, by what dark magic Sherard couldn't imagine.

A third sphere, he noticed then, was coming straight at his head.

The gold lion's-head stick trembled in his grip. Tom agreeably released it. The stick met the incoming sphere—which had no apparent rotation, an unnerving phenomenon that made it impossible for him to judge its velocity—with a level swing that sent it flying, intact, in the direction of an eagle soaring leisurely above the canyon across the road. The sound of impact was more rifle shot than home-run clout.

The other two spheres appeared to pick up their pace, rising in the air thirty feet or more, then falling toward him. Again he had no sense of their speed, but the walking stick took the measure of the spheres and swung twice more, faster than his eye could follow. Two more line drives out over the canyon.

That left the ever-growing sphere that had absorbed the bullet from Courtney's pistol. It came at Tom also, hopped like a knuckleball when the stick took a powerful hack at it, and veered off toward the woods. About the size of a basketball, and with a sunny glow inside where the bullet at its center was melting, dissipating in copper droplets.

Tom heard the battle-toughened Courtney cry out in terror.

"Simba!"

The walking stick flew to his outstretched hand. He followed the glowing sphere into thick woods, depending heavily on his stick to get him past rough footing on an uphill track. The sphere sailed easily around thick conifer trunks, bounced airily over ledges and windfalls until it reached a small clearing where the other sphere had come to rest, huge now, at least six feet in diameter and shining like a lighthouse mirror.

Courtney Shyla was, remarkably, inside the brightness of the sphere, condemned to an agonizing, futile struggle, still screaming, to judge from the terrible contortions of her face. But he couldn't hear a sound from her.

As Tom watched in agitated but helpless horror the flesh of Courtney's face began to melt like butter in a chafing dish. Beads of rendered flesh and superheated brains dappled rainlike the inside of the sphere while her bared bones took on a dread appearance, flashy as the red crystal of the ancient skull that had so fascinated her in the magician's house.

When her heated eyeballs drifted from their sockets like dead planets orbiting a dwarf malevolent sun and her limbs went slack inside her clothing, gloves drooping from skeletal hands, Sherard, nothing in his mind except escape from the probability of his own entrapment and gruesome death, ran, certain that both spheres had become too large for the magic that the walking stick could muster: the magician's virtuoso spell had the force of timeless evil behind it.

Ran, in spite of grinding pain in the knee no surgeon could completely make right again, with no idea of how to defeat what lay behind, what followed him now, although he didn't risk a second glance to gauge the lessening distance between himself and the buoyantly pursuing sphere: a slip, a bad fall, death would be there to suck him in like poor Courtney. Shock inspired speed and agility; flight summoned cunning. What did the spheres feed on so glibly other than flesh, what gave them motion?

The air itself, perhaps, charged as it was by the light of a midday sun.

Sherard looked for darkness in the woods and, as he was growing drastically short of breath, found it: a seam in the face of a bluff beneath an overhanging ledge, and falling water from a subterranean source fed by the melting of winter's snowpack.

He wedged himself into the seam a dozen feet or so and watched the slow dance of the pursuing sphere outside the lazy waterfall, flushed a pearly pink, unable to reach him. Nor was it able to maintain either its size or buoyancy once the sun moved on and early darkness fell on this side of the mountain. When the last beam of the sun withdrew, the sphere went with it.

By then it was past three o'clock in the afternoon, according to his watch. Shuddering in the sunless chill and wet from the dripping walls of his hideaway, he resolved to remain where he was until full dark. Thinking of Courtney Shyla's scintillant bones lying now in shadow on the forest floor, could he ever find the words to describe her fate? Implacable evil, he reflected, took a lot of explaining to the uninitiated. He didn't feel adequate to the task, but it wasn't a moral choice. Courtney would have to be accounted for, to those who cared for or loved her.

2:15 P.M.

Implacable evil.

That wasn't exactly the last thing on Bertie Nkambe's mind as her long lunch with Charmaine ended. The fashion show sponsored by the Vegas Neiman Marcus store as lagniappe for the luncheon guests on the terrace overlooking a bracelet of pools around a sandy island with palm trees had partly distracted Bertie for a while; but the sight of tanned young honeymooners, preschool children squealing like minks in the wave pool, and a gin-rummy foursome of old bronzed men with roadkill chest hair, looking like mobsters long gone to seed, only reminded her of another body, that of the luckless Lewis Gruvver, who soon must be accounted for.

Her cautious probing of Charmaine's mind (for Bertie it was the mental equivalent of touring barefoot dark pathways salted with sharp objects and white-hot coals) convinced her of little more than the sad fact that nothing very human was left of this winsome girl, almost exactly her own age, whom Mordaunt had arrogantly claimed for himself. There could be no punishment to fit a crime this terrible. But Bertie resolved to do her best.

While they had eaten their light lunch, enjoyed a glass apiece of sauvignon blanc, and chatted about nothing of importance, including the cutthroat ritzy business of high fashion that was conducted by sophisticated greedheads for whom fawning was a high art and neurasthenic designers of varied specious charms, Charmaine was at all times watchful behind her lovely smile, in the way of an animal that hadn't begun to satisfy its blood hunger with a plate of thin-sliced prime rib and tomato in aspic. Bertie was not as unsuspecting as the late Mr. Gruvver might have been; she knew she was certain prey of Mordaunt, the deed entrusted to his ensorcelled cutie. How and when the attack would come was Charmaine's secret. What Charmaine couldn't know was that it would be neither a novelty nor much of a challenge to Bertie, who was very much at home in the distorted netherworld to which Charmaine had only recently been introduced, through the Trickster's beguilement, or by a ritual darkening of her soul.

Too bad, Bertie thought. But it was hard to grieve for your would-be executioner.

She really didn't want anything more to do with Charmaine as they dawdled over espresso. Charmaine had a murder to confess to the appropriate authorities while Bertie and Eden, once she returned from Los Angeles, concentrated on the undoing of Lincoln Grayle.

Too late, however, to gain a reprieve for Charmaine and who knew how many others like her in Grayle's adopted playground, obliviously flaunting its pleasures and voluptuous frenzies while it continued to spread like a monstrous canker on the very lip of hell.

Their conversation had been, for more than two hours, trivial and gossipy while Bertie tried to guess where Charmaine would be coming from next; tiring of this effort, Bertie introduced a new topic, using her words like a blunt instrument.

"Why was it necessary to kill Lewis Gruvver? Weren't you in love with him?"

Charmaine continued to smile; it was as if she had to hear the question a second time, like an echo in her mind, before she could react. Then the casual good cheer faded from her face; she licked her lips in an expression of feral hostility.

"Are you crazy?"

"I saw him, Charmaine. Faceup in the fish pool under the floor in the bedroom of your villa. What did he do to deserve it?"

Charmaine's fingertips caressed the white linen tablecloth in front of her, right hand moving to the sterling handle of a knife partly concealed beneath a linen napkin.

Bertie said, "Touch that and you'll be wearing it in your right eye."

"We were getting along so well," Charmaine murmured.

"You think so?"

"I didn't kill him. I made it clear. I couldn't do that to Lewis. Even though he didn't matter to me anymore. The Great One understood. He made . . . other arrangements."

"Who does matter to you?"

Charmaine caressed her lips instead of the tablecloth, looking fulfilled in a way that Bertie found almost unbearably obscene.

"Who did kill him, then? The Great One himself? But that's not his style, is it?"

Charmaine shrugged one shoulder and smiled secretively.

"Oh, it was—"

They both looked up at a badly timed interruption, the third or fourth (Bertie couldn't remember) time since she had been seated for lunch, causing the usual stir of interest among those in the know fashion-wise, which seemed to be everybody on the terrace today, followed by those who felt themselves important enough to drop by the table to express their pleasure in encountering a supermodel in the ravishing flesh.

"Oh, Miss Nkambe," said the artistic designer of the luncheon show from Neiman Marcus, a woman with an obvious history of facelifts, nonetheless radiant in five figures' worth of resort wear, jewelry, and neon-purple lip gloss, "I didn't want to bother you before, but it is just such an honor to have you here today! I hope you enjoyed—"

Bertie held an outstretched hand tenderly for a couple of seconds, saying, "Yes—very nice—Pru, is it?" This from a name tag attached by a small safety pin to a crewelwork beach jacket. "Beautiful show. They could take lessons from you in Milano."

"I am so delighted to meet you, and if you're going to be in town for a while would love—"

"Just passing through," Bertie said with a regretful smile, "catching up with old friends; but thank you, Pru." She returned her attention to Charmaine just as a semibald man wearing impenetrable dark glasses walked boldly up to the table behind her, saying in a loud, sobbing voice, "I wuh-warned you to stay away from my bruh-brother, bitch!"

And shot Charmaine in the back of the head with his .40-caliber semiautomatic pistol.

8:25 P.M.

Eden Waring walked off the Gulfstream jet that had returned her from Los Angeles after a series of events she could have done without and delivered her into a new series of events so shocking it made breathing difficult whenever her thoughts returned to dwell on them.

She ducked her head beneath an umbrella being held for her but which only partly deflected a grit-laden wind with a few drops of rain in it; the wind was gusting up to fifty miles an hour and had delayed her flight back. She slumped into the back of a limousine, hollow-eyed and with an aching head, and was driven to North Las Vegas Hospital, then around to the emergency entrance, avoiding the main body of the media crews clustered in floodlit self-important knots as close to the buildings as uniformed security people allowed them to be.

Two Blackwelder Organization detectives met Eden and escorted her through a minor electrical storm of camera flashes inside the ward and upstairs to the intensive care unit, where Tom Sherard was waiting.

As soon as Eden looked into his eyes she knew that Bertie wasn't dead. Not yet anyway. Time for tears then, angry tears, tears of exhaustion.

They were shown by a hospital administrator to an empty office where they could talk privately. They sat side by side on a small leather sofa. Eden wanted the overly bright ceiling lights off; she didn't want to have to look at Tom's face for now. The view through open venetian blinds was west; just at one edge of the framing windows was the Lincoln Grayle Theatre in the dark body of mountains: star bright, the only star visible on this cloudy night.

"How long was Bertie in surgery?"

"Five and a half hours."

"Is she conscious?"

"No. Nor breathing on her own."

"This is my—" Eden began, her body tensing as if she were in danger of flying to pieces.

He used both hands to turn her face to him. He smelled, faintly, of damp clothing and evergreen woods.

"Don't ever say, or even think, that again."

The pressure of his fingers close to her temples hurt; but she didn't mind the hurt. He could have shaken her, slapped her, anything, she would have accepted it, only a small part of what she felt was due. She went on hating herself but wanting to kiss him. More tears; Tom relaxed his grip but Eden kept her head still, just licked at whatever drops trickled close to the edges of her mouth.

"What is Bertie's—what do they call it, prognosis?"

"Too early to tell. The bullet that killed Charmaine Goferne passed completely through her head; what remained of it struck Bertie in the left temple, but at greatly reduced velocity. It shattered bone but didn't penetrate her brain. Otherwise she would have been killed instantly. The lovelorn Mr. Crigler—as the cops are perfectly willing to have it—continued to fire in what was described by onlookers as blind rage. Bertie was hit twice more as she fell to the floor, and one of the waiters took a slug in the ribs; no major damage. Mr. Crigler saved the last round for himself and died with no further explanation for his actions, other than what he shouted at the girl before blowing out her brains."

"Tom, there's a body in the villa next to ours—"

"Yes, the investigators discovered the late Mr. Gruvver a couple of hours ago. Shot once in the temple with what should prove to be a .40-caliber semi. So the official version has it that Bertie was an innocent victim of a love-triangle killing. We'll leave it that way."

Eden pulled his hands away and lay against him. "And all of this was stage-managed by the magician. To get Bertie out of the way. He was afraid of her powers, of what together we might do to him." There was a gleam in her eyes of contempt, but when she realized just how alone she was now with Bertie near death, her expression revealed no less fear than she was ascribing to the magician.

He felt compelled to tell her, "Mordaunt has accomplished more than that today. Gwen is . . . gone." Sherard explained what he and Courtney Shyla had discovered at the magician's house on Mount Charleston, with emphasis on the photos Gwen apparently had used to access the era in which she might now be living. He said nothing about the rest of his harrowing day, and Courtney's fate. There was no point in overloading Eden's nervous system.

"I didn't think it was possible to take her away from me! It's like I've lost—" Eden sat up and shook her head slowly. "Part of my own soul. He had no *right*. He doesn't own . . . either of us." She rubbed her reddened eyes, and trembled. "But what do I do now?" she concluded miserably, staring at Tom. Her left eye was turning in from tiredness and he was reminded of his late wife, whom Eden so closely resembled. His heart absorbed the impact like a hammer blow.

"Whatever is done, we will do it together," he said fiercely. "Understood?"

"Yes," she said, and put her hands in her lap, began to rock gently from the waist up. "But, ah—sorry. Can't think straight. I'm so tired. Tom, I know . . . I did some good in L.A. Did I tell you?"

"When you called from the plane. Sounds as if the Patriarch is one potential victim Mordaunt's surrogates won't get their hands on."

"So I did some good," Eden repeated, reassuring herself. She looked around the office they'd borrowed. "That must be a bathroom in there. I need to . . . freshen up." She stood but didn't move away from him immediately, as if she were unsure of her footing. "Then, if I could just lie down for a couple of hours—"

"I'll see to it that you're driven back to the villa."

Eden shuddered. "No, please! I don't want to go there. I want to be close to you, and Bertie. The couch is big enough for me. And you'll come immediately if there's any change in Bertie's condition."

"Of course I will. Is there anything I can get for you now; a sedative?"

"Not now. But if I can't sleep—" She bent to kiss him. It was chastely meant, but she was still trembling; he was a man and had to know what she wanted above all else just then. Particularly when there was every chance she would never see him again. Eden took some breaths to shore up her stamina, smiled, and headed for the bathroom, brisk in motion but devastated in spirit. In spite of which she managed to call back to him with a semblance of cheer, "Two hours, Tom? Then maybe we could have something to eat."

Following a dress rehearsal that had lasted nearly three hours because of the introduction into his act of new illusions requiring some complicated props and machinery, the magician had begun to unwind, nude and alone, beneath colored lights in the spectrographic chamber of his duplex dressing suite. The colors he had chosen to bathe his pineal gland, solar plexus, and the soles of his feet were a lush purple and indigo. Aromatic oils were diffused into the chamber. He orchestrated both hues and oils with a keypad by his right hand as he lay faceup on a simple massage table.

Those remaining in the Lincoln Grayle Theatre after dress—stagehands, office personnel, and the night security force—knew not to disturb the magician during this period of meditation and recuperation. If he *was* to be disturbed, the circumstances had better justify it.

He frowned and touched a key in response to a call and the face of one of his assistants appeared on a plasma screen overhead.

"What is it, Perk?"

"Sorry, sir, but there's a young woman outside the theatre who insists she has an engagement with you tonight."

"Perk, that's such a tired routine. I'm surprised at you."

"But—she asked me to give you a message that seemed to imply there is a relationship of some sort."

The magician said with a stir of interest, "Tell me."

"She said, 'I want Linc to know that what began at Shung-wa-ya"—he stumbled over the pronunciation—"must be finished tonight.' "

The magician sat up on the table.

"Let her in, Perk! Give me five minutes, then bring her to my suite."

He sat on the edge of the table for ten seconds, blankly astonished, then ran a hand through his unruly hair, still a little damp from his recent shower, and laughed.

Within five minutes he was combed and dressed in white beach-comber pants, sandals, and an unbuttoned long-sleeved shirt. He was pouring Tuscan wine into two glasses when Eden was shown into the suite.

"*Jambo!*" he said, holding up one of the glasses in a welcoming salute. "And I must say I like the sound of 'hello' better than good-bye. Which is where we left it, I believe, at Kenyatta Airport."

Eden acknowledged him with a smile of such diffidence it was as if she had neglected to bring a personality with her—or at least the lively spirit to which he had been attracted on their first meeting. Her hair was shorter now, and redder. Cut with some flair, as if she'd found time to visit a salon, or Bertie Nkambe's personal hairdresser. Which reminded him.

"I heard about Bertie. Terrible, just terrible." Perhaps he was referring to the fact that she hadn't been killed instantly.

A muscle jumped in Eden's face, affecting one eye, but otherwise she didn't respond, just continued to look around, eyes skipping over his face a couple of times as if he were furniture.

"Will she make it?" he persisted.

"I don't know. I can't talk about it."

"Would you like to sit down? How about some wine?"

"Yes, thank you."

She took the glass from him, still not meeting his eyes, moved sideways to a grouping of comfortable leather chairs amid a collection of props, puzzling to someone outside the profession, that had been employed by magicians a century ago. She had a sip of wine, holding her free hand close to the glass as if she were afraid of a clonus that would cause her to spill the contents on his Turkish carpet. Her lips did tremble slightly. Her eyes were rimmed with a fine mist of perspiration. They were restless, as if she couldn't focus on anything for more than a second or two. He wondered if she were in shock.

"Do I get to do all of the talking?" he said genially, sitting next to her on the arm of a cream leather sofa. Eden was wearing a shawl-collar cashmere sweater and a blue skirt. No ornamentation except for a plain gold chain around her neck with a pendant made of a dark lump of metal that didn't look as if it had monetary value. He didn't remember having seen her wear it in Africa.

"I'm sorry," she murmured. Another sip of wine braced her. She lifted her head and was able to look at him. "I don't mean to be . . . bad company."

"It's understandable. Still, as long as you're here . . ." His expression was a mixture of pleasure and skepticism.

Her eyes wandered off again, to a framed one-sheet of a magician in Chinese dress. "I had no idea your theatre was so huge."

"Why don't I give you a tour? While we talk about our 'unfinished' business."

"There's not much to say, really. I thought about . . . what choices I have left, and I've come to be with you. For as long as you want me."

"Quite a change of heart."

Eden finished her wine in a couple of swallows and stood.

"But there are conditions. Of course I know what—who you really are. You wanted Bertie out of the way. It's done. Even if she recovers she won't be the same. You have no reason ever to hurt her again. And you *won't* hurt Tom."

"Granted," the magician said with a shrug. "He's no problem to me."

Eden walked toward the double doors in the vestibule of the suite. More framed posters there. Movie monsters. The Creature from the Black Lagoon. Boris Karloff's Frankenstein. Surrounded by them Eden looked threatened, haunted.

"One other thing. I want Gw—my doppelganger back."

"In all sincerity, Eden, that's out of my hands. She's in a . . . slightly altered state, and on her own now. I don't even know if she made it to where she was going."

"You've taken away so much from me. Has anyone ever denied you anything?"

"Not for long. As I reckon time. Don't be afraid. It won't be such a bad life, Eden."

"You mean after the nightmare you have in store for me? I don't want to see it coming. *I don't want any memory of it later.* Can you do that, Magician? Take away my mind until it's over?"

"If you'd like you may sleep through insemination and your pregnancy. Which should reach full term in about seventy-two hours."

"Don't shit me," Eden said in a snarly tone.

"True. Spectrographic enhancement of your vital life-giving processes. Theoretically it ought to work. My all-too-human flaw is, I hate to wait."

Eden held her bowed head in the palm of one hand, like a sorrowing bride.

"And what, theoretically, am I expected to give birth to?"

"If only it has your eyes," he said, "I'll be pleased."

"Thank you. I need to walk now; otherwise, I swear to God, I'll turn to stone. So give me the hurry-up tour. Bring the bottle. Wine will relax me while I'm learning more about the wizardry of Murdaunt the Great."

10:18 P.M.

Tom Sherard found the note from Eden taped to a sofa cushion in the empty hospital office.

> TOM:
>   THE TERRACE OF THE
>   LINCOLN GRAYLE THEATRE.
>   SHOWTIME WILL BE
>   TWELVE MIDNIGHT.
>   I WILL ALWAYS LOVE YOU.

The windows in the office rattled, further aggravating his nerves. How had she slipped out of the hospital without his knowing?

Midnight.

Why?

Sherard checked his watch. He could have used more time.

But if Eden was with the magician now, he might already be too late.

11:55 P.M.

He had shown her everything behind the scenes, a hidden and mostly subterranean complex of tunnels, trapdoors, elevators, flying rigs, suspension systems that could hold an elephant steady twenty feet above the stage floor. They had visited his menagerie of blue-eyed tigers and snow-white lionesses, and other lissome felines that were a combination of leopard and lion.

Eden, having regained her normal tongue and a measure of self-assurance after consuming most of the wine from the bottle she had with her, was unimpressed.

"That's genetics," she said of the crossbreeds. "I know a little something about genetics." She leaned against an unpainted concrete wall, eyes simmering in subdued lighting. "Now tell me your *real* secrets, Magic Man."

"Like what?"

"Like how you raise blood lust to the level of insane murder in an otherwise average, well-behaved teenage kid like Jimmy Nixon. And, like, where do shape-shifters come from—f'r instance, that saber-toothed baboon I met in the pasto—the, y'know, 'cause you were there too, don't deny it; the Pope-astolic Palace."

"Interesting mutation. I never know what I'm going to get. That's the fun part. So it was a saber-toothed baboon you destroyed?"

"Damn right I did!" Eden said, leering with pride. " 'N with little help from my own brand of magic." She held up the bottle to a worklight in the tunnel outside the menagerie, sized up with a squint the inch of dark wine remaining, and drank it unsteadily, the rim of the bottle clicking against her front teeth. A few drops dribbled off her chin.

The magician watched her with the same forbearance, mild amusement—and continued skepticism—that he had shown Eden for more than an hour.

"C'mon," she said, lowering the empty bottle and issuing a challenge, "if we're gonna have a true, lasting *relationship,* gotta level with me. Hey! Speaking of the relationship, have to call you something. What do you suggest? Linc? Or, no, more appropriate, how about *Morrie?* You get it, don't you? Short for *Mor*daunt."

"Linc will do for now, Eden."

" 'Kay. So, Links. How 'bout another bottle wine? I am *really* starting to get loosed up here, no shit. That's how you want me, right? *Purrrr*feckly relaxed." She hiccuped and smothered a giggle with the back of her free hand, stealing a glimpse of the face of her watch as she did so.

"Maybe later," the magician said indulgently. "Why not take a break from the booze for now? You're sweating. I don't care for that. I don't like having women who sweat around me. Which they tend to do, onstage, when we've got flames going—"

"Just like in hell? Oops, my bad. Sorry. Listen, about sweating. That's what my glands are used to doing. Pour out the juice. I played basketball since I was in third grade, you know. Sweat's just bodily essence. If a man I happen to like sweats, it turns me on. That's something personal I'm letting you know, Links."

"There's a great deal about Eden Waring I'm eager to learn. But we have many years ahead of us."

"Kind of warm in this tunnel. Keep the animals cozy, right? Keep *your* animal warm too, Links? The one I heard so much about, came sniffing 'round my bed at Shungwaya. Scary son of a bitch. So let me in on it. The *big* secret. How can you take ordinary human beings, make them into monsters?"

"If you know how to stimulate the pineal body and the endocrine system by the use of spectrography, human evolution can be accelerated to warp speed. The trigger is then implanted in the brain through the time-honored power of suggestion."

"Human evolution? Devolution, I'd call it," Eden said wisely.

"Whatever. They serve our purpose, luv."

She wagged a forefinger at him, face going slack; but her eyes were frightened. "Nuh-uh! Changed my mind. 'Clude me out."

"But I need you. It's a most interesting experiment in genetics, Eden. I'm so looking forward to seeing just what it is you give birth to three days from now."

She jerked away from the wall as if she had been stuck there, lurched toward him.

"I'm scared! Why can't it just be you and me, Links? You and me."

"Because what you see as Lincoln Grayle is only an insignificant part of who and what I really am. We want to realize, in the person of a child, what is most powerful in each of us."

Eden tried to snuggle against him. He resisted the thrust of eroticism with a grimace of displeasure, but couldn't prevent her hand from clamping onto his penis.

"Isn't *this* good enough?" she said, whorishly kneading the brute sausage. "It's what *I* want, Linc. Give it to me, please? Right here. Now. I am so ready!"

"I'm not. It can't happen when—unless I—and you need to sober—"

Eden became dead weight on his arm, as if she were having a spaz attack. When he tried to hold her up off the floor she recovered with all of the nimble footwork that had made her a star point guard and, squaring up to him, smashed him full in the face with the butt of the empty wine bottle. His nose shattered and his head was driven into the wall behind him. Blood flew as his lungs emptied.

She hit him again, backhanded, and the bottle broke against a wedge of cheekbone before he hit the floor rolling, just beginning to feel the awful pain.

Eden stood astride him momentarily, still holding the jagged neck of the wine bottle, his blood dripping down her face.

"I believe I could use some fresh air," she said, perfectly lucid. "You'll find me on the terrace—Links, honey."

She walked away, steady after a first stagger-step, wiping blood off her face and trying to keep her gorge down. She headed along the tunnel toward the freight elevator that would take her to stage level. Wanting to scream but she couldn't get it out of her throat. The adrenaline rush was rapidly burning the alcohol out of her blood. She thought she could make it. Outdoors, the cold night air. But his blood. A little of it had passed her lips. She spat and spat.

As Eden ran into the large elevator, big enough to lift an elephant, she heard the roaring of the mutant big cats in their menagerie cages. She felt a livid itch on her lower lip and knew she was about to break out in hives.

Something entirely different from the magician whose face she had just ruined would be rising from the bloody floor of the tunnel, finding her spoor.

Eden looked at her watch again.

Showtime was eighty seconds away.

If she lived that long.

11:59 P.M.

The strong winds that had afflicted the Las Vegas area and caused some temporary power outages had abated and the clouds were breaking up as the cold front passed through, affording glimpses of a waning moon above the summit of Spring Mountain.

He wouldn't be needing the moon tonight. At four thousand feet Tom Sherard had settled into his hide overlooking the Lincoln Grayle Theatre, approximately one quarter mile away at two o'clock and seven hundred feet below his rocky perch. He sat cross-legged in spite of the painful stress on his bad knee, the stock of the .447-

caliber rifle his father had ordered for him on his first birthday (stocks had been replaced several times from the day he took his first reduced-powder shot at the age of six) against his shoulder as he calibrated the scope.

Directly east lay a golden field of shimmering lights sown like the wages of sin for miles across the high desert floor. A toy version of King Arthur's castle at one end of the Vegas Strip; the red thread of a roller coaster wound around the needle of the Stratosphere Tower at the other.

Below Sherard the terrace of the theatre looked like the flight deck of an aircraft carrier, with huge concrete planters for trees and three fountains, not operating at this hour. The superstructure of the theatre, five stories of beehive glass cut like a diamond into thousands of facets, filled the front of the cavern that had been blasted out of the mountain to accommodate the theatre and kitchens where assembly-line meals were prepared for sixteen hundred guests on show nights.

He couldn't see past the facade from where he was, but he knew from the magician's Web site what the semicircular lobby inside looked like: gold-veined travertine floor, chandeliers resembling stalactite sculptures in an ice cave, each weighing a quarter of a ton.

A pair of nightwatchmen in a golf cart were moving slowly around the terrace. He sighted in on one of them, crosshairs just below a jowly neckline, feeling now the familiar slow-boiling anticipation of a blood stalk at the root of his throat, in the pulses of his temples.

The watchmen concluded their circuit of the terrace. A door opened in a wall bearing a fifty-foot-high mosaic of Lincoln Grayle. The golf cart disappeared into the lower depths of the theatre complex.

Sherard moved the stock of the Holland and Holland rifle from the padded shoulder of his hunting jacket. He closed his eyes, clearing his mind of the shot he was going to take, and waited.

MIDNIGHT

Eden ran through the levels of the darkened theatre and crossed the lobby, emerging into the brilliance of ten-k floodlights aimed at the theatre's facade. The temperature behind the cold front had dropped to the mid-thirties at this elevation. She was still perspiring from the heat of the menagerie tunnel and began to shudder as she turned and backed away from the entrance doors, circling a fountain, keeping it between her and the were-beast she was certain would be coming after her.

As she moved she had a look around the empty terrace, glanced at the stars appearing now in the sky. One hand against her breasts, cupped over the talisman that Leoncaro had urged on her. She was bleakly aware that whatever blessings accompanied it would be only of limited value. Bertie had believed—and look what it had gotten her. None of her powers had been adequate to anticipate and deflect an assassin's bullets.

Now that she was out in the open fear evaporated from her skin. Bertie lay gravely wounded in ICU but Eden felt satisfaction in remembering what the magician's face had looked like after she'd smashed most of it to pulp. The sharp neck of the wine bottle was still in her left hand. Probably futile as a weapon, given the power coming her way, the retaliation she had provoked.

She let go of the ugly little talisman and wiped the hollows of her eyes. The drops of Grayle's blood and her perspiration she flung from her fingertips appeared to hover in the floodlit night a few feet from her, taking on some of the fire that seemed also to glow within the crystal chandeliers visible inside the theatre. Light of her Light; a sub-conscious recognition, a gift of apprehension as, there on the terrace where it seemed to Eden she had been waiting until half past Eternity instead of less than a minute, something was happening.

The most wonderful *something* she had known in her life. There was just nothing to compare with the sight of an ordinary golf cart coasting out of a doorway in a wall near the left foot of another huge version of Lincoln Grayle, this one composed of many thousands of black and white tiles. You couldn't look anywhere in or outside of his theatre without encountering the likeness she had done a brutal job of deconstructing in reality.

Eden wasn't thinking about that right now; she could only smile incredulously at the sight of Bertie Nkambe behind the wheel of the ghostly cart as it crossed the terrace on a diagonal, coming straight for her. Bertie looking in the pink instead of unconscious beneath a ventilator mask in the hospital Eden had left a little less than three hours ago. Bertie, giving her a familiar blithe wave along with a big white dimpled smile.

Incredible to see her, but wonderful: of course she knew about Bertie's considerable healing powers . . . Eden could not control her tears.

"Bertie?!"

"Hi."

"But you—"

"C'mon, we'll take a ride. Tell you about it."

"No! Bertie—Grayle—he—we've got to—"

"Hey, nothing to worry about! I saw him. He's down and out. You clocked him good."

"Saw—?"

She braked the golf cart a few feet from Eden and beckoned, still smiling, a hand jauntily on one hip. Didn't appear that a single hair on her head had been disturbed by Mordaunt's assassin. To Eden's weary eyes she looked, matter of fact, as if she'd spent hours getting dolled up for a cover shoot.

"Time for us to skedaddle outta here, Eden. Saddle up and let's ride, partner."

Still Eden hung back, light-headed from the confusion, the assaultive conflict of her senses.

"Bertie, where's t-Tom?"

"Tom?" Her smile changed, just a little, as if she'd heard something obscene.

"Didn't he come with you? He's—" Eden ventured a couple of

steps toward the golf cart, shielding her eyes from the hot glare of a nearby floodlight. She failed to notice crimson drops of moisture she'd discarded into the air frantically rearranging to spell out a warning.

Beware

"—Supposed to be here," Eden concluded weakly. "I left him a note?"

Bertie's good humor vanished. Her back hunched like that of a sullen cat. She looked around the terrace swiftly, then in an instant of raw apprehension raised her eyes to the cliffs flanking and rising above the Lincoln Grayle Theatre, pale to the darkness of the sky from the leak light of the powerful floods and the glow of faceted glass.

Bertie's slanted eyes seemed to elongate as she took in the silent seated form of Tom Sherard, a distant wink of light off the lens of his rifle scope. Her recognition of danger was swift but not as swift as the bullet Tom sent her way. The .476 solid slug took out two ribs and splashed most of one lung, knocked her flat and hard beside the golf cart.

A human being and most animals would have died instantly from hydrostatic shock. But this Bertie wasn't human, only a cunning copy. It was the copy Eden saw struck with a meaty wham and knocked down but not Bertie struggling to assume yet another form on the deck even as the big bellowing echo from the Holland and Holland reached her ears, rolling across the face of the mountain. Sure as hell wasn't Bertie stretching out and getting up on all fours, claws grating on stone, blood billows issuing like condensed red breath from a leer of a mouth and coal-black nostrils.

Eden scuttled backward and recoiled from the scorch of a hot floodlight. The were-beast that was making a screaming effort to achieve its full shape from the abandoned form of Bertie Nkambe— *that* was to be the Trickster's last great illusion—wasn't having an easy time making the shift. Mindful of the sharpshooter on high, instead of coming at Eden it turned and loped toward the safety of the theatre, still incomplete and lopsided from the drag of a Bertie-leg, knee to foot, that remained unassimilated, a sight that wrenched Eden's violently beating heart. Then Tom fired again, hitting and disabling the striped high shoulder of the tiger.

The were-beast plunged through a glass door and skidded ten feet on slick travertine, then collapsed in a spill of coughed blood out of gun range.

There was another message in the air for Eden made of her sweat and tears, a message from the center of her being.

Destroy

Eden looked up where she thought Tom must be, but couldn't locate him. She walked deliberately across the terrace as the were-beast crawled along the floor inside the theatre, howling miserably, leaving a blood swath beneath the great blazing chandeliers, white as ice sculpture.

(Ice, glass—what did it matter? What mattered was to focus properly, channel the Dark Energy she felt as a hot-wire tingle back and forth across her scalp, causing the hair of her head to stand and strain at the roots.)

A smoke-tinged rosette opened in one of the facets on the hivelike facade. And she hadn't even been trying, just gave it the merest glance, the wild heat converging from both eyes as another blister formed on her lower lip.

The talisman smoked between her breasts. Her nipples were electric. She was on fire, but a fire she could bend outward and direct according to her will; it meant her no harm. She looked up again, leisurely, past insignificant clouds to a starfield that lay close across the heavens. It assumed from a cataclysm of seething light and energy a familiar form: her own. Recognition gave her cheer and a confidence that was beyond godlike.

Now, if she could make an elephant fly—

(Best not to leave any part of it standing. Not a single magical door or tunnel through which the Trickster might make his escape.)

Eden stood ten feet from the facade of the Lincoln Grayle The-atre, perhaps twice that distance from where the deformed magician was making an effort to pull his final act together—

—And dropped a quarter ton of melting chandelier on top of him.

Because—oh, yes!—she could definitely make an elephant fly!

The feline shape of Mordaunt was indistinct within the crude drop of glowing glass. Only the grotesque hyena head and strong shoulders of the tiger were still visible. Its screams difficult to bear. Eden added another slow-moving mass of molten glass to what was already on the floor, continued to pile it on until all of the chandeliers were melted and down. They composed an ingot like a softly pulsating, liquid star eight feet deep on the travertine floor.

The glass would, perhaps, take a week to cool and harden com-pletely.

Eden backed away from the theatre until she was nearly at the outer edge of the terrace. Her celestial simulacrum lay cozily on the brow of the mountain, intensely radiant. Stars in her eyes, stars in her hair. All of them spinning in concert with her earthly mind waves. She looked down and saw that she had risen a couple of feet above the terrace floor. She felt a curious lack of childlike wonder. Still she enjoyed her casual buoyancy, a bodiless sort of freedom, and the enormous light show playing in her brain as she initiated the meltdown of the theatre's facade, more trudging tons of sizzle glass.

But all of the added weight was too much for the terrace supports and the whole thing collapsed suddenly; Eden thoughtfully watched it go, great smoking globs of glass and slabs of concrete tumbling down the mountain, setting trees aflame, blocking the only road to the theatre. The floodlights were out. The Trickster's show had gone dark.

Beginning to feel depleted, Eden let herself drift a couple of hun-dred feet through the dark rising cloud of smoke and dust until there was solid ground beneath her feet again.

1:55 A.M.

Tom Sherard drove the back roads of the valleys and desert until at last he saw her, a lone slow-moving figure at the edge of a long straight road to nowhere.

He slowed down to a crawl and kept pace with her in the rented SUV and she never looked his way. She walked with her head up, eyes fixed on the dim mountainous distance.

He pulled ahead of her, turned the SUV in her direction, all lights blazing. She must have been nearly blinded but she kept walking until he stepped into her path. Then she just stood there, swaying a little, looking intently at his face. Her own face was grimy, her clothing filled with dust. Breakouts on her lower lip from hives. She began to tremble, as if she were just feeling the cold.

"Where are we, Tom?"

"I don't know."

"Then let's stay lost. For a little while longer. Can't we, Tom?"

She fell forward then, eyes closing, as if she were falling out of the sky.

6:58 A.M.

The ringing of Sherard's cell phone shocked Eden from her doze.

She left his side where she had been warm and content, crept out from beneath the thin blankets on the bed they shared in a nondescript motel, the first they had come to, in a desert town that might have been in California or Utah. The room had a single inadequate radiant heater and the floor felt like an ice rink to her bare feet. Eden rummaged in pockets of his hunting jacket and came up with the phone. Answered.

She listened for twenty seconds, let out a soft cry as she sank down trembling on the side of the creaky bed, turned her face to Tom.

He raised his head, blinking to get the sleep out of his eyes, and stared at Eden.

"Is it about Bertie?" he asked.

"She's awake and alert. Still on the ventilator but doing, they s-said, miraculously well."

His face relaxed into an expression of gratitude and then irony at the echo of the word *miraculous* somewhere in his mind.

"All right, then. That's my girl. She's begun to heal herself."

"C-can she do that?" Eden blubbered.

"In many instances. Will you please get under the covers? You're shaking to pieces."

She had never felt more naked than in this decrepit room, four stained walls, a loose window that let in a whistling wind, a bed, the man she had made love to in the shower, soapy and voracious, then again minutes later in the bed. He was now looking at her with unexpected composure when she'd dreaded that he would push her away from him like a cheap pickup he already was tired of, regretted. She was embarrassed by her own body and bones, the sore on her lower lip, the still-unbanked fire in loins and breast, not because he'd done badly by her but because each orgasm she'd experienced had seemed only a promise of greater bliss to come.

"It's all right, Eden," he said, sympathetic to the rage of emotions in her face.

"Oh, no, how can it be all right?! I went haywire; betrayed Bertie, my *God,* insulted us both, not to mention the memory of my—"

He reached up impatiently with both hands and pulled her down hard on top of him, Eden gasping in surprise, the rough stuff a new slant on the man and the situation. But his hands relaxed immediately while still keeping her close.

"We were both haywire, as you put it, for a time, and with damned good reason. I didn't know if you were alive or dead. Drove aimlessly, one road after another. How did you manage to get so far so quickly? No, it doesn't matter. The look on your dirty face when I found you. I had to make love to you as quickly as I could, and nothing short of a bullet in my own heart could have stopped me. Quite the typical aftermath of a successful hunt. That's one aspect of it. But we made love to bring ourselves back to life. Now we will deal with it. Nothing has happened for us to be ashamed of, or grieve over, or waste time in recriminations."

"How can I d-deal with being in love with you?"

"But you're not, Eden."

He held her face against his chest while she shuddered in protest; then, to her chagrin and panic, he began to laugh.

"Nothing's funny! And how do you know what I—"

"Affection, gratitude, youthful desire is what you feel. Everything that we hope may define and enrich our long-term friendship."

"We haven't had the chance to—"

"I have no misgivings about making love to you, Eden. We've behaved humanly, not badly. But—"

Eden thought she saw herself, vaguely, a diminished spirit in the high gloss of the pupils of his eyes. She was very still against his body, afraid of what he must say next. Obeying the wants of the flesh had broken something that might not be repairable—a valuable charm that had bound the three of them in a magical circle.

"—But I would feel cheesy should I use this night as an excuse for an affair that would be good for neither of us. Tonight may have been fated; now we must try and get on with what is most important in our lives. Think about what lies ahead of you, Eden. And for Bertie and myself. You've grown in your powers, awesomely so, but only half of Mordaunt and what he represents lies buried behind us. You are still missing someone of vital importance to your evolution as the Avatar. Cry now if you must, but let that be an end to it."

After half a minute the motionless Eden said, "I won't cry."

"Not yet. But you will."

"I think that I have to . . . go away for a while. By myself."

"Of course."

"I don't know what I'm going to say to Bertie."

"Shouldn't that be up to me?"

"Damn, damn, *damn*."

"But she will get over it."

"So sure of yourself, aren't you?"

"Not in these matters."

"Will I have to hate you before I get over you?"

Unhappiness in his eyes. "I said I was out of my depth here."

She dug her fingers into his shoulders until he winced, a creature of unrest, kneading away her growing frenzy and her own sense of loss. She tossed hair out of her eyes. Hollywoodish.

"Screw her, leave her."

"You haven't been listening worth a damn."

"Then say what I want to hear!"

"I've told you the truth. Now take your well-earned holiday and think it over, Eden."

"I can bring this room, shit, this crummy goddamned motel down around our heads. I can destroy both of us here!"

"You can do disastrous things. I bear witness. Go ahead, throw all of your toys out the window and break your crayons. It won't change the picture of yourself in your coloring book."

Eden slumped against him with a low and mournful sound.

"All right, little beauty. All right, now."

He stroked her rigid shoulders and the cold nape of her neck.

"Just hold me a little while longer, Tom." Her body quaked but her voice had lost its spiteful grit.

"For as long as you like."

"And tell me that you're hurting. Even though it's not much of a hurt."

"If I confess to that, you'll know rather too much, won't you? Could present an obstacle in the relationship we must work very hard to maintain."

"Oh, boy, all the answers. The voice of pure reason. Tom Terrific, truth-bringer."

"Speaking of hurts, actually it's your bony knee digging into my bad one, and that does hurt plenty. I may whimper."

Eden shifted her weight, briefly thinking about giving him a hard nudge in the groin with her knee. Those little sulfurous bubbles of spite still showing up in the bloodstream. But she was deadly tired and, after strenuous sex, parts of her body felt like leftovers from

The Rape of the Sabine Women. Presumably he was already sore enough.

She kissed him, sensing no reluctance on his part, relaxed, and let her mouth linger beside his, lips moving speechlessly. Then she rolled away and raised on one elbow, looked at him. Eyes drowsy, refocusing slowly.

"I do love you. Someday you'll know how much. Our relationship will just have to live with that. Now let's get out of this dump; the wind coming in around that window is beginning to depress me. Whether or not Bertie can heal *her* wounds, how easy can that be and meanwhile she'll need us."

EPILOGUE

Jubilation County, Georgia
July 22, 1926

Cap'n Hobbs ridin' here
Black horse rider
Buckshot in his gun, huh!

Hammers on the Dumas line
Buddy don't you fall, huh!
Jesus done forgot his long-time man
Oh buddy don't you fall

Crazy in my head, huh!
Hurtin' in my soul
Hear that hammer ring, boy
Down in the dark hour's dream

His name was Jericho Smith.

Smith, and the others on his chain, the guards around them each broiling day, knew that much about him, but not much more. What they knew best was to leave him alone.

Not that Smith was dangerous or a troublemaker, one of those hapless convicts on the squad chain who made life even more difficult for themselves with an incautious word, a slack work ethic, or a wrong look at a harassing guard, which earned punishment brutal beyond the pains of a long day's labor with hammers, shovels, pickaxes. There were other Negroes on his chain with powerful frames, but Smith was the tallest, his shoulders wider, his arms more powerful than any of the rest. He set a tireless pace at the track-laying site with his nine-pound hammer while the labor gang's slow chorus accompanied the spike-driving, steel-ringing strokes. Hammers on the Dumas line.

Smith knew what those words meant, because the straight stretch of railroad track was where he had spent all of his conscious life. The track that came out of the woods half a mile to the west, lying alongside a flat cotton field and a red dirt road straight as the track itself. He knew *west* because that was where the sun set every day. He didn't know where Dumas was. He knew only the horizon and the chain and the eighty dark men he worked with, the narrow road and the dusty cotton field. The birds on the telephone wire and the insects in the dry weeds of the ditch. The same clouds in the same sky, day after day. The heat and sweat and moaning and work. The brutal guards, the man on the black horse who ruled the guards and whose name was Hobbs. A thin man with war wounds, part of his face wrenched sideways, one eye rigidly pale as ice. Wore jodhpurs and polished brown boots and a campaign hat. Tobacco in one cheek. Smith knew just when Cap'n Hobbs would lean down from the saddle and spit vilely in the dust. All day long. The same times, the same way.

The Dumas line never seemed to get longer, for all of their hard work and track-laying. Every day he swung the same hammer at the same spikes in the same place until it was time, sun growing red in the sky, to lay 'em down.

But who was Jesus? he sometimes wondered. And what were those dreams of the dark hour?

It was the dark hour during which he lay down on a thin filthy mattress (*Know it musta been a bedbug, chinch can't bite that hard*), his head on a pillow covered with an evil-smelling flour sack, the collective sweat and grime of his days, linked to the "building chain" after the prisoners' evening feed of fried sowbelly, cornpone, and sorghum, their unvarying meal. Lay down as he knew he must but not to sleep. Or if he slept he had no memory of what sleep was like. Close his eyes and open them again to the rousting cry, still dark outside, torches in the prison camp yard, trucks waiting, pee and eat and go to the squad chain, jolt down another rutted clay road to the Dumas line, wait for a glimmer of light in the east to pick 'em up and go to work.

Smith never spoke to any of the other prisoners during the short ride to the Dumas line or while they rested, after the midday feed. Yet he knew all about them without having to ask, just as he knew everything he could want to know about the guards or Hobbs, the black horse rider. He knew names and knew their crimes, much of it petty although there were men on his chain who had committed rape or murder. He knew secrets and torments. They just came to him, unbidden, like flies to the dried salts on his skin. He knew about sweethearts, children, despair. What he knew nothing about was himself. Where he had come from, why he was there.

Hobbs leaning down from his saddle to spit, straightening with an angry sweep of his good eye, looking out for the men he would remove from the chain that evening, give them the strop, then a medieval pillory in which prisoners were locked into wooden stocks, left to hang in midair by their wrists and ankles until they passed out.

The sweat began to sting their eyes by nine in the morning.

Wiping it off here!

Wipe it off.

Smith couldn't tell time, and of course he had no need to, but he knew exactly at what point in his daily labors the mule wagons would plod by on the road. He knew when the six crows would float down to alight, one at a time, on the sagging telephone line. He knew when, having raised his hammer above his strong shoulders for the hundredth or two hundredth time, he would catch a glimpse of a hawk in full wingspread above the pine woods and marvel at its freedom. He knew when he would shift his eyes and find Cap'n Hobbs looking hard at him, and he knew with that little push he could give things in his mind the captain's good eye would be made to shift away from him, and there would be no blood-biting lash for Jericho Smith after the day's work, no pickshack locked to his already-burdened legs, no sweatbox assigned out of idle malice. Bored and ignorant men could turn vicious on a whim.

Yet they all sensed it was wise to leave Smith alone.

The man chained to his immediate right had stolen twelve dollars from a market to feed his children. He had been sentenced to eight years on the chain.

Smith wondered, at a certain time of each day, what his sentence was for, and how long it would last.

The thief had developed a hernia working on the chain. Smith knew exactly when he would sink to his knees, paralyzed from agony, and the guards would come to take him off the chain, cursing him as they loaded him roughly into the back of one of the prison camp trucks.

Screams.

Jesus done forgot his long-time man.

Smith wondered where the prisoner with the hernia was taken, yet he was always there in the torchlit yard the next day, which was this day, and the day before, waiting patiently to become another link on the chain.

Smith knew how easily he could get off the chain if he wanted to; in that bright corner of his mind where he instinctively Knew Things he had seen himself sever the links just by concentrating for a few seconds. But what was the reason for leaving the chain? Where would he go? Tomorrow, inevitably, he would be back in the yard. They all would, even those who had come from "somewhere." Towns and homes and families they thought about daylong, their hopes and silent cries for release passing through Smith's receptive mind.

But he had nowhere to go. Dreams, memories, were denied him. The chain—the first and final place—was home, just as tomorrow was today, and today was yesterday. He was there simply to endure.

Oh buddy don't you fall.

The man with the hernia had been taken away.

Hobbs, scowling, leaned out past his horse to spit chewed tobacco.

And Smith raised his hammer.

As he had done countless times before, as he always would do.

Then he noticed, out of the corner of his eye, something completely unexpected, compelling in its newness. Something *different.*

He stood there transfixed, arm and shoulder muscles bulging.

Crazy in my head, huh! went the refrain up and down the squad chain.

But, as they grunted *huh!* in rhythmic expectation of the hammer's fall, Smith was motionless. Men with hammers and pickaxes faltered and stared at him in stark disbelief.

A taxi had appeared on the road, and was slowing opposite the chain gang on the embankment.

Smith couldn't read and had no concept of what the word DUMAS
TAXI slanting through a yellow shield on a front door of the taxi
meant. But in the part of his brain that Knew Things he was aware
that this day was meant to be different, with consequences to himself.

The black horse threw back its head, reacting as if a bee had wandered up its nose. Cap'n Hobbs nearly lost his seat.

Work had stopped. Everyone was looking at the taxi.

A back door opened, and a young woman in a summer dress and a
wide-brimmed hat stepped out into the rust-colored road. She held
the crown of the hat to her head because of a sudden breeze and
gazed up at the chain gang.

"God damn you, Smith! Starin' at a white woman there? Nigger,
you bring that hammer *down*!"

Smith.

The young woman smiled, and looked in his direction.

In his mind where he Knew Things, Jericho Smith heard her
voice.

You're Smith? Come on then. We've got places to go.

The breeze freshened; red dust blew. Smith laid his hammer down.

Walked away from the shackles and chains that fell from his ankles
like paper cutouts.

Shocked silence, punctuated by the cocking of hammers on Cap'n
Hobbs's eight-gauge sawed-off.

Smith glanced at him and the dust rose in a furious cloud and
swept Hobbs away from his horse, lifted him twenty feet into the air
while Smith shrugged a biting fly from a sweaty shoulder and walked
on down the embankment toward the waiting girl.

He jumped the ditch while most of the men on the gang and the
guards watched Hobbs cartwheel squalling through the dirt mael-
strom that surrounded him. His horse wheeled and ran. A few of the
prisoners were more intrigued by Smith, who had paused to speak to
the girl. She gestured to the open door of the taxi.

A boy of fifteen or so with hard-to-comb blond hair and more
than a touch of hobgoblin in his face, so ugly he was sort of cute,
looked out of the taxi with a cranky expression, said impatiently,
"C'mon, it's time to go! Leave late, get there late."

The young woman held out a hand to Jericho Smith.

"I'm Gwen," she said. "For Guinevere. And the Stinkpot's right. We'd better be going; it took me long enough to find you."

"Who am I?" Smith said uncertainly.

"Big guy, we'll talk about it on the way."

"I have to do something first."

Smith turned, looked hard at the long line of prisoners on the railroad embankment and the brutal guards who seemed not anxious to fire on him, standing as close as he was to the pretty young woman.

The chain writhed and upended a score of prisoners before flying harmlessly to pieces, freeing them. A few of the men turned to the guards, who ran for their lives. But the rest just stared at their feet for several moments before layin' them down a final time and scrambling away in all directions from the never-to-be-finished Dumas line.

"There," Smith said. For the first time in his harsh existence he felt the unfamiliar tug of facial muscles. He was smiling. In the mind sanctuary where he had always Known Things recognition stirred as he looked again at Gwen.

"I don't know who I am," he said. "But I know who I want to be."

"And who is that?"

"You will do," Jericho Smith said.

To Be Continued in *Avenging Fury*